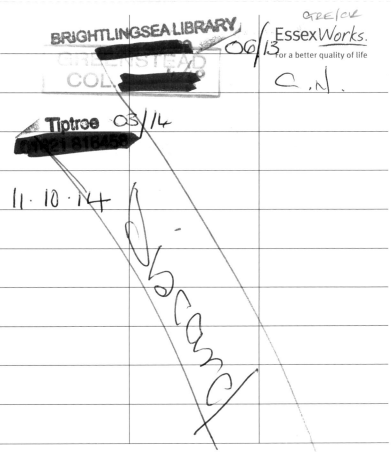

D1326150

30130500353613

J.A. Kerley worked in advertising and teaching before becoming a full-time novelist. He lives in Newport, Kentucky, but also spends a good deal of time in Southern Alabama, the setting for his Carson Ryder series. He is married with two children.

IN THE BLOOD

TV evangelist Reverend Scaler made his fortune from firebrand attacks on the sins of modern America. But Scaler has preached his last sermon after being bound and beaten to death in an apparent S&M session. Detective Carson Ryder has his own problems. He's edgy and unpredictable, seemingly unmoved by the discovery of an abandoned infant in a boat — nearby, a burnt-out shack, a body and signs of a struggle. Scaler's tangled personal life reveals bizarre connections between the cases. And it seems the baby fighting for its life in hospital has powerful enemies. Ryder can't seem to save himself but can he save the life of an innocent child?

Books by J. A. Kerley
Published by The House of Ulverscroft:

BLOOD BROTHER

J. A. KERLEY

IN THE BLOOD

Complete and Unabridged

CHARNWOOD
Leicester

First published in Great Britain in 2009 by
Harper
An imprint of HarperCollins*Publishers*, London

First Charnwood Edition
published 2010
by arrangement with
HarperCollins*Publishers*, London

The moral right of the author has been asserted

British Library CIP Data

Kerley, Jack.
    In the blood.
    1. Ryder, Carson (Fictitious character)– –Fiction.
    2. Police- -Alabama- -Fiction. 3. Suspense fiction.
    4. Large type books.
    I. Title
    813.6–dc22

    ISBN 978–1–44480–198–9

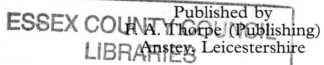

Published by
F. A. Thorpe (Publishing)
Anstey, Leicestershire

Set by Words & Graphics Ltd.
Anstey, Leicestershire
Printed and bound in Great Britain by
T. J. International Ltd., Padstow, Cornwall

This book is printed on acid-free paper

To Janine and Duane Eby,
always beautifully there

1

'It's almost midnight, Anak. Would you stop throwing that goddamn harpoon?' Rebecca Ahn stood on the porch of the tiny, weatherbeaten house, glaring at Anak Jackson.

'I'm bored,' Jackson said. 'What else is there to do here?'

Bathed in the thin illumination of a lone light on the side of the house, Jackson crunched across the sand to yank the six-foot lance from the scrubby palmetto doubling as his target.

'Dr Matthias said to keep a low profile, Anak,' Rebecca said. 'Not get noticed. Not yet.'

Jackson stared into the surrounding blackness. There wasn't another dwelling for a half-mile.

'Who's gonna complain, Bec? The moon?'

Jackson returned to his former position, lifted the spear to his broad shoulder. He had used true harpoons in his youth, for seals mainly, throwing with respectable accuracy according to the Inuit elders on his mother's side. And wasn't *spear-chucker* a derogatory term for blacks? He was doubly blessed. Or cursed.

The spear sliced through thirty feet of sultry night air to *thwock* into the base of the tree.

Ahn said, 'At least throw that thing during the day.'

'It's too freakin' hot,' Jackson complained. But he went inside and returned the lance to a corner of the living room, a display of cheap

1

furniture and mildewed walls. He walked a short hall to a bedroom, tiptoed inside. He returned seconds later.

'Is everything OK back there, Rebec? Have you handled the fee — '

Rebecca pointed to a damp spot on her T-shirt. Jackson smiled and pushed his hand into his jeans pocket, pulling out a candy tin. He popped it open and produced a half-smoked joint. He lit, inhaled deeply and let the smoke dribble out through his nose as he spoke.

'This doing-nothing shit is making me stir-crazy, babe. The doc promised he'd find us decent jobs, a place to stay in Mobile, right? Then he runs off to the other side of the world to — what did he say? — 'descend staircases'. What the hell does descend staircases mean?'

'Dr Matthias will do everything he said when he gets back, Anak, he always has.'

'You're too trusting, Rebec. We've known Matthias for maybe three months. He's spooky, too freakin' weird for me. And if he sticks that goddamn needle in my arm one more time, I'll . . . '

'I trust him. Be patient. And don't smoke inside. It's not good.'

Jackson started to argue; caught himself. 'My bad. Sorry.'

He rattled open the screen door and stepped into the night. The air smelled of the estuary behind the house, the Gulf's falling tide exposing dead fish, broken clams, clots of seaweed. The erstwhile neighborhood had been home to shrimpers, but that was before hurricanes shattered the houses and grounded the boats hundreds of yards inland. The house was the sole dwelling standing on jigsaw-cut channels separated by marsh grass and hummocks. Built in the forties of oak and cypress and hand-hewn joists, it survived the winds and water while the shacks and trailers had been blown as far west as Galveston Bay.

Anak took a final hit off the roach. He scratched at his full-face black beard, what Rebecca laughingly called his Rasputin beard, a reminder his blood had once lived in Russia. When they were stoned, Ahn made up fabulous stories about their distant forebears' bloodlines traveling the earth to meet, Anak's originating deep in Russia, taking centuries to cross eastward to China, north to the Bering Strait, into Alaskan Inuit tribes — where it met another traveling strain that had originated in Africa! It was like magic.

Rebecca's blood, as she told it, her storytelling voice sweet and musical after she'd smoked weed, had its genesis in the Middle East, moving through Europe to the US, pausing in the Swede-land of Minnesota, then pushing into Canada. Rebecca joked that Anak carried half the world in his veins, she carried the other half in hers.

Pretty little fairy tales that disappeared at dawn.

A light drew Anak's eye toward the distant road. The lane to the shack was a hundred yards distant, the turn-off obscured by scrub trees and kudzu. Two sets of lights, two vehicles. The lights

3

stopped by the gate. Went black.

Anak brushed mosquitoes from his eyes and stepped down to the sand. He was jogging up the drive for a closer look when a spotlight blazed from a vehicle. Anak dropped to the ground and watched the stark white beam of a searchlight sweeping the trees, the kind of high-intensity lamp mounted on cop cars, or used by poachers to jacklight deer, freezing them in light to await the bullet.

The searchlight died. Anak listened into the dark. Someone had passed the gate, someone else was creeping through the trees. Anak realized the road through the gate was the only easy way off the marshland edging the Gulf of Mexico.

A hunter all his life, Anak saw the pattern of a trap. He pushed from the ground and ran to the house. He snapped off the living-room light, the only remaining illumination coming from the bedroom down the hall.

'What is it?' Rebecca said. 'What are you doing?'

'Someone's coming.'

'Jesus! Who?'

'Thieves, maybe.'

Rebecca looked toward the bedroom. 'Remember the doctor's warning? That some people would see us as dangerous? We've got to hide the — '

Anak waved her silent. 'Get to the rowboat. Cross the channel and hide. There's a paddle inside. Don't use the oars, they creak.'

'You're coming too,' Rebecca said.

Anak looked to the old shark lance in the corner shadows.

4

'Anak!' Rebecca hissed. 'Come on.'

Anak spun to her, blue eyes blazing. 'Get out!'

The back door opened and Rebecca slid her slender body through the gap of a broken deck rail and jumped to the sand. She ran toward the water clutching a tight bundle, then crept to the end of the fifty-foot pier where a small green boat rocked.

Voices!

Not from the house or drive. From the water. Rebecca flattened against the pier, watching a searchlight's beam hit the shack, flick off. Someone had confirmed the shack's location.

Trapped.

Rebecca held the bundle tight. She heard the electric whine of a trolling motor as the boat moved closer. Heart pounding, she knelt on the salt-crusted pier, seeing a folded tarp in the rowboat. She wrapped the bundle in the tarp, tucking it beneath the middle seat. She loosened the boat's ropes to swing it beneath the pier. There were a few inches between the boat's top and the dock's underside. She'd crouch in the boat and hope the intruders would pass over above her.

A voice from the water said, 'Something's moving over there!'

The light snapped on, trapping Rebecca in white clarity. Behind her, from the house, came the sound of breaking wood, a door kicked in. A few seconds of breathless silence . . .

Replaced by a scream and the sound of gunfire.

Rebecca spun toward the house and began

running. *Get away from the dock!* her mind screamed. *Lead them away from the dock.*

She was a dozen feet from the house when the back door exploded open and a hideous image appeared on the deck: a man with eyes impossibly wide, his mouth frozen in a soundless scream . . .

And a harpoon bobbing from his abdomen.

Rebecca froze. The man's hands clutched at his gut. He vomited blood down his shirt, staggered through the rotten deck rail, and dropped into the sand in front of Rebecca.

A pop of gunfire. Pain seared Rebecca's head. She felt sand rush to her face, grit slide into her mouth. Voices screamed all around. More popping sounds. Someone yelled, 'I can't find it . . .'

The world spun into hazy colors. A thousand miles away, Rebecca heard footsteps on the dock. As the feet approached she turned away, drawn to a strange scene before her eyes, like a movie she could enter at will: a young woman naked on a beach with multi-stranded light arcing from her belly to the sky. The arc glittered like the Northern lights, bands of color pulsing like heartbeats.

The woman on the beach was her.

What Dr Matthias said was true, Rebecca thought as she spun into darkness. *I have a rainbow inside me.*

2

'People should be sleeping at this hour,' Harry Nautilus muttered.

Beside me, I heard the metallic click of his fishing reel. To the east, the horizon held the blue glow of approaching dawn.

'It's the best time to fish,' I countered, whipping my lure into the low waves of the Gulf of Mexico.

'Fish should be sleeping at this hour.'

Harry'd stayed in my guest room last night, expecting to fish today. I'd not planned to awaken so early, but hadn't been sleeping much lately, kept awake by the files on my desk at the Mobile Police Department, a dozen mean and horrific homicides in the past two months. When I'd looked at my clock — 4.37 a.m. — I figured we'd catch the early-shift fish.

'Coffee, bro?' I said.

'Don't ask, just pour.'

I reeled in my line, set the rod in a tubular spike in the sand. I pulled a thermos of homebrew from my tackle bag, half cheap-ass Mexican espresso, half New Orleans-style coffee with chickory. I'd filled the thermos three-quarters full, topped it with scalded milk, added a quarter-cup of demerara sugar and a tot of Kentucky bourbon. Liquid zip-a-dee-do-dah with a jolt of my-oh-my.

'Crap,' I said, rifling through the bag.

'What?'

'I forgot mugs. Be right back.'

I started jogging to my stilt-standing beach-front home a hundred yards away, across dunes bristling with sea oats. I live on Dauphin Island, thirty miles south of Mobile. It's my second home on the site, the first having been knocked cockeyed by Hurricane Katrina.

'Wait a sec, Carson,' Harry called from behind me. 'There's something out on the water.'

I turned and wandered back to Harry's side. Squinting into the dark, I saw a small craft out thirty yards or so, an aluminum rowboat rocking in the waves. It was nearly swamped, water licking its gunnels, the side-slipping tide pulling it parallel to the beach. It was a ghostly sight, like a lifeboat from the *Flying Dutchman*.

'Jeez,' Harry said, frowning at the empty boat. 'You think someone got knocked overboard?'

I sighed and pulled off my T-shirt. 'More likely it slipped its moorings. I'll swim out and grab it.'

'It'll beach soon enough,' Harry grunted. 'Get the mugs. I need coffee.'

I glanced east. A half-mile away lay the wide mouth of Mobile Bay. The tide would draw the boat into the path of watercraft soon to pour from the bay into the Gulf.

'The damn thing's a navigation hazard,' I said, kicking off my moccasins. Harry rolled his eyes as I sloshed waist-deep in my tattered shorts, threw my hands in front of me and dove. I set my bearings on the boat and pulled a lazy freestyle in that direction.

It took a half a minute to reach the craft. I

grabbed a trailing painter, the bow rope, which suggested someone's knot hadn't held the boat to the dock. The sloshing craft was too unstable to board, so I put my hands on the gunnel and kicked high enough to glance inside, seeing only a cheap plastic tarp floating on trapped air. I pulled it toward me, planning to jam it under a seat so it wouldn't drift away and foul someone's propeller.

The tarp began unfolding. I felt something wrapped in the plastic. With my legs kicking in the water and my biceps on the gunnels, I unwrapped the tarp. A second package dropped out and floated in the water. A pink insulated bundle . . .

Topped with a baby's face.

A wave crashed over me, not water, but horror.

3

The furious downdraft of the approaching medical helicopter created a sandstorm on the beach. I felt its roar against my back as Harry knelt over the baby and performed rescue breathing. He'd grabbed the infant when I was splashing wildly in shoulder-deep water, simultaneously trying to back-swim to the shore and keep the kid high and dry. Harry had 911'd the Dauphin Island paramedics, who'd sent the medivac chopper.

'I'm not feeling any breathing,' Harry yelled. Jimmy Gentry of the Dauphin Island cops had arrived two minutes back and was using a flashlight to wave the 'copter toward the sea side of the dunes. The flashers on his cruiser strobed blue and white across my partner's face. Harry looked terrified.

'Keep going, brother,' I said. 'The cavalry's almost here.'

Harry pinched the tiny nose and tried to puff air into the baby's mouth. I hunched over the pair and held my opened shirt wide to block some of the sand. The helicopter yawed above our heads.

When the chopper's rails were still wavering above the sand, two people vaulted from its innards. It was bright enough to make out a guy in his twenties and a woman in her mid thirties. She had a medical bag in her hand and a serene expression on her face, like it was the third time she'd done this today. Despite the quiet expression she outsprinted the guy, skidded to her knees beside Harry, took the child. The woman was long-legged, her hair so blonde as to seem white. The blue eyes looked better suited to someone selling saunas in Stockholm than jumping from helicopters in South Alabama.

'The kid was in the boat,' I told her, my words tumbling over one another. 'Wrapped in a tarp. The boat was sinking, but the tarp was floating. I don't know if it's, if it's . . . '

She held the baby close and did a series of palpations and checks. Harry fell back on to the sand, gasping. The woman spoke quickly to her companion in medical jargon. He ran to the chopper, plucked a mic from the wall and began relaying instructions to the crew at the hospital.

'Alive?' Harry asked the woman.

'Barely,' she said. Baby cradled high against her bosom, the doc stood and retreated to the chopper. Her assistant was already in place and reached for the child. The blonde doc pulled herself into the craft. Seconds later it was roaring toward Mobile.

Harry shook his head as the chopper disappeared into the sky. 'I don't know if I ever got a breath from the kid. It was too small for me to feel a pulse. I was afraid I'd break something.'

'You guys did a great job,' Jimmy consoled. 'We'll know more when the kid gets to the ER. How it's going to play out.'

Jimmy meant brain damage. Out on the water, when I unrolled the tarp, the infant's eyes — I'm sure it was under six months old — were closed with no sign of life. But its skin had been ruddy, not the blue of oxygen deprivation. Still, any brief stoppage of breath would start cells dying in the developing brain. Plus there was the aspect of exposure. And infection from aspirated sea water.

I doubted the prognosis was good.

Jimmy headed back to his office to set agencies and investigations in motion. I looked at Harry. He had picked up his rod and reel from the sand and was breaking it down.

'You're done fishing for the day?' I asked.

He stared at me.

'We just landed a baby, Carson. How can we top that?'

★　★　★

We retreated to my place for long-awaited mugs of coffee. When I brought them to the living room, Harry had switched on the local morning news and was frowning at the tube. I saw a semi-familiar face on the idiot box: Jeffords Tutweiler, a tall, lean, middle-aged man with black hair gone gray at the temples, an almost-pretty face that reminded me of Roger Moore. He was at a lectern, thumbs atop, hands down the sides. He looked like he wanted to pick up the lectern and heave it at the reporters sitting in a row of folding chairs. Behind him, I saw a mound of dirt with a dozen shovels buried halfway up the blades.

'*I don't think this is the proper venue for*

deliberately provocative questions,' Tutweiler was saying through tight-pursed lips. *'Today is for celebrating enhanced educational opportunities across the South.'*

'What's going on?' I asked Harry. 'Some kind of groundbreaking ceremony?'

'The endless expansion of Kingdom College,' he grunted.

The camera panned to the left of the guy at the lectern, showing a dozen dignitary types, including Senator Hampton Custis and three state representatives. The camera passed Custis to highlight a face familiar to everyone who used the television for devotional purposes, and nearly anyone in America who watched the news: the Reverend Richard Bloessing Scaler. Scaler's round, plump face was without mirth and, actually, without much activity at all, save for the occasional pursing of lips as if figuring out a puzzle in his head. He was so focused on the solution as to seem oblivious to both the hubbub a few dozen paces away and the political powers attending his ceremony.

'It's not a provocative question, Dean Tutweiler,' a reporter responded, *'but a simple one. Your institute has been called racist because it didn't accept black students until recently. And grudgingly, it seemed. Was Kingdom College founded on separatist principles?'*

The Dean shot a glance at the founder of Kingdom College, Richard Scaler. If Tutweiler was looking for help, he received nothing; Scaler stayed in his own head, miles away.

13

'Reverend Scaler and I have explained the position of the college to the point of distraction. Students of African-American descent weren't initially considered for admittance because of the many excellent institutions specifically geared for such students, a helping hand to folks who couldn't afford college. Our original intent was to provide the same — equal — helping hand to less economically blessed students of Caucasian parentage and meant no insult to those of other — '

His words were cut off by hoots and jeers. The news camera panned to a couple dozen people at the back of the crowd, held in check by steel barriers manned by cops. They were a mix of black and white, many holding signs equating Kingdom College to a racist institution, calling it *Jim Crow College* or *Old South University*. Scaler looked up and read the angry statements in turn, his face devoid of emotion. Senator Custis looked irked. The lesser political types noted Custis's irritation and quickly affected irritated looks of their own. Audience members turned in their seats and jeered back at the demonstrators.

Scaler remained impassive.

'What's with Rev. Scaler?' I said to Harry. 'Normally he's racing back and forth, pounding his bible, promising hellfire and damnation to anyone who doesn't agree with him.'

'Maybe Scaler's starting a new phase,' Harry said, taking a sip of the coffee, eyes widened by the bourbon blast. 'He's been through, what? — maybe a half-dozen phases, starting when he was hardly old enough to tie his shoes.'

I returned my eyes to the television. Richard Bloessing Scaler, though only in his mid fifties, had been a fixture throughout my thirty-six-year life. What the Jackson and Osmond families were to under-age singing talent, the Deep South was to youthful preaching talent. Kids as young as five and six preached at tent revivals, bible in one hand, microphone in the other, exhorting the flock to come to Jesus in sing-songy voices normally associated with whining about being fed vegetables.

Scaler had been a star on the circuit, a chubby little whirlwind who could preen and thump with the best of the bunch. I recall him from taped interviews, staring at the camera with a sincere face, his hair pomaded, dressed in a sky-blue suit, spouting verses of such precision and attribution that interviewers were certain he'd been prompted by his parents. His answer was always the same: 'Oh no, sir' — or ma'am, for the young Scaler had the mandatory impeccable Southern manners — 'from the first time I opened the Good Book, His words jumped from the pages to my soul.'

Scaler faded from the scene when an adolescent, re-emerging in his mid twenties as the pastor of a rural church in west-central Alabama. Perhaps small congregations weren't to his liking, for within two years he was building his television empire, his flamboyant style and personality perfect for the camera.

Something in the intervening years had politicized him toward the hectoring style of

15

right-wing politics launched from many Fundamentalist pulpits. The bible was thumped, the
finger pointed, the warnings declaimed. Opposing views were mocked. Comedians needed only
to crouch and scream to convey Scaler to the
audience.

Seeming almost desperate to succeed, he'd
created his own religious broadcasting empire
— the Kingdom Channel — and within a few
years he'd amassed the funds to begin buying up
large tracts of land and building Kingdom
College.

Alongside hyper-conservative religious views
came a bent more toward the Old Testament
than the New. Hurricanes, tornadoes and
earthquakes were warnings from God, post-
industrial plagues of locusts and famine. Though
other prominent preachers had jumped on the
bandwagon, Scaler had been the first to proclaim
Hurricane Katrina's assault on New Orleans as
the retribution of a miffed deity.

'God hath sent his terrible wind and flood to
wash away the filthy lifestyle of the Sodomites,'
he had intoned to national cameras a day after
Katrina had turned the nation's longest ongoing
party into a tragedy. 'Praise the name of Jesus
who smiteth all his enemies!'

When a bothersome local reporter pointed out
that the two major neighborhoods of the city to
be mainly spared — the French Quarter and
Garden District — were where most gay New
Orleanians resided, while the mostly black Ninth
Ward was the hardest hit, Scaler seemed lost for
a split-second, then suggested God had used the

Ninth Ward to demonstrate what might happen if the gays didn't repent their sinful ways.

'Are you saying, Reverend Scaler,' the reporter had asked, 'that God drowned citizens in the Ninth Ward as a warning flare for the gay population?'

Sensing a problem, Scaler had screwed himself to his full five-foot-eight height and launched a bombastic response, his standard solution to rhetorical difficulties. He jabbed a righteous finger at the reporter. 'I'm saying God stirred up the sky and the sea and sent a warning. People should have been smart enough to see it as the hand of the Lord coming and moved from the swath of His cleansing.'

Scaler's clarification sparked howls, but he remained undeterred through the publicity furor, perhaps because applications for Kingdom College went up by forty per cent and donations to his ministry went up fifty. The increased donations added new acreage to the holdings and a new library and dormitory to the campus, creating, as one editorialist put it, 'The only structures built by Hurricane Katrina.'

Beside the distracted Scaler was his wife, a plain woman with an awkward nose, her major role in Scaler's drama restricted to the utterance of *amens* after his pronouncements and singing hymns in a reedy, nasal voice. There were pronounced spaces between her outsized upper incisors, giving her a rabbity look. With a fluffy paste-on tail and penciled-in whiskers, she would have made a convincing Halloween bunny.

I saw the bunny shoot a couple of side-eyed glances Scaler's way, as if surprised by his

17

newfound taciturn demeanor. She aimed a perplexed glance at the senator, who looked back and shrugged. Despite the gesture, I thought I saw a split-second of fear cross his face.

'Reverend Scaler,' a reporter asked, turning from Tutweiler, *'you built this college and remain chairman of the board of regents and spiritual advisor. Will you not share a few words with us on what has to be one of the major accomplishments of your life?'*

Scaler blinked several times, then rubbed at his right eye. He held out his hand, fingers moving in a grabbing motion. An assistant quieted the hand by giving it a microphone. Scaler leaned toward the mic, his eye closed tight. *'I have something troubling occurring in my eye,'* he said. *'An affliction that's been ongoing. I promise I'll have an important statement within the week. One that will — '*

'What's wrong with your eyes, sir?' a reporter called. *'Will it involve surgery?'*

'No, no . . . nothing so drastic. Thank you all for coming out on this momentous day.'

'But, Reverend, surely you can — '

Scaler held up his hand. Blinked. *'I'll speak soon. In fact, I am already speaking. When my words are in the light, they will ring from earth to sky. This I promise.'*

'I don't understand, Reverend. You're speaking and yet you're not speaking? It doesn't make sen — '

But Scaler had already handed the microphone back to the assistant and resumed his look of distraction. Tutweiler cleared his throat and

18

continued his platitudes. The camera cut to a reporter from a local affiliate, a sturdy young woman with the distinctly un-Southern name of Jonna Arnbjorg.

'*And that's the news from the groundbreaking ceremony for the new library and dormitory at Kingdom College here in West Mobile. Most of today's events featured Jeffords Tutweiler, Dean of the college, with only a few puzzling remarks from the often-controversial Reverend Richard Scaler, blaming an eye affliction for the uncharacteristic brevity of his input.*'

'If Scaler has an eye problem,' Harry groused, thumbing the TV off, 'he got it from four decades of wearing blinders.'

But, truth be told, Richard Scaler's narrow field of vision appealed to a great many people. In a Bible Belt state like Alabama, few in office dared to challenge the uncompromising views of the Reverend Richard Scaler, knowing it could mean fast passage to another line of work.

Outside the sun was rising and would soon transform the air to hot syrup and the sand to a griddle hot enough to sear the soles of your feet. A Dauphin Island copmobile was approaching, Jimmy Gentry's face behind the wheel. He continued to the end of the street where the asphalt crumbled into the sand, exited and walked to the beach, hands in his pockets. He stood in the wet sand at the water's edge and looked seaward.

Harry and I wandered out. 'S'up, Jimmy?' Harry called before Jimmy saw us approaching. 'Expecting twins?'

Jimmy dipped his finger in the foam of a broken wave and held it aloft in the breeze, discovering what my face had noted: a southwest wind, the basic rule this time of year. He plucked a foot-long piece of driftwood from the sand, a spar bleached by salt and sun. He chucked it out a couple dozen yards, watched it bob eastward.

'You know tides better than me, Carson,' he said. 'Where you think the boat came from?'

'West somewhere. If the boat was launched on an ebb tide, it would have floated out into the Gulf, reversed on the incoming. There's a lateral drift because of current and the west wind.'

Jimmy said, 'Or the kid could have come from a boat way out on the water. Someone dropped her in the rowboat, kicked it away.'

Jimmy's words flashed pictures into my head. A blur of faces, one small and utterly helpless. A horizon of gray water in all directions. A tiny boat rocking alone on pitching waves.

Though I'd seen every form of human cruelty and thought myself professionally inured to emotion, the pictures kicked the breath from my lungs. I felt my knees loosen and my eyes dampen at the thought of human hands placing a baby in a boat, human eyes watching it float away. I took a deep breath, blanked my mind of the images, and slipped my shades over wet eyes, as though the sun was bothersome. I turned back to my companions.

'Coast Guard know anything?' Harry was asking Jimmy.

'They're gonna check suspicious-looking boats

out on the water. But they figure anyone doing that kind of thing would be long gone.' Jimmy shook his head. 'Of course, you guys would be zeroed-in on that kind of mentality.'

Jimmy was referring to Harry and my participation in a special unit in the Mobile Police Department, the Psychopathological and Sociopathological Investigate Team, or PSIT. We were the sole members of the unit, laughingly called *Piss-it* by everyone in the department. If a case showed signs of involving a seriously damaged mind, it landed on our desks, generally superseding our normal caseload of shootings, stabbings, and the like. The PSIT reviewed over a dozen cases a year, with only one or two that truly fit the psychological parameters. I learned something from every case, generally something I didn't want to know.

'I don't envy the DI cops,' Harry said as we crunched back across the sand to my home. 'How would anyone figure where the kid's journey started?'

I grunted my sympathy. The Dauphin Island Police Department was made up of ten full-time cops and five volunteers handling a mainly upscale resort community. Petty theft, drunkenness and speeding were the major crimes. However that kid came to be in that boat, it would be sad and strange and probably ugly beyond anything the normal mind could conceive.

Turning back to the sea, I tried to imagine it from jet height, the blue of the water and the green and white of the island and mainland. If I

21

knew enough, I could superimpose arrows over the image: the direction of last night's currents and wind.

I didn't have those arrows. But I knew someone who might.

4

Dr Kurt Matthias was on the hunt, walking with a slight list through the Hong Kong market, the bag slung over his brown-jacketed shoulder tipping him a few degrees to his left. The bag's interior rattled with his footsteps, glass tubes clicking together like ice.

The air brought Matthias's nose the smells of incense and soya, fried eel and garlic. When the air shifted, it brought the scent of sea water, some dockage only a few blocks distant, the babble of the market occasionally broken by the blast of a freighter's horn. In the maze of booths, melons vied for space among spices, clothing, and jade carvings. Smoke wafted from charcoal burners, and heat from the coals joined the heat rising from thousands of bodies in the market. A hodgepodge of languages and dialects mixed with the screech of parrots and the cackling of caged chickens.

Matthias's eyes sought faces as if they were quarry. He criss-crossed through the stalls, watching, measuring, gauging nose structures, distances between eyes, the size of ear lobes and lips, chins and chests.

There: in an oily mariner's uniform, a man with pan-flat Mongol cheeks and forehead, the nose not the Central Asian button, but hooked, a magnificent beak of a nose — Indian? Arabic? In that same face: ice-blue eyes and jutting chin of

23

some Nordic race. His waist was slender, his shoulders hard and broad. He was a head taller than most in the crowd, their fully Asian genes never having traveled more than a few hundred miles. The man was leaning against a wall and smoking a filterless cigarette, hands in the pockets of his jeans, cold blue eyes scanning the crowd as if weighing options. Matthias studied the man and gave his thoughts free rein . . .

A Viking tribe rages through English country-side. Rape and pillage and children with Nordic eyes set loose like spores through the Anglo-Saxon population. Centuries later a spore sets adventurous sail to Calcutta, emissary and conqueror. Ships and ports and lighthouses through the human dark. Blue Aryan eyes in a Hong Kong marketplace.

Matthias crossed the street to the man. Eyes turned his way like pinpoint jets of flame.

'You know English?' Matthias asked.

The man ran his hands through his hair, not the coal black of the Orient, but shaded to auburn. He pinched his fingers an inch apart; the gesture saying, *I speak English this much.* Matthias noted the man's hands were overly large for an Asian, the fingertips spatulate.

'I have money for you.' Matthias pulled crumpled bills from his pocket and gestured the blue-eyed man from the swirling crowd of bargainers.

Curiosity overcoming confusion, the man pinched the wet stub of cigarette from his mouth and threw it to the street. He shadowed Matthias to a darkened alley stinking of lust and urine and

24

the spoor of rats. When a drunken man and woman coupling against a damp wall saw the pair approaching, they cursed and staggered away.

Matthias set his bag on the alley cobbles. He leaned against the wall where the couple had been fornicating, opened his bag, and explained his strange needs to the blue-eyed Asian.

★   ★   ★

Larry Hayward blinked at Harry and me through half-glasses and spun a dried starfish on his desktop. Larry was an independent marine biologist who had retired from the Eighth District of the National Oceanic and Atmospheric Administration. He'd spent so much time in scuba gear he'd been dubbed Merman by his colleagues.

Now retired and in his early fifties, Larry ran a consultation service from his home on Dauphin Island, a three-tiered white building — four, if you counted the pilings holding the structure above the sand — the tiers growing smaller toward the top, so that the house resembled a wedding cake on stilts. His office walls were covered with charts. His window peered across the mouth of Mobile Bay, Fort Morgan visible across the eight-mile stretch of blue.

'NOAA has tidal data we can use,' Larry said, considering my question on currents. 'I just have to access their mainframe.'

We followed Larry's flapping sandals to a room of instruments and computer monitors. A fifty-gallon saltwater aquarium was in the corner, a dozen gray commas flicking within. I recognized the critters, almost.

'What kind of shrimp you got here, Larry?' I asked. 'They look like Gulf models, but not quite.'

'Good eye. They're hybrids. I'll spare you the Linnaean nomenclature and just say they're Gulf shrimp bred with a species of Chinese shrimp.'

'They come already marinated in soy sauce?' Harry mused.

'There's a nasty virus potentially endangering Gulf shrimp. It's common in Chinese waters and the Oriental shrimp are resistant. They've dealt with the virus for hundreds of years, evolved defenses. I'm studying how the hybrids fare against the infection.'

We turned from the shrimp experiment as Larry sat down before a large screen, talking half to us, half to himself as he pulled a keyboard to his Hawaiian-print chest.

'What was the time of day, as near as you remember?'

Harry said, 'Four fifty-two in the a.m.'

'You hooked into the atomic clock in Denver, Harry?'

'I'd just looked at my watch, amazed Carson had me up so early.'

'Four fifty-two it is, then. Let's see . . . an eastward drift of three knots per hour. Add a tide just past slack and starting to flow. I won't go into the hydraulics, but if the boat was launched from shore it needed to have been drawn sufficiently seaward by an ebb tide to avoid beaching near the launch site.'

I saw the screen reflected in Larry's glasses: charts, graphs, columns of numbers. A coastal map began building on the monitor. Larry leaned back and tapped his chin.

'There are all sorts of influences and permutations. But the wind was calm that night. That's good because it's a non-factor; shifting wind might have made this a moot exercise.'

'You're getting somewhere, I take it?' Harry said.

'Halfway. I've got the current-drift models in place. Now we run things in reverse. The boat was spotted here, right?' Larry tapped my stretch of beach on Dauphin Island.

I nodded. 'Just outside the sandbar, a couple hundred feet.'

Larry ticked numbers into the computer, lost in an ebb and flow of time and tide. Ten seconds passed and the computer made a *bong!* sound. I saw a section of coastline change from dark brown to vibrant pulsing orange.

Larry jabbed a finger at the highlighted section. 'The craft was most likely launched from somewhere within three hundred yards of beach centered here. Sorry to be imprecise, but there are a lot of variables.'

Harry leaned close to study the marshes and estuaries and patches of sand abutting the blue Gulf. I looked over his shoulder.

'Where are you pointing, Doc?' Harry asked.

'A bit southwest of Coden. A marshy estuarine with a few small inlets from the Gulf. Not much there any more — the area got redesigned by Katrina.'

I said, 'I'll pass the info to Jimmy Gentry. He can do with it what he will.'

Harry studied the monitor again. Turned to me. 'I'm up for a nice little drive. Somewhere a bit south of Coden. How 'bout you, Carson?'

I shook my head. 'It's not our case. We've already got two deskloads of death and weirdness.'

'It might be a chance to do some good.'

I started to respond, but found no words. I shrugged and stared at the ragged stretch of coast, feeling a strange chill at the base of my spine.

5

Harry and I picked up chow at a po'boy joint on the DI Expressway before we turned west. Harry ate as he drove, brushing crumbs and lettuce from his chest to the floorboards. We pulled off I-10 and dropped southwest toward the coast, not the white sand shores of tourist Alabama, but land with dense expanses of brush and sea grasses. The road was an armadillo graveyard, the car-struck beasts studding the tarmac like scaley mines.

I heard a passing vehicle at our backs and saw Harry shoot a glance into the rear-view mirror as his hand tensed on the wheel.

'Check this out,' he said quietly.

I looked up as a large black pickup truck passed, three males jammed in the front, another in the bed. They were in their twenties and thirties, shirtless, heavily tatted, crosses and swastikas and lightning bolts. The driver was wearing a plastic Nazi-style helmet and drinking from a can of Miller. They stared at us as they passed, not a happy look. A Harley-Davidson logo filled the rear window. Celtic runes decorated the bumper, bookended by Confederate battle flags.

Though no one was in the oncoming lane, the truck swerved in front of us. Harry jammed the brake as I slapped my hand to the dash. The pudgy guy in the bed grinned like a Jack-o'-lantern, turned for a one-handed grab of the chrome light bar atop the cab, and dropped his pants, showing us his hairy white ass.

The driver hit the accelerator and I heard the roar of a V-8 as the truck blew away at what had to be a hundred ten.

'Man,' Harry said, 'I can smell the ugly.'

We drove another few miles, turned hard south. The Merman had printed out a satellite shot of the area in question. We angled down a few sand-and-shell roads that led to shattered boats and the mason-block foundations of houses reduced to driftwood and termite fodder.

'I don't see anything,' Harry said, staring into scrub pine and land as flat as a billiard table. 'Not that I know what I'm looking for.'

'Check over there,' I pointed. 'A dune where a stretch of pine got blown away.'

We stopped and got out. The sun was climbing toward noon and the air was close enough to induce claustrophobia. Insect sounds rose in waves from the stunted trees. We swatted biting flies from our faces. Harry ramped a hand over his eyes and studied the trees.

'There. Something's not right.'

I followed to a sand-drifted stretch of road. Uprooted brush covered a metal gate. The gate blocked a slender lane, barely more than a scattering of broken shells in the hard sand. Since storm-uprooted trees were everywhere, the camouflage was effective.

We tugged away brush, sweating like stevedores, then drove down the lane, branches screeching against the car doors. Six hundred feet later the lane terminated in a webwork of marshy channels. I saw the hulks of shrimp boats in the sand, prows pointing upward like they were sailing out of hell. In the distance were a few tumbled houses, once home to shrimpers, now rotting wood and rusting metal. We saw a house trailer half-flattened and blown over on its side. It looked like a shoebox someone had kicked down the road.

'Over there,' Harry pointed. 'I see a dock.'

We jogged to a rickety pier extending into the marshy channel. Harry passed me, stepping carefully to the end of the dock, boards creaking beneath his feet. He dropped to his knees and studied one of three old tires nailed to the sideboards of the dock, the bargain version of boat bumpers.

'Check out the tires, brother,' Harry said.

I knelt and studied the surface of the rotting rubber. Saw streaks of paint worn into the now-gray whitewalls. It seemed to match the bilious green of the rowboat. But green was a popular color for boats.

I nodded. 'There's a chance the kid got launched from here.'

'Cars, check behind the trees.'

Harry pointed to the far side of a stand of short trees. I saw truncated pilings, ragged black spikes pointing at the sky. We pushed through brush and found the burned-down house once supported by the short pilings, a tumbled pile of blackened wood and sheet-metal roofing.

'It burned recently,' I said, squatting to puff at a soft pile of soot. 'Otherwise rain would have

31

pounded away the softer ash.' I walked the edge of the debris pile, seeing burned and broken supports, a fried chair and couch, a blackened toaster.

'Uh, Cars . . . ' Harry said. 'Step over here. Carefully. I've got something.'

I walked over and looked down to see several feet of twisted cinder with a bulb on top, a former human being. I'd seen this phenomenon a half-dozen times after structure fires.

'Oh shit, a dead body.' I pulled out my cell. 'I'll call it into the county police.'

Harry tugged my sleeve. 'You're missing the interesting part. Look closer. Down by the belly.'

I crouched close. Details congealed in the shadows and I saw an object emerging from the charred abdominal area: four feet of scorched steel rod entering a blackened shaft of scorched hardwood. What was left of the corpse's hands were clutching at the shaft.

'That what I think it is?' Harry whispered.

I stared at the pierced corpse. 'If you're thinking harpoon, I'm thinking you're right.'

6

'I ain't surprised at a dead body. More'n one came outta this neighborhood over the past few years.'

Sergeant Elvin Briscoe of the local constabulary spit tobacco juice on the ground and leaned against his dusty cruiser with thick arms crossed and his mirrored shades low on a gin-blossomed nose. He was a barrel-bodied man in his mid forties with a ruddy face and equine teeth stained with tobacco.

A dozen feet away, two techs from the Medical Examiner's office photographed the torso prior to pulling it from the debris. Behind them, the forensics team scoured the surrounding land for evidence.

'This was a violent community?' I asked.

He shrugged. 'Got worse once the white folks left.'

'White folks?' Harry said.

Briscoe looked at me. 'Used to be a shrimper's community, white people mainly, until a few years back. Then the Vietnamese pushed in and the whites moved out.'

'Why'd they move?' Harry said, knowing the answer, just wanting to hear it confirmed.

Briscoe shrugged and spat a second strand of tobacco juice into the weeds. He wiped his mouth with the back of his hand, looked at a hawk circling above, a black dot in a blue sky.

I thought maybe Briscoe didn't hear. 'Why'd the Caucasians leave?' I asked.

Briscoe turned his gaze from the sky to my face. 'Guess the whites wanted to be with their own kind. Plus most of the, uh, Orientals didn't speak English. Just jabbered monkey-speak.'

Harry said, 'And all these years I thought they spoke Vietnamese.'

Briscoe turned away and spat juice. Rubbed it into the sand with his boot.

'This fire happened recently,' I said. 'Since last Friday.'

'No way you can know that,' Briscoe scoffed.

I nodded downward and kicked a pile of ash. Watched a plume float away on the breeze.

'Friday's when it last rained. The ashes are unsettled.'

Briscoe feigned a yawn. 'Guess that's why you're a detective, Detective.'

'You know who lived here?'

'We never patrol back here cuz no one lives here any more. Or I didn't think so.'

'You never got a call about a fire?' Harry asked.

Briscoe gazed with amusement at the surrounding desolation. 'Who would call one in?' he said, like talking to himself. He belched and looked at me. 'You were saying something about a kid found in a boat?'

'Launched from here, maybe. That pier.'

'How about you move your ass a couple feet?' someone said behind us.

'How about you fuck yourself?' came the response.

We turned our heads to the voices. A chunky,

fiftyish guy from the Alabama Bureau of Forensics was jabbing a finger at the deputy who'd arrived with Briscoe, a hard-muscled man in his early thirties wearing a too-tight uniform shirt to emphasize the swollen biceps. The deputy slapped the finger away.

'Whoa,' I yelled, spinning from Briscoe and running to the altercation. 'What's the beef?'

The red-faced guy from forensics, Al Bustamente, pointed at the deputy's spit-shined black Wellingtons. 'Bubba here's standing in the middle of what appear to be footprints. I guess no one told him that professionals don't put their feet in evidence.'

I saw the county cop's eyes tighten. 'What are you saying?'

The cop was a collection of granite muscles, but Bustamente had a fast fuse and hot mouth. And as a member of the state's department of forensics, he also had jurisdiction. 'I'm saying I don't give a rat's ass if you're ignorant, all I want is to make a cast of the prints. Is that too tough to understand, you hick moron?'

I saw the deputy's jaw clench and his arms ripple, the punch cock. I jumped in front of him, knocked the punch aside with my forearm, like blocking an incoming missile. I was left staring into the deputy's eyes from a foot away.

'Get outta my way,' he snarled. His words smelled like unwashed teeth. His breathing was shallow. Veins bulged on his forehead and he seemed dangerously close to unhinged.

'Get hold of yourself,' I said. 'A man's been killed here.'

'I don't give a fuck if — '

'Baker!' Briscoe's voice from behind me. 'Git to the car and you git calm. Now!'

I stepped aside, made an effort to keep from massaging my forearm, aching from the deputy's sledgehammer blow. The guy mouthed something at Bustamente, turned and walked to the cruiser like a programmed robot. Bustamente shook his head, knelt, commenced pouring compound into one of the footprints he'd spotted. Crisis averted. I returned to Briscoe. He was picking his teeth with a thumbnail.

'Your man always such a pain in the ass?' I asked.

Briscoe nodded toward Bustamente. 'Seems lardass over there called Baker ignorant, a hick and a moron. You take that kind of talk yourself?'

'If I'm an ignorant hick moron,' Harry interrupted from a dozen feet distant. 'But since I'm a professional, I don't generally plant my shoes in the middle of evidence.'

Briscoe looked into the distance. I saw his jaw clench, his eyes tighten. He turned them to me.

'Looks like we got everything under control here. See you.'

I said, 'You're planning on checking ownership of this house, right, Sheriff? Track down whoever was inside?'

'Sure. Have a nice drive back to the city, Detective.' He winked. 'Hope you get that lost pup returned to its kennel.'

Briscoe ambled away to talk to his deputy. The festivities seemingly over, Harry and I climbed back into our car and left the scene to the medical and forensics teams. We could drop the case back into the arms of Jimmy Gentry, since it was in Dauphin Island's jurisdiction. Jimmy, unfortunately, would have to deal with Briscoe.

We drove a couple miles, Harry strangely silent. Usually he wanted to kick around details while a scene was still fresh in his head even if it wasn't our jurisdiction or case.

'Can you believe Briscoe?' I shook my head. 'A pity Jimmy'll have to coordinate an investigation with that rube.'

'Besides the banter about monkey chatter and pups,' Harry said quietly, 'what did you notice about Sheriff Briscoe?'

I ran the interaction through my head. 'He was semi-literate, a heavy tobacco user and probably a heavy drinker . . . '

'Did you notice he never looked at me when I spoke?'

'What?'

'Just like I wasn't there. The invisible man.'

'Briscoe did that?' I said, looking at Harry.

'During the introduction phase, he shook hands with everyone but me. He turned away, faked a sneeze and moved to the next guy.'

I recalled Briscoe's big howling a-choo. Pretending to wipe his hands, moving to me with a big hand but a wet-rag shake. I replayed the scene and only in retrospect saw the slight.

'Shit,' I said. 'It went by me.'

'Briscoe was having a great time fucking with me, him knowing it, me knowing it, the muscle-bound deputy knowing it. I got the impression Briscoe was showing off for his deputy.'

'I'm sorry, bro,' I said. 'I didn't see what was happening.'

'You weren't meant to.'

We moved down the road another mile, me thinking about the small and ugly drama that had sullied the air at the crime scene, a display of racial condescension I'd missed totally.

'How much do they piss you off, Harry?' I finally asked. 'People like Briscoe?'

Harry was silent for so long I thought he hadn't heard my question. After a mile of farm fields, hawks and watermelons our only audience, Harry turned my way.

'Pull over.'

'You mean now? What are you — '

'Pull over, Carson. Right here.'

I braked to the sandy berm. Harry pushed open his door. By the time I got out, my partner was striding into the field. He appraised a head-sized sugar-baby melon, knelt, snapped it from the vine. He balanced the melon on a rotting fencepost and returned to the car.

'Harry?' I asked.

In one sweeping motion, Harry snatched his nine millimeter from the shoulder rig, pointed one-handed at the target, snapped off three shots. I saw a spray of pink from the rear of the melon, and it toppled to the ground, cracking open to reveal red innards.

Harry replaced his gun and got back in the car. I pulled back on to the road. He thumbed replacement rounds into his clip and returned the weapon to the holster, staring out the window at the cotton fields.

7

Come Monday, the Homicide Division was its usual kick-off-the-week self, a dozen overworked dicks sucking caffeine and yapping on phones, checking what snitches might have dredged up over the weekend. Lieutenant Tom Mason, our hound-faced commander, was in his windowed office staring down at the weekend reports. He had his mouth open and was drumming his flues with his fingertips, making music inside his head.

Harry arrived at eight and sat across from me. We worked with desks butted together to converse face to face. Plus it gave us a bigger space to hold about twenty pounds of homicide files and paperwork, though overflow avalanched to the floor daily. Harry was wearing an orange blazer over lime-green pants, his polo shirt was plum, his shoes burgundy. If environmentalists figured how to convert the color wavelengths in Harry's wardrobe into electricity, the polar bears would be safe forever.

I coughed and sniffed, the summer pollen counts high. Harry shot me the narrow eye. 'You breathed down sea water, right? When you were racing the baby to shore?'

Aspirated sea water could lead to some hellacious infections. I shrugged it off, mumbling about something in the air.

Harry said, 'You haven't been looking real healthy the past couple of weeks, Carson. Maybe your resistance is down.'

'I'm fine.'

'The hospital's a ten-minute drive. You can get a shot or whatever.'

'Earth to Harry: I feel fine.'

Harry sighed and pitched his pencil to the desk. 'Come on. We're going to the hospital. It's closer and insurance pays, right? We can get you a shot and . . . ' he paused as if having a sudden thought, 'see how the kid's doing, health-wise.'

Harry had segued from the first rationale to the second so smoothly I realized the whole conversation had been an excuse to visit the boat baby. I'd pretty much pushed the incident to the back of my mind, wanting nothing more to do with the kid. The case belonged to the DI police.

'Do you really want to know how it's doing?' I challenged. 'The kid could be terminally ill. Or brain-dead.'

Harry closed his eyes, conflict tightening his face. He sighed.

'I have to know, Carson. I held the kid. I breathed into her.'

Minutes later we were at the hospital. An emergency room resident I knew shot me up with a syringe full of antibiotic and wrote script for some pills. Rolling my sleeve down, I looked for Harry, didn't see him. I found him on the fourth floor in paediatric intensive care, peering through the window separating the sterile unit from the hall and waiting area.

I walked tentatively to Harry and peeked in the window. Machines and monitors owned the real estate inside the unit. Our rescue was third in a line of five babies in Plexiglas boxes. Two kids were squalling, two were twitching or stretching. Ours was as still as clay. I felt myself staring. But it seemed as if I was watching from a vast distance, like the child was an image on a screen.

I felt my body take a step backward and I bumped into Harry.

'She looks terrible,' Harry groaned, stepping past me to press his hands against the window. 'Just terrible.'

'You're responding to the tubes and wires,' said a cheery voice at our backs. 'She's doing far better than we expected.'

Harry and I turned to see the blonde doc who'd sprinted from the helicopter. A brass badge on her breast said *Angela Norlin, MD*.

'You're sure?' Harry asked, skeptical. 'She looks like she's — '

'She's asleep, that's all,' the doc said, bright eyes scanning the read-outs on the monitors. 'Her temp's up a bit, but minimal. All in all it's a very promising report. Surprising, too.'

While Dr Norlin studied the machines, I circumspectly studied her. The slight crinkle of skin at her eyes and across the backs of her hands told me I'd been off a few years in my age estimate, and I now figured her for late thirties. A nicely crafted late thirties.

'Do you specialize in helicopter paediatrics?' I asked.

'When we got word there was a baby in trouble, the medivac folks sent me instead of the regular medic.'

41

'A smart move on their part, I expect,' Harry said. 'Why are you surprised she's doing so good?'

'Usually by this time we'd have had to flood the victim's system with high-level antibiotics. There's a potential for side-effects that can actually hinder progress. Baby Doe has some infection, but it's low grade, and standard antibiotics are keeping it in check. Her immune system seems in exceptional condition. The power of her immune response is surprising everyone.'

'The little lady must have good genes,' Harry said, scrutinizing the kid. Her skin was tawny, the eyes almond shaped, the dark hair curly.

'What race is it, Doc?' I asked.

Doc Norlin shot me a disapproving glance. 'It's a she. As far as race goes, to me it looks like human.'

I'd never had much interaction with children.

They were all *its* to me until old enough to communicate, at which point they became interesting. But the *it*, combined with a racial query and what I'd been told was an accent more cracker than cosmopolitan, probably made me sound a tad Cartoonish. Not a good cartoon.

'I just mean . . . an, uh, ethnic identity might give investigators an idea what to look for in the parents.'

'I'm concerned with her health, not her ethnicity.'

I was trying to think of something to say that would make me sound reasonable and intelligent when Harry reached for my sleeve.

'Watch out, Carson!'

Pain stabbed my ankle. I jerked around to a cart at my back, its deck piled with towels and cleaning supplies.

'Jeez, I'm sorry,' said the thirtyish guy pushing the cart, somehow looking more smug than apologetic. 'I rolled around the corner and didn't see you.'

'It's . . . all . . . right,' I grunted, leaning against the wall and rubbing my Achilles tendon. The corner was a dozen feet away; the guy must have been temporarily blind or daydreaming hard.

I set my foot on the ground. Limped a few feet down the hall. Turned and came back. I waited for Doc Norlin to inspect my potentially broken ankle, but she seemed blind to my pain and suffering.

The guy started to roll the cart away, but paused to look at the kids. He tickled his fingers at them and smiled as though greatly pleased, then pushed on. Babies have that effect on some people.

'So you think the kid'll pull through, Doc?' Harry asked, turning back to the window. He tapped the glass and made an eyes-wide, tongue-boinging series of faces through the glass. He cooed and babbled. Harry was one of those people unhinged by babies.

'The prognosis is guarded, Detective Nautilus, but I'm hopeful. Especially with the strong immune response and general good health, given what Baby Doe must have been through.'

Harry's goofy grin descended into a frown.

'Baby Doe? Is that what you're calling her?'

'Standard procedure. They assign the name in Records.'

Harry studied the child for a long minute. 'Can't you pick more descriptive names?'

'What's wrong with the temporary designation?' I asked.

My partner stared at me like it was the dumbest question he'd ever heard.

'Baby Doe's a generic name, Carson. No one should be generic.'

8

Leaving Harry to talk baby this-and-that with the blonde doc, I told him I'd meet him at the car and set off down the hall to the can, remembering to limp to keep the weight off my wounded extremity. The orderly who'd rear-ended me was leaning beside a hand-dryer and talking on a cellphone. He glanced up, mumbled, 'Gotta go, Miriam. We'll talk later.' He snapped the phone shut and ducked out the door without acknowledging my presence.

Outside I found Harry leaning against the car, beaming like a child at Christmas.

'Isn't it great,' he said. 'The kid's gonna pull it off.'

'Pull what off?'

'Live. Have a life.'

'Sure,' I said. 'Who's driving?'

We were cut off by the dispatcher. '*Harry? Carson? We have a call regarding a possible 10–54D at 824 Bellewood. You anywhere close?*'

The code for a dead body. I grabbed the mic.

'Ryder here. Harry and I are maybe four miles. Why us specifically?'

'Caller is Hispanic and not speaking entirely in English, but she keeps screaming about *trabajo de diablo* . . . the work of the devil. Plus she's screaming *sangre*. Blood. Sounds like a weird one, so I figured we'd best have the Piss-it boys check it out.'

45

'Let's hit and git it,' Harry said, jumping behind the wheel and pulling a 180 in the street. It was a maneuver he loved but had never mastered. The rear tire banged the curb, jumped up, burned rubber, dropped back into the street and screamed like a scalded banshee until the tires bit. 'We're en route,' I told the dispatcher when my breath returned.

I hung up the mic and held tight as Harry put the pedal to the floor. He switched on the siren and in-grille lights and we blew past other vehicles like two tons of rabid metal.

The address led us through a wide white gate, down a long lane canopied by trees, and into a circle of a dozen single-story cabins surrounding a bonfire pit. The cabins were simple and rustic. The land was studded with live oaks veiled in Spanish moss. Longleaf pines towered above. It was a clean and pastoral setting, radiating calm.

On a slight hill behind the cabins were three crosses made from telephone-pole-sized logs, the center cross taller than the others. A grouping of white rocks at the base of the rise proclaimed *Camp Sonshine*. We were in a church camp, one of many in southern Alabama.

'Over there.'

Harry pointed to a larger cabin outside the circle, two stories tall and set in its own copse, almost hidden in the dense green canopy. It was more house than cabin; the director's quarters, I figured. I saw a woman in front of the structure, her face in her hands. We roared up the drive and bailed. I ran to the woman, Hispanic, in her forties.

'What is it, ma'am? What happened?'

She jabbed fingers toward the house, speaking Spanish through her tears. She bordered on hysteria and I couldn't catch a word. I put my arm around her shoulders, walked her to the end of the porch and eased her into a wicker chair.

'Calm down, ma'am. Speak English if you can.'

I held her hand as she took a few trembling seconds to gather herself.

'I clean cabins,' she said. 'When I come I find a man ees *muerte*, dead. *Madre di Dios. Es de trabajo de diablo.*'

'Is anyone else inside?'

'I saw no one.'

I patted her shoulder again, thanked her. Harry had eased open the door and was peering inside. Harry called, 'Police.' Waited. Called again. No response, the cabin as silent as an undersea tomb.

We entered and saw why the woman had been screaming.

A man was hanging upside-down beneath a suspended staircase, a rope tight from his ankles to a hardware-store pulley on the upper staircase. His purple and blood-swollen head swayed a foot above the plank floor. His eyes bulged hideously, the whites turned red by gravity-exploded veins. Rivulets of blood ran from his eyes to the floor.

The man was wearing lacy women's panties and metal clamps bit into his nipples. A black ball gag filled his lipstick-smeared mouth, and something like a black cucumber was lodged in his anus. His toneless, fatty back and buttocks

47

were striped with welts. His hands were bound behind his back with a red scarf. His hair was wild, like whirlwinds had blown across his scalp. Six dead candles lay at points around the carpeted floor, white and thick, the wax pooled and hardened on the carpet. It looked like a scene from a demonic Tarot card.

'Lord Jesus,' Harry whispered.

I crept to the body, pressing a puckered thigh with my index finger and studying a pool of congealed brown on the floor.

'The blood's caked and rigor's gone. He's been dead for hours.' I looked closer. 'A lot of blood, but I don't see any wounds beyond superficial: lashes on his back and ass, broken skin on his nips.'

'Every time I find one of these scenes it creeps me out for days,' Harry said. 'I never understood B&D.'

'More like S&M,' I corrected. B&D was Bondage and Discipline, a sexual practice where people get a kick out of being restricted in their motion and spanked or whatever. Sadism and Masochism was like B&D on steroids. Some people liked to see how much pain they could take; for them the pain was mixed up with pleasure — the more it hurt, the better the sex.

It was all way beyond me.

Harry walked to the front door, checked side to side. 'The housecleaning lady's booked. She's not coming back, at least not for a while.' He ducked back inside, started a visual inspection. 'Let's you and me take the place apart. I'll toss the back rooms.'

Harry stepped through the doorway and took a fast stutter-step, grabbing the door. He muttered, 'Shit.'

'What is it, bro?'

'Water on the floor. I just about slipped on my ass.'

I walked over, saw a puddle about two feet around. I got on my hands and knees and sniffed.

'Weird,' I said. 'It smells like sea water.'

I wondered if there was a broken pipe in the walls and what in the pipe would give leaked water the scent of the ocean. Harry stepped around the puddle and headed to the back bedroom. I returned to my inspection of the front room and the area around the body.

I found the guy's clothes in a side closet, brown silk, custom made. No ID. I picked up the jacket and bingo, felt a wallet in the breast pocket. I shook the wallet from the clothing to the floor. Alligator skin and slim, a designer billfold. I riffled a corner of the bills and watched a parade of hundreds flash by, followed by fifties and ending with a single plebian sawbuck. Well over two grand.

I noted a driver's license tucked in a pocket of the wallet, picked it free. I stared at the ID a long moment before walking back to the body. I spun the head to face me.

'Harry,' I called toward the back.

'What is it, Carson?'

'You ever wonder what TV preachers do in their spare time?'

9

Waiting for the techs, we called the department to explain the situation. Tom Mason agreed that we had to inform Mrs Scaler of her husband's death immediately. The news media would soon darken earth and sky like a plague of locusts. Better us than a dozen reporters at her door with clicking cameras and hollered questions. As soon as the body got into the system, the hunt would be on.

'You say it looks like an S&M situation?' Tom said. I could hear his grimace.

'Yup.'

'Hold that info tight for now and keep everyone close-mouthed. You're looking for someone else who was there?'

'Someone had to haul Scaler in the air and stripe his back. I'm thinking a big, blonde Valkyrie-type of dominatrix.'

Tom sighed. 'This is the sort of thing makes me yearn for early retirement. Keep it all on the QT until we know more.'

Harry and I did a corny hands-in-the-air pledge and made the techs swear not to reveal details of the scene. It was pure theater, since the others had worked high-profile cases and knew that leaks did nothing but stir the media and impede the investigation. We were just reinforcing the closed-mouth ethos.

We released the scene to the forensics folks

and went to the Scaler household. The holy man's home was an imposing, white-columned antebellum structure a football-field's length from the street, high wrought-iron fence in front, its own gated community. A sprinkler system was watering the grass, intermittent geysers hissing rainbows against the air. The wet lawn seemed luminous in the sun. I saw a swimming pool to the side, tennis courts beyond. Banks of azaleas blazed with color.

The gate was open and we roared up a tree-lined driveway, passing a five-car garage, four bays holding expensive vehicles, all shiny white and showroom clean, the fifth bay containing a golf cart with a fringed shade.

'That looks like about a half-million bucks' worth of vehicles,' Harry noted. 'Wonder what the cart's for?'

'To drive to the street to fetch the mail,' I joked, then realized it was probably true.

We parked in a roundabout pinioned by a marble fountain spraying water a dozen feet into the air. The butter-colored glass and lead sconces framing the expansive mahogany front door were large as torpedo launchers. Ringing the doorbell felt akin to ringing the doorbell at Oz, except Oz's doorbell didn't *bong* the opening notes of 'Onward Christian Soldiers'.

On-ward Chris-ti-an sol-di-ors, marching as to war . . .

The soldiers marched three times before the door opened. Instead of Mrs Scaler, we found a nervous and diminutive Latina in her fifties.

'I'm very sorry,' she said. 'Mees Scaler has

51

been take to the hospital.'

'What happened?' Harry asked.

'She fall down the stairs.'

'Where? When?'

'Las' night. I was called to stay and watch the house. That's all I can tell you. Mees Scaler ees at hospital called the general.'

We raced to Mobile General and found a P. Scaler was in room 231. Entering, we saw a small presence on the railed bed, eyes closed. A heavy bandage crossed her nose. Her eyes were purple-black with contusion and I saw stitches in her lip.

'You take it, Carson,' Harry said. 'A solo.'

A solo was when only one of us handled an interview, usually when the person being questioned was ill or infirm or intimidated by cops. Going in alone offered a better chance of bonding.

I nodded and slipped into the room. Cleared my throat at P. Scaler's bedside. Her eyes fluttered open.

'Oh my,' she apologized in a soft mumble, 'I'm not dressed for visitors.'

I showed my ID and introduced myself. 'What happened to you, ma'am? And please don't talk if it hurts.'

She nodded toward a water cup on the bedside table. I filled it, angled the plastic straw downward, put my arm behind her back and helped her sit a few inches higher. Patricia Scaler seemed to weigh less than a pillowcase filled with straw. She took a few sips, nodded her thanks. I eased her back down.

'Silly, clumsy me,' she said, talking slowly. 'Wearing high heels down stairs . . . heel caught, fell down the steps. Doctor says broken nose, some teeth to be replaced. Thank the Lord. I could have broken my silly neck.'

I heard a throat cleared at our backs and turned to see a slender MD at the door, Harry at his side. Harry pointed at the doc and shot me a come-hither nod.

'Excuse me for a moment, ma'am.'

'Of course, sir.'

I stepped to the hall. 'What is it, Doctor?'

He looked uneasy. 'Under those dressings it's pretty easy to discern three contusions to the side of her nose. Ever see that before?'

'Sounds like knuckles. You're saying she was beaten?'

The doc shrugged, looked uncomfortable. 'I'm not sure it would hold up in court.'

Harry stepped close. 'When was she admitted?'

The doc looked to the chart for confirmation. 'Eleven twenty. But judging by aspects of her injuries, I'd say she tried to tough out the pain for at least three hours before calling for transport. Maybe more.'

A simple toothache would send me racing for the oil of cloves and shortly thereafter to the dentist. I couldn't fathom waiting for hours with three teeth snapped off at the gum line. It must have been agony. And that was without adding in the busted nose, another excruciating injury.

I stepped back into the room, pulled a chair to the side of the bed. Patricia Scaler's eyes flicked to me. To the physician at the door. Back to me.

'What's wrong? Something's wrong, isn't it?'

I nodded. 'It's your husband, ma'am. I'm afraid that — '

'He hurt someone, didn't he? He couldn't help it. He was angry. He has to be alone when he's angry. It was my fault. I made him angry.'

'You're saying your husband hurt you, Mrs Scaler?'

'What? No one hurt me. I fell down the stairs.'

'You're sure? It looks like you've been struck.'

Her small white hands knotted into fists. She pulled them to her chest, nails of one hand digging into the back of her other hand, as if in subconscious punishment. Tears poured down her face and on to her gown.

'It's my fault, all my fault,' she murmured. Her eyes lifted to me. 'Where's Richard now?'

I closed my eyes, took a deep breath. 'Mrs Scaler, I hate to be the one to tell you this . . . '

10

I left the poor woman weeping into a pillow, her small body racked with grief. I dropped further questions about the abuse, but was sure her husband had been the cause of injuries that would take cosmetic surgery to undo.

We walked into the path of three men in expensive business suits, the center man fiftyish, bald as a bullet, with badger-mean eyes under bushy black eyebrows. He was built like a guy who knew his way around a weight room. I felt an intensity coming from him, much like I'd feel heat. Or maybe it was the musk-heavy cologne that telegraphed his presence from a half-dozen feet away.

He held up his hand like a North Korean border guard. 'What did you do in there?' he demanded, dark eyes flashing. 'What did she tell you?'

'Who's asking?' Harry said.

The guy snapped a card from the jacket of his pinstriped suit, jabbing it between Harry and me. 'I'm the Scaler's attorney, James Carleton, III. Anything Mrs Scaler told you is — '

'Anything she told us is part of an investigation into her husband's death,' I said, looking at lawyer-boy's card like it had diphtheria.

'Mrs Scaler is an ill and injured woman,' Carleton snapped. 'Anything she might have told you is subject to interpretation.'

'Here's what she told us, sport,' I said, taking the guy's card, tearing it in half and pushing it down into his outer pocket. 'She said she was being followed by a lawyer who lacked the hormones to grow hair and wore cologne that smelled like the underparts of a rutting hog.'

Harry stepped between us, always better at diplomacy. 'Mrs Scaler told us she accidentally fell down some steps. We informed her that her husband was dead. She started crying. Anything else you need . . . sir?'

The guy's lips pursed so tight I thought they'd invert.

'Well . . . we'll just see about that.'

He pushed past, the two other legal types sucked along in his perfumed slipstream. I heard him rush to the woman's bedside, his growls muted to murmurs of consolation. The door closed.

'Jeez,' Harry said, shaking his head as we continued down the hall. 'What was that all about?'

'Damage control, I reckon. Let's beat feet out of here.'

★   ★   ★

On the way back to the department I got a call from Dr Clair Peltier, director of pathology for the Alabama Forensics Bureau, southwest region, wanting to see me and Harry. We were minutes away and Harry shortened them by nudging a few lights from red to pastel green.

Harry and I sat across from Clair in an office of bookcases and bound files. A vase of flowers

56

from Clair's garden topped her impressive oaken desk, the scent of roses and lilacs masking the harsher scents of the morgue.

There was a time not long ago when Clair and I explored a physical relationship that had, after a blazing start, arrived at a quieter station. We were more than trusted friends, less than constant lovers. Contemporary culture hadn't found a term for our relationship, which was probably good.

'So what killed the good reverend?' I asked. 'Off the record.'

'Best guess? A cardiac event. The man was fifty-seven, overweight, and his muscle tone tells me he wasn't into regular exercise. This was a sado-maso event, right? That in itself can be stressful.'

'You don't suspect foul play?'

'The welts on his back and buttocks were superficial. There were no scrapes or contusions like you'd find in a scuffle. Outside of the nipples and back area, his body was unmarred. You find who the other party or parties were?'

I shook my head. 'We're waiting for word on latent prints. He was found in a church camp, so all sorts of campers and counselors have been through. It was closed for the season for renovation.'

'So Reverend Scaler had a whole camp for his playhouse?'

'Swim, hike, make a leather wallet, get your butt whipped. Scaler must have been a happy camper.'

Harry's phone rang. He excused himself and

slipped into the hall. I studied Clair. Her eyes were as blue as the Caribbean and I wanted to dive into them and backstroke somewhere far away from the present. She stood and moved close. The familiarity of her perfume made me dizzy. Hearing no one outside the door, our lips touched.

'I haven't seen you in weeks, Carson. You look strained, tired. I know you've got to be running on stress and adrenalin. Are you OK?'

I smiled, did a super-hero pose. 'I'm immune to stress.'

'No one is.'

'I'm no more tired than you, Clair.' I nodded toward the room where the autopsies took place. 'You get the victims after I do, right?'

'It's different for me. I don't have to look into their lives or hear their stories. I never find who they really were. That's what you do.'

A recent memory moved me to the window, like my eyes needed real light. I let out a long breath and turned back to Clair.

'A couple weeks ago I went to a drive-by in south Mobile. The deceased was a nineteen-year-old kid named Alphonse Terrell. When we found the body his thumb was in his mouth, his last instinct before dying.'

'I recall seeing the paperwork on the body. What about it?'

'My first case after I made detective was a woman named Twyla Terrell.'

'Oh Lord, Carson . . . was she the mother? Sister?'

'The mom. Mama had been shot by a

boyfriend in the kitchen. I remember the kid, Alphonse, standing in the corner, a skinny twelve-year-old. Alphonse was sucking his thumb, Clair. Staring at his mother's body, tears pouring down his face, sucking his thumb like a baby. I walked him outside, trying to say things with meaning and comfort, failing miserably.'

'That's terrible, Carson. I'm so sorry.'

I shrugged. 'Mama gets shot, sonny gets shot a few years later. It's just the way things have become, Clair. Like leaving a legacy.'

Clair moved closer and took my hand. 'It'll get better, dear. We've had spikes in the homicide rate before. They always pass.'

'Of course,' I said, pressing a smile to my face. 'Like bad weather.'

Harry appeared at the door and I turned to leave. As we stepped from Clair's office she called my name. I turned to see her thumb and pinkie beside her head in that funny mimic of phoning. There was no humor in her eyes, only concern.

'Call me, Carson. Let's get together soon, right? Talk?'

I nodded and turned away.

★　★　★

When we got to the car, Harry took driver's position.

'Where to from here?' he asked.

'We find who Scaler paid to work him over. Given the money he had in his wallet, he could afford the best.'

59

'How come she left the money?'

'Either she freaked when her client's heart popped, or took her money and a big tip. Scaler could have started the night with twenty grand in his pocket.'

We didn't keep a list of dominatrix types, since they tended to avoid interaction with the legal system, particularly the high-money babes who kept a lower-than-low profile as they went about their business.

However, they generally set up shop in a part of town where clients could come and go without attracting attention from the neighbors, so we skirted the inner-city, looking for informants past and present. We passed by a half-dozen hookers lounging in the midday heat, trading tales and gossip in front of a payday loan store.

'Hey, Harry — looking gooooood,' one of the hookers crowed, a tall transsexual-in-progress named Shanelle who resembled an Oriental Whitney Houston. We'd dealt with her a few times as an informant, and Shanelle had taken an immediate shine to my partner.

Harry flicked a wave and a wink as we pulled over, causing Shanelle to shriek and fake an attack of the vapors, one hand palm-forward over her forehead, fanning with the other as she faux-fainted into the arms of her colleagues.

'Talk to you a minute, Miss Shanelle?' Harry asked.

Shanelle recovered, giggled, and strutted over like she was working a Paris runway. She was wearing a brief white top to display heavy silicone orbs, a black leather miniskirt high above the knobby knees, and plastic shoes like those Croc things, only with four-inch platforms. They were spray-painted metalflake gold.

I leaned out the window. 'Hi, Shanelle. Love the shoes.'

Her false eyelashes fluttered like excited butterflies. She tapped her toes together, looking down.

'You don't think they're too conservative, Carson?'

I shot a thumbs-up and a wink. 'They're sexy and sassy.'

Shanelle beamed and put a shoe on the window frame while bending to look at my partner. 'What do you think, Harry? They pretty, ain't they?'

'They're lovely, Miss Shanelle,' Harry said. 'But I've got a question even more important than shoes.'

'Anything for you, Harry Nautilus.'

'We're looking for a dominatrix. Any around?'

Shanelle grinned and batted the lashes. 'Harry, if you need a spanking . . . '

My partner sighed. 'The person we're looking for is probably one of the highest priced ladies in the market. A pro's pro.'

'She ain't in no trouble is she, Harry?'

'Not a bit. Just questions.'

'The girl you looking for. Is she black or white?' Shanelle asked.

Harry looked at me. I rolled the question over in my head. 'Almost certainly white.'

'And real expensive, you said?'

61

'That's what we're thinking.'

Shanelle thought a minute, gave us an address not overly distant.

'Is that all you need, Harry?' Shanelle purred through the window.

'For now, Shanelle. But remember, Carson and I always appreciate you keeping your pretty eyes and ears open for any weirdness or — '

'Whoooo-eee,' Shanelle whooped like a crane, turning to screech at her cadre a couple dozen paces away. 'Harry Nautilus says I got pretty eyes and ears.'

The girls called back taunts and howls. Shanelle said, 'Bitches. They don't understand what we got going, right, Harry?' She did kissy-mouth, complete with sound effects.

Harry sighed a final time and waved goodbye. Fifteen minutes later we were in a warehouse district between the city and the bay. A small apartment held a few mailboxes by the front door, one of them assigned to M.L. We headed up the stairs, found a single apartment occupied the entire floor, the door built of cleated metal. Harry banged the metal, making a booming sound like a hammer on a ship's superstructure.

'Police. Open up.'

We heard a rustle of motion, a door slam inside. We'd checked for a back exit, found none. 'Police,' Harry repeated.

The door opened to reveal a powerful-looking woman in her mid thirties, a silky robe from her shoulders to the floor. I saw black boots sticking out, expected they laced up to her knees, standard fare. She was smoking a cigar and emitting smoke through chrysanthemum lips as red as blood. Her puffy explosion of jet-black hair was striped red down the center. The cat-bright eyes were large to begin with, further widened by make-up dusted with flecks of gold. Even with the robe it was apparent the lady had a splendid exercise regimen.

'Mistress Layla?'

She blew a plume of smoke to the side. 'Who's asking?'

We showed ID. She looked close, a careful type.

'May we come in?' I asked. 'We won't need much of your time.'

'*May* you come in?' she said. 'How polite. Gentlemen are always welcome here.'

She moved like rhythmic water and led us down a short dark hall to a small sitting area with a loveseat and a chair, passing a side door on the way; a closet, I assumed, by its proximity to the front door. The walls were flocked red wallpaper, the trim was burnished brass. Along with the cigar odor, the air smelled of incense and sweat. A velvet curtain hung behind the couch, covering the door to the arena, I supposed.

'Who else is here?' Harry asked, looking at the curtain.

'No one's back there,' she said, sitting on the couch.

'May I take a look?' I asked. 'Specialized décor has always fascinated me.'

'I'd be delighted if you would.'

I pushed through the curtain to the windowless room behind. Twenty by twenty, high beamed ceiling, three walls black, the fourth raw

63

brick. Steel hooks and rings and loops were situated at intervals along the walls as chain-holds. One hook held leather straps, still damp with sweat. A small table held an assortment of whips and flails. Smaller tables around the room held candles. There was an antique four-poster bed in a shadowed corner, beneath it I saw a gleaming steel bedpan.

I returned to the sitting area and smiled at Mistress Layla. 'The rings look very solidly anchored. The exposed brickwork is a nice touch.'

'Thank you. My dungeon always gets compliments.'

A fair amount of cops might have made snide comments or tried to be funny, but Harry and I always tried to treat folks with respect. One, it was the right thing to do. And two, over the years it had given us a solve rate that was the envy of our peers.

'You say you're working, ma'am?' I asked.

I saw a glance flick to the closet down the hall. She didn't try to hide the look.

'Yes.'

'This won't take long. We're checking into a for-hire situation. A man hired a dom to ball-gag him, suspend him by his ankles, give him a plugging and a whip job on the back and buttocks.'

Mistress Layla stubbed out the cigar in a crystal bowl. 'Your presence tells me the man must have been robbed. Or hurt.'

'He was . . . injured,' I said, realizing how little we could say without revealing the victim was Richard Scaler.

'We're trying to find out how it all went down, ma'am,' Harry said. 'There's no indication that anyone is in trouble. I want to stress that. This is purely a gathering of loose ends.'

'Good to know,' she said. 'Where did this, uh, event happen?'

'I can't tell you,' Harry said.

A small smile. 'When, then?'

'In the past week.'

'You want to see my appointment book, gentlemen? No names, but times. If someone was hurt, it wasn't me. My clients don't get anything but what they need, which is a little time out of themselves. I've made my reputation on creating imaginary situations where humiliation and fear prevail, but safety is a word away.'

'I believe you,' I said. 'You ever work anywhere but here?'

'Not often. All of my materials are here.'

'Have you worked off-site in the past two weeks?'

'Not in months.'

I felt she was telling the truth, further strengthened when Mistress Layla consented to giving us her fingerprints. We wiped down a Coke can, she gripped it, dropped it in an evidence bag. We'd compare them to the hundreds of prints and partials found inside the cabin, but I didn't expect a match.

She frowned in thought as I zippered the bag.

'Did you say the client was upside-down, Detective?'

'Yes, ma'am.'

'Gagged?'

I nodded. 'With hands bound tight behind his back, a double knot.'

She leaned back in the loveseat, tapping her chin like an engineer presented with a structural anomaly.

'That's not too common, being upended. It drains blood from the sexual organs and diminishes pleasure. Add the gag and bindings and it's a position almost too helpless for most people. Tied to a bed or wall or using a harness suspension is one thing, but everything is disoriented when you're upside-down. There must always be the knowledge that the . . . *event* can be turned off in an instant. That's the difference between pleasure and terror.'

I said, 'Tell us about your competition, Mistress. I don't expect you have many peers.'

She nodded at the compliment. 'You're very kind. My colleagues are few in number, ranging from Pensacola to Biloxi. More in New Orleans, of course.'

'We need names, ma'am. If you'd be so kind.'

She raised a penciled eyebrow. 'You'll not mention my name in your travels?'

'It would be intolerably poor manners.'

She smiled and nodded, found a pen, wrote for a minute and passed us the names, a half-dozen. We walked the hallway to the door. I paused at the closed door along the side, pulled it open. Inside, on the floor, crouched a naked man in his forties, one hand in his lap. I know a two-hundred-dollar haircut when I see one, and I was seeing one.

'Hello,' I said. 'You're under arrest.'

The man looked up, breathless with fear and excitement.

'This is part of the act, right?' he whispered.

'Yes,' I said. 'Isn't Mistress Layla something?'

He moaned the word *incredible*. I closed the door and we walked outside to the car. In the next two hours we visited three local names on Mistress Layla's list. All claimed alibis, which we'd check, and gave us fingerprint samples to clear through forensics.

It was getting late in the day. Harry sighed and pointed the car back downtown. We went a few blocks and he brightened at the thought of something.

'Hey, Carson. We go by the hospital on the way back. How's about we stop in and see the kid, then grab a beer. She'll cheer us up.'

The beer sounded decent, but I'd had my fill of hospitals. I figured I'd end up sitting on a plastic couch for twenty minutes while Harry pulled faces and made goofy noises at the kid, which, being in a plastic box behind a glass window, it never even heard.

I said, 'Drop me off at my truck.'

'You don't want to check the kid, Carson? How about grabbing a beer? You've been looking a bit stressed out lately, so maybe some downtime would — '

'I'm not stressed, Harry. I'm simply over-worked. I want to go home.'

'It'll kind of take me out of my way to drop you at your truck then circle around to — '

I held up my hands in defeat. Harry pointed the grille toward the hospital. We found Doc

Norlin at the nurse's station conferring with an orderly. When she saw us, she brightened. Or maybe it was Harry that sparked the smile.

'I've got good news,' Norlin said, her hand sliding behind my partner's elbow as she walked him to the unit, me following, not shooting glances at Norlin's trim backside. When we turned the corner toward the viewing window, I stopped.

'Carson? You OK?'

'I'm fine. I'll wait here.'

Harry began waving his arms at the kid. He tapped the glass, cooed like a pigeon. I looked away, embarrassed for my partner and waiting until his initial burst of emotionalism had subsided to making kissy faces.

Norlin smiled at Harry. 'Returning a nearly drowned baby to health is like a marathon,' she said. 'Sometimes the runner never finishes. Little Jane pulled it off like a hundred-yard sprint. I've never seen anything like it.'

Harry studied the kid, mumbled something, and spun away, pacing down the hall like on a personal mission. Reaching the end of the hall, he looked out the window for a few beats, still mumbling, then spun on his heel and started back. Doc Norlin's eyes were fixed on Harry, seemingly fascinated by my outsized partner. He returned, crossed his arms, leaned against the wall.

'How about Noelle, Doc?' he said.

'Pardon me, Detective Nautilus?'

'As a name for the kid,' Harry said. 'Noelle.'

'You mean like in Christmas?' the doc asked, a

quizzical smile on her face.

'Like in Noah,' Harry said. 'But with an *elle* because she's a girl.'

'Moses would be better,' I suggested, 'given the small boat on the water.'

Harry dismissed the notion. 'You ever try and convert Moses into a feminine name, Carson? Moselle's a German wine, Mosina sounds like crap, ditto for Mozette . . . '

Norlin said, 'You worked all that out in under a minute, Detective Nautilus?'

'How about it, Doc?' Harry said. 'Think it's a keeper?'

Norlin smiled twin rows of luminous Swedish teeth at my partner. 'I'll talk to the administrator, but I doubt it'll be a problem. If it is, I'll take you along to help convince her.'

My partner grinned like a love-struck adolescent. He turned to the glass. 'Noelle, Noelle,' he crooned.

Norlin studied Harry with curious eyes. 'You seem quite concerned about the little lady, Detective.'

'I came in on a boat myself, figuratively speaking,' Harry said.

11

Doc Norlin said we could hold the kid if we put on robes and masks. Harry looked like he'd just won the Super Lotto, and I retreated to the cafeteria until he'd had his fill. We were three steps outside the hospital when Harry's phone rang. He studied the number, grumbled and dialed.

''S'up, Shanelle?' he said, listening for a moment before dropping the cell back in his pocket and giving me a look that was a silent groan. 'Shanelle says she remembers something weird.'

I grinned. 'Like, maybe the first twenty or so years of her life?'

We were at Shanelle's preferred intersection in minutes. She thundered to the corner like a knock-kneed Clydesdale in heat, holding her wig tight as the clogs banged pavement.

'I remembered some weirdness, Harry, right after you left. I had to tell you.'

'Lay it on me, Shanelle.'

'It was maybe two months ago. My feets was killing me and I took a break in that little park over on Walter Street. This guy was on a bench like he was reading. But his eyes was watching everything, especially people walking by. I could see he was after something that wasn't in his book.'

'Companionship,' I said. 'At least briefly.'

'The man got up and wandered over and asked could he talk to me. Then it got strange. Not the bad kind, the question kind.'

'Question kind?' Harry asked.

'Questions like he was trying to get to know me. Weird shit about my family. What race was my mom and dad, did they come from another country? I said I hardly knew either of them, and what the fuck did it matter? He asked could he put something in my mouth.' Shanelle pursed her lips in an exaggerated kiss pucker. 'I said before anything gets between these lips, hon, it pays fifty bucks.'

Harry said, 'And?'

'We went to his car down the street. I stretched out on the seat and let him spend his cash.'

'He, uh, put his penis in your mouth?'

'He jabbed a Q-Tip around my tongue a couple times, pulled it out.'

Harry shot me puzzled. Turned back to Shanelle.

'What happened after that?'

'He asked did I work around there. I said, 'Sure, come back anytime, Doc, and we'll — ''

'Doc?' Harry said. 'He was a doctor?'

'He said his name but I forgot. Martin? Matthews? Murphy? I remember his last name had a M in front. I told Dr M. to come around anytime and ask for Shanelle. He said he might, depending on how things turned out, but never did. A shame. I'da loved to see him every day, Harry.'

'Why's that, Shanelle?'

'Fifty bucks for sucking a Q-Tip?' She gave my partner's shoulder a poke. 'Harry, you don't even have to gargle afterwards.'

Harry sighed and pointed the car back toward the station. 'What do you think that was about, Carson? The doc or whatever with Shanelle and the Q-Tip?'

'Probably some social-services type doing a health survey,' I said. 'Port cities are the crossroads for a lot of things, germs included.'

'So you don't think it's anything?'

'I just hope the Q-Tip got burned after it was analyzed,' I said, slumping in the seat. 'Let's get the hell out of here.'

'Beer?'

I was worn through. 'I ain't into it. I'm going home.'

Harry dropped me at my truck. I headed home, pulling into my drive as my neighbor Lucinda Best walked past, something other-worldly on a leash beside her. Miz Best is seventy years old and a volunteer at the county animal shelter. She often brought canines home to gauge their temperaments.

I'd seen some odd critters at her side, but none so odd as the apparition currently pacing her shoes. Its body was thick and heavy chested, the hair tightly grained, suggesting Lab or shepherd, but the long fluffy tail hair said collie. The legs were slender but the feet were like oven mitts. The head was square and wore basset-length ears. Its eyes were huge and bright and inquisitive. The powerful body was spotted brown and white and black, though the back legs

72

were brindled. The creature looked like a Dr Seuss character.

The animal regarded me politely, not seeming to find my stare ill-mannered. I expect the odd beast was used to being stared at.

'Howdy, Miss Best. That's the weirdest-looking pooch I've ever seen. What's the breed?'

'I call him Mr Mix-up because he's pure Heinz . . . fifty-seven varieties. I expect this doggie's got about everything in him a doggie could have, Abyssinian to Zuchon.'

I smiled. 'So he's a mutt's mutt.'

She tut-tutted me with disapproving eyes. 'Don't say mutt like it's a pejorative, Carson. It's a badge of honor.'

'Aren't pedigrees the way to go?' My knowledge of dogs was limited to the occasional amused viewing of the Westminster Dog Show. My father was an unhappy man and dogs might have brought happiness into our home, thus they were forbidden. I once had a pet hamster for about three days, a gift from a classmate for my upcoming ninth birthday. My father found it beneath my bed and fastballed it into the dining-room wall during my birthday party.

Miss Best said, 'I once heard you and Harry talking about a trip to a horse track in Kentucky, didn't I?'

'We went to Keeneland in Lexington a couple years back.'

'What's a thoroughbred horse do, Carson?'

'Run fast.'

'What else?'

'Uh . . . '

'Running fast is all they do, Carson. Besides being fragile and subject to temperamental fits and all manner of illnesses. Show dogs are beautiful, but also prone to all sorts of maladies. Mutts may look odd, but statistically are healthier, more intelligent and, if you ask me, happier.'

I looked down and couldn't argue the point. I swear Mr Mix-up was grinning at me. Miz Best and I both turned to the sound of a door slamming and saw Mrs Warnock stepping from her house down the street, a ball of yellow fluff on a glittery leash. The ball of fluff saw Mr Mix-up and exploded in a frenzy of leash-pulling and yapping. It resembled a rabid yo-yo.

'Mrs Warnock's dog, Trixie?' Miz Best whispered. 'A two-thousand-dollar blue-ribbon purebred. And it has allergies, hip problems, ear infections. You can probably detect its demeanor.'

'All too easily,' I said, waving at Mrs Warnock and stepping quickly away before the yapping ball of insecurity ran over to urinate on my shoes, something it had done twice in the past.

'Need a faithful companion, Carson?' Miz Best called to my retreating back. 'I know a doggie that needs a good home.'

I smiled and waved, pretending not to hear. There was ample daylight left for a run along the strand, but my remaining energy fizzled away as I tied on my running shoes. I kicked them into the corner and made a sandwich; ate half, finding it tasteless. Clair's voice echoed in my ears.

Are you eating, Carson?

Was I fine? Was some kind of sickness making

74

me pale? She'd said that too: *pale*. Lately, though I'd awaken with a modicum of energy, it waned as the day passed. Had it always done that?

I pulled my laptop from my briefcase, leaned back on the couch, and Googled *pale, lethargy,* and *hunger, lack*.

The engine returned thousands of responses. I saw the word 'cancer' in one of them and shoved the computer back into my case, trading it for the remote. I'd never been a big TV watcher, save for the occasional news update and weather info. In fact, I'd never had anything besides standard channels until last month when something in me decided to invest forty bucks a month in a dish that delivered the world to my living room.

Puffing pillows beneath my head I channel-hopped until I found a show where married couples traded spouses and families and everyone got on everyone else's nerves until they were ready to kill each other. I'd watched it before, oddly enchanted. It was related to my work, but I didn't have to do anything about it but laugh and drink beer until I fell asleep.

★   ★   ★

On the way to work the following morning, I stopped at a convenience store for a coffee and some aspirin to get the couch-kinks from my neck. In the checkout line I noted an example of the speed of the tabloid press, the front page of *World-Week News*, showing a photo of Scaler in one of his patented preaching stances, half Elvis, half auctioneer. The headline was direct:

Famous Preacher Found Dead in Church Camp; Heart Attack Suspected.

The subhead was, *A Fighter for Moral Values.*

It was a tabloid aimed at the political right, and in the past had championed Scaler and his denunciations of homosexuality and liberalism, as well as quoting his veiled slights to people of color. The hagiographic article lifted Scaler to angelic height, ballyhooing his enterprises and advancing a contributing cause of Scaler's cardiac arrest as the 'continued assault on the ideals of Kingdom College by the Left'.

There was a brief mention of Mrs Scaler, painting her as 'a quiet and supportive housewife who often accompanies her husband on his acclaimed television show'. No mention of the good Rev's fondness for using the missus as a punching bag, of course. I wondered how many years the abuse had been going on.

When I got to the department, Harry had checked with the hospital: Mrs Scaler was awake and stable. We'd allowed her a little time to convalesce but now needed to interview her in depth. I hoped lawyer-boy Carleton was off filing a tort or whatever.

Harry and I climbed into the Crown Vic. I took the wheel and pulled out into the streets, the sun already searing at eight thirty, haze thick in the air. When we got to the hospital, I saw a familiar face at the door of Mrs Scaler's private room: Captain Brock Surewell, our departmental chaplain. Surewell nodded us aside and spoke in the modulated whisper that formed his duty voice.

'Mrs Scaler has her nutritionist with her, an Archibald Fossie.'

'Nutritionist?'

'I guess he's also a personal friend.'

'How's she taking things, Brock?' Harry asked.

'She's devastated. But holding on. It's the grace of God; her faith is as strong as iron. Still, go easy with her, guys.'

We entered the room slowly. Mrs Scaler was abed, looking like she was sleeping. Her face remained a mask of bandages. The room smelled of salves and disinfectants. A man sat beside her, making notes on her chart. He looked up at my approach.

'Police,' I whispered.

He nodded and pointed to the door, meaning, *I'll come to you.* We stayed in the hall. Archibald Fossie looked less like a nutritionist than a retired sixties activist: slender as a rope, salt-and-pepper hair going bald up front, long behind the ears, frameless bifocals. He wore a cockeyed red bow tie against a rumpled denim shirt, suspenders holding up khaki pants. His eyes were faded blue against a tan so smooth and even it looked like a table job. He owned a deep and consoling voice, conveying a bedside manner even after leaving the bedside.

'How is she doing?' I asked after he introduced himself.

'As good as can be expected, I suppose. I'm not sure if the horror has connected yet. I'm hoping she . . . doesn't feel like hurting herself.'

'She's suicidal?'

He pushed back his hair, frowned. 'Not any longer. At least, I don't think so. There was an attempt four years back. She chased a bottle of Xanax with a pint of Southern Comfort. She was alone in the house, no one expected for hours. It was certain death.'

'What saved her, Mr Fossie?'

'She staggered drunk through the patio door. When it broke it activated the burglar alarm. The cops rushed her to the emergency room for a stomach pumping.'

'She's improved?'

'Her faith saved her by giving her the strength to continue. But I think there's not much left of her spirit, if you know what I mean. Do you have to question her?'

'We didn't get to talk much yesterday. She was in pain. Do you know why, Doctor?'

'She said she fell down the stairs. Something about high heels.'

'Do you believe her?'

Fossie turned away.

'Sir?' I said.

'God help me, I don't believe her. I think her husband beat her. I think he's done it before. But all I ever got from Patricia was denial. She stumbled over a hose in the yard, tripped in the garage, walked into a door . . . Damn him.'

'You didn't get along with Reverend Scaler?'

'He thinks of nutritionally oriented health as akin to New Age crystal therapy, or maybe even witchcraft. Since her, uh, incident, Patricia's become very nutritionally oriented, part of a regimen I've designed to keep her body healthy. When the body's in balance, the mind follows. Richard tolerated me because keeping Patricia healthy potentially helped him avoid embarrassment.'

'You don't sound like a big fan of Richard Scaler.'

'Everything was his. *His* home. *His* cars. *His* ministry. *His* television network. God gave it to him for being Richard Scaler. Patricia was just an object to him.' He paused and blinked through his lenses. 'Do you really have to talk to her today?'

'Yes. We'll go as easy as possible.'

'Thank you.' Fossie walked down the hall toward the waiting room.

Harry leaned low. 'You want to go in solo?' he asked. 'You think that's better?'

I did and entered the room, cleared my throat. Patricia Scaler's head turned to me, eyes open, frightened. I re-introduced myself, said, 'I'm sorry for your loss, ma'am. Did the chaplain explain a few things?' I meant the grim details of Richard Scaler's death. 'Or Mr Fossie?'

She avoided my eyes. 'Both men spoke of unsavory topics, while trying to be gentle. I suspect Archie — Mr Fossie — of hiding uglier aspects of my husband's final evening. It's his way.'

'Then you know your husband went to Camp Sonshine after he left you. He met someone who may have been there when the heart attack occurred. Do you know who Richard might have met?'

'I have no idea. I never want to know.' She turned away, as if that would make the ugliness disappear.

'Mrs Scaler . . . I want to help. And I won't go telling what you say to anyone who doesn't absolutely need to know. They'll keep the information tight and confined. What happened that night?'

Her eyes turned inside. The second hand swept round the clock twice before her lips moved.

'Richard was having one of his bad times.'

'Bad times?'

'The stress of his work sometimes caught up with Richard. He'd have these moments. He'd question his works, his life. The moments never lasted more than a day or two. It's been said Mother Teresa had terrible doubt.'

'Your husband's, uh, episodes of doubt. They were infrequent?'

'Yes. But terrible to behold and coming more often of late. It was like the Devil was spearing Richard's soul. Richard never made sense when he was like that. One time he spent a whole night yelling about serpents, following me around like he was preaching a sermon. I hid in bed, terrified, until Richard passed out on the floor downstairs.'

'You have no children?'

'God made it impossible for me to bear children. He thinks I would be an unworthy mother.'

I nodded, unable to argue with a thought process I could not understand. I put my hand over hers. 'I'm sorry, ma'am. For all that happened.'

Her other hand fell over mine as soft as a falling leaf. She started to weep. I pulled the chair as close as the bed would allow.

'We were happy once,' she said through her tears. 'But for the last few years it was like we lived separate lives in the same house. The more famous and successful he became, the less I was to him. I didn't try hard enough. It's all . . . my fault. Everything.'

'It's not your fault, Mrs Scaler. Not a bit.'

'I must have driven him to such women. Made him need such terrible things.'

'Please, Mrs Scaler, Patricia, you need to — '

'I'm no good. I should have died long ago.'

Tears continued to flow from her closed eyes. I held tight to her hand. 'As a cop I've seen every possible kind of relationship, Mrs Scaler. I think you were trapped in a marriage that had become loveless. But I suspect you stayed because you thought leaving would hurt your husband. That's not a failing, that's devotion to an ideal. You performed a great kindness at a terrible price.'

Her eyes fluttered open. She stared at me for a long moment. 'Thank you,' she whispered. 'Thank you so much for that.'

'May I ask for your help over the next few days, ma'am? Could you think about people you might have seen with your husband. People he didn't usually associate with. Can you think about that for me?'

'I'll try, sir. But I, uh . . . '

'But what, ma'am?'

81

Hands fluttered beneath the blankets. She swallowed hard. Her head turned away with shame.

'I stopped thinking a long time ago, sir. I believe it was part of my job as Mrs Richard Scaler.'

12

Harry was waiting at the nurses' station down the hall, talking to an intern. Fossie was on a couch outside the door, reading a book on herbal supplements. He saw me and set the book aside.

'How's Patricia?' he asked.

'She's feeling guilt at not being the perfect little wife. She thinks she didn't contribute enough to holding the relationship together. What kind of life did she and her husband have, Mr Fossie?'

Fossie shook his head. 'The marriage was like a play, I think. But like almost everyone, I only saw the performances, not what was happening behind the scenes.'

I nodded, started toward Harry, stopped.

'You're a nutritionist, sir?'

'Nutritionalist is the actual term. I have a practice on the southwest side of town. And, of course, I advise several institutions.'

When I was in college I dated a woman who was studying nutrition. Some of what she said about vitamins and whatnot seemed over the top, but a lot of it made sense and, I'd noted, it had been borne out by subsequent research. My then-girlfriend had used the word *holistic* like a mantra, but now medical doctors used the word; score one for her.

And just maybe I needed a little holism or whatever. 'Are you taking any new patients?' I asked Fossie. 'Is that what they're called?'

'Clients. And I'm actually seeing fewer and fewer clients — my glide path into retirement. Are you talking about yourself, Detective Ryder?'

'I've been feeling a bit off,' I confessed. 'Just recently.'

He studied me for a moment, the blues eyes moving from feet to hair. He took my hands and studied my nails. Put a thumb against my neck and felt my pulse.

'Where do you live, Detective?'

'Dauphin Island.'

He smiled, clapped my shoulder. 'You're in luck. I have a private patient on the west end of the island, an invalid, we go back years. I'm due to see her this evening. How about I stop by and give you a little work-up?'

I gave him my address and he returned to Mrs Scaler's bedside. I briefed Harry on the interview, said not to depend on much from Patricia Scaler, the woman about as beaten down as anyone I'd ever seen, except maybe for my mother. I started back to the car.

Harry said, 'Gimme a couple minutes. I want to see the kid.'

'She'll look just like she did yesterday.'

'Which is fine with me.'

I jammed my hands in my pockets and lumbered toward the PICU a few feet behind my partner. Harry nodded to the nurse at the station, a heavyset young woman with a country-singer mane of artificially red hair that needed a prettier face to pull off the rural-hip statement. She was penning information on

84

charts, sucking a can of Mountain Dew, and nibbling from a bag of FunYums. She'd seen us there before and gave a wiggle-fingers wave.

'We took Noelle off the antibiotics this morning and her temp's holding steady; all other signs are good, including neurological tests. It's like a miracle.'

Harry jogged to the window of the ICU. Yesterday the kid had been third in a row of five hose-studded Plexiglas boxes. But the box was empty and the two in front of it were askew, as if they'd been pushed out of the way.

'Where is she?' he called to the nurse.

'Who?'

'Noelle.'

The nurse tossed aside the FunYums and padded over. She looked into the station, gasped. 'Oh my God,' she said. 'Oh my God.' I saw that beside the empty baby box were tubes and wires hanging limp from bottles and monitors. An IV line ended with a needle and tape, like the kid had been ripped from its lifelines.

'Oh my God,' the nurse said. 'Oh my God.'

Harry sprinted to the nurses' station and picked up the phone, telling hospital security to lock down the building. He ran back to us.

'If the kid's inside, she'll stay inside.' He turned to the nurse, voice firm but gentle. 'When was the last time you checked on Noelle?'

'N-not long,' she stammered, about to burst into tears. 'Maybe five minutes.'

'Did you see anyone near?'

'I . . . wasn't looking this way.'

Harry pulled his cell. 'I'll call it in and get an

Amber Alert in process in case the kid's on the street.'

An Amber Alert was an urgent bulletin in child-abductions cases. An acronym for *America's Missing: Broadcasting Emergency Response*, it was named for nine-year-old Amber Hagerman, abducted, raped and murdered in Texas in 1996. After the horrible crime, it was discovered local law enforcement agencies had information that might have led to the girl's rescue if only they'd had the means to widely disseminate the info. Thanks to changes inspired by the '96 horror, Harry's call would get the kid's description on radio, TV and other media outlets, as well as to all necessary agencies in a wide area.

Bam! Bam!

Gunshots. Harry abandoned his call, grabbing the nurse, pushing her inside the room with the babies. 'Get the kids safe and don't come out,' he growled. She nodded, eyes wide, and went to work rolling the baby boxes and attendant machinery to the rear of the unit. I grabbed my weapon, ran to the connecting hall and looked down. The shot had sounded muted and I was thinking it had been fired in a closed room.

Bam. Bam. Two more shots. Each from a different gun.

Harry was calling for backup. I looked down the hall. Past the central bank of elevators was a whole other section of building, a recently added wing. I heard a fusillade of connected shots, *brrrrrrrrp*, a weapon on automatic fire echoing from somewhere in the other wing. Cold fear flooded my spine. I ran to the junction of the wings and peered around the wall past the elevators. I smelled the raw bite of cordite in the air and I heard screams from a distance. I ran in that direction. Someone, a woman, was shrieking for help.

I slowed at a nurses station, the hub of four spoking halls. Spilled coffee and cups were on the floor alongside paperwork abandoned when staffers fled. I leaned cautiously into the near hall and saw a guy in a security uniform lying on the floor three dozen feet distant, his head held up as two nurses and another security guard bent over him, working furiously. Judging from the man's wounds and the blood flow, they were wasting their time. Glass was strewn everywhere. The walls were pocked with a dozen holes. I looked at the guy performing CPR.

'Where's the shooter?' I yelled.

He pumped the downed man's chest while trying to talk to me, nodded to the staircase at the other end of the hall.

'Male, bearded, tall. He ran there . . . to the stairs.'

'He ran down, right?' I asked, figuring the abductor was headed for the street.

'No, man. He ran up.'

Up? No one escaped a hospital by going up. 'Did he have a baby?' I asked.

'He had something . . . in his hand, I couldn't tell . . . what it was. All I really saw . . . was the freaking machine gun.'

I ran to the stairs, checked, saw nothing and stepped inside, running up to the fifth and final floor. Looked around the corner. A tall bearded guy in an outsized white jacket at the end of a brief hall, fifty, sixty feet away. Motorcycle boots with chains stuck out of his white pants. His sleeves were pulled up to reveal forearms blue with tattoos. A wide window was behind him, the skyline of Mobile in the distance. A heavy steel door was in front of the guy and I figured it went to the roof, the only level left. A security camera was perched atop the door and the guy was yelling into the lens, an angry rant in a tinny nasal whine.

'SCARED MOTHERFUCKERS COULDN'T DO THE GIG, BUT I DID! WHO HAS THE BALLS NOW?'

In one hand I saw the weapon, a machine pistol with a long clip. In the other hand he had the kid clutched by the front of its gown. It was screaming.

'SHUT THE FUCK UP!' the guy roared at the kid. He thumped his chest with the weapon. Shrieked at the camera. 'LOOK AT ME! FUCKIN' LOOK AT ME!'

I slipped the door open. There was no way to get a clear shot as long as he had the kid close. He kept screaming at the camera, getting louder.

' . . . always treating me like I was FUCKIN' HALF THERE!'

When he turned a half-step away to peer out the window into the night, I slipped through the door, scooting across ten feet of floor to a cleaning cart pushed against the wall. There were no rooms off the hall and I figured this section of the top floor was where the roof systems like A/C and drainage joined the building.

'TERRY LEE IS A FUCKING HERO!' the guy howled. 'Yeeeee-hah!'

No patients or staffers. Just me and a raving lunatic with a stolen kid and an automatic weapon. With nothing between me and him but the medical version of a dessert cart.

'*Psssst!*'

I heard the hiss, turned to see Harry crouched in the staircase. We had no chance to shoot for fear of hitting the kid. If we tried for a leg shot the perp would probably lift his weapon and blast Noelle. The guy was on the back edge of a bad nightmare.

'I dedicate this day to ADOLPH . . . ' the guy railed, sounding like he was approaching a violent orgasm. 'And GEORGE, and JAMES AND JOHN AND BUFORD AND PASTOR BUTLER . . . '

'I called for a hostage negotiator,' Harry whispered.

'He'll never get here in time,' I said, skinnying between the cart and wall. 'The guy's falling faster than a Manhattan crane.'

'Hey!' Harry's big voice boomed from the hall. 'Hey, Buddy. Let's talk for a minute.'

The guy wheeled and squeezed the trigger of the freaking Uzi or whatever. A one-second burst filled the air with about thirty slivers of angry lead. I tightened into a ball, heard two slugs *bing* into the cart, more thump the wall. The recoil had kicked his hand back and most of the bullets jumped high, sending puffs of acoustic tile falling from above, a yellow snow on my shoulders. I looked back at Harry. He was grimacing, tucked tight in the stairwell. I heard the dead clip fall, a live one jacked into place.

'My talking's OVER for fucking EVER!' the guy screamed. I watched from a corner of the cart as he paused, shot a glance at the camera, added, 'DIE, YOU FUCKING PIG!' and punctuated it with another fusillade. I ducked. The rounds were closer, thudding into the wall above my head, piercing the stair doors at chest height. Harry was behind mason-block wall, but I knew ricochets were zipping through his space.

I peeked past the edge of the cart, saw the guy shake the kid at the camera like it was a rag doll. 'DO YOU WANT THIS MUTANT TO BE THE FUTURE?' he roared. 'A FUCKING CLONE?'

He rotated the screaming baby to look into its face. For a second he looked about to slam it into the wall. But the camera seemed to call to him and he jammed the kid back under his arm. 'I'M BAD TO THE FUCKIN' BONE!' he screamed at the lens, then turned to our end of the hall, eyes wild. 'SHOOT ME!' he howled, pulling Noelle to his chest, hand around her neck. 'GO AHEAD AND SHOOT ME! I DARE YOU!'

He lifted the weapon. I pulled as tight into myself as possible. Heard muttered cursing. I peeked around the cart in time to see him banging the gun against the wall, then pulling the trigger. Still nothing.

A jam.

'FUCKING CHEAP-ASS SHIT!' he roared,

throwing the weapon to the floor. 'FUCKING JEW GUN!'

'STOP!' Harry yelled. He stepped out into the hall, his gun aimed, hands quivering, unable to do anything with the baby tight to the man's chest.

The guy's wild eyes turned to Harry. 'Oh, wouldn't you just know it,' he said, almost to himself. I stood from behind the cart, my weapon double-gripped.

'It's over,' I said. 'Set the kid aside and you get to live.'

For a moment, the guy seemed to retreat inside himself. For a couple of seconds the madness in his eyes was overtaken by sadness. He seemed, in that moment, almost sane, almost human.

'No, I don't,' he said.

'Come on, partner,' Harry said, taking a step down the hall. 'Put the kid on the floor now, and you end the day breathing. Whatever's bothering you, we can get it fixed.'

'No,' he said. 'Nothing fixes what I got.'

The guy crouched lower and kept Noelle before him like a shield. He snuck a glance at the window behind him. Five stories up. He studied the window again and started giggling, like he'd had a great thought.

'Oh Jesus,' Harry whispered, 'not the window.'

The man pulled Noelle even tighter. He looked behind him again, gauging the steps to the glass.

'Let's see if your goddamn mutant can fly.'

'NO!' Harry yelled. 'DON'T DO IT!'

The guy yelled 'EIGHTY-EIGHT!' then spun and launched himself at the center of the window, a screaming baby beneath his tattooed arm. We froze in horror as the scene unfurled in slow motion: the laugh, the spin, the lunge toward the center of the glass . . .

The dull thump as the man bounced backwards to the floor, scrambling on the white tiles. He recovered instantly, wrapping his hands around the kid's throat, lifting her in front of him, half of the madman's grinning face hidden behind the child.

Harry squeezed the trigger.

13

Dr Lee Hsiung, professor emeritus of Biology, University of Hong Kong, creaked in his office chair. Hsiung's walls were a photo gallery of the professor with preeminent scientists from around the world. Highlighted was a black-and-white photograph of a young Hsiung receiving a hand-shake and a plaque from Francis Crick. Beside it was a photo of an older Hsiung beside Dr Kurt Matthias. Hsiung was smiling, Matthias, dour and distracted.

Hsiung leaned forward, smiling at his visitor. 'Markets are everywhere in Hong Kong, Dr Matthias. They're a potent stew of humanity.'

Matthias sat on an ornate teak and silk couch, briefcase at his side.

'That was what I was looking for, Dr Hsiung,' Matthias said. 'A potent stew.'

'I don't recall you as interested in travel, Doctor. You were always a man of the laboratory. It was a big event when you'd leave the US for a symposium. Of course, given your reputation, the world's geneticists came to you. May I ask why you've become such a seasoned traveler?'

Matthias waved the question away. 'New projects, new horizons. I have, in the past few years, become very interested in fieldwork.'

Hsiung lifted an eyebrow. 'The past eight years, perhaps?'

Matthias's eyes turned dark. 'Something like that.'

Hsiung shook his head. 'Your views were not much accepted, old friend.'

'Not accepted?' Matthias's eyes tightened to slits. 'My views were misread. Spat on. Misused by the most disgusting creatures. A moronic Afrocentric politician in New York used his opposition to me to run for Congress. He won.'

'You never managed to elucidate your — '

Matthias's hand slapped the desk in anger. He stood and walked to the window, silently watching a hundred students walking the commons below.

'I don't explain myself to the gibbering masses. Certainly not to liberal spear-throwers, self-appointed centurions of political correctness. Damn them all.'

'You were vilified, Kurt,' Professor Hsiung said quietly. 'I've not beheld such an uproar since *The Bell Curve*.'

'What does not kill us makes us stronger, Lee.'

Hsiung reached in his desk and produced a stack of computer readouts, the research Matthias had asked for. Hsiung studied his visitor with sad eyes.

'Yes, Dr Matthias. I would expect you to say something like that.'

★ ★ ★

The kid was gone; the screaming, terrified child had been handed off to Doc Norlin, summoned as soon as we kicked the weapon away from the abductor's hands. We figured he was dead — Harry had aimed as far from Noelle as he could, tagging the perp on the outside rim of his eye socket. The slug had taken the inside track, removing a handful of head meat as it exited the rear of the skull at the end of its brief but potent visit.

People had started arriving. Hospital security. EMTs. Terrified staffers peeking around the corner before moving in our direction. Harry and I were still catching our breath. I stepped over the body to the window. Looked down five stories to the parking lot.

'He ran at the window like a rabid gazelle,' I said. 'Dove into it full force. What happened?'

Harry tapped the pane with the muzzle of his .40. It didn't *tick* like glass but *thonked*.

'Hurricane glass,' a security guard behind me said. 'In all the windows. You might as well try to jump through steel plate.'

Forensics arrived to process the scene. Harry put uniforms to work taking statements. Before the upper-departmental types arrived for our own statements, Harry and I hustled to the paediatrics unit where Doc Norlin had just returned from the kid's body scan and was getting her re-hooked to the various tubes and monitors.

'How is she?' Harry asked.

'Outside of abrasions and contusions, she appears unharmed, thank God. Not a bone out of place. I'm about to have the blood work updated, but she seems fine.'

Harry let loose a sigh that sounded like a dam breaking. He leaned against the wall for support. The doc started drawing blood for work-ups and we returned to the murder scene. The air smelled like a shooting range. We found the guard who had been furiously trying to save his colleague's life. It had been, as suspected, futile. The guy, young, dressed in a blue uniform, looked beat down, eyes red, knees unsteady. The body had been collected but the floor was bright with blood.

'What happened?' Harry asked, leading the shaky guard to a chair at the nurses' station. I found a coffee machine, brought him a cup.

The guard wiped his eyes, sucked down half the coffee. 'Homer was in the monitoring station, watching the six cams. I was up from the first floor, on break, asking if Homer wanted to go bass fishing next Saturday. He said 'Hold on,' 'cause he spotted some guy in a suit creeping down the hall, a back-pack in one hand, a parcel in the other. Homer called for the guy to stop. The guy turned and shot with a pistol. Homer shot back. Then the guy pulled something heavyweight out of his pack, turned and fired a burst.' The guard nodded at the glass, the pocked walls. 'Everything fell apart.'

'Can we see the security footage from the camera upstairs? The one at the end of the hall?'

'The roof-door unit? Sure.'

We followed him to the security station. He dialed up the camera in question, racked the recording to just before the event, started it forward. We watched the door open at the end of the hall. The abductor approached, running. He'd slung the backpack over a large shoulder, holding Noelle cradled down his forearm like a

96

football. The lens had a fish-eye configuration, giving the psychologically warped scene a visual warp as well, a funhouse mirror at a psychotic carnival. He started to go beneath the camera — entering the door to the roof — but looked up and saw the device. He backed up and stared directly into the lens. His face was distorted, not by the lens, but by a defect or injury, a lopsided face that probably scared the hell out of kids.

The guy again started for the roof, caught himself. Returned and continued to study the camera, looking between the lens and the end of the hall. Something blossomed in the twisted face.

'He was heading to the roof to finish the action,' Harry said. 'The camera stopped him like a brick wall.'

'He decided to leave a message,' I said. 'A spur-of-the-moment suicide note.'

'But what was all that stuff about mutants and clones?'

'I'd say a head filled with speed and psychedelics. And some kind of psychotic delusion.'

Harry asked the security guy to rewind to a specific moment. The perp raged at the camera.

'*LOOK AT ME! FUCKIn' LOOK AT ME!*'

Harry turned to me. 'There's an old movie with an actor name of James Cagney. *White Heat*. Cagney plays a gangster with a mama complex; it's actually a psychologically complex movie, Cars. You should check it out. Cagney's character is as cold-blooded as a snake and pure psychotic to boot. Long story short: beloved

Mama dies, the gangster goes full whack. Kill-crazy. There's some more stuff about an undercover cop — a guy — who Cagney seems to want to please, just like Mama. Cagney's character gets trapped in a tank yard by the police, flees atop a huge storage tank, a million gallons of gasoline. He decides it's his day to die and he's going to go out with a bang. He starts firing into the gas tank beneath his feet. As it explodes, he's screaming, 'Look at me, Ma. I made it. I'm on top of the world.''

'Turning a dead-end into a blaze-of-glory moment?' I mused. 'You think that's our boy?'

'Given that no helicopter was waiting to pluck him off the roof, I think he was planning to fight the cops until he and the kid were killed, or dive overboard with the kid in his arms. Then he saw the camera and decided to have the finale right there.'

'Look at me, Ma, I made it?'

Harry nodded. 'He was making a movie for someone.'

'But for who? He mentioned five names: Adolph, George, James, John and a Pastor Buford. And a number: eighty-eight. You know what that means.'

I'd seen it tattooed on prison inmates. Eight meant H, the eighth letter of the alphabet, thus, HH for Heil Hitler.

Harry said, 'Guess we got us a white supremacist type. So we wait to see if forensics can ID the perp. I imagine he's got an arrest record about a half-mile long. Then maybe we can track down all those names he was ranting.'

'I got another way to do things,' I said. 'It'll take a trip to Montgomery . . . '

'Can't do it now,' Harry said, looking at his watch and sighing. 'It's gonna take the rest of the day to make our statements and fill out the paperwork.'

'We'll leave first thing in the morning,' I said. 'It's a good time to get in some veterinary research.'

'Veterinary research?'

'We're gonna study the underbellies of ugly animals.'

* * *

When I finally got home, I sat in the quiet of my living room and let the day dissolve. I wanted to call Clair, but knew I'd start babbling and when she asked why I was calling, have no answer whatsoever. The silence in my head grew so loud that I cranked on the TV and filled my eyes with a show about beautiful, soulless people purposefully stranded on an atoll.

At nine thirty I heard a knock on the door, opened it to find Archibald Fossie in suit pants, shirt and tie, sleeves rolled up, wearing a dapper straw fedora with bright paisley band.

I slapped my head. 'I forgot. We had an appointment tonight.'

He looked at me closely. 'You look like you've had a long day, Detective. I'll stop back in a few days.'

I glanced down and saw a barn-shaped black bag in his hand, the kind doctors carried when I was a little kid. It was reassuring, like a talisman from the past.

'Come in,' I said, grabbing his sleeve. 'The day's been a bowl of boiled dung, but I need something. Maybe you've got it.'

'I hope so,' he said, stepping inside as I closed the door against the heat and mosquitoes.

'Can I get you a drink?' I asked.

'Got any Scotch?'

I couldn't help laughing. 'Not a glass of soy milk?'

A sly grin. 'Alcohol can be healthy in moderation. Though for you, I'd prescribe red wine, four or five fluid ounces a night.'

'Duly noted.'

I got Fossie a neat single-malt kept around for Harry's benefit, poured myself a tumbler of red wine, deciding to start nutritional therapy tonight. Fossie reached into his bag and produced a stethoscope, hung it around his neck.

'I'll need you to undress, Detective. Down to skivvies is fine.'

I complied and sat on a dining-room chair as Fossie poked and prodded, thumped and listened. He studied my tongue, my hair. He had me walk across the room and back, making notes on my carriage. He had me do two minutes of push-ups, re-listened to my heart. I told him how I'd been feeling — lack of appetite, vague pains in my gut, lethargy, occasional lightheadedness, insomnia.

'The major machinery sounds fine,' he said, dropping the steth into his bag and plucking several vials out, pouring capsules into paper packets. 'In the meantime, here's a concoction to help you sleep: L-Tryptophan, valerian and a bit of melatonin. These others are vitamins, heavy on B-complex and good for stress.'

'Stress? Really?'

'So is ginseng. Here's some ginseng extract. Natural medicines, one and all. Take two of each every morning, two in the early afternoon. None after four p.m. I'll write up a diet I want you to follow, low fat and high protein.'

I nodded and followed him to the door. 'What do I owe you?'

'Find out the truth about Richard Scaler,' he said quietly, hand on the knob, looking into my eyes. 'Discover what he really was.'

I said, 'You spend a lot of time at the Scaler home, right, Mr Fossie?'

'An hour a day or so. I'm actually on retainer, another thing that drove Richard nuts. I go to the co-op, buy fresh fruits and veggies, take them to Patricia. Or I grind herbal medications and mix infusions. She likes to watch and talk while I work.'

'What's she talk about?'

'Her childhood. The pre-Richard days when she was carefree, a high-school girl with her whole life ahead of her. The conversation is therapeutic. I'm usually there in the morning. With the, uh, unfortunate event, I plan to stop by in the afternoon or evening to make sure Patricia's all right.'

'You don't really think it was an unfortunate event, Mr Fossie. Not if the Missus got free of a man who was hurting her.'

He closed his eyes, loosed a sigh. 'Being free of that self-righteous beast is the best thing that ever happened to Patricia. But she's not ready to let herself know that. Though she already knows it deep inside. Does that make sense?'

'Yes. And if you really want me to uncover the truth about Scaler, there's a way you can help. I need to know who was with Scaler on his last night.'

Fossie's eyes looked dubious behind the glasses. And maybe a bit scared.

'It doesn't sound ethical.'

'You want me to reveal the truth about Richard Scaler? Give me something that provides insight into his secret life. See if you can find a calendar entry. Something on his desk. A phone number scrawled on a Post-it. Anything.'

When Fossie escaped into the night, I didn't know if I'd succeeded in enlisting him. Expecting little, I washed Fossie's prescribed capsules down with the last of my wine, falling into a sweet and dreamless sleep more satisfying than any I'd had in weeks.

14

It was eight thirty a.m. when Harry and I pulled into the failing strip mall on the south side of Montgomery. The offices I sought were on the end. There had once been windows, but they had been bricked over after a shoebox loaded with four sticks of dynamite exploded on the sidewalk outside. The two occupants of the office had been back in the files, or they would have been shredded by glass and shattered by concussion.

Nothing was taken for granted any more. There were no windows and the door was metal.

Near the entrance to the lot I saw a hulking bubba type slouched in a battered pickup with the door open. He had a square face and had gone days without shaving. His plaid shirt had the sleeves cut off, showing hard and tattooed arms. He shot me a look, flicked the cigarette to the pavement. I checked my rear-view and saw him pull a cellphone.

'You see that guy, Cars? Mean-looking piece of work.'

'Probably just sitting and eating,' I said. 'But around here's where you should let your natural paranoia shine.'

'Cuz it ain't paranoia if they're really following you, right?'

'Bingo.'

I parked at the far end of the building. There was no name on the metal door, just a number.

But I knew the name: Southern Legal Defense Program. Though the name suggested a program to help indigent defendants, the SLDP was a monitoring organization that kept close tabs on hate groups. The organization had contacts ranging from law enforcement to prison leadership to informants inside the groups. In a recent case information supplied by the SLDP and a couple of similar watchdog groups helped convict two former Klan members of a series of lynchings that had occurred in the early sixties. The Kluxers were now in their late seventies, and I was delighted they got their earthly retributions in before whatever lays in the distance exacted the Universe's toll.

Much harsher, I hoped.

There had, predictably, been the usual cracker chorus bemoaning the perps' current ages and calling the investigation a vendetta against a few old men, as though time had washed their crimes away. I recalled video footage of their lawyer, a beady-eyed guy in a loud suit, standing at the courthouse mics after the guilty verdicts, yodeling about injustice to a crowd with few but vocal sympathizers.

Thus the bomb, one of several revenge schemes aimed at the group in its forty-year existence.

I'd known the SLDP's director since my first year on the force, back when I was in uniform. A murder had occurred on my beat, horrific, a fifty-year-old black man beaten to death with ball bats.

I'd been asking around on the street about the

104

unsolved murder — it couldn't even have been called a case because I was in uniform — for a couple months when I got a call out of the blue from a guy named Ben Belker. It was curious that he'd heard about my interest, because I was just a beat cop. Belker said I should talk to a guy named Hawley Cage.

Long story short: Cage turned out to be a member of a group called Aryan America Only. Except he was also an informer for the SLDP. Cage told me of interesting boozy conversations he'd overheard at a meeting. Long story shorter: I vetted the info, passed it to the dicks on the case, and a month later they arrested two psychopathic Klanners who'd killed the old guy after he'd yelled at them to slow down in the street because kids lived in the neighborhood.

It turned out Ben Belker had worked for the SLDP for years as a field operative and was now its 'survey director', meaning he assimilated and analyzed data on hate groups to make sense of their comings and goings. If anyone was anyone in the various movements, Ben kept tabs on them.

Ben was at the door as I entered, as skinny as a sapling, brown hair looking like it was combed with a wolverine, big eyes widened by nerdish black-frame glasses. A pen stain soaked the pocket of his work shirt. His shoes were gray Hush Puppies, one untied. He clasped me in a hug as tight as an auto compactor. When we released he slapped the side of my head. Harry seemed content to stand back and watch the drama.

'Jeez, what was that about?' I asked, rubbing my head.

'When was the last time you were here?'

Time has never been exact to me. I tried to recall my last visit.

'Has it been a year, Ben? Year-and-a-half?'

'Three. After promising we'd get together at least twice a year.'

'My bad.'

'OK,' Ben grinned, 'I've hugged you 'cus I love you, smacked you because you're a prick, now introduce me to Harry Nautilus and let's get down to business.'

Harry frowned at the mention of his name.

'Have we met before?'

Ben held his finger up in the *hang on* motion, went to a computer, tapped a few keys. He waved us over to look at the screen. I saw Harry and me in a crowd in Mobile's Bienville Square, a prominent civil rights leader at a podium a dozen feet beyond. The event had been two years ago.

'Here's another,' Ben said, pulling up a second photo from the same day. Both shots were slightly unfocused. 'And I think there's one more . . . '

Harry didn't look happy, but kept his counsel and watched Ben select from a sheet of tiny photos, making an enlargement that fit the screen.

'Voila!' Ben said. Harry and I leaned forward to see a shot of the two of us standing outside the front door of a local hotel. I was on the radio, Harry looking to his side at a crowd of sign-holding protestors. I remembered the day: a liberal Massachusetts senator had been visiting Mobile and Harry and I were put on guard duty along with half the force.

'I know there's an explanation I'm going to accept.' Harry's tone said it would be a challenge. Harry wasn't big on unauthorized surveillance of himself.

'We weren't specifically taking surreptitious photos of you, Detective,' Ben explained. 'This guy here, ten feet away, is who we were tracking. Arnold Meltzer. He's the head honcho of the Aryan Revolutionary Army, a pivotal white power splinter group attractive to a lot of biker gangs. You just happened to be there.'

Harry took a second to let it sink in, nodded acceptance. He studied the photo of a wisp of a man in his fifties, dressed in a light seersucker suit, his face almost totally hidden behind sunglasses. His mouth was a tight pucker, like he was about to lift a clarinet to his lips. He looked as threatening as a canary.

'This guy's a Klan type, you mean? A real baddie?'

'These days, the danger is a lot bigger than the Klan. Thanks to the internet, white supremacist types are more organized than ever.'

'Obama's presidency doesn't change things?'

'People this broken just feel more threatened. It's made them even crazier, full-blown para-noiac. The movement used to weed out the worst psychotics, but now it gives them leadership positions.'

Harry re-studied the photo of Arnold Meltzer.

'And this little fella's a leader?' He sounded dubious.

'Don't be fooled by Meltzer's stature. His ideas make him dangerous. As well as his influence and money.'

'Where's the money come from?'

'Outlaw bikers are big in the drug-running biz. Mules. It's whispered Meltzer's into that big-time, like a contractor. He's also the figurehead for the White Power movement in the South, revered by supremacists.'

Harry scowled at the photo. 'I was nearly rubbing shoulders with the scumbucket and didn't know.'

Ben said, 'He's not in any police files. I was scanning through the photos when I saw Carson. From his descriptions, I figured that was you next to him. I blew the photos up and saved them.' Ben grinned at me, a loopy Cheshire cat. 'Something to remember Carson by since he never writes, never calls, never . . . '

I put my hand on Ben's shoulder. 'I'm here now, Ben. With another photo for you to consider.' I pulled three death photos of our baby abductor, handed them over. He stared, shook his head.

'Never seen him before. What'd he do?'

'Tried to steal a kid from a hospital.'

'I saw that bit of weirdness on the news,' Ben said. 'I should have figured you'd be in the middle of it.'

He picked up a magnifying glass from his desk and studied closer. 'I know that tat on his shoulder: WR. It shows sympathy with a specific biker gang.' Ben turned to the open door to the back offices, yelled, 'Wanda!'

A second later a heavy thirtyish woman with braided hair pushed her head through the door. She wore one of those formless dresses people wear when they don't give a damn for fashion.

'Yo?'

He held up the shot and she stepped into the office. 'This is Wanda Tenahoe,' Ben introduced. 'She coordinates the info on biker gangs; a big job, but Wanda has a photographic memory.'

'It's good,' Ms Tenahoe corrected in a bright, musical voice at odds with her first impression. 'Not photographic. Let me take a peek.'

She studied the photo. Yanked her thumb for Ben to move from his desk so she could sit. She pecked keys, faces flying past on the monitor. I wondered if the SLDP had face-recognition software. They seemed to have everything else to gauge the whereabouts of people, not just in locale, but spanning decades.

The computer beeped and four photos unfolded on the screen.

'Here we go,' she said. 'Your baby-snatcher's name is Terry Lee Bailes. There's not much on him because he wasn't singled out for individual surveillance, meaning he's not considered particularly dangerous.'

I looked at Harry, mouthed *not dangerous?*

'I've got a few photos of him peripheral to other investigations. Here they come.'

We leaned close to the monitor. In the first two pix, the man we now knew as Terry Lee Bailes was on a scruffy, dented Harley parked with a dozen other bikers outside a roadhouse. The third was the same bar, a different day, a few different participants.

'That's the Southern Gladiators' clubhouse over by Jackson,' Tenahoe said. 'It's a bar where a lot of the WR biker-types hang out.'

'WR?' Harry asked. 'White something-or-other?'

'How'd you guess?' Tenahoe grinned. 'White Riders. They're a nasty lot. Not real organized, not real smart, but murderously mean and loving to prove it. They're also allied with the Aryan Revolutionary Army, its security and enforcement wing.'

Something caught Harry's eye. He leaned close to the photos, scanning between them. He pointed to something only he had seen.

'Look how their bikes are parked. The gang's machines are lined up straight and so tight they're almost touching, but here, five or six feet away, is Bailes's bike. Both times.'

'He's not part of the group,' I said, suddenly seeing it. 'It's subliminal. He couldn't park his bike up close and personal to theirs. The physical distance reflects a psychological distance.'

Harry nodded. 'He's not fully accepted by the group.'

'Incredible observation,' Tenahoe said, staring at Harry with undisguised admiration.

The last shot was Bailes with two other guys, smoking and talking. One guy's palm rested on Bailes's shoulder, like they were buds.

'Who's the guy with his hand on Bailes?' Harry asked.

'The guy the shots were meant to catch,' Tenahoe said. 'Donnie Kirkson. He's a low-life scuzzer who operated as a conduit between movers and shakers like Arnold Meltzer and the rank-and-file types like the White Riders. Kirkson's nasty business: aggravated assault, breaking and entering, wanton endangerment, drug busts, sexual assaults. He's not bright enough to be a chief, but he probably killed or kicked the shit out of someone Meltzer considered an enemy, so he moved up to the equivalent of middle management.'

'You said 'operated', past-tense,' Harry noted.

'Kirkson got caught having sex with a fifteen-year-old runaway. He befriended her, then loaded her with alcohol and dragged her to a motel for four days. Kirkson took a six-year prison fall. He went in last winter.'

I looked again at the spread of surreptitious photos, always amazed at the minutiae Ben and his people could garner.

'Anything else you need?' Ben asked.

I handed him the list of names Bailes had ranted at the camera.

'Lessee here,' Ben said, tapping the list. 'You know Adolph, and you know 88 is Heil Hitler, right? The James is probably James Burmeister, who randomly executed two black people on the street. John is probably John King, who dragged a black man to death behind his truck — '

'I remember that,' Harry said. 'The victim's name was Byrd.'

'Right. Buford would be Buford Furrow, who opened fire on pre-schoolers at a Jewish

111

community center. And Pastor Butler is Richard Butler, the founder of the Aryan Nation, a supposed man of God who proclaimed Hitler a prophet, Jews the descendants of Satan, and blacks as mud people.'

'So Terry Lee was giving a big ol' shout-out to previous hatemongers?' I said, feeling sickened.

'A lot of these screwballs believe in Norse myths — the Aryan thing, right? — your boy Bailes was probably figuring he'll get his name scribed on the walls of Valhalla, right beside Adolph, Buford, James and the rest of the glee club.'

Harry and I thanked Ben and Wanda Tenahoe and started to the door. Ben said, 'Anything else you need, Carson, just ask. We've got decades of info on low-life scuzzballs, with more coming in every day. Plus a wide range of operatives, informants, and sympathizers who keep up on the whereabouts of the worst of the lot. Some of them, we can tell you what they had for supper last night. And what pizza company they called to deliver it.'

Harry stopped and turned. 'You know when they make phone calls, Mr Belker?'

An uneasy smile from Ben. 'We might have a sympathizer or two in the phone companies. Folks who slip us call records of certain nasty individuals. Unless that's illegal, in which case this is all conjecture.'

'Must be conjecture,' Harry said, jamming his hands in his pockets and heading for the door. 'Hell, I didn't even hear it.'

15

'That's some network those folks have,' Harry said, putting the cruiser in gear.

'It's been in place for years. Some of their operatives are dedicated enough to take heavy risks, like being undercover in dens of hate. And as Ben alluded, they're not above edging around the law to get the job done.'

'Keeping tabs on white supremacists has got to be one of the stranger job descriptions. How'd Belker get into the gig?'

'You remember the twenty-year-old white guy who came down South in 1973 to register voters, unionize the factories — Thomas Belker? Ben is his boy.'

It was one more ugly act in a national history of ugly racial acts. After only a week of trying to unionize a paper mill in a small town on the Sippi-Bama border, Thomas Belker had been abducted and beaten severely. Like many of the attacks of the day, the perps were never found.

Though Belker had the fortune to survive, his wounds were crippling and constantly painful. He was an icon of the populist movement, the naïve but hopeful kid from New York City who went to the Deep South to fight the segregation and work abuses that had lingered into the seventies. Pete Seegar had written a song about Thomas Belker, and his name was invoked at civil rights commemorations.

'I remember the day it happened,' Harry said. 'I was just a kid. When I got older, there was something in me that wanted to track down his address, say thanks. But then I'd wonder what I'd say, how I'd say it. And, of course, I never knew where to write.'

'Ben's dad lives in Brooklyn,' I recalled. 'Send a letter.'

'It's a different time now,' Harry said quietly. 'And I still wouldn't know what to say.'

★   ★   ★

A little more checking revealed that Bailes had lived in a trailer on the southern side of Mobile. I expect the motor court had started out nice back in the fifties, but time and weather had taken a toll on some of the lots and units. Others were in decent shape with sculpted hedges and neat little lawns. I figured these were owner-occupied, the park a mix of owned and rented units.

Bailes's trailer was a rental, not a surprise. I suspected it had been in place since the court opened, its lines blocky and tired-looking. It was green, which probably helped disguise the mildew, but not much. Paint isn't generally fuzzy.

Harry and I walked rickety steps to the door and he slipped the lock in a five-count. The door bottom squealed across the warped floor, needing to be lifted to swing clear. We stepped inside to a smell that wrinkled our noses.

There were plates on the table with cigarettes

stubbed out in unwashed food remains. Maybe Bailes hadn't done the dishes because there was a motorcycle engine block in the sink. If there was a décor motif in the trailer, it was Empty Beer Bottles, the Miller Lite period. A secondary motif was Aryan: a 'flag' made from a sheet and hand-painted with a black swastika, poorly, draped over a slumping couch. I figured it was a thematic venue for reading *Mein Kampf*. Except for the couch, it was all outdoor furniture, probably swiped from patios. The smells of smoke, beer, garbage and mildew fought, with garbage the easy winner until Harry set the overflowing can outside and we opened the windows.

I checked the cabinets, finding canned goods, packets of tuna, popcorn, a five-pound bag of instant mashed potatoes, all from cut-rate outlets. The fridge held beer and ketchup and a package of gray hot dogs. Harry took the bedroom, emerging after a five-minute toss.

'Nothing in there but a porn collection and white-power pamphlets and books.'

We found mountains of porn in our jobs. I used to regard the bulk of it with an ironic amusement, but the content had darkened and now there were widely available magazines and websites that made me avert my eyes and wonder if we were all the same species.

Harry got down on hands and knees to check under the couch. He rolled his eyes, muttered, 'Oh shit.'

'What?'

He pulled out a mousetrap with a shriveled

body dangling from the clamp.

'Looks fresher than the hot dogs,' I noted.

We finished up. Aside from the white-supremacist and biker trappings, Terry Lee Bailes remained a cipher. Stepping outside into clean air blowing up from the Gulf, I resisted the impulse to strip to my skivvies and let the sun burn away any vampiric bacteria from Terry Lee Bailes's stinking trailer.

We heard the near rumble of motorcycle engines and saw a trio of bikers through a copse of cypresses acting as a windbreak between the trailer park and the road. They braked to turn into the park. I saw the advance biker look our way and shout behind him and the trio fired their engines and thundered away.

'Goddamn I hate them big motorscooters,' grumbled a voice at our backs.

We turned to see a tight, wiry guy in his seventies. Though small of frame, he had the shoulders and stature of a man who'd once been fit and hard, his carriage as erect as a fence pole. He wore pressed khakis and a white strap tee, a blurry blue anchor tattooed on a bicep. His hair was short and steel gray.

'You're cops, right?' he said, narrowing an eye.

'As true as the day is long,' Harry said.

'Bailes in jail?' the guy said, looking hopeful.

'Bailes is in the morgue.'

For a split-second it seemed the old guy was about to clap his hands in glee. But maybe he was gonna play air accordion.

'Did you know Mr Bailes, sir?' Harry asked.

'Our biggest conversation came after he

116

moved here few months back. Thought he was some big-ass Hell's Angel or something, a tough guy. I worked as an oiler in the Merchant Marine since I was seventeen years old. I never gave anyone shit, but I never took any either, you know what I mean?'

'I expect I do.'

'He come a-roarin' in here the first couple nights on that damn Harley, gunnin' the engine outside my window so I couldn't hear the tee-vee from two feet away. The third day I heard him coming and put my forty-five in my belt . . . I got a permit, you wanna see?'

'I'll take your word, sir.'

'I jammed that hogleg in my pants and headed to the door. Bailes pulled up under my window. The sound was like a goddamn train wreck that kept going. When I stepped outside he put a finger in one nosehole and cleared out the other one on the ground. He gave me a shit-eating grin with that lopsided face and said, 'Loud enough for you, Pops?''

'Your reply, sir?' I asked, knowing it was going to be the highlight of my day.

'I pulled that pistol out and said, 'Almost as loud as your screamin's gonna be when I blow a hole through your leg and into the crankcase.''

'Bailes's response, sir?'

'From that day on he cut the engine when he got close, glided up between the trailers.' The old sailor shook his head. 'Gutless little pissant.'

16

'Gutless?' Harry said as we climbed back into the car. 'Bailes creeps into a guarded hospital, fights a duel with a security guard, tries to hop out a window when cornered? Nuts, maybe. But not gutless.'

The computer in the car beeped and displayed an address. I shielded my eyes against the sun and studied. 'Bailes's mother, current surname Teasdale,' I said. 'I'll go tell mama her baby boy is gone. You want me to drop you off first?'

Given that Harry had fired the fatal shot, I didn't know if he'd want to be there when I informed Bailes's mama. He'd stay in the car, of course, but it'd still be an uncomfortable nearness.

Harry considered my offer for a couple of beats. 'Thanks for the thought, bro. But I'll be fine in the car. I'll call the hospital for the latest on Noelle.'

'That'll do the job, I suppose.'

Mrs Bailes/Teasdale lived in a scrofulous bungalow along a drainage canal. Vehicle carcasses lined the street, waiting for repairs the owners could never afford. The yard was dirt and weeds. A silver GMC pickup sat in the drive, tool chest in the bed, not generally a lady's kind of vehicle.

I waited for a pair of motorcycles to roar down the street, knocked again. For a split-second I noticed a strange sensation, like my knocking made a kettledrum sound. I looked around, making sure no one was playing a big drum nearby, but nothing. I knocked harder, but the drum effect was gone.

'Who the hell is it?' a male voice barked from inside.

I held my ID to the window on the door, saw the curtain slide, eyes inspect. The door opened to a big muscular guy in his early forties, with sun-bronze skin and a Fabio-style hairdo. The guy pulled a red crushed-velvet bathrobe around him, hair still wet. The bathrobe was probably an XX-Large and seemed to fit just right. I didn't like him on general principles.

'Sorry to disturb you,' I said. 'Does LaVernia Teasedale live here?'

He began swinging the door shut. 'Never heard the name before.'

I put up my hand to stop the door. 'Records show she pays utilities on this house. If Miz Teasdale is here, I need to speak to her. If she's not, I'll be back.'

'What would a cop want with LaVernia?' the hulk growled. His biceps rippled like fluid stone.

'That's between me and her.'

'She ain't here. I dunno when she'll be back. Maybe next week.' He tried the door-close again, I did the one-finger doorstop. I looked across the room, saw the ashtray and pretty much knew by the smell what I'd find. I slipped under the guy's arm and across the floor.

'Hey!' he barked.

'Wrong,' I said, holding up the half-smoked

joint plucked from the ashtray. 'Not hay, sport. Grass.'

'Aw fuck,' he said. 'You gotta be kidding. An' I ain't never seen it before anyway.'

I pocketed the doob. The house was dark, curtains drawn. I saw discount furniture in the living room, a couple of porno mags on the couch. I heard giggling in a back room, female. It sounded like a voice on the phone.

'Didja like it?' the voice asked. *'Was it all in focus?'*

I could see into the dining room. Instead of a table and chairs, there was a king-size mattress on the floor, a couple pillows. A movie camera was tripoded in the corner. There was a still camera on a table. In the opposing corner a black tripod held a floodlight, also angled down at the bed. Wires ran from equipment to a laptop computer on a low stool near the bed.

The guy saw where I was looking. 'Now what? You got a problem with people making home movies?'

I've never been opposed to sexuality. I've celebrated it with gusto when time and companion are right. And I don't give a tinker's damn what anyone does in the privacy of their home. But the keyword is *private* and beaming intimacies out over the internet for the entertainment of thousands of viewers seemed to defeat the word 'intimate'. Plus, given the appearances of most who mingled body parts for viewing, the programs were an affront to aesthetics as well.

'Here's the way it is, star,' I said, tiring of the

120

repartee. 'Either get Miz Teasdale, or tell me where I can find her. Elsewise you are gonna find your ass in jail.'

He sneered. 'My lawyer will pop me in ten seconds.'

'Indeed, star,' I agreed. 'And I'll happily put your ass in there for free. But your lawyer will charge five hundred bucks to get it out.'

He started to say some smart-ass thing. I was about fed up with star-boy. I waggled a *no-no* finger with my right hand, said, 'Get the lady.'

He scowled but folded, looking to the back of the house. 'Vernia!'

'What?'

'A guy wants to talk to you. Some cop.'

A door opened in a back room; bedroom, I assumed. A petite teenaged girl stepped into the shadowed hall wearing a white blouse and short plaid skirt, the kind of dress worn by parochial schoolgirls. She had on blue knee socks and patent-leather loafers. I was about to turn and bust bathrobe boy for statutory rape when the girl stepped into the living-room's light.

I saw her youth was a façade of make-up, a lie of cosmetology. Squint and she was fourteen, open your eyes and she was forty-something. The effect was freakish, like a mummy with ten coats of pink paint, or something from a Ray Bradbury sideshow.

'I ain't done nothing wrong,' the girl protested. Her whisky-soaked voice was three hundred years older than her appearance and suggested she'd done plenty wrong, but was pretty sure I wasn't currently catching her at it.

'LaVernia Teasdale?' I asked, still spooked by the carnival face. 'Formerly Bailes?'

'It was Bailes for four fuckin' months. That was twenny-something years ago. Whadya want?'

'You're Terry Lee's Bailes's mother?'

She lit a cigarette and let the smoke drift from her nose as she talked. 'I ain't seen that chicken-shit kid in forever. Two years, mebbe.'

'How long did he live with you?' I figured there wasn't much to be gleaned here, information-wise, but I tried for a bit of background before I laid the ugly news on her.

She shrugged. ''Til he was fifteen, sixteen? He kept running off, nothing I could do. So one day I just didn't call the cops to look for him any more.'

'That was the last time you heard from him?' I asked.

She shrugged. 'He calls mebbe once a year. He gets his ass in jail for some pissy-ass thing and calls me whining for bail money.'

'You ever give him any?' I asked.

'I don't steal the shit. Why should I pay his bail?' She grinned. 'Terry Lee still got a face like a squished basketball?'

The casualness of her words roiled my stomach. I breathed down anger and let a few seconds pass.

'I'm sorry to tell you this, ma'am,' I said, 'but your boy's dead.'

A look of mild confusion. 'You mean like . . . dead?'

'Yes, that's the dead I mean.'

She frowned at the news. Stubbed the

122

cigarette dead in the ashtray.

'What am I s'posed to do now?'

'You might ask how he died,' I suggested, feeling my jaw muscles clench. 'Or grieve. Or pray for his soul.'

None of my proposals seemed appealing. She looked to Fabio Hair for a second opinion. 'What am I s'posed to do, Sweets?'

'Sweets' looked at me, a frown of concern on his broad face. He stepped close for a man-to-man conference. 'This thing with Terry Lee,' he asked. 'It gonna cost her anything to deal with?'

'He was over twenty-one,' I said, hearing drumbeat thunder in my head. 'There's no paternal obligation, legally. If the State drops Terry Lee into an unmarked hole, it won't cost a penny. But she might consider a small service, something to honor his life.'

Vernia Teasdale nee Bailes was eavesdropping.

'I ain't got money for no fancy services and shit,' she brayed. 'I got a tough life.'

The drumming in my head ramped into a roar, like an overloaded dynamo. From beside me the coffee table launched from the floor into the smelly little room to the side, taking out the camera and the lights and causing sparks to pop from a junction box on the floor.

The action seemed in slow motion. I remember a lot of yelling, but by the time I walked out, Mrs Teasdale and Sweets were nicely quiet.

When I got in the car Harry looked between me and the house.

'You OK, Cars? You're kind of red in the face.'
'It was warm in there.'

He raised a curious eyebrow. 'But everything went fine, right?'

'Hunky-dory, bro. How 'bout we get a move on?'

17

Harry seemed deep in thought for a few miles, now and then shooting me a glance, as if uncertain about something. He took a deep breath, blew it out, sounding like he was changing gears in his head.

'You hear anything from the Dauphin Island cops on their part in the Noelle case?' he said. 'Have they gotten anything from Briscoe?'

'I talked to Jimmy Gentry yesterday. He said Briscoe was all promises, but hadn't really checked on anything like the ownership of the burned-down house.'

'Racist bastard,' Harry muttered. 'How about you check, Carson? Briscoe ain't gonna do squat for me.'

I sighed, picked up the phone, got the deskman, asked for Sheriff Briscoe. A gruff male voice answered like the mouth was at home watching TV and eating pizza and not in a supposedly professional law-enforcement agency.

'Yeah, what?'

'Briscoe?'

'Speaking. And it's Sheriff Briscoe.'

'This is Carson Ryder. And it's Detective Ryder. I'm calling about — '

'I know what you're calling about, Deee-tective. We ain't got nothing on harpoon man.'

'Nothing?'

'Like in zero. You ever have one of those cases

has nothing to grab hold of? That's this one. No one lived close to that place, no one heard anything, no one saw any fire. I'm about to close the books.'

'It's only been a few days since — '

'The place was probably used as a meth lab. Some meth head got pissed at another, jammed a spear in his belly. Still had enough brains left to burn the place down 'fore he ran off. I gotta go. I got work to do.'

'Let someone else sort the mail, Briscoe. I need ten seconds of your twenty-second attention span.'

'What the hell are you — '

'Two things, Briscoe. One, the forensics lab found no residue of the chemicals used to make methedrine, and two, harpoons aren't used to make meth either. A man was killed in that shack and, like you said, you're the sheriff. Maybe you recall from your oath of office that the title comes with some expectations.'

The phone clicked dead. I sighed, dialed the county property evaluator's office. The owner would be listed in tax records, a no-brainer. The woman who answered was one of those personality-free, efficient types I love, answering my question within thirty seconds.

'The residence was owned for fifteen years by a Lewis Johnson. It sold twelve years back for twenty thousand dollars to a . . . to a . . . Oh my, I'd better spell it for you.'

I started to take down the name — and kept taking down the name — hoping the lead in my pencil lasted.

'Chakrabandhu Sintapiratpattanasai?'

Harry attempted to pronounce the name, no way of knowing if he was even close. He'd pulled over and parked, the better to devote his attention to the name.

I shrugged. 'For all I know about Thai, it's pronounced Chuck Smith.'

'Male or female?'

'I'll assume male. Records show that CS bought the place a dozen years back, which dovetails with the upsurgence in Thai shrimp fishermen moving into the area.'

'Address? Phone?'

'No listed address. Phone disconnected five years back.'

'Probably switched to a cell and stiffed the phone company.'

'Wonderful,' I said. 'A name we can't pronounce, a phone we can't call, an address that ain't listed.'

'It's an immigrant community,' Harry mused. 'Extremely close-knit, I expect, the protection of the tribe. We have to assume that somewhere in the area is a Thai who has knowledge of his kinsman's — CS's — whereabouts.'

'So where from here, Mr Anthropology?' I asked.

'Let's go to lunch and see if we can dig up some family Thais.' He grinned at me, the first time in days he'd looked happy about anything but Noelle. 'Pun intended.'

★ ★ ★

We ended up at a tiny Thai restaurant and grocery in Harry's neighborhood. We'd eaten there a few times, always a delicious experience. We sat in the eight-table dining area, the walls green and embellished with posters of Thai temples. Paper lanterns gave a soft light. The room was fragrant with garlic and ginger and chilis. The owner, a man in his early sixties, came out to meet us. Harry pulled him aside and spoke for a few minutes, and the man gave a half-bow and returned to the kitchen.

'Well?' I asked.

Harry said, 'Mr Srisai thinks he speaks English worse than he does. He's calling someone who might help us. It'll be a few minutes.'

We ordered pad Thai and pad see yew, trading halfsies. Harry doused his with nam pla, I went heavy on the chili paste. We ate and watched visitors to the adjoining grocery select from a variety of vegetables that were unfamiliar to me, save for ropy knots of ginger and fragrant sprays of cilantro. I saw a blue beamer pull from the street to the rear of the restaurant. I listened for the back door and heard it through the potwash din of the kitchen.

Two minutes later, the kitchen door opened to reveal a short, slender man in his mid twenties. He wore sandals, unpressed khakis and a T-shirt from the University of Alabama. His short black hair was arrayed in abbreviated spikes, like being hip, but having to temper it for the office. The soft angles of his round face were further softened by owlish eyeglasses. We did introductions, shook hands. Kiet Srisai was the owner's eldest son.

'You a student at the U of A?' I asked, nodding at the shirt.

'A recent graduate. Architectural engineering. I'm working for a firm a couple miles from here. Father tells me you have questions about Thai fishermen down the coast.' His English was excellent and musical.

'The shrimpers near the border. The ones hit by the recent 'caines.'

He nodded. 'I knew the community, small, maybe a dozen families. They came here to the restaurant and grocery when in town. Very close-knit. They were scattered like leaves by the hurricanes. Some blew off to Texas, others to Louisiana. Others as far as California. Most will be near water, that's all I can say. All they know is fishing.'

I again studied the name on the note page, handed it to Srisai. 'Such a long name,' I said. 'Is that common?'

'It's the Chinese influence. Native Thais tend toward simple, short surnames, like Srisai. Immigrants from China had to register a name with the government, a minimum of ten characters. But favored combinations of letters got taken. No duplication is allowed, so the names are increased in length to be unique. Many are over twenty characters long.'

Harry said, 'And I've been trying for decades to get folks to spell Nautilus right.'

Srisai's face went from affable to apologetic. 'Also, and perhaps this will add to your burden, Thais often change their names. In Thailand, names have mystery and meaning. Thais are very

129

superstitious. If bad luck befalls a person, they might change their name to change their luck.'

Harry frowned. 'Getting blown out of job and home by a series of hurricanes might be interpreted as pretty bad luck. So the person we're looking for under this name . . . '

Srisai nodded. 'Might not be using that name. At least not fully.'

'Can you help at all, Mr Srisai?' I asked.

'The fishing community is very inwardly focused, Detective. They're also viewed with suspicion by the locals — many look on them as interlopers and stealers of jobs. The fishing people have sometimes been the focus of overzealous law enforcement.'

'The kind that says, 'We don't need you here'?' Harry asked.

Srisai nodded, sadness in his eyes. 'Yes. Thus your, uh, police ties might be a difficulty in getting people to come forward.'

I looked Srisai in an owlish eye. 'Someone killed a man with a shark spear, Mr Srisai. A harpoon straight into the belly. The death was neither immediate nor pretty. A fire was started to hide the body. All we want is information.'

Kiet Srisai studied the name I had handed him. He folded the paper and put it in his wallet.

'I'll put out the word. Our family is known and respected. People may respond if they know anything.'

I reached to the table and picked up the fortune cookie that had accompanied the meal. 'So fortune cookies are in Thailand as well as China?' I asked Srisai.

'The cookie idea actually originated in San Francisco years ago, in Chinatown. It's not a Thai tradition. But the, uh, natives seem to like the concept, so we . . . ' Srisai smiled sheepishly, spread his hands.

'Give 'em what they want,' Harry finished. He looked at me. 'What's it say, Carson?'

I slipped the paper strip from the broken cookie. Stared at the tiny writing.

Small steps will eventually take you a great distance.

18

Back at HQ, Tom Mason saw us as we walked into the detectives' room with steps neither small nor large, and gestured us into his office. Tom was behind a metal desk as file-laden as ours, though he lined up the file edges better. Tom was in his mid fifties, rail-skinny, with a face as wrinkled and lugubrious as a basset hound. He was totally unflappable and spoke in a country drawl so slow that waiting for words was like watching cold molasses drop into a biscuit.

'You're off anything with the baby snatcher involved, Harry,' Tom said. 'You had direct involvement in the case, and killed the chief suspect. It's over on the kid case for you.'

'Come on, Tom,' Harry complained. 'I can still work the edges.'

'Procedure says it ain't gonna happen, Harry. Anyway, here's the case I need you guys to put to bed,' Tom said, holding up the morning *New York Times*. The biggest headline read, *Rev. Scaler Found Dead in Church Camp. Details Pending Autopsy.*

'The Scaler case?' I said. 'It's not a murder. The guy died of a heart attack while wearing panties upside-down.'

'First,' Tom said, 'we don't know anything for sure, right?'

I turned from the blinds. 'Not a hundred per cent. Maybe ninety-nine point — '

'Secondly, it's high-publicity, gonna get higher. You guys are the first team, and the city council and chief are gonna want me to tell them the first team's on the case, right?'

'That's just diddle-squat politics,' I groused.

'Playing diddle-squat politics is what keeps me in the corner office. Scaler's yours for now. Find out who was with the Rev. in his final moments, get all this ugliness figured out.'

'Why?' I continued to protest. 'It's all gonna be kept under wraps. Half the politicians in Washington attended Scaler's services and prayer breakfasts. Everyone knows Scaler's support put Senator Custis in office and kept him there. You know what'll finally come out: Scaler died of a heart attack while writing pietistic sermons at his church camp. The dom who beat Scaler's butt will be threatened by one of Scaler's lawyers and offered money by another. Stick and carrot. She'll clam tight. Richard Scaler's reputation will stay pure as the driven rain.'

Tom walked to his window. 'You're probably right, Carson. But we're gonna do our job because that's what we do, right?'

I shrugged. We did our job all the time and nothing ever changed.

Harry chimed in. 'What about the baby snatcher? I want to stay close.'

'You want to take it, Carson?' Tom asked. 'You've been handling it so far. Or should I assign it to someone else?'

'Give it to Barret and Osborne. I'll fill them in on what background we've got. It's a freak thing. They're all freak things these days.'

133

Tom said, 'You don't think the guy specifically targeted the boat kid?'

'Noelle,' Harry corrected.

I said, 'There's no way a brain-dead fuck-up like Bailes could have known which kid to pick. You got a half-dozen infants in the sick-kids ward, another dozen in the regular paed unit. Bailes called the kid a clone and a mutant in his rant, like maybe he saw *Star Wars* a few hundred too many times. Or maybe he thought the hospital was breeding them. You can't get into a psycho's mind, Tom. When Bailes got caught he made an I'm-a-tough-guy speech to the camera and tried to take the gravity elevator.'

'Carson's right, Tom,' Harry said. 'I can't see how Bailes could have been looking for a specific kid. It had to be pluck'n'run, a random grab.'

'Give the goddamn case to Barrett and Osborne,' I said. 'If we're gonna pursue the Scaler investigation, we haven't got time for — '

'I want the abductor case,' Harry repeated.

'It ain't gonna happen, Harry,' Tom said, shaking his head. 'The shooting, remember? Departmental rules are clear.'

Harry looked at me. 'Carson? How about it? You can work Noelle's case, right?'

'I'm working the Scaler case if that's what Tom wants. *We're* working the Scaler case.'

Harry's eyes were no longer looking, they were pleading. I dropped my head, muttered something that must have sounded like surrender.

'OK,' Tom said, holding up his hand to indicate *discussion over*. 'Carson's got the baby snatcher case. But that can of worms isn't high priority as long as Scaler's in the air, no pun intended. That's the case I need shed of right now.'

We left Tom standing at his window and hustled toward the garage; it was time to pick up our tack hammers and beat on the Great Wall of China, trying to reduce it to rubble. We climbed into the car. Harry looked my way.

'Thanks for taking Noelle's case, bro. It makes me feel a lot better.'

I turned to my partner, pulled my mouth wide with my fingers, blinked my eyes and waggled my tongue. I said, 'Gaaaaa. Gaaaaaaa.'

'Uh, what's that mean, Carson?'

'What real choice did I have?' I said.

19

I dialed the college, got the general switchboard, was shunted to Tutweiler's office. He'd been a longtime friend and business partner of Scaler's. We figured he might have something interesting to say.

I asked the female voice when Harry and I could come and talk to the Dean, suggesting fifteen minutes from now would be a good choice. I heard her muffle the phone with her hand, talk to someone, Tutweiler, I supposed. She came back on.

'Dean Tutweiler can meet you tomorrow after lunch, say one o'clock? He has fifteen spare minutes and wants you to know he's a firm supporter of the police.'

'I was thinking more like within the hour.'

'He's very busy,' she said. 'He's having a difficult week.'

'Not as difficult as his boss, ma'am,' I said, hanging up. I heard that drumming in my head again, like my irritation had developed a soundtrack. I frowned at Harry. 'We have an appointment for tomorrow. Let's go confirm it now.'

We passed the boundaries of the college minutes before coming to its buildings, the border denoted by plastic strips flapping from pine poles in the ground: surveyor's stakes. A billboard-sized sign proclaimed we'd hit Elysium, after a fashion, providing a twenty-foot-long artist's soft-edged rendering of the institution in the near future, a cityscape of architectural splendor and curving streets embracing dormitories for tens of thousands of the faithful. A white cross was displayed in the upper-right-hand corner of the signage like a beaming sun.

It took us another half-mile to get to the college, a cluster of boxy concrete buildings. As we drew close I saw a large white tent awning near a hole in the ground: the site of last week's ground-breaking ceremony. Students, faces scrubbed and backpacks tight with books, wandered by. No one wore jeans or tanktops or miniskirts. I attended college in the early 90s, briefly at the University of South Alabama, then, more seriously, at U of A. Those venues seemed a world distant from this quiet campus.

We followed signs to the administration building, took an elevator to the top floor, entered an anteroom, behind it a wide room with a round cerulean desk at the end, making the receptionist look as if she were stuck in a big blue inner tube. We walked fifty feet of fancy parquet flooring.

The receptionist was in her late thirties, a bit chubby, with a small and pretty face beneath a swirling tower of golden hair.

'Can I he'p you gennulmen with — '

'Mobile Police,' I said. 'We need to see Dean Tutweiler.'

'Uh, I'm sorry, but he's not in his office.'

'But he's in the building, right?' I said. 'Or nearby?'

'Uh, yes, I think.'

I nodded toward the open door at her back. 'We'll wait inside his office, ma'am. Thanks.'

The office was more akin to a CEO's sanctuary than a religious academic's lair, though a massive podium in the corner held a huge leather bible, a purple bookmark tucked into some pithy passage. Turning back I heard approaching footsteps outside, followed by Tutweiler speaking as though giving dictation to be chiseled into granite tablets.

'Call the PR people and tell them to meet me at 11.45. No, make that 11.50. In the Mary Baker Eddy room. Tell them to start working up a statement on the school's position vis-à-vis the enemies of Christianity and Truth. Richard's enemies. They know the drill.'

Tutweiler veered from his receptionist and into the room, tall and dark and splendidly suited in the thin-lined black of a banker. He saw us and his eyes darkened at foreigners in his sanctum sanctorum.

'Can I help you?'

I remained seated and flipped open my ID wallet. 'I'm Detective Ryder with the Mobile Police Department and this is — '

Tutweiler shot a not-subtle glance at his watch. 'Can it wait, officers? I've got a meeting with the board and the faculty advisors group. The donors committee. Right now I've got to return a call to *People Magazine*.' He turned away, reached across his desk and lifted the phone. It was a fancy one with a shitload of buttons. I wondered if one of them was reserved for God.

'Please have a seat, sir,' Harry said, using his quiet voice. It's about as deep as the Marianas Trench with the timbre of Thor's hammer striking a small planet. 'I promise this will be fast and easy and you'll be back on track in a brief while. Is that all right?'

Tutweiler didn't look like he was going to break into song, but he set the phone down and took the chair behind the desk, more a throne, actually, red velvet with gold leaf over embossed wood, the high back a carving of Adam and Eve holding hands in Paradise. They looked like adolescents. There was no serpent in sight.

Tutweiler angled his throne and leaned his head back, the better to display his imperious profile, half Caesar, half Heston. Harry said, 'We're trying to find out about Mr Scaler's last few days and if you can help us with — '

'*Reverend* Scaler was his title. You could also use *Doctor* Scaler, another of his titles.'

I looked up. Tut was definitely getting on my nerves. 'Reverend Scaler had an MD?'

Tutweiler narrowed an eye my way. 'A PhD.'

'Impressive. From where?'

'The Southwestern Arkansas Institute of Bible Studies.'

'Forgive me for not recognizing the school, sir,' I apologized. 'Is it an accredited institution, like, say, the Harvard Divinity School?'

Tutweiler's jaw clenched. 'The Southwestern Arkansas Institute holds the highest possible accreditations, those from God.'

'Of course,' I said, writing earnestly in my notepad. I wrote *pompous pinhead asshole.*

139

'Was anything bothering Reverend Scaler recently?' Harry asked Tutweiler. 'We saw TV footage of the groundbreaking for the new structures. He seemed distracted, not his usual self.'

'I'm probably far better acquainted with Richard's usual self than you gentlemen are,' Tutweiler sniffed. 'He seemed fine to me. What makes you think otherwise?'

'For one thing,' I said, 'he went five minutes without begging for money.'

Harry shot me a glance. Tutweiler reached for his phone.

'What's the name of your superior?' he said, nose in the air. 'I don't have to put up with this.'

I jumped from my chair so fast it tipped over backwards. I slammed my knuckles on Tutweiler's desk, leaning forward until the Dean's eyes filled with my face.

'Here's what you're going to put up with, Brother Tutweiler. Right now no one knows the Rev. was hanging upside-down with whip marks scalded across his fat white ass. Or sucking a ball gag the size of a lemon. Or wearing lipstick and frilly women's panties with a dildo jammed into his last supper. Those little details might never surface if we get some straight answers to our questions.'

Tutweiler turned white. The phone returned to the cradle. The Dean of Kingdom College stood and walked to the window, gazing over the spreading green commons four stories below. Students walked casually across the bright grass, as fresh and clean-scrubbed as if pulled from a casting agency for a *Happy Days* remake. Tutweiler sighed and turned to us.

'The past year — maybe longer — Richard seemed to grow more and more erratic. He stopped writing his sermons. He sat by the lake. He disappeared for days sometimes. It was getting worse.'

'How so?'

'A week before he was scheduled to address the National Fundamentalist Council, he told me to cancel the engagement. He's been the keynote speaker for years, it's always a powerful address, covered by the international media. He said he wasn't going to deliver the speech. I was floored. It's a huge event for both of our organizations. After the Reverend delivers his speech we always get huge . . . ' he paused, winced.

'Donations,' I finished. 'Don't be afraid to say the word 'money', either, Dean. It's the truth, right?'

'Yes,' he said, looking away. 'Donations. To continue our many ministries.'

'Detective Nautilus and I heard Reverend Scaler mention an eye problem in the news clip. Macular degeneration? Cataracts? Something as simple as conjunctivitis?'

For the first time, Tutweiler looked totally perplexed. Dumbstruck.

'Dean?' Harry asked.

'I have no idea, Detective. I never heard him mention his eyes before or after that day.'

'It seemed a big deal at the time,' I prodded.

Tutweiler shrugged. 'Got me. The whole eye

141

thing came straight from the blue.'

We hammered at a restrained Tutweiler for a few more minutes. He had nothing earth-shaking to add, save for a solid alibi for the three days pre and post his boss's murder, a symposium-cum-revival in Albany, New York. For verification he mentioned several congress people and aides. When we headed out, he made no mention of my behavior. His voice was subdued.

'Can . . . all these sordid details . . . uh, can they . . . '

'Things may leak out,' Harry sighed. 'But I imagine we can keep a lid on the worst aspects.'

The door closed at our backs. We went to the cruiser. Harry paused before he put the car in gear. Looked at me.

'Carson, did you plan that action in Tutweiler's office? You looked about to jump across his desk and strangle him.'

'An act planned from the git-go,' I said, waving it off and hoping it sounded like the truth.

20

We returned to the department, flipped a coin. I lost and had to write up the events of the day. I was feeling worn and bleary-eyed and it took an hour to document the case thus far. I made copies of the full materials and dropped them in the box outside Lieutenant Mason's office, then wandered to the meeting room. The door was closed and I saw Richard Scaler sermonizing on the screen of the computer. The video was jittery. Though I couldn't hear the audio, my mind heard his angry rants, the crowd *amen*-ing Scaler's every screeching condemnation of those not fitting the straitjacket confines of his theology.

When I entered the meeting room Harry sat forward and paused the action.

'A Richard Scaler film retrospective?' I asked.

'Tutweiler got me wondering who Richard Scaler really was. How the reality jived with my images of him. It's pretty sad what I found so far. Wanna look?'

Though weary, curiosity pulled my chair closer to the screen. Harry tapped a key and the action re-started.

'This one I pulled off YouTube. Scaler preaching at a tent revival in Louisiana in the early sixties. The kiddie-preacher stage.'

The uploaded video was black and white, grainy, probably shot on what was called a super-8 camera, the film negative about as wide as your average lady's pinky nail. Richard Bloessing Scaler was about seven years old, a little dab of pudge on a big broad stage. He danced, twirled, cajoled, all the while *amening* and *hallelujahing* in a comedic, high-piping voice. The crowd ate it up, some fainting, others speaking in tongues, others shaking as if standing in water while holding a shorted toaster. And always, moving through the crowd, the hat asking for money.

The film floated out of focus, re-entered on a scene that appeared to be backstage at the just-completed revival, billows of white cloth backdrop as Scaler's parents sat in folding chairs, the young Richard between them.

'*He's got the spirit all the way through,*' Daddy Scaler drawled. '*They come from fitty miles to hear my boy preachin' the Lord's word.*'

Richard Scaler Senior looked like a refugee from a Depression-era dust storm, a bone-skinny scarecrow with a nasal Oklahoma drawl. He wore overalls and a plain shirt, and I figured it was more costume than clothes, telling the dirt-poor audience he was one of them.

Mama Scaler was grossly obese; no way to gloss it, a lump. Her eyes seemed lost in her fleshy face. I felt sorrow at her condition until she looked into the camera. Her eyes were as cold and glittering as the eyes of a rattlesnake, and projected a force I could not explain, even through the bad lighting and grainy film. She stared at the camera as if determining whether to ignore it or kill it.

144

'How often do you preach, Richard?' the interviewer asked the chubby little kid.

'*Every ni* — '

'*Two* — *three times a week,*' Daddy Scaler interrupted, shooting a wide grin at the kid and patting him like an obedient retriever. '*He'd preach day'n'night if we let him, but uh course, he's got school an' things.*'

I'll bet, I thought.

I saw Richard yawn and begin to slump, dead tired after hours of preaching and altar calls. His mother's hand shot in from behind and grabbed the kid's jacket at the shoulder blades, yanked him erect like a sack of meal. It was meant to be hidden, but Mama Scaler was unfamiliar with camera angles.

'*Stand up straight, boy,*' Mama Scaler side-mouthed. '*An' smile. These people are takin' pictures.*'

I looked at the seven-year-old and saw a wooden marionette. The camera scanned the departing crowd. The camera had lights and the faces looked back at the lights with confusion or fear or anger.

'*I notice the crowd is all white,*' the interviewer said. '*Do you ever let Richard preach to colored audiences?*'

Mama Scaler backhanded the question away like it was a fly. '*Negras is made by Satan an' doan have the men'l powers to unnerstan the word a God Ahmighy. All they wanna do is stir up trouble ennyways.*'

'*What kind of trouble do they stir up, ma'am?*'

'*What kinda question is that? I'm not sittin'*'

here to be talkin' 'bout no filthy negras.'

'*It was just a question, ma'am,*' the interviewer said. '*Could you tell us how much the typical revival pulls in, and what percentage of the proceeds are yours?*'

A look of disgust quivered through the flesh of Mama Scaler's face. She looked at her husband and said, '*Get 'em the fuck outta here.*'

Daddy Scaler rocketed from his chair with his finger pointing.

'*This goddamn interview is over right now —* '

'*They're simple questions, Mr Scaler. Mrs Scaler? Might you know what percentage of the — *'

Scaler pushed his hat at the camera lens. '*Doan you be talking to mah wife out my permission. Git outta here right now. ZEB! ETHAN!*' he called to someone off-screen. '*Come kick these goddamn nigger-lovin' Communists outta here!*'

The camera shifted sideways. A flurry of grunts and curses and the camera fell to the floor, showing a two-second scuffle of shoes and boots. The screen went black.

Harry said, 'The copyright on the full documentary the clip came from — titled *God's Country* — is 1959. It tracks several revivals across the South. That's where the film ends for the Scaler journey.'

'Little Richy would have been . . . '

'Seven,' Harry said. 'And already a two-year veteran of the circuit.'

'It's obvious Mama Scaler's got spiders in her wiring,' I said. 'Probably psychotic. Stuff like that can mess a kid up bad.'

'Your mom . . . ' Harry said. 'She was the opposite, right?'

'Scared of everything. It was righteous fear — my old man would explode if the temperature was a half-degree different than what he wanted. She made church mice look bold by comparison.'

A half-beat pause. 'How do you think that affected you? Not just your mom, the whole childhood-fear thing?'

'Not as much as it affected Jeremy,' I said.

Jeremy was my brother. At age sixteen he'd killed our father and later he'd been imprisoned for killing five women, the crimes starting soon after my father had been torn apart in a wood. After years of living in an institution for the criminally insane, he'd escaped last year. I had nearly been killed trying to safely return him to the institution. The chase had ended in the revelation that Jeremy had not killed the women. Or at least that's what I wanted to believe.

Jeremy was still out there, free, and I heard from him every three or four months, a brief phone call, a cryptic postcard. He never said where he was, I never asked. He was smart enough to stay outside forever, I figured. He was a genius at camouflage, exterior and interior.

'I guess I'd have to agree there,' Harry said. 'At least, from what I know about your bro — '

'I don't want to talk about it, Harry. I'm done.'

He nodded. 'Sure. Let's get back to the Reverend Dick, preaching in 1995.'

Harry resumed his control of the keyboard, pulling up another video. The gestures were pure Scaler, dramatic and exaggerated, from his popped-wide eyes to his ten-league-boot steps. He'd yowl out a statement, cross the stage, yowl out another. His suit was white, his shoes were white, his belt was white, his shirt and ties were white. The only dark was hair and eyes. His body was about two decades older than the boy we'd just seen on stage, almost three decades younger than the body we'd seen cut down from a staircase last week. The body was also about thirty pounds lighter. I was surprised at how lithe and youthful Scaler was, and how good looking.

'*Who built this country?*' he railed at what appeared to be an audience of several hundred. '*The Europeans who arrived on these shores? The people who were sent by God to build the greatest nation ever seen on the face of the earth, a shining star of freedom? Yes, the nay-tives were here, it's true, can't be denied. In-di-ans.*' Scaler did a woo-woo-woo motion at his mouth to the delight of the crowd. He arm-flapped across the stage in a parody of pow-wow dancing, twenty feet of insult to the sacred rituals of others. '*Were terrible things done to the In-di-ans in the name of Nation? Of destiny? Again, it can't be denied. It also cannot be denied that the native tribes worshipped plants and animals and the heads of idols carved on poles outside of teeeeee-peeeees . . .*' Scaler paused and glared into the crowds to let his words sink in.

'Totem poles were northwestern tribes,' I said. 'They didn't live in tipis.'

'Shhh,' Harry said, pointing back to the computer. Scaler shook his disgust at plant and animal and idol worship from his face, lifted his bible and pointed to it with a stern finger.

'*When you worship false gods and idols, you anger the true God. He sends an army to smite you in the name of justice and redemption. Could that army be the soldiers of Columbus? The armies of Cortés? The God-blessed American cavalry rescuing women and children trying to pioneer the plains of this great land?*'

'Yes,' the crowd roared. 'Yes.' I could see the front rows of the audience. Several turned to one another, patting backs and shaking hands, transported in the bliss of Scaler telling them that what they'd wanted to believe all along was true.

'*The same God who saved the children of Israel at the expense of the blaspheming Egyptians now comes to save the Christian children of the plains at the expense of the marauding infidel In-deee-ans?*'

Yesses and amens and hallelujahs. Scaler raised a palm for silence. It took two seconds for the place to turn as still as a windless desert. He appeared in the throes of decision, then spoke in a stage whisper:

'*I can't he'p but think that this leads to an overwhelming fact: God lifts the righteous, drops the unholy. It's how he makes his work known . . . So despair not for those fallen to the Lord's swift sword . . . those of Sodom and Gomorra*

149

— they did not heed the lessons. Do not despair for those charred by God's truthful lightning — they did not listen to His clear words. Do not despair for those who constantly beseech, 'Help me, help me. Give me this, give me that . . . ' They have not heard the words of God, to lift thyself by thine own bootstraps . . . '

'Adidas 3:19,' I whispered. 'Pull thyself up as you would thine laces.'

'*For they have set themselves at odds with God and His works and His servants and messengers. For they have set themselves at odds with us!*'

'Them and Us,' Harry said, turning off the computer with a sigh. 'Can't beat the old favorites.'

21

After a night of the deepest sleep in a month I awakened to the sound of piccolos being assaulted by tubas. I pushed aside the curtains. Outside in the street was Miz Best and the improbable dog, Mr Mix-up. True to its multispecies make-up, the ridiculous beast was squealing one moment like a lap poodle, roof-ing the next like a basset.

I went to the kitchen and ate a banana — 100 per cent natural and organic — popped my B-vites and ginseng and turned up the TV to block out the idiot mongrel. Ten minutes later I was leaving, hair shower-wet, shirt unbuttoned, stepping into shoes as I walked out the door. Miz Best had walked to the beach and was on her return trip. Part of the dog must have been Lab, because it was sopping from a plunge in the water. It saw me and exploded from Miz Best's hand, dashing across the sand like I was a bowl of gravy. It ran two circles around me, planted its feet in the sand, and shook. Water rained from every direction.

I looked at Miz Best. Her eyes were worried.

'Sorry, Carson. Mr Mix-up doesn't usually go to strangers. You're the first person he's run toward. Mr Mix-up's running out of days and we can't find him a home. He's too odd-looking, I think. You know anyone who wants a dog?'

I looked at the star-crossed critter, whomping

its feet into the sand while its tongue lolled, alternately squealing and roof-ing, wanting me to touch it or whatever they want.

'Sorry, Miz Best,' I said, putting my hands in my pockets. 'He'll have to take his chances like the rest of us.'

On the way in I stopped at my standard convenience store. Having been made more nutritionally aware by Fossie, I got a banana and a Clif's bar. My eyes did the usual scan of the newspapers. A headline caught my eye:

Rumors of Scaler's Mystery Meeting Before Death

The subhead read: *Famous Preacher Seeing Woman?*

I sat out in my truck, chomping and reading. The details were squishy: police suspected Scaler might have met someone at the cabin that night, odds were it was a woman. But the copy made no mention of a dominatrix and the rest of the sordid actuality. I imagined an enterprising reporter had gotten wind that a couple of detectives wanted to question a woman in conjunction with Scaler's death, put two and two together.

Though I had no love for Scaler and his hard-line, uncompromising ilk, I hoped the story would go no further. It would be tough enough on his wife to have the suspicion of an affair out there, far worse if the reality was known.

★　★　★

Harry had to prepare for a court appearance on one of the murders we'd investigated a couple months back. I was feeling more energetic than I had in days, wondering if all I'd needed was sleep, vitamins and a better diet.

I decided to head up to Holman Prison and confront Donnie Kirkson, the guy in Ben Belker's surreptitious photos, the one biker who had any interest in Terry Lee Bailes.

At Holman, a guard was assigned to accompany me. After passing through a series of barred doors and gates, I stopped and looked out a grated window to the yard. It was like recess in one of Dante's circles of Hell: a couple hundred cons, their shadows extended in the late-afternoon sun. Most had self-segregated into the three primary tribes: white, black and Hispanic. They were hanging out on tables or flipping a basketball or spotting one another while pumping iron. A trio of black guys jogged the perimeter, brown dust flapping from their feet as they padded by below, cutting a hard right to give wide berth to a man on a chinning bar.

The guy weighed three hundred pounds and was chinning all of them easily, his biceps as round as phone poles. His body shone with sweat and his shaved head glowed in the sunlight. I saw a slight black guy mince to the monster. The little guy made some form of entreaty to the hulk swinging on the bar. Without breaking his fluid motion, the behemoth said something brief and the little guy clapped and skittered away.

'Who's that on the chin bar?' I asked the guard.

'Thunderhead Wallace. An' it looks like he's

153

got a date for later.'

'Thunderhead?'

The guard grinned and clenched his fist, letting his arm dangle between his legs for a second.

'Boy's got a wang that'd shame Johnny Wadd. Likes to polish the internal plumbing of a whole stable of punks. 'Bout the only time he ain't fucking something is out there in the yard.'

'What's he in for?'

'Accomplice on a bank heist put him here, but he also has priors for indecent exposure and bestiality.' The guard chuckled. 'If you can believe it, ol' Thunderhead got caught at a cattle farm — '

I held up my hand. 'I'll pass on the details. You know much about Kirkson?'

'A nasty little shit who hangs with the Aryan Nation types, thinks he's something. The girl he took to the motel and soaked with alcohol? Same age as my daughter. I'd like to get Thunderhead to take Kirkson to a motel.'

'You're kidding, right?' I said to him, feeling an odd notion bubble to the top of my brain, a thought encircled with inspirational light.

The guard looked from side to side. Didn't see any supervisors.

'I mean ever' goddamn word, buddy.'

I thought for a few more moments as we walked, pulled the guard aside before we got to the block. We spoke briefly, me laying out my case, maybe embellishing a few points. He took me to an office, set me in the chair, said, 'Third drawer on the left, in the file marked *Transfer*

Directives.' He added the word, 'Hurry,' and stepped outside, looking up and down the hall before closing the door.

I was out in under a minute, patting my pocket. The guard was looking the other direction; he said, 'I never saw anything.'

'Of course,' I said, following him to a holding area, a gray-walled ten-by-ten cell with a table and three chairs waiting. I sat and drummed my fingers on the tabletop while Kirkson was fetched from his cage. He'd added a few pounds since the photos with Bailes; prison food does that, starch and carbs. But he'd kept the muscle def; under his dirty yellow mullet I could see hard shoulders and a thick neck. His arms were ropy and heavily inked. He preferred to lean against the wall rather than sit. He lit a Marlboro. I asked him about Terry Lee Bailes.

'I'm not sure I remember that name,' Kirkson smirked, true to form.

'Come on, Donnie. Let's not start our relationship on a false note. I've got pictures of you two together. What was Bailes like?'

Kirkson blew out smoke and grinned at the ceiling. The smartass was thinking *deal time*. This was a guy who'd plied a confused fifteen-year-old runaway with alcohol and taken her to a motel for four days. Now he expected us to fix things so he got time off for talking about Bailes.

'What was who like?' Kirkson said.

When I said nothing, Kirkson sneered. 'What's in it for me? You better be talking time off. Big time off, you got that?'

'I can find others who knew Bailes,' I said.

'Sure,' Kirkson taunted. 'That's why you're here. I'll say it one last time: What's in it for me?'

I pulled a trifolded page from my pocket, snapped it open. It was yellow, a page from a carbon duplicate form. It was a bogus transfer, a cell-reassignment form. I'd filled it out all by myself, signing the warden's name with a big wardenly flourish.

'What's that?' Kirkson grinned. 'The deal that tells me I'm outta here in six months? It fuckin' better be.'

I handed Kirkson the sheet. He was still grinning as he started reading, but was staring wide-eyed and gap-mouthed by the time he reached the warden's sig at the bottom.

'You . . . can't do this,' he stammered.

'It's already done, Donnie,' I said, my turn to smirk. 'Your new bed is being made as we speak.'

'My lawyer won't let — '

I leaned against the wall and folded my arms. 'You're between lawyers, Donnie. Remember? One quit in disgust. Then you fired two in a row. It'll take days for the court to appoint new counsel. Sleep tight.'

'It's a fucking set-up. A lie!'

I shook the page in the air. 'Official form, official signature.'

'No way. It's like a death sentence!'

'Not if you play your cards right, Donnie-boy,' I crooned. 'I suggest you shave your legs, practice your pucker, and invest heavily in Vaseline. Or maybe motor oil. Word has it Thunderhead Wallace likes to drive all night.'

'You filthy son of a bitch. You BASTARD!'

'Hey!' the guard outside yelled. 'Keep it down, Kirkson. Or you'll go back to your cell. I hear you're getting a new one.'

'On your way to your new cell, Donnie . . . ' I said, putting the page in my pocket like I was preparing to leave, 'you might want to stop at the commissary and get that Vaseline. They sell it in fifty-gallon drums?'

'THIS AIN'T AMERICAN!'

I reached out and hooked my finger into Kirkson's front pocket and drew him so close I could smell the fear rising from his armpits.

'Really, Donnie? In my America, thirty-one-year-old men take fifteen-year-old runaways to a shelter or a social worker, they don't fill them with vodka and take them to a motel.'

I poked Kirkson backward with a stiff finger. He grunted, spun away, and sucked the cig to the filter, squished the butt on the floor. When he turned his eyes showed surrender.

'Terry Lee was a fuck-up, all right? He was like a big stupid kid. Why you need to know about him?'

'If he was such a fuck-up,' I asked, 'why were you friends with him?'

Kirkson shrugged, studied the floor. He actually seemed confused by my question.

'I always kind of felt sorry for Terry Lee. We both had shit for families. He was so fucking ugly and always trying to be cool and say the right words and act like some kind of stone killer, a mad dog.'

'He wasn't?'

157

'Terry Lee Bailes was a Chihuahua with a loud bark. He looked the look and talked the talk, but he couldn't walk the walk. Underneath all that leather and ink was pure chickenshit.'

It didn't make sense. No chickenshit would slip past hospital security, steal a kid, then, cornered, try to leap to a grisly death. I put my hand on the chair behind Kirkson, leaned close.

'Bailes tried to steal a kid from a hospital, Donnie. When someone got in his way and the event went south, Bailes grinned and tried to jump out a fifth-floor window. No second thoughts about taking the long dive to the bottom floor.'

Kirkson looked at me. 'Wait a minute. You mean you didn't find it out?'

'Find out what?'

'When you did the thing with the . . . ' Kirkson made a knife-cut motion from his groin up to his neck.

'The post-mortem?' I said. 'The autopsy? Those things take a few days to get to, Donnie. Thanks to great citizens like you, there's a stack of dead bodies at the morgue. It's a take-a-number operation.'

He grinned. 'That explains it.'

I jammed him into the wall. 'EXPLAINS WHAT?'

He held his hands in front of his face. 'Take it fucking easy — Jesus! Terry Lee was dying. He had cancer in something by his liver. It always kills you. It hurts like hell and you die screaming.'

'Pancreatic cancer?'

'That's the shit. Terry Lee visited here a week back and told me. He was crying like a fucking baby. I told him to man up, live the rest of his life like there was nothing to lose.' He grinned. 'Cuz there wasn't.'

22

Heading back to Mobile, my heart started pounding like a drum and my skin felt tight. I figured it was the irritation of highway driving, an idiot behind every third steering wheel and slow-moving semi-rigs backing traffic up for miles.

I veered down a ramp and took the back roads south, driving through piney woods with trees straight as arrows, crossing slender bridges over black-water swamps. I roared around a bend and saw a typical roadhouse bar, a mason-block building with painted-over windows and a heavy metal door. A sign saying *Al's Hideaway* hung over the door on a rusting iron frame. A dozen pickups and cars were on the dusty, crushed-gravel lot. A portable sign near the road proclaimed *Big Picher of Beer $8*.

I was thirsty and hot and what energy I'd had was fading. I veered into the lot beside the building, skidding sideways in the gravel.

It was as cold as a refrigerator inside. Three men sat at the bar, another five played cards in a back booth. Two chalked cues and stalked pool balls at a table. I heard a decades-old Conway Twitty song on the juke: 'It's Only Make Believe'.

Eyes found me, held for an evaluative two-count, turned back to the serious work of heavy drinking.

The man behind the bar was a porcine guy in his thirties, a bandana covering his pumpkin head. His shirt advertised Colt Arms. His voluminous jeans were held aloft by a black leather belt clasped by an ornate silver buckle big as a dessert plate. He was pulling beers from cases at his feet and racking them in a cooler. He didn't look happy at being distracted from his labor, muttering *shit* and padding over.

'Whatcha need?' he asked.

'A couple RCs. And a half-pint of Maker's.'

He reached in a cooler, scrabbled through some bottles, produced two RCs, dropping them in a bag with the bourbon.

I headed toward my truck and put the bottles in the passenger seat. I heard a bite of tires on asphalt as a big-ass Dodge Ram veered on to the lot. The driver gunned the engine for no reason but to announce arrival. He swerved to send a rolling cloud of dust my way and jammed the brakes to skid to a stop. A bumper sticker said, *DON'T LIKE MY DRIVING? CALL 1-800-EAT SHIT*. In the back window was a Confederate battle flag, only at the crossing of the bars was the grinning face of country singer Hank Williams, Jr. The license plate was from Ohio.

Ohio?

The door pushed open and out jumped a jostling beer belly overlaying a large frame, six three or four. The belly's owner had a wide chest and heavy biceps, and I took him for a laborer on a construction site or maybe a loading dock. He looked at me, seemed to sneer at the sports jacket, like I was a lost tourist. He flicked his

161

cigarette to the dirt, hawked up a gob of phlegm, fired it at the butt, missed by two feet.

The passenger was smaller, with tight tiny eyes and dirty fingernails tapping the side of the truck. His wispy beard, long trailing mustache, and hard-edged face made my neurons fire three random words: *syphilitic hillbilly Confucius.*

'Get a case for the cooler, Beefer,' Syphilucius whined, a nasal wind as flat and nonmusical as air dribbled from a balloon, the tone straight from the plains of a Midwest backcountry nowhere.

Beefer. I looked at the driver and the name fit, probably applied while a high-school lineman pushing aside smaller players like a fat bull, stomping their ankles when he saw the chance. He maybe went on to some second-tier college on scholarship, but found that elbow-spearing opposing players' necks didn't make up for slow legs and an inability to remember the play-book.

I looked at the sullen, obnoxious Beefer. My eyes went to the comedic flag on the cab and the bumper sticker. I looked at the license plate. I felt a fast and scarlet anger sizzle through my guts and a deep thrumming in my brain. Normally I would have pushed the irritation out with a few quick breaths, moved on. But something kept my feet planted.

'Hey, buddy,' I called to the wide back.

He turned. Eyes squinted in a flat red face. 'Huh? You talkin' to me?'

I nodded at the flag in the rear window. 'I like the flag. Looks good.'

He was pissed at my stepping into his day,

162

bewildered by what seemed a compliment to his truck's attire. It was a wash, so he nodded, turned away toward the roadhouse.

I said, 'Hey, buddy.'

He stopped, wheeled. This time there was no confusion, only ire.

'What now?' he growled, squaring in my direction and pulling off his shades. I removed my sunglasses, absent-mindedly polishing them on my shirtfront.

'What's it mean to you?' I asked, looking at my glasses, not him.

'What the hell you talking about?'

'The Stars'n'Bars. The flag of the Confederate States of America. What does it mean?'

'It means I'm a rebel. That's what it fuckin' means.'

I puffed breath over my lenses, studied them closely. Resumed polishing. 'What are you rebelling against?' I asked.

He moved two steps my way, fists closing. 'Stop with the fucking questions, freak. You got a problem with my flag?'

'*Your* flag?' I twirled the glasses in my fingers and nodded toward his bumper. 'But the license tag says Ohio.'

'So the fuck what?'

'Ohio was a member of the Union,' I explained quietly. 'Not the Confederacy.'

He moved closer, now a half-dozen feet away. 'What the fuck does that have to do with anything? Get outta my face before you get hurt.'

I turned and took the three steps to my truck, opened the door, set the shades inside. Closed the door and turned slowly back to the Beefer.

'What was the capital of the Confederacy, Rebel Boy? It's what any Southerner would know. I won't ask you what famous battle was fought in Manassas, Virginia. I won't ask you the year the war began. Just prove you know enough about the Confederacy to tell me its capital.'

'What is your fucking problem, asshole?'

'Children who play games with symbols they don't understand.'

'Fuck him up, Beef,' the guy in the truck tittered. 'Fuck him up bad.'

I'd had enough of Confucius and headed that way, but was sucker-punched in the side by Beefer, faster than I thought he'd be. His grapefruit-sized fist knocked me sideways.

I dropped to one knee, gasping. He circled around my back to put a kick into my kidney, but I surprised him my diving toward him, grabbing his foot at toe and heel and twisting with all I had. It brought him down like a sack of wet manure and he swung his fist as he fell, the punch hitting my shoulder. I didn't want to match strength to strength so I blunted two roundhouse swings, head low, looking for the moment.

He jumped into me to try to get his hands around my neck, and for a split-second his fat throat was open. I drove a knife-hand chop into his larynx.

Game's end. Beefer's hands fell from my throat and clutched at his own. I stood, resisting the notion to punt his head like a football and instead crouched beside him as he struggled for breath, my hand clutching his hair.

'The war began in 1861,' I whispered into an ear so close to my lips I could have bitten it off. 'Manassas was the site of the Battle of Bull Run. The capital was Richmond, as in the state of Virginia. Say it.'

'Hur-ugh,' he rasped.

I yanked his head back, the better to see the fear in his eyes. 'The name of the capital of the Confederacy.'

'Rug-mom,' he gargled.

I threw Beef's head toward the ground and spun to the truck, yanked open the door. The syphilitic hillbilly Confucius held his hands in front of his face, babbling, 'No, man, I didn't disrespect you. No, man . . . '

I yanked him from the truck and sent him skittering across the parking lot. I tore the flag free of the rear window. I climbed in my truck and drove away, jamming the flag under the seat.

I felt like crying, but didn't know why. So I started yelling as loud as I could. The feeling passed by the time I reached the next curve.

★   ★   ★

When I rolled in, at half past seven, Harry was still there, looking through YouTube videos in the side conference room. I wondered if he was checking out more background on Scaler or just playing around.

'Do I smell mint juleps?'

I opened my mouth and showed him a green

tongue. 'Tic-Tacs,' I slobbered. 'Mint flavor.'

He frowned and sniffed the air. 'I could have sworn I smelled whiskey, too.'

'Because you associate mint with whiskey,' I explained. 'It's how the mind works. Now sit your ass down and let me tell you what I got solved.'

I conveyed my conversation with Kirkson.

'That begins to explain things,' Harry said, after I'd run through the play-by-play. 'Bailes was on the way out. Looking at nothing but pain and a plot in Potter's Field.'

'A man with no future. Remember when he got quiet? I said to him, 'It's over. Set the kid aside and you get to live'?'

Harry thought back. Nodded. 'Bailes said, 'No I don't.''

'Bailes knew he was a goner, so he decided to act out some weird-ass fantasy,' I said. 'Kirkson inadvertently helped light the fuse by telling Bailes to get his shit together and man up. Then do what he wanted because he was in the no-consequences zone.'

'Why did Bailes get weird? What was the fantasy?'

'No one will ever know what Bailes was thinking. When you've got a mama like that and a face like that there ain't no way to turn out normal.'

'What if there's more to it, Carson?'

'There isn't.'

'We've got to make absolutely sure.'

'I've got two goddamn cases on my plate, Harry. One is a preacher who died while getting whipped as part of his sex life. The other is a delusional man-child who tried to jump out a window with an infant. Both are over. THE PEOPLE ARE DEAD!'

It finally seemed to penetrate Harry's leaden skull. He thought for a few moments, shifted gears.

'Hardasses like Kirkson never tell cops anything without a trade. How did you get Kirkson to spill?'

I *ahemed* and told him the story of my on-the-spot creativity with the fake transfer.

'Jesus,' he whispered, jumping up to close the door. 'You could have gotten your ass fired. The guard's ass fired. Why did you take such ridiculous chan — '

'It worked,' I said, waving my hand in the done-with-talking mode. 'That's what's important. Why don't you call Clair and ask if she can get a pathologist to run the ripsaw through Bailes tomorrow after Scaler's funeral so we can confirm the rotten pancreas and file this case under *Dying Freak's Last Wish*?'

Harry paused, picked up the phone. I went to the can to take a leak. Washing my hands, I saw a wide red smear on my face, an abrasion from the set-to with Beefer. Harry had looked straight at it and hadn't mentioned a thing.

When I returned to the meeting room, Harry was gone, a note in his place:

Post on Bailes @ 11.30 a.m. tomorrow. Scaler's funeral at nine.

167

I went home, took a couple of Fossie's sleeping pills, and watched a show about groups of people racing around the world. Everyone was angry at everyone else and I drifted into a rich and welcome sleep as they screamed at one another in an airline terminal in Singapore.

23

Scaler's service was at the Kingdom College chapel. My head was thick with sleep and I arrived late at the department. Harry and I had the misfortune to fall in behind Senator Custis's motorcade as it traveled the final miles to the campus, four black Yukons book-ended by State Police officers, two on motorcycles, two inside cruisers. Sirens wailed, lights flashed. Senators did not move with stealth.

We kept a distance of a hundred feet behind the parade, careful whenever a clot of folks on the long drive leading to the bounds of Kingdom College held aloft a sign praising Custis. His black Yukon, the last in the quartet, would slow to roll down the smoked black window so the senator could wave and shine his teeth at the onlookers.

After our fifth slow-up in two miles, Harry cranked down our window. I watched as he stuck his face into the oncoming breeze and sniffed. He pulled his head back inside and rolled up the window.

I gave him a *what-was-that-about?* look.

'Just smelling the self-importance,' he said.

'How thick is it?'

'Like a ham loaf.'

The motorcade turned from the main road to a stretch of two-lane, the final half-mile before crossing into the confines of Kingdom College. A dozen men and women rose from lawn chairs positioned at the grassy green intersection and applauded as a news crew shot video. Two men held aloft signs proclaiming, *Custis: The People's Choice* and *Custis For Family Values.* The signs were red-and-blue type over a white background with a full-color shot of Custis's face in profile. I figured the senator's PR team had scoped the route and passed out signs much in the manner of Jesus distributing loaves and fishes.

I looked ahead to the opaque rear window of the senator's vehicle and smelled something worse than ham. Senator Hampton Custis had become emblematic of a class of politicians using fear to fuel their drive to power. Though the Civil Rights movement was years past by the time Custis made the jump from a rural county prosecutor to a senate seat, he'd based his campaign on the greasy residue of Jim Crow, speaking of a 'golden age' that had disappeared, oddly enough, when blacks gained full voting stature.

Like many Southern politicians who had risen from humble beginnings to heights of power, he maintained a thick rural accent, although amused reporters often noted his speech became much less mush-mouth in the halls of Congress than on the stump.

Custis's ascension had been fast and not unmarked by controversy. After college, he'd returned to his Alabama home town and practiced small-town law, advertising on bill-boards and park benches: *Divorces, $100!* While in his late twenties he ran for county prosecutor when both the incumbent and main competitor were affected by scandal. He won by a few votes and made his mark as a strict law-and-order type.

Seemingly able to smell news cameras, Custis learned to speak in sound bites provocative enough to gain face time on the national news. He called a group of conservative gays, 'pansies that got in the wrong boat somehow'. Another was, 'Any woman who's considered abortion for any reason is a murderer in her heart.' In a renowned 1983 trial of three white men arrested for raping a black woman, Custis's office lost or 'misplaced' crucial evidence, the loss allowing the perpetrators to go free.

In the late eighties, Custis's office was surreptitiously investigated by the SDLP, prompted by the discovery that, where blacks and whites were accused of the same crime, the blacks were 320 per cent more likely to be jailed. There were also accusations of pay-offs and bribes.

Snarling about 'political assassination', Custis had jumped from the embattled prosecutor's office into a senate race. In the primary, he defeated a respected moderate senator by accusing him of insufficient patriotism and liberal sympathies because the man had once said that slavery had been a blight on the South. A concurrent rumor campaign held that the incumbent had either fathered one black child and one Hispanic child, or a single child of both persuasions. Though the stories were unfounded, the rumors were so well-seeded that the

171

incumbent spent half his campaign refuting them.

After winning the primary, Custis drummed up wads of money, advertised constantly, refused one-on-one debates with a black opponent — '*I want to talk direct to the people, not jabber with some lib'ral*' — and won the general election by point-zero-two per cent on a viciously contested recount.

Canny enough to realize his victory had been secured not with ideas or personality but money, Custis had since devoted himself to amassing the kind of largesse to keep him in office and his contributors in tall cotton. He received much, and gave much to the campaigns of his fellow lawmakers. In Washington DC, honor withers in the face of money, and Custis was allowed great berth in biases and pronouncements.

After seemingly hours in the wake of Custis's motorcade, we flashed our ID at the impromptu security point still a mile from the college. The general public had been channeled to a side road. Free of the need to wave, Custis's motorcade picked up the beat to about eighty-five mph and rocketed away.

We flashed ID again when on the campus, were sent to a lot reserved for non-security cops, press, buses, and mid-range celebrities. Our IDs bought fast entry through a side door. The main floor was a melee of sweating bodies reeking of deodorant and cheap fragrances. We hiked to the balcony.

The stage of the chapel was about eighty feet

wide and fifty feet deep, the depth necessary for the pulpit, the band, and the choir's eight rows of risers. The area was lit from six stories above by a lighting system an arena-rock band would have admired. Two huge video monitors flanked the stage.

Taking front and center of the stage was Richard Bloessing Scaler, his suit white, his casket hammered brass, his hands laced over a black bible. Above the casket was the pulpit, looking like the helm of a sailing ship, if helms were white and gold and inlaid with mother-of-pearl.

The bereaved elite sat in velvet-upholstered chairs behind the pulpit. Closest to the casket was Patricia Scaler. She was in the requisite black with a veil so dense it seemed opaque, as if she had believed it would wall her off from the thousands of incoming mourners and reporters. I felt deep sadness for her.

I saw Fossie beside Mrs Scaler, his eyes drifting over the crowd. After a few minutes I saw her move from Fossie's side to Senator Custis. She leaned low, spoke a few words, and sat beside him. He put his hand over her forearm, gave a squeeze of reassurance.

Sitting in the other chairs — many still arriving — was an assemblage of what I assumed were friends and people from the college and various Scaler media enterprises, though I could recognize only two: Dean Tutweiler, looking amply doleful, and the lawyer Carleton, sitting beside the Dean and whispering in his ear, probably putting the funeral on the clock.

Looking down into the front rows of the congregation, I recognized several other notable right-wing televangelists, out to pay their respects to a colleague in the industry. Or maybe making sure he was dead.

We watched a half-dozen orations which, save for the vocalizations, sounded the same. Between speeches the choir sang hymns. When I'd shoot a glance at Mrs Scaler she remained in the same position, unmoved by so much as a breath, hiding in the fortress of her grief.

After nearly an hour of hagiography, Custis took his position at the podium, the main event. He tapped the mic and asked for more volume. The senator cleared his throat, then opened his hands toward the man in the casket below the podium.

'*I've known this beautiful man since his days as a simple country pastor in a small church. It feels like a hundred years, such has been the Reverend Richard Scaler's influence on my life and devotion to our Lord. Here lies a true man of God, a warrior for righteousness, a soldier of Heaven, the vanguard scout for the legions of Truth and the point man for Jesus Christ our Eternal Savior . . .* '

Custis's voice boomed from the walls. Amens arose from the crowd. I heard Harry mutter something. A sixtyish, blubber-necked white guy in the pew beside us turned to see a black guy talking to himself. Blubber-neck couldn't hide his disgust.

Harry looked back. I couldn't see the expression on my partner's face, but the white guy turned even whiter and snapped his head back to Custis's eulogy.

'... *Richard and I were two sons of the South, scions of small towns close to one another. It was a simpler time then, a better time then ... before the hippies and the nay-sayers and the America-haters took to the streets, before the Godless heathens stormed the gates of rectitude ...* '

More *amens* from the crowd, though I saw less-hardened faces looking uncomfortable at Custis's opportunistic language. The raw politician in Custis sensed the same, backed it down.

'... *Then the seventies came with what Richard later called his 'finding' period. Finding who he was, discovering his full potential as a preacher, though he had preached since the age of four. He could have given it all up, my friends. Or stayed in his small country church away from the great responsibility he later undertook. I knew him then just as I knew his beloved Patricia then, and I hope that my friendship was some inspiration to him ...* '

I took as much as I could stomach and left, Harry on my heels.

When we arrived at the department, Tom Mason whistled me to his office. 'You can come along, too, Harry,' Tom added.

I sat, Harry stood. 'Got us a li'l problem here,' Tom said, looking at me.

'Which is?'

Tom picked up a sheet from his desk, put on reading glasses. 'A woman name of Vernia Teasdale and a Mr Jameson Daniels signed a

175

complaint avowing that, lacking proper cause, you entered their domicile yesterday and broke camera equipment, a table, and caused them to be in fear of their lives. They say you scared them so much they locked themselves in the bathroom until you left.'

I shook my head. 'Teasdale is the mama of Terry Lee Bailes, the guy who tried to abduct the baby at the hospital,' I explained. 'I was there to inform Mrs Teasdale of the death of her son. She became emotional. The man with her didn't like me causing her distress. They were shooting a porn movie or performing for an internet audience when I arrived. A marijuana roach was found on the premises — seen when the door was open, proper cause. The afore-mentioned man took offense at my ability to arrest him. There was a small scuffle. Objects fell.'

'No one was arrested because of . . . ?' Tom asked.

'I didn't want to place the woman under any more emotional duress, Tom. She was having a tough day, her son dead and all.'

Tom studied a pair of rap sheets. 'Both of 'em got records, low-life stuff: misdemeanor dope busts and three DUIs on Teasdale, Daniels has grand theft auto, second-degree assault. It'll turn into your word against theirs, and the judge'll throw their charges out like a week-old biscuit. I don't see a problem here, do I?'

'Nope,' I said. 'Because there is none.' I laced my fingers behind my head and smiled at Harry. He frowned back at me.

What? I mouthed.

He looked away. I stood and headed out the door, went to my desk. When I turned back, Harry was still in Tom's office, only this time the door was closed.

24

Harry was scheduled for another meeting at the District Attorney's office, which left me to attend the autopsy on Bailes. Leaving Harry still in with Tom, I went to the morgue. The pathologist handling Bailes was Ernie Hemmings, a rotund black man with huge sleepy eyes, octagonal glasses, and a constant smile as bright as his hairless pate. I always saw Ernie as a character in *Alice Through the Looking Glass*, the Cheshire Pathologist, maybe.

Ernie was studying a report as I entered.

'The blood screen on Bailes,' he said, frowning at various numbers on the pages. 'We got some interesting hits including a Prozac-type substance. Plus the stuff you'd expect, like THC and meth. And one big surprise, Stenebrexia.'

'What the hell's Stene-whatever.'

'I suppose you could call it a psychotropic dis-inhibitor. It was developed to help people with inhibitions and anxiety disorders, like stage fright and agoraphobia. But the stuff interacts poorly with other drugs, common ones like Prozac and the ilk. It can actually promote anxiety, plus odd behavior and acting out.'

'But if the stuff dissipates fear, it could have helped Bailes step into the hospital.'

'You're right. It could have made it easier. Thing is, Stenebrexia is only legally available in a half-dozen countries, the US not one of them.'

'Pharmaceuticals seem able to float over borders, right?'

Ernie nodded, turned to study Bailes's misshapen face. 'Maybe the guy was afraid of his mirror. Anyway, time for the show.'

When Hemmings pushed the scalpel into the swastika tat on Bailes's sternum and pulled it south, I started from the room.

'You're leaving?' Hemmings said.

'I'm not paid enough to watch you root through garbage. I'll be back.'

I jammed my hands in my pockets, went out a side door, and cut to the parking lot. I found a coffee shop with a television and watched CNN — abducted woman of the week, children starved in a basement, a man poisoned to death by his wife — until I duked the clerk five bucks to switch to the Weather Channel. When I returned to the morgue, Hemmings was lacing Bailes's abdomen shut with stitching like shoelaces. The Frankenstein stitches fit the lopsided face.

'He was pretty eaten up inside, right?' I asked.

'Pardon?'

'Pancreatic cancer? Terminal?'

Hemmings frowned and tapped Bailes's gut. 'Our boy here might have died of hepatic failure in twenty or so years if he kept drinking and drugging. Outside of incipient hardening of the liver, the guy was basically healthy, Carson. Who told you he had cancer?'

I re-ran Kirkson's words in my head . . .

'*Terry Lee visited here a week back and told me. He was crying like a fucking baby. I told*

179

him to man up, live the rest of his life like there was nothing to lose.'

I was sure Kirkson hadn't been lying. The details were too real, plus Kirkson had the image of being bunked with an aroused Thunderhead Wallace to keep him truthful.

'That's not the question,' I said. 'The question is, who told Bailes he was sick?'

Hemmings shrugged, snipped off a stitch. 'You gotta figure it was a doctor, right?'

★   ★   ★

'Dr Bascomb? Are you there?'

Dr Bernard Bascomb, senior biomedical researcher at New Zealand's University of Auckland School of Medicine, was reluctant to turn his eyes from the slender ankles of his new research assistant. She was currently hunched over a microscope in the bright lab outside his office, her ankles trim and elegant and, given the ample revelation of calf beneath the back of her lab jacket and the floor, very European, though his researcher was obviously part Maori.

'Dr Bascomb? I say, are you there?'

The latter heritage was reflected in a darker skin tone, high-cheekboned facial structure, and her musical, integrated name, Alicia Apatari. She was a lovely creature who, at twenty-two, would consider him a doddering old clutcher, though he was barely sixty and could play badminton like a forty-year-old.

'Hello-oo . . . Dr Bascomb?'

He would have loved to have considered Alicia

Apatari's Euro-Maori ankles all afternoon, but Bascomb's intercom was buzzing and the evil crone who intercepted visitors was yowling his name like a dyspeptic cat.

'*Dr Bascomb . . . are you there? Doctor?*'

Bascomb's finger jabbed the response button. 'What is it this time, Miss Trendle?'

'*You're there, then.*'

'No, I'm not here. I departed a half-hour ago.'

A pause as she digested the information. Then, irritation. '*You have a visitor. A Dr Matthias from the US. He said he had an appointment.*'

Bascomb shot a glance at his calendar and winced. He was a day off.

'Yes, yes . . . send him in.'

The receptionist's voice dropped to a whisper. '*This Matthias, Doctor. Is he the one that had all the, uh, publicity a few years back? When he said American black people were . . .*'

Bascomb rapped the case of the intercom with a chubby knuckle. 'Is the machine not functioning, Miss Trendle? Or did I not make myself clear? Send Dr Matthias in.'

'*To be sure.*' The receptionist's voice had gone sub-zero.

Bascomb's hands swept over his desk, arranging and tidying. A messy desk suggested an untidy mind. And the mind about to enter his office had been — no, was — one of the most distinctive in genetics, no matter what so many others thought.

Idiots. Retrogrades.

'Hello, Bernard,' a voice said as a face appeared at Bascomb's door, small and tan. The tanned flesh fit, Bascomb noted; Matthias's retirement had taken him to one of the US states on the Gulf of Mexico.

'Kurt!' Bernard said. 'Make yourself at home in my small dominion.'

Matthias entered. He wore a black suit sculpted to a hard, diminutive body, a jockey's body, Bascomb thought. *Would I be surprised if he rode into my office on a black horse? Probably not.* Matthias's pinpoint eyes were like green lasers behind gleaming wire bifocals.

Bascomb leaned over his desk to extend his hand, remembered Matthias didn't like to be touched. He turned the motion into a shuffling of papers as Matthias sat in a wingback chair across from Bernard's ample oaken desk. Matthias set the rattling brown briefcase down by his side.

'Excuse the clutter, Kurt. My needs exceed my space. A man of your distinction must have had a much larger office. I mean, must, uh, *have* a much larger office.' Bascomb reddened at using the past tense.

'Everyone knows I'm retired from the university life. I'm working for a private concern. And, of course, I have several patents that provide a bit of income.'

'Good for you, Kurt. We haven't been face to face since . . . when? The symposium in Lucerne? Eight years back? You were still advising on the Human Genome Project, Kurt. I remember your monograph on the A allele and genetic drift. A triumph.'

Matthias backhanded the praise away, a man

182

swatting a fly. 'At the time. But the field evolves so fast. Unlike us, Bernard. We get stuck in . . . ' Matthias paused, seemed on the verge of saying more, demurred, changed the subject. 'Your email of last week said you were able to get the research I requested?'

'What there was. You've been seeking the same sort of research in Australia, I expect?'

'There's a decent body of research over there,' Matthias said. 'The Aborigines, you know. I also had a secondary interest in the country's Asians. You know there's a Chinatown in Sydney? A rather expansive one?'

'The Dixon Street area. You were there, I take it?'

'I had to do field research in the vicinity. As well as in the outback.'

'Who was your contact in Australia, Kurt? Marnick at the AGRF? Or someone from the U of Queensland?'

Matthias's eye hardened. 'I'll keep that name confidential at present, Bernard. I hope you'll understand. I intend to do the same with yours.'

Bascomb shrugged and looked away, thinking it perhaps wasn't such a bad idea, given past events. He reached to the corner of his desk, pulling a four-inch stack of papers in front of him. 'Some of your specifics, especially race-mixing, are not an area of official governmental inquiry, at least not in decades. There are some rather surreptitious references on miscegenation with the Aborigines, data acquired on the QT. But there's a hefty dollop of other information. Bureaucrats love to amass data, don't they?'

Matthias nodded. 'Sometimes it's even useful. Is there much on the Maori? Their diseases in youth and the infirmities of age?'

'Including some revisionary medical history. It was thought that Maoris didn't suffer the ravages of diseases of the aged, but now it's suspected that's because the Maori don't live to a ripe old age, statistically. Those that do have a significantly higher susceptibility to degenerative diseases.'

Matthias leaned forward. 'Any personal thoughts on the racial anomaly, Bernard? Between the Maori and the European races?'

Bascomb tented his hands in front of his lips, sighed across his fingertips. 'The Maori suffer from poor quality of overall healthcare, mainly. Another theory is that the European influx brought all manner of unfamiliar and destructive diseases to the native peoples. The diseases still affect the Maoris as a race; those with more Maori blood, naturally, suffer the most.' Bascomb pushed the file across his desk. 'Anyway, you may wish to agree or disagree once you read the findings. Here's everything from the Ministry of Health, plus information from the district health boards in Maori-heavy districts. Some of it's confidential — bureaucrats again — and I blanked out the official letterhead so you're not stopped at the airport and suspected of smuggling out state secrets. Though I expect you'd be in more trouble if the files pertained to breeds of sheep rather than humans.'

'Breeds of human,' Matthias whispered.

'What?'

'Nothing,' Matthias said, waving away the question. 'Just tasting a turn of phrase.' He tapped the sheaf of papers. 'Individual health reports are defined by race?'

'Yes, almost always.'

'That will be helpful. Now, let's talk a moment about ports, Bernard.'

Bascomb smiled. 'The wines or — ?'

'The ship sort. I currently live near Mobile, Alabama, a very old port city. I'm interested in New Zealand's ports, particularly the older ones. Where the European immigration occurred. Any immigration, actually.'

Bascomb shrugged. 'Most of our English immigrants sailed from Liverpool. I'd guess the majority came ashore here in Auckland. But there's New Plymouth, Port Chalmers, Wellington, and half a dozen other ports. You'd have to speak with a historian for exact dates and numbers of the influx. I can quickly connect you to one at the university.'

'Thank you, Bernard, that will be helpful. It'll set me up for a few days of simple field work, collecting various samples.'

'Can you give me more input on your particular aspect of study, Doctor?' Bascomb asked.

Matthias tapped his fingers on his knee. He seemed to retreat into himself for a long moment, then stood abruptly, picking up the dark brief-case.

'It's probably safest that you don't know, Bernard.'

★   ★   ★

'Kirkson was lying about Bailes having the Big C,' Harry said, rolling a pencil between his palms, taking a full minute to absorb the results of the autopsy. 'It's the only thing that makes sense.'

'He wasn't,' I argued, leaning forward, planting my arms on my desk. 'You know me, I can spot a con's lie before he even makes it up.'

Harry paused his rolling. Started it again. Said, 'Usually.'

'What's that mean?'

'It means we all have good days and bad days.'

'And what the hell does that mean?'

'It means . . . ' Harry stopped, blew out a breath. 'Never mind.'

'Why would Kirkson lie?' I prodded.

Harry ticked off three answers on his fingers. 'Because he didn't know anything. Or to get you out of his face. Or to jerk you around. Or all three.'

The idea that a piece of talking excrement like Kirkson had lied to me sent a hot wave through my gut. I felt my fists tighten. I slammed one on my desk, sending a stack of files to the floor.

Harry studied the fallen paperwork. 'Carson, you ever think about a vacation? Taking a couple weeks and running off to the Caribbean or something?'

'Why?'

Harry's cellphone rang. He stared at the files on the floor and yanked the phone from his pocket. Spoke for a few seconds, then dropped the phone in his pocket and looked at me.

'That was Glenn Watkins in forensics. They

need to see us right now. It's about something at Scaler's death scene.'

★ ★ ★

'Sea water?' I said to Watkins, standing in his office in the main lab at forensics. 'How can you be sure?'

He passed over the report, a simple one-page sheet. 'Standard-issue sea water, judging by algal composition and salinity. We've also got decent hits on petrochemicals, gasoline, oil. The water came from somewhere near boats, I expect. Marina, shipyard.'

'You were right, Carson,' Harry said. 'It was sea water I slipped in at the cabin. Great catch.'

I'd been right, but had no idea what it meant. I shook my head and turned for the door. I remembered a question I was going to ask when I first saw Glenn on the scene.

'I thought you were semi-retired, Glenn, and just working in the lab a couple days a week.'

Glenn sighed, shook his head. 'You didn't hear about Al?'

'Al Bustamente?'

'He got jumped a couple days ago, beaten bad. Somebody snuck up behind him in the carport at his apartment complex. It was night. The assailant worked Al over with a pipe or blackjack, then ran off with his wallet. Broke both wrists, some teeth.'

'Keee-rist,' I whispered.

'Al'll be back in six to eight weeks, but he's

187

hurtin' right now. I'm standing in 'til he's in the pink.'

I left, shaking my head at one more case of Evil overwhelming the Good. Passing through the pathology annex I saw Clair inside the second lab. I kept my head straight, as if reading maps in my mind and not noticing my surroundings. I made eight steps before I heard her voice.

'Carson? You got a few minutes? There's something I want you to see.'

I started to claim a harried schedule, but followed her slender form into the lab, a wide room of counters and instruments, vials and tubes and things cooking over blue flames. My nose was assailed by a scent of decay hiding beneath antiseptics and deodorizer, knowing I'd smell it for an hour after leaving the building. I was never sure whether the odor had entered my clothes or my mind, but it lingered nonetheless.

She led me to an exam table. I beheld six feet of twisted cinder with a bulb on top, the former human being Harry had discovered staring from the remains of the coastal fire, though Clair didn't know that. The cinder had been further mangled by an autopsy, or whatever opening a charcoal briquette was called. On a nearby table was a rolled-up towel. She nodded at the elongated cinder.

'This appeared, sent in by the county police over the weekend. The body was found near the Mississippi border in a burned-down shack in the swampy middle of nowhere.'

'I know the gentleman,' I said, 'though we've

never been on speaking terms.'

'What? How?'

I explained how the deceased and I had met. I didn't go into the details of Harry's treatment by Briscoe, or how my partner's anger had resulted in an exploded melon not long thereafter.

'Then you know of the harpoon?'

'Actually, Clair, it's a fish lance, used to kill sharks and marlins and whatnot. But it's a harpoon at heart. Maybe someone thought our dead man was a whale.' I paused. 'Was the sheriff here when you performed the autopsy, Clair?'

'We called and told his office the date and time. No one showed.'

'You sent the reports over, right?'

'The prelims were faxed as soon as they were done. I called Sheriff Briscoe personally to make sure they'd arrived.'

Briscoe. The racist bastard's name bubbled in my gut. Flashed anger to my face, suddenly hot.

'His response?'

'He yawned into the phone. Said something about Katrina blowing some people over to Texas was the best thing to happen in a long time. That was basically the extent of our conversation. He sounded like what you'd call a major-league asshole.'

'He is, but he's not my problem, thank God. Gotta go. See you later.'

I made it four paces. 'Carson?' Clair called.

'Yes?'

'I asked you to call me a couple days back. In the past I would have heard from you within a half-day.'

I stared at her. 'Half a day?' I said. 'Is that my programmed response time?'

'I only meant . . . you're usually so careful about calling back.'

I slapped my forehead in an exaggerated gesture. 'Somehow I forgot to tattoo that on my arm: *Call Clair now.*'

'I didn't mean for you to — '

'You want me to call you, Clair? You got it.'

I pulled my phone from my pocket, made an elaborate show of inputting her number. Across the room in the small utility office, her phone started buzzing.

'Hi, Clair,' I said, staring at the floor as if she wasn't there. 'This is Carson returning your call. I couldn't do it within the time you wanted because I've got a dead preacher out there. This particular asshole was famous and politically connected and I've got to pretend like it's a big deal. Oh, Clair? In addition to citizens stabbing and bludgeoning and shooting one another twenty-four goddamn hours a day, there are people putting babies in boats and setting them loose on the ocean.'

I flicked the phone shut. Looked at her with a raised eyebrow.

'There. Are we all caught up?'

25

I awoke the next morning to find the television on and a mustache drawn over my upper lip. I found a mascara pencil on the living-room table alongside a mirror. I vaguely recalled Clair wondering what I'd look like with a mustache, but that had been months back. I took my vitamins, brewed my tea, and ate two apples and a bowl of oatmeal, wondering if I should just throw out the bacon and sausages in my fridge; not on my healthy list. Or maybe toss everything and start anew by filling a trolley at the health-food store. As I ate, I listened to an Italian flutist on NPR. I found the sound lyrical and intoxicating, the most soothing sound I'd ever heard.

I whistled flute sounds all the way to HQ and was steeping a teabag when Harry arrived. He wore a red linen jacket over an iridescent green polo shirt, yellow pants, black running shoes. The ensemble was so loud I should have heard his approach.

'Is that *tea*?' he asked, aghast at the bag floating in my cup.

'Ginseng with rose hips. I'm off coffee. And I'm going to learn to play the flute.'

A pause. 'Good, I guess. Got a minute? I want you to see a videotape I found on the web. I need your opinion.'

I followed my partner to the computer in the

side meeting room. I saw blue sky through the window, a storm's dark edge to the south. Harry took a chair and pulled the keyboard close. I watched over his shoulder as he went sailing through cyberspace.

We'd entered Scaler's home and I saw Scaler sitting restlessly at his huge white desk. There was a blue mug on the desk, a white remote, and a spiral-bound report.

Scaler plucked a white linen handkerchief from his pocket and dabbed his forehead. He tucked the cloth back into his pocket, subconsciously tugged his lapels straight, the final motion of a performer before taking the stage. He frowned into the camera, his face and voice subdued, like at the groundbreaking ceremony.

'*A parable,*' he announced. '*I paid a man to do work for me. I had built a house and wanted assurance its foundation was solid.*'

He stopped and gathered the handkerchief from his pocket again, dabbing a head shiny with sweat. He sighed and hung his head. All I saw was the crown of his head and eroding hair at front and back. When he lifted his head, a transformation, the sorrow in his eyes replaced with anger.

'*I PAID a man to do WORK for me. I had built a HOUSE. I had built a house on SMUG-NESS and SELF-RIGHTEOUSNESS and LUST for POWER AND GLORY. Though I inherited the foundation and built with the help of many . . .*' he paused, as though weighing a word, ' *— false friends. I tell you freely that I BUILT THIS HOUSE WITH MY OWN HANDS.*'

Scaler spoke through clenched teeth, punctuating words with rhythmic explosions of volume. It was his audience voice, his drama voice. But I'd always heard overblown stagecraft behind his pulpit pronouncements and dancing runs across the boards; this anger sounded deep and painful. His head drooped.

'You found this with the other Scaler stuff on YouTube?' I said.

'No. It took some looking. I couldn't sleep, found it at three a.m.'

'Why didn't you find it with the others?'

'There's maybe five hundred Scaler vids on various sites. It's a long haul to see them all.'

I glanced back at the screen, Scaler's head still down, hands rubbing his face.

'What's it filed as?' I asked.

'It's listed under Truth,' Harry said. 'Then under Scaler.'

'What?'

'Shhhh,' Harry said, pointing at the monitor. Scaler was back. He straightened his lapels and continued:

'The man I had hired was the expert in the world at his work. He came to my door one day. I said, 'Come in, Brother, and prove the perfection of my house for I am the great Richard Bloessing Scaler and God has spoken to me since my childhood.' I said to my learned expert, 'Tell me the truth of the perfection of my house.''

''I am sorry, Reverend Scaler,' came the learned man's response. 'I cannot.''

''HOW DARE YOU TELL ME I CANNOT

193

HEAR THE TRUTH!' I railed at the learned man of science. 'WHY CAN YOU NOT TELL ME THE TRUTH?''

Scaler waited for the anger to drain from his face, replaced it with fresh sorrow.

'And my learned man said to me, 'Because it will cause your house to crumble into ashes.''

26

'Bizarre,' I said, unable to pull my eyes from the screen. 'Is that all there is?'

Harry held up a finger. 'He's got a coda.'

I turned back to the monitor. Scaler was dabbing his head and face with the handkerchief again. Beads of sweat had gathered in the thick folds beneath his tragic eyes. He tucked away the cloth and turned back to the watchdog lens.

'*Excuse me. I wanted to get this recorded before my will failed. Sometimes the best place to hide a truth is in plain sight. Thus it will live in the Tower of Babel. I have made mistakes, I have walked a lie. I have been led astray by false companions over years. If I don't falter, many things will soon come to light. I will tell you the truth through the Trinity, and what I now believe to be —* ' Scaler put one finger atop the other to indicate a capital letter — '*the Truth.*' He slid his finger down to the first digit, forming a cross. '*The Way and the Light,*' he whispered.

He stared at his gesture. His hands fell to his lap and he began weeping. I saw him reach for the white remote control and the video died.

'It's cryptic deluxe,' I said. 'The ravings of a madman?'

'Actually, it's making more sense to me,' Harry said. 'I think Scaler himself put the video on the web. Hiding his truth in plain sight.'

'The Tower of Babel,' I said, suddenly catching

Harry's drift. 'His video tucked away with ten million others. One grain of sand in an hourglass.'

'But what's this 'truth' he's talking about?' Harry said.

'The parable, the analogy to the house . . . I figure house either pertains to himself, or to his empire.'

'I like the second one, myself,' Harry concurred, sighing and flicking the computer off. 'The empire as his house of worship, the church enterprises, fits well with the parable house. But Scaler and the institution were pretty much one and the same, so it could be representative of both.'

'In either case, something's been built on sand,' I noted. 'But he didn't know that until the 'expert' did work for Scaler, work seeming to undermine Scaler's mysterious edifice. Is the expert Christ?'

Harry frowned and tumbled it through his head.

'Not making the nut for me. There's something in it that doesn't have the reverent tone I'd expect if Scaler was using Jesus as his expert.'

'It's Richard Scaler, bro. The scuzzball would — '

Harry waved me silent. 'For thirty years I've been looking at Scaler and every time I did I swear I could smell something bad in the room. But now that I've been through his sermons and tapes a dozen times . . . ' He shrugged, like he couldn't understand his coming words. 'I believe he's sincere.'

'*Sincere?*'

'The bible has passages of great compassion and love, often butted against passages of vengeance and pain. It seems to me that self-titled men of God define themselves through the passages upon which they build their theology. I don't agree with Scaler's selection. But I think the guy actually felt he was following scripture.'

'Scaler?' I scoffed. 'He was an ignorant cracker bullshit salesman.'

Harry said, 'A girlfriend gave me a book of poems by a guy from the sixties, Richard Brautigan. He had a short poem about a schoolroom where once a day the teacher pulled a red wagon across the floor and that was all the kids knew.'

I waved my hand in front of his eyes, said, 'Earth to Harry.'

'Don't you get it, Carson? If that's all you're taught, that's all you know. Especially if it starts when you're in the cradle.'

'You're giving Scaler a pass because he's been a preacher for fifty-odd years?'

'I give Scaler a semi-pass because I suspect he got pumped full of fundamental hate-ology as a kid.'

'Just because you start life as a blank slate doesn't mean accepting what others write there.'

'I don't understand that level of self-delusion, Carson, but I understand the process that creates it: Endless spewing of hate and aspersions. To deny a parental belief questions the entire family.'

'You think Mrs Scaler might help make sense of this?' I said. 'Hubby's weird monologue?'

'You've been there, so it's your call.'

I pulled my black briefcase from beneath the desk. I kept my old Apple iBook in it, used the computer for moving files from work to home. I pulled out the computer and handed it to Harry.

'Let's give the lady a show.'

★ ★ ★

The housekeeper led me into the Scalers' home. She wore an apron and had a feather duster tucked in the strap. I was surprised to find the living room painted rose instead of the white I recalled. Accents were scarlet and sun-yellow, a bold deployment of color. I smelled fresh paint in the air. Saw ladders and drop-cloths.

'Is Mr Fossie around?' I asked.

'Mee-star Foss-see he ees een the room named Jim,' she said.

'Jim?'

'*Si.*' She began pumping her arms up and down.

'Ah,' I said. '*Gracias.*'

Wandering to the back of the house, I heard a moan and a squeaking sound and stuck my head in the exercise room, the gym. Fossie was sitting on a quadrilaterals machine, legs under the padded bar, trying to lift with the pin in the fifteen-pound block. He saw me and, startled, let the block clank down all of the four inches of elevation he had managed.

Fossie unwrapped himself from the machine clumsily as I pretended to look the other way. He did a couple of side stretches and a toe-touch attempt, making as if shaking off a major-league workout.

'She's having the place re-painted?' I asked, nodding toward a stack of folded drop-cloths.

He dabbed his face with a towel and nodded. 'The rooms have too many memories. Patricia wanted the change.'

'You're spending a fair amount of time here, I take it?'

'I have the time, and it makes Patricia feel secure to have me here. At least until she's better. How are you feeling?'

'I'm sleeping better. And I think some of my energy's returning. It comes and goes.'

'Good. But returning your body and mind to a balanced state doesn't come as quickly as getting a shot of penicillin for an infection. Regimen is the key. Keep taking the vites and avoid processed food. Don't stay up late. I'll drop off more vitamins when I'm out on Dauphin Island in a day or two. Maybe add a bit of Tibetan ginseng to the mix, perhaps some kelp.'

I nodded my thanks and started to climb the stairs, but paused.

'Mr Fossie?'

'Yes?'

'Have you had any luck looking for . . . ' I ended the sentence with a raised eyebrow, got a look of guilt in return.

'I-I will. It feels strange to look through things that aren't mine. Like I'm ransacking.'

'Don't do anything that makes you feel ill at ease,' I said. 'But you're the one who wanted us to uncover more about Richard Scaler.'

He nodded and looked happy to retreat. I continued up the stairs and knocked on the door.

'Mrs Scaler? It's Detective Ryder. May I come in?'

'Just a second, please.'

Her voice sounded as faded as the last time, a tired wisp of sound. The second-hand of my watch made three revolutions until I heard the voice again.

'Come in, sir.'

Patricia Scaler was a-bed, one that configured every whichaway. It was a huge bed, king-sized at least, and she had the head elevated. She seemed lost inside a fluffy yellow robe, the sleeves at her fingertips; her husband's robe.

'How may I help you, sir?'

'I need you to help me make sense of something odd, ma'am.'

'Your words frighten me, sir. But I'll do what I can.'

I pulled the laptop from my flight bag. 'Are you familiar with sites like YouTube?'

'A warehouse for pictures? Richard mentioned it.'

'You're basically right. YouTube is a huge databank, hundreds of thousands of videos that — '

'Who keeps all the videos?'

'Pardon?'

'Who sorts and arranges all the videos? Is it like the Mormons having all the names inside the mountain? And who sends you the pictures when you want to see them?'

'It's all digital, ma'am. The videos are in computer code. They're kept in computer memory.' I wondered if she'd ever used a computer.

'What a scary world it's become,' she whispered. I wondered if I held up the granola bar in my bag would it frighten her? *Behold the amazing concoction of grains and raisins!* I also wondered if she'd ever been under the care of a shrink to help her counter her timidity.

I turned my laptop so Mrs Scaler could see the screen. She was emotionless as the odd video played, either thinking so hard it overwhelmed expression, or trying to blot out thought. When the screen faded to black, her hand reached out and covered mine.

'This, this storehouse . . . did it tell you how the pictures of Richard got there? Where they came from?'

'There are ways to prevent that sort of thing, though we'll try. Did you understand anything Richard was talking about?'

'No. Richard was having . . . one of his bad days. Like I told you about.'

'Would you know the expert he refers to?'

'God? The divine specialist in everything?'

'Um, I get the impression this was someone your husband hired. A less omniscient expert.'

'I wouldn't know, Richard was gone so often. He'd go out at night, be gone for hours. I was terrified the police would stop him. Then I wanted them to. To make him see into himself, to stop.'

'To see himself doing what?'

She looked away. 'He'd come in and go to his bedroom. There was the smell of strong drink. And strange perfume. And smells I couldn't identify, ugly things.'

'No one else saw this?'

'We'd do the show and he was Richard, then we'd get away from all the workers and audience and people from the college, and he became someone else.'

She dabbed at her eyes with a tissue. I turned the laptop off, waited for it to beep itself to sleep. I noticed Mrs Scaler's mouth was less puffed, the damaged teeth attended to, perhaps with temporary crowns. She had put on a bit of make-up, giving her pale face a semblance of color.

'You've had dental work done, I take it?' I said, small-talk to fill the dead air.

'The restoration is just starting. But little by little God is fixing my body.' The eyes turned expectant. 'Will I see you again, sir? I hope to.'

'I . . . truly don't know, Mrs Scaler.' I stood.

'May I see you to the door?' she said. 'I'd very much like that.'

'Certainly.'

'Let me visit the little girl's room first.'

She sat up and tugged the robe tight, slipped her small feet into the slippers and padded off to a dressing closet. My gaze fell over her tight-robed derriere and watched it bob in a rhythmic motion before shame pulled my eyes away.

I took a final look at the room, saw a photo on a corner dresser that caught my eye, drew me over. I hadn't seen it before.

It was an eight-by-ten head shot of a woman, typical portrait pic. A relative of Patricia Scaler, I figured; there was a family resemblance in the eyes and ovoid facial structure. But where Patricia Scaler was plain at best, the other woman was lovely, with a fairy-princess nose and straight and gleaming white teeth behind lips so full I wondered if they were enhanced. Her cheekbones were model-high, her jaw firm and symmetrical. Bright highlights shone in rich auburn hair. Her skin was firm and tight and she looked in her mid thirties.

Though the woman was — in the jargon — a hottie, the photo itself seemed cold and mechanical. There was a name printed lower right: Blackburn Studios.

I heard a throat cleared at my back. Mrs Scaler had returned so quietly I hadn't heard her. She was in a loose-fitting pantsuit and watching me study the photograph.

'I, uh . . . '

'Don't be embarrassed, sir. You're a policeman. I expect you're allowed to search my room.'

'I, uh, wasn't searching, ma'am. I was just looking and saw the, uh . . . '

'The picture. It drew you in, right? Like it was calling you?'

'I have to admit it did.'

'That's my sister. Isn't she lovely?'

'She is rather attractive, Mrs Scaler.'

Her eyes fixed on me. There was something in them I couldn't read.

'*Rather* attractive, sir? Some say she's gorgeous.'

I smiled and set the picture down. 'Your sister's very pretty.'

'She has her pick of men, you know. A banquet. But she's very selective.'

'Pardon me?' For a moment I felt as if I'd wandered into a chapter of *Great Expectations*, Miss Havisham speaking to young Pip. It fit in its own small and sad way, aspects of Mrs Scaler seemingly minted in Victorian times.

We walked slowly downstairs, crossed the room to the door. Patricia Scaler held out her hand. It was surprisingly firm and I figured she gardened.

'I wanted to thank you for your time, sir. I'm sorry you had to listen to the failures of the lives in this house.'

'May I make a suggestion, ma'am?' I asked. 'I don't mean offense, it's just my take.'

'Of course, sir.'

'You can't change the past, but you have a much different future than you did a few days ago. That's the direction I'd be looking.'

*   *   *

I went back to the department and grabbed Harry. We had two more dominatrixes on our list supplied by Mistress Layla, one of them over in Pensacola. We did the visits and the interviews and came up empty-handed. We were running out of leads, and left with the horrible feeling that, unless forensics pulled some kind of evidence from the cabin, or someone unknown stepped forward with new information, the case would always have a question mark at the end.

We got back to town at seven in the evening. Harry tottered off for his fix of Noelle, and I stopped by a health-food store for organic brown rice and quinoa, another of Fossie's recommendations. By the time I got home, I was too tired to fix anything and fell asleep on the floor watching Andy Griffith re-runs. Somewhere in the night I dreamed of the beautiful woman who was Patricia Scaler's sister, jolting awake with her breath in my throat.

27

My sleep was as thick and juicy as a thirty-dollar steak, eight hours' worth. In the morning I drank tea on my deck, though I couldn't tell what kind, the writing on the package so artsy as to defy translation. I ate something rectangular made of lentils and popped my vitamins. I got a call on my way in, a number I hadn't called before, no ID on the phone. I pulled to the side of the road and popped it open.

'Ryder.'

'Detective Ryder, this is Archie Fossie.'

'What can I do for you, sir?'

'I'm over at the Scalers'. I-I found something in Richard's office. It seemed kind of hidden.'

'I'll stop by.'

'Can I meet you on the corner? I don't want to alarm Patricia.'

'Fifteen minutes.'

Fossie was on the corner when I arrived, pacing in circles beneath a magnolia tree. I swooped up, pushed open the passenger door.

'Get in, we'll take a ride.'

He slipped in my truck. 'I told Patricia I was going for a walk. I should be back soon to prepare her meals for today.'

'What'd you find?'

'Just a phone number. It was on a Post-it, like you suggested. Stuck under the monitor on Richard's computer.'

I looked at the number. A cell. It probably didn't mean anything, but what seemed an out-of-the-way location might pan out.

'You thought to look under his monitor?' I asked.

'Richard spent hours at his computer, writing books and sermons. I figured anything he needed would be close at hand. You supplied the idea, I just did the looking.'

I pocketed the Post-it. 'Miz Scaler mentioned Richard going out late at night, returning hours later. Ever see that?'

'Three weeks ago. I came in the morning before going to my office. Richard pulled in behind me in one of those huge white cars. He looked half crazy and his clothes were rumpled, his, uh, zipper down. His pants were stained.'

'What happened?'

'All I wanted was out of there. I asked him if he'd kindly take a bag of fruits and veggies and a couple of prepared dinners into Patricia.'

'And?'

'He asked me if I was having a relationship with her — not using those terms. My mouth fell open and I told him no, of course not.'

'What happened from there, Mr Fossie?'

'He started laughing, a filthy, dirty sound, and said he could understand, because it was like . . . like fucking cold grits.'

I thanked Fossie and dropped him back on the corner. 'Keep looking, Mr Fossie,' I said. 'It's what we need.'

'It makes me feel like a creep. A spy or something.'

'You're working for the good guys. And by the way, I'm sleeping again.'

He smiled for the first time, flicked a wave, hustled back toward the Scaler edifice.

I got into the office to find Harry at the coffee urn and studying doughnuts. Though it was Sunday, half of the detective's desks were occupied, the price of a murderous season.

'You should eat more oatmeal,' I advised. 'A healthy mind and body and all that.'

Harry leaned low over the pastries to scrutinize a danish. 'I'm sure these sprinkles are organic.'

'I just got some info from Fossie,' I said, digging in my pocket for the Post-it. 'Probably nothing, but worth a try. I put him on scoping out the Scalers' place, an inside man.'

Harry gave me a frown, like he did after I mentioned my little scam at the prison.

'How'd you pull that one off, Carson?'

'Fossie's been giving me a little advice on a healthy diet. He prescribed some herbs to help me sleep. It's working.'

Harry nodded. 'My aunt takes that herbal stuff and it did miracles for her. What's Fossie think this number means?'

'He's got no idea, but he found it — '

'Harry! Carson!'

We turned to see Tom Mason leaning out his office door with phone in hand. 'Got a body at 513 Broad Street,' he called. 'The Hoople Hotel.'

I jammed the Post-it back in my pocket. 'Ah, the Heroin Hilton. Let's go dance with the roaches.'

We were at the Hoople five minutes later, Harry wheeling the big blue Crown Vic half on to the sidewalk and shutting down the screamer. Two radio cars were on scene, and a crowd was gathering, vacant-eyed homeless types shambling beside gum-chewing hookers dressed like Whore Barbie. Streetwise studs with white tees and sideslung caps watched from a distance, afraid of getting nailed on outstanding warrants. When I stepped from the car a crack vial crunched under my heel. The air smelled of stale beer from the bar across the street.

We ducked past a uniform and into the Hoople. It was a resident hotel mainly occupied by old-line junkies who worked sporadic, low-pay jobs and needed a place to crib and fix and stay out of the way of normal people.

I saw a young uniformed officer at the desk counter, keeping the clerk from bolting. The clerk was Hispanic, in his thirties, maybe four-foot-ten and ninety pounds. His anxious eyes told me his immigration status was nebulous. Harry asked for directions and the uniform turned to point at the rickety steps leading upstairs.

'Third floor, Detective, room 321, about midway down the ha — '

That was all the clerk needed. He dropped low and bolted, trying to squeeze past us and out the front door. Harry's hand flashed out and grabbed the guy by the back of his collar. When Harry lifted, the clerk was suddenly in the air, feet still running as Harry whirled around and set him down in the opposite direction, where he ran into a wall, just like a cartoon.

Helping the guy up, dusting off his shoulder, Harry said a few words in Spanish, telling Mr Jaime Critizia we were not going to inform La Migre — Immigration — unless he repeated his attempt at running.

The guy nodded acceptance and collapsed into a metal chair. We headed upstairs to the third floor, saw an open door midway down a hall less than two shoulders wide, a uniformed cop leaning against the wall, Officer Jerry Gilmore. He looked up, shook his head.

'Add another one to the year's growing list of corpses, guys. Someone called it in anonymously just a few minutes ago. Me and Ryan were down the street, ran over. Found the guy inside, still warm.'

We peeked into a linoleum-floored room scarcely larger than a parking space. Surprisingly, the room was clean and tidy and recently painted. Two large philodendrons perched atop a table by a window, probably the only window in the place that had ever been washed. I saw a painting on the wall, an inexpensive copy of Van Gogh's *Starry Night*. The place resembled the digs of a fastidious college student, not a room at a low-rent sleeper.

Across the room the view wasn't so pleasant: a body on a single bed, a bronze-skinned male in his early forties or thereabouts, jeans, no shirt. His head was shaved. His eyes were open and so was his mouth, a strand of dried vomit tracing down his cheek and throat to the sheet. I figured he'd been a good-looking man in life, his body lean, his features strong and chiseled and exotic.

At the head of the bed, beside a grated window streaked with grime, Sergeant Orville Ryan stared down at the corpse while scribbling notes in a spiral-bound pad almost lost in his plate-sized paw. Somewhere in the room I discerned the dank scent of the sea.

'What is it, Orv?' Harry strode over and looked down at the corpse, said, 'Oh,' like things were self-explanatory. I wandered in and saw the cheap plastic syringe on the floor beside the bed, the blackened spoon used to heat the drug, melt it into water or spit that would liquefy it for sucking it up the needle. I snapped on latex gloves as I crouched, lifted the body's arm and looked at the inner section from bicep to wrist, saw a webworm of scabs and collapsed veins, the stigmata of a veteran junkie.

'Looks like a classic OD,' I said, trying to hide the hopeful note in my voice. If the death was accidental, it wouldn't fall under our aegis.

'Dead on,' Ryan said, looking up over the reading glasses perched on the tip of a bulbous nose. 'He was aimed this direction, just a matter of time.'

'You knew the guy, Orv?' Harry asked.

'Name's LaPierre O'Fong, officially.'

'O'Fong?'

'To hear Red tell it, years back someone on the Irish side of his family married the Chinese side and somehow — as a joke or maybe meaning it for real — the family changed its name to O'Fong. It got into official records and stuck.'

'That's some kind of family story,' Harry said.

211

'He came from some kind of family, to hear him tell it. He went by Chinese Red, or just Red. He'd been on and off smack for twenty-plus years; on, mainly, starting in his late teens.'

I studied the guy's features closer, saw Asian genes in the delicate nose, almond eyes. He wasn't Caucasian or African or Hispanic or Asian, but somehow he was all of them and more. His open eyes were staring at the ceiling, like watching a movie in a theater where only the dead got tickets.

'Chinese makes sense,' I said, looking at the face. 'Where's the Red come from?'

'Red's natural hair was the color of rust. He'd started shaving his head because of me,' Ryan said. 'When I'd see that red rug ducking down an alley I'd pull over and roust his junkie ass.'

'You didn't like him, Orv?' Harry asked.

'I liked Red plenty, Harry. Smart guy, sharp. I wanted him to clean up full time, maybe do something right for the next forty years. Every time I'd roust him I'd give him the speech, pass over a list of detox centers. He'd climb free of the shit, fall down two months later. I'd heard through the grapevine that he'd cleaned up again. Guess it didn't last.'

'How'd he make his living?' I asked.

'Car detailer, when he was clean.'

'And when he wasn't clean?'

'He hustled. It was another thing I'd roust his ass for; leaning a wall by the docks, winking at rich white guys in Lexuses. He was a good-looking guy. It made scoring off horny old guys pretty easy.'

'Bust him lately?'

'Not in three-four months. I hoped he'd seen the light.'

'He hustle down here by the docks?' Harry asked.

Ryan nodded. 'Red preferred being where he could walk to the water. He liked to watch the ships come and go, said the water felt like home.'

'He had fish genes, too?'

'Red called himself a breed of the world, Harry. Said his daddy's side of the family was Australian Aborigine-Irish-Italian and his mama was Thai and Chi and Russian and French. He said the ocean touched all those places so the ocean was as close as he could get to home.'

'A genetic smorgasbord,' I said. Chinese Red's multilateral heritage was nothing new in a port city like Mobile; I figured the world's ports were the planet's most efficient melting pots.

'The ocean was home?' Harry said. 'That's kind of poetic.'

'There was poetry in Red's soul, Harry,' Ryan continued. 'Like he'd made peace with his life, and just wanted to enjoy it, the dope notwithstanding. A shitty end to a life that might have had some promise.'

Ryan pushed up from his crouch. He nodded to the cop at the door. 'Tell the bus drivers they can have the body, Jerry. Chinese Red has sailed for home.'

The bus attendants came for the body. They grunted the dead weight from the bed toward the gurney.

With Harry looking between the body and

213

Ryan, I saw a blue denim pant leg sticking from the shadows beneath the bed, a dark spot on a rolled-up cuff. I tweezed the pants out with my fingertips. When I saw the familiar stain I pulled latex gloves from my pocket and snapped them on.

'What is it?' Harry said.

'Blood,' I said. 'A decent amount on the pants. Dried, but I'm sure it's blood.'

I got down on my hands and knees. Pulled a white wad from beneath the bed.

'Got a T-shirt, too. Same stains.'

Harry looked between the deceased and the clothes. 'I don't see any wounds on the body. Let's get the clothes to forensics. Have them verify the blood's his when they get the chance.'

When I stood I felt dampness in my knees. Looking down I saw wet splotches.

'The carpet's soaked,' I said.

'Piss, I expect,' Ryan said. 'Red's bladder let loose before he fell on the bed.'

I leaned my nose close to my wet knees. Sniffed. I expected to smell urine, but didn't.

'It smells like sea water,' I said, befuddled.

'What was that?' Harry said.

'I said it smells like — '

'No. From outside.' Harry canted his head toward the open window.

'Dead guy! Dead guy!' A woman screamed for a second time. 'There's a dead guy in the street!'

We ran down the stairs, followed the woman's screams around the corner. We saw a body facedown in an alley, hands splayed like the guy was hugging the pavement and kissing its surface. I slid up beside him like a ballplayer sliding to home plate. I pressed the back of my fingers to his neck, felt nothing. Harry had his phone out to call for assistance.

'They's a man dead over here!' a male voice howled. I saw a head sticking from the vestibule of a ragged building, waving at me, at Harry, at anyone watching to please come help. Ryan and the uniformed officer came from the Hoople, looked our way with confused faces. I did a palms-up gesture of helplessness.

Another shriek of despair from across the street. A woman came running from an apartment. 'My boyfriend won't get up. I don't think he's breathing. Help me!'

'What the hell is going on?' Harry whispered, watching a brace of radio cruisers screaming on to the far end of the block.

'I don't know,' I said, my heart thumping just under my chin. A little girl wandered up, not over eight years old. She tugged at the back of my pants.

'Mister? Mister?'

I turned and looked down, tried to affect a smile. 'We're pretty busy here, dear. What is it?'

She pointed toward the next block over. 'They's a man laying on the steps in front of my house. He look like he sleeping, but he won't wake up. Why he doin' like that?'

28

The block had been cordoned off. Scared people stood in tenement doorways or huddled on corners as lights flashed from over a dozen official vehicles. Bodies were being loaded into ambulances, evidence was being gathered. I saw Orville Ryan accompanying one gurney to an ambulance, seeing O'Fong off to the next world. I felt sorry for Ryan; he'd believed in Chinese Red.

Clair Peltier had arrived a few minutes into the mayhem, alerted that something major was going down. I'd nodded her way when she arrived and let her work. Now, with the hubbub dying away, Harry and I wandered over. I studied my shoes while Harry spoke.

'Any ideas, Doc?' he asked. 'Is it what it appears?'

She nodded. 'I get the feeling someone forgot to cut a batch of heroin. Those poor folks got into some smack so pure it shut them down.'

Mobile wasn't known for the quality of its heroin, usually brown scag, Mexican tar, and other bottom-level crap so stepped on by greedy local dealers that ten per cent heroin to ninety filler was a general rule. Pure heroin would have been like slamming nine extra bags into a vein at once, almost instantly depressing the machinery to the Off setting.

As part of the response, news organizations and social agencies with contacts in junkie-land were being alerted, soon to issue warnings about the deaths and potential for more problems. *If you don't know it, don't shoot it*, was the mantra being prepared. Hopefully, what we had were a few isolated cases, a mistake along the pipeline.

'How about an adulterant?' Harry suggested. 'A toxin in the junk.'

'I'd lean that way,' Clair said, 'except the reactions suggest OD from all directions. But I'm going to no-comment the media until I get a for-sure verdict.'

I looked across the street and saw reporters bunched up like runners at the start of the Boston Marathon, held back by uniformed cops. When the scene was released they'd run rampant.

'Carson?' Clair called to my retreating back.

I looked over my shoulder. 'You're looking better,' she said quietly, and hustled off to consult with her crew. I turned back to Harry. 'If it's all accidental OD's, we're off the hook. Clair seems to think that's the way it'll fry up. What next?'

'Back to our regular grind,' he said. 'And that means Scaler. You were saying Fossie found some kind of number in Scaler's office?'

'Stuck on the underside of his monitor.'

'Why not give the number a ring; see who answers? Probably best to use the clean phone.'

Our clean phone was a pre-paid cell we used when we wanted a call to be anonymous, not tipping off the recipient who was on our end. We mainly used it with skittish snitches. I pulled the phone from the cruiser, dialed. Four rings and pickup.

'Hello?' said a voice sounding both hesitant and oddly familiar.

'Who's this?' I asked pleasantly.

'Who's *this*?' the familiar voice on the other line responded.

I said, 'I got this number from a friend who said I probably needed to call it.'

A beat. 'What was the friend's name?'

'He's well known and doesn't like his name used,' I said.

'Hmmmm,' the voice said. 'Who were you wanting to speak to?'

We were both being cagey. I looked around while my mind raced for the next line. Across the street I saw Orville Ryan standing beside Chinese Red's body with a cellphone at his ear. Ryan was frowning, like he was stymied.

'Ryan?' I ventured. 'Is that you?'

I watched his mouth drop open. His eyes scanned the street until finding me. We stared at one another over sixty feet of concrete. I watched Ryan's lips move as the phone spoke.

'Hi, Carson. Fancy talking to you.'

'Did I just call your number, Orv?'

'You called Chinese Red's cell, Carson. It started ringing in his pocket.'

★   ★   ★

I was putting in my fourteenth nervous pace lap around the forensics lab when Glenn Watkins rushed in with the test results. The implications made the test supersede all others that would occur today.

'No mistake,' Glenn said, snicking the results with a fingernail. 'It's a match. The blood on O'Fong's shirt and pants is Scaler's.'

'Scaler paid a black junkie prostitute to work him over?' Harry said.

'Blood doesn't lie,' Glenn said. 'These clothes must have been what O'Fong wore when whipping the Reverend.'

'Lawd, this case is a muthafucker.' Harry budgeted himself two spoken MFs annually and he'd just spent half his budget on Richard Scaler.

'There's more,' Glenn said. 'You know the water found in O'Fong's digs in the Hoople?'

Harry nodded.

'Sea water. The same composition of sea water found on the floor at Scaler's death scene. A second indication they were together.'

'But what's the water mean?' Harry said. 'You got any idea, Carson?'

But my mind was elsewhere. Scaler preaching as a child, bible in hand, mouth wide. The adult Scaler charging to and fro on the stage ranting about sin. A model-handsome black prostitute slapping Scaler's fat ass with leather while the preacher twirled upside-down in red panties.

I started laughing: tears running, gut-lurching, red-faced laughter. Glenn watched open-mouthed.

'What's wrong, Carson?' Harry asked.

'Scaler beat mousy Mama and it got his engine revved. He called his sex buddy, Chinese Red, and headed to Camp Sonshine for some butt-pluggin' and whip lovin'. Muhhhh-muh-muuuh,' I moaned orgasmically, spinning in circles, pretending I had a gag in my mouth.

'Muuuuh-Muuuuuuh. Muhhhhnnnnnnnnnn.'

I mimicked spitting out the gag. 'Case closed,' I announced. 'We can all go home.'

Which is exactly what I did. It was one p.m. and I figured I'd done enough. I stopped at the library on the way to pick up books on playing the flute, creating with mosaic, identifying creatures of the woodlands, and Bolivian cooking.

★   ★   ★

The following morning my still-on television woke me at seven. Though foggy with sleep, I performed my morning rituals, washing down my vites with Ginseng tea and downing a wheatberry salad I'd bought at the health-food store on my way to the library. It appeared I'd purchased eight of them. Despite my sluggishness I felt stress-free and had a leisurely drive to work.

I walked into the detectives' room. Harry shot me a glance, picked up the ringing phone. I watched him open his desk drawer, scrabble through it, shove papers aside on his desk as I walked up.

'Paper,' he grunted, making the scratchy motion with his fingers.

I pitched him a notepad and he wrote a few lines, saying *uh-huh* and *gimme the name again* and finally '*I owe you one, Kiet.*'

He set the phone down. 'That was Kiet Srisai at the Thai restaurant. He's got a name and place for a guy who might have owned the burned-down house. He's over in Mississippi, just across the border.'

'I'm not driving all the way over there on my own.' I crossed my hands behind my head. 'And you're not allowed to deal with anything pertaining to the Bailes case. I'll get the Dauphin Island cops to make the trip.'

Harry shot a look over his shoulder at Tom Mason's office. Tom was on the phone, turned away. Harry lowered his voice and leaned close.

'I figure if we spend all our time on the way to Sippi and back talking about Scaler, that's the case I'm on, right?'

29

Chakrabandhu Sintapiratpattanasai blinked lizard eyes at me and seemed as puzzled by the English language as I was by his name.

'No understand what you word say.'

We were on a no-name strip of beach in Mississippi, west of Biloxi. The land stretched from the water north for a hundred miles before there was anything that could be charitably called a hill. It was the billiard-table flatness that had allowed Katrina's storm surge to steamroll the communities for miles inland. Sintapiratpattanasai was a short man, heavy and square, with jet-black hair glistening with pomade. Even though the sun was high, he wore a dark three-piece suit, his tie tight to his thick neck.

I put my badge wallet back in my pocket and tried rephrasing the question. 'We're trying to track down ownership of a piece of property. About a quarter acre that once had a house on it.'

Sintapiratpattanasai frowned. 'Ay-ker? Prop-tee?'

I'd seen this act before and so had Harry. He pulled his handcuffs and nodded toward the Crown Vic.

'OK buddy, put out your hands so I can cuff them and let's take a walk to the car.'

Mr S. startled back three steps, barked, 'You from Mobile in Alabama. This Mississippi. You have no jurisdiction here.'

'That solves the language problem,' Harry said.

'We're not here on any problem relative to you, sir,' I said. 'We're here about a property you own or owned.'

'Where this property?' he challenged.

I gave him the address.

'Own four houses there for years. I rent to fishermen, shrimp fishermen.' He wagged his head. 'Tough bidness. Fishermen move when Katrina blow houses down in Alabama. I buy houses here now. Do rent.'

I'd seen Sintapiratpattanasai's kind before. The archetypical slumlord, he'd buy houses or apartments on the cheap, fill them with poor like rabbits in a warren. Any repairs came late or never.

'What did you do with the house?' Harry asked.

'Sell.'

I heard a roar of heavy motorcycles to the north and craned my head to a pair of riders on Harleys burning hell-for-leather along the road. The bikers seemed to be looking our way.

I turned back to Mr S. 'Who did you sell the place to, sir?'

'Man come, say he need place. I sell. This two month back.'

'What was the buyer's name?'

'I think. I remember in a minute. Or I have written down.'

'Why did he need the place?'

'He like to fish. Not boat, but fish . . . ' Sintapiratpattanasai jigged his hands as if casting

223

a rod. 'He was soon retire and fish all day long. Use house for fish house, fix up.' He paused and recalled the moment. 'Ten thousan' dollar, for that place? He either sucker or using somebody else's money.'

'Did you use a lawyer, anything like that?' Harry asked, trying to find a paper trail. 'Or handle the transaction at a bank?'

'Man gave me money, I sign paper saying house his. No big deal need banker. Banker is bullshit, take money to watch you sign paper.'

'You received a check?' I asked.

Sintapiratpattanasai held out his right palm and jabbed it hard with his left forefinger. 'Fuck check. Cash money.'

I shot Harry a look. The transaction had all the signs of a street deal. Someone needed the property for a short time, paid for the privilege. But the deal was off the official books. The State would eventually find no taxes were being paid, check into things, but Sintapiratpattanasai had made his money, had a valid receipt, and the buyer had used the property and was long gone.

'Did you keep a copy of the paper you signed?' Harry asked.

'I keep everything so no get fucked by US government.'

'Can we see the paper?' Harry asked.

'Come in office and I find.'

We followed the landlord to a large black Lexus parked in the shade of twin palms. He popped the truck to reveal a pair of orange crates stuffed with files.

'Your office?' Harry asked.

'I own forty-seven properties all down coast. I need to know who pays so no one get free ride. People try cheat me all the time. They don't come to me, so I go to them.'

I pictured Sintapiratpattanasai driving his files from place to place, checking names, making sure the rent came in on time. If not, there would be penalties, surcharges, evictions. All quite legal.

Mr S moved to the crate tucked the farthest back in the truck. 'These old files. Alabama. No more property in Alabama.' He snatched up a file, pulled out an envelope, found the receipt in question within the envelope. I took it and stared at the page.

'It's freaking indecipherable,' I said. 'It looks like a damn prescription. I can read 'Kurt', I think. But the rest? Mathews? Masters? Martinas?'

Harry took a look, shook his head.

'The receipt is built to show nothing but a transfer of money from someone to Mr S for a quarter-acre parcel and four hundred-square-foot house, with six-foot-wide common access to a pier. Ten thousand dollars, paid in full.'

'You see my name, don't you?' the landlord asked. 'All right and legal bill of sale?'

'Clear as a bell,' Harry said.

The landlord started to tuck the page back into the envelope. Harry reached out and tapped the man's wrist.

'We'd like a copy of the document, sir. Can we take it and return it after we inspect the page?'

The landlord went to the back door of the

Lexus. 'I make you copy.'

He opened the back door. A mini-copier was seat-belted on to the back seat, plugged into the outlet on the plenum. Beside the copier was a fax machine. On the other seat was a cooler. Lunch and supper, I figured, business on the fly. Sintapiratpattanasai pulled us a clear copy. It didn't make the buyer's name any more decipherable.

We followed him back to the trunk. He folded the receipt, and slid it into the creamy white envelope. Harry noted the saw printing on the envelope, grabbed it from the landlord.

'Did the buyer give you this envelope?' I asked. 'Did it have the money inside?'

'Already spend money,' Sintapiratpattanasai said, suspicious of a shakedown. 'Money all gone.'

'Did this envelope come from the buyer?' Harry repeated. 'Answer the question.'

'Buyer man have money counted out and inside.'

'What is it?' I asked.

Harry said nothing. He simply passed me the envelope.

'No,' I said, closing my eyes, trying to blot out the outside, inside and everything in between. 'This isn't happening.'

It was a tithe envelope for Kingdom Church.

30

'A coincidence,' I insisted on the way back. 'How many zillions of sheep did Scaler have in his flock? They'd all have tithe envelopes, right?'

'What are the chances of two outrageous cases connecting like that?' Harry countered.

Harry was driving. After finding the envelope I wanted to shut my mind off as my eyes watched treetops and power lines make fast shapes against the sky. We were in farm country: melon farms, cotton farms, timber farms, now and then the stretching green baize of a sod farm.

'Why would Kingdom Church buy a rundown house in the middle of nowhere, Harry? They've got a college, dorms, chapel, TV operation, three church camps, about a thousand acres scattered between Alabama and Mississippi. Why a quarter acre in the middle of bleak nowhere land?'

'To hide something.'

'A baby?'

He shot a glance over his shoulder. 'Here's the problem, Carson. I can't work the Noelle case, just Scaler's. But if they've turned into the same case . . .'

I pulled out my phone and dialed. 'Mr . . . uh, Sinapir, Sentasipp . . . this is Detective Ryder. Stop the no-English riff. We spoke fifteen minutes ago. Did the cabin you owned have a harpoon or shark lance anywhere around?'

I listened, hung up. 'There was a bunch of old

227

crap in the shack, to use Mr S.'s words. Fishing rods, a lead anchor, a life vest, and what he called a rusty spear on hooks over the front door.'

Harry drove and thought for several seconds. 'Maybe it's the only weapon the cabin's occupants have when someone shows up with bad intentions. Grab and stab.'

'Yeah, but if the person or persons with bad intent have a more developed arsenal, like guns, the spear-thrower's just taken his one shot.'

'Forensics found footprints from the cabin to the pier, small, like a woman's shoes.'

Three had been found along a stretch of sand, washed over, as if obscured by someone dragging a tarp or blanket down the trail. If the obfuscation had occurred at night — like all else did — it would have been easy to miss a couple prints.

I said, 'Let's say the woman is running from the inside action, bad things. Someone in the house throws the harpoon in defense. Meanwhile the lady is out the back door with Noelle in hand.'

'She puts the kid in the boat. But something bad happens. Noelle washes out on the tide, floats to Dauphin Island.'

I said, 'Is the person in the shack the person who bought the place with cash in a tithe envelope from Scaler's Circus of Worship, first name Kurt, second name indecipherable?'

'The landlord said the buyer was an older guy in a suit. Smallish in stature. Shades. Hat.'

'The landlord said it was a good suit, right?'

'He said, 'Man wear good suit, first-class.''

'Mr Landlord would know,' I said. 'Clothes are important to him, part of looking like a businessman and not an itinerant slumlord.'

Harry gave it some thought. 'So the man who paid for the cabin using a tithe envelope from Scaler's church might not be the man found dead inside?'

'Clair said the body inside was a male in his mid twenties to early thirties. The landlord's description fits an older man, but not Scaler.'

Harry looked grim. 'It's all smoke and mirr — whoops. Train ahead. Looks like we stop a bit.'

Freight-cars were pouring from the pine forest like they were being assembled in the trees and set on the track. The train sounded like it was going somewhere it wanted to go and I got out to watch, Harry following. We left the engine on to keep the AC pouring into the Crown Vic and stepped into the bright sun. I rolled up my sleeves, and sat on the hood to watch the four-engine freighter highball pass, boxcars, tankers, hoppers, container flats — swaying and squealing and rumbling, the sound added to the staccato clanging of the crossing signal, a raucous cacophony of journey and commerce.

On the other side of the crossing, in jittery motion, I saw two motorcycles roll up, with men riding tandem. Outsized silver-studded saddle-bags were slung over the tails of the hogs, big-ass Harleys, and I could hear the unmuffled four-strokes over the howling clatter and metallic squeals of the train, the riders gunning the accelerators as if challenging one another to something. They wore full-face racing helmets, which seemed a bit odd. They appeared to be talking to one another, passing time as the train passed.

'The end's near,' Harry said.

For a split-second my mind heard it as an eschatological statement, until I saw the rear of the train a few hundred yards up the tracks. I craned my head farther and saw a black pickup truck moving in on us from behind. Three men inside. Chrome light bar.

Why was it so familiar?

The motorcycles roared louder. The train squealed and shivered the earth. The trestle bells tore holes in the air. I took a final look across the way.

What?

The barrel of a short shotgun swung past the knees of one of the riders. He was off the bike and getting back on, probably grabbed the gun from the saddlebag. He held it close, hidden.

The rear of the train clattered past. I spun to Harry.

'Ambush!' I yelled. 'Get in the car!'

The first explosion took out the passenger-side window as I was diving inside. The air filled with cubed glass. I hugged the floor, hearing rounds chunking into the Crown Vic's chassis, the truckers firing from behind. The rear window crumpled. My legs were still outside and I drew them as close as I could while pulling myself inside with whatever I could grab. Harry had done the same on his side, simultaneously pulling out his weapon. His face was taut and I expected mine was the same. We'd fallen into serious shit.

I stuck my head up, pulled it back. The bikers were crossing the tracks slowly, dodging the trestle gates. They could pull to the side and thump heavy rounds through the Crown Vic's doors until Harry and I were more metal than meat. But I'd also seen a small gray structure on the far side of the tracks, a deserted gas station or something.

'We're trapped,' Harry said.

'There's a building over there,' I yelled. 'I've got the wheel. Push on the gas.'

Harry's arm was trapped beneath him, but he jammed an elbow into the accelerator. The car lurched ahead, Harry's arm slipping from the gas pedal. The car stopped dead.

'Lay on it, Harry!'

He flopped sideways and pressed his body against the pedal. The car made a grinding sound and roared forward. I felt the vehicle crunch through the crossing gates, felt the downgrade as we slammed over to the far side of the crossing. I jammed the wheel hard to the right, forgetting to tell Harry to roll off the gas. We were still accelerating when we hit the structure. I heard a thunderous crash. The engine roared, died.

'Harry?' I yelled. 'You all right?'

I heard a grunt. 'I can't move, Carson.'

If the bikers made a concerted run, Harry and I would be easy targets on the floor, deer in the headlights. Rounds started slapping the upper compartment, not the lower doors. I kicked open the door, slipped out, dropped. Another slug whanged off the roof of the Crown Vic.

We'd landed in a defunct local station, slamming the wooden wall at enough speed to crash three-quarters through to the inside, dropping half the roof at the rear of the Crown Vic, a pile of four-by-four timbers that were keeping the first couple feet of airspace free of slugs. I heard Harry struggling in the car, smelled gasoline, burned rubber.

A concentrated burst of fire tore into the broken wood around me. I fired from beside the lumber pile, no idea where the rounds went. I saw one of the bikes readying a run at us, the gunner thumbing red shells into the tubular magazine. The driver cranked the accelerator.

I flattened on the concrete as the duo roared closer, the bike weaving to screw up my aim. A blast from the shotgun tore through shingles two feet from my head, filling the air with asphalt dust and wood chips. The gunner on the other bike was fast-firing a pistol.

It was an insult, like the bastards had singled me out for all this bullshit. Every damn day was a fresh challenge from a new enemy. The guy on the bike fired until his magazine emptied, and I saw the driver skid-spin away as the shooter reloaded.

I heard drums thunder in my head and felt an anger so hot it made my skin glow and my heart was roaring so loud it drowned out everything else in my world. I stood from behind the cover, the crap impeding my aim. I flicked the clip from

232

the butt of the Glock, pulled another from my belt, heard a bullet tumble past my ear as the rider and shooter turned for another charge. The shot gunner pulled a blast high and to the side.

'Carson!'

I turned and saw Harry. He'd gotten out the car. I waved, turned back to the action.

The Harley bore in, the shooter grinning as they approached, waving the muzzle side to side. I heard a puff at my right ear, then my left. I raised my Glock. I saw the shooter grin, he figured he had me.

I pulled the trigger three times. As if in slow motion, I saw the guy in back touch at his side. He panicked and grabbed the driver's arm, jerking the handlebars and sending the machine down. I saw sparks as pedals ground into concrete.

I heard firing from behind me. Harry.

A guy in the truck unloaded with everything he had, cover fire. Two others lifted the gunshot guy into the bed, one of them yelling, 'It's all right. I got you. You'll be all right. Hang in there, brother.'

The driver of the fallen bike was muscling it up, the passenger on the other bike racking the shotgun. I heard Harry laying out shots, glass breaking, a ricochet. Someone out front yelled, 'Go!'

The firing stopped. I heard tires squeal and engines roaring in retreat.

I turned to see Harry, gun by his side, his jacket ripped half off, the lining hanging to his knees.

'You all right?' I said. 'You hit? You said you couldn't move.'

'My jacket got caught on the goddamn pedal, couldn't tear loose.'

He wavered, looked around at the shattered station, black smoke, totaled Crown Vic, crossing gates like shattered candy canes, the ground littered with shotgun shells and bright brass casings aglint in the sunlight.

Then he looked at me for an uncomfortably long time.

'You walked straight into them.'

'Seemed the thing to do,' I said.

31

'Yeah,' I heard Harry say into his cell, talking to the State Police. 'Carson put a round in one of the perps.'

'I caught him in the lower right abdomen,' I called to Harry. 'Punched through intestine. I expect he'll make it if he gets to a hospital, has everything cleaned and sewed and gets pumped full of juice to ward off peritonitis.'

Harry passed the info on. The Staties would check the hospitals and clinics stat. Plus visit physicians' offices in the area, making sure no one was being forced into playing emergency room for a gunshot victim.

The State Police did themselves proud, arriving in four minutes, the tech squad rolling the big traveling lab down the road a few minutes later. The ranking officer from the Staties was Sergeant Waylon J. Plummer, a black guy in his early forties. It had always mystified us why he bore the name of one of the South's preeminent country stars, Waylon Jennings.

One day, unable to take it any more, we'd asked. Turned out Waylon's mama was white and she'd decided that eleven hours in labor outweighed the ten minutes Daddy had invested in the whole process, giving her naming rights, and she'd chosen to honor her favorite singer in the whole world.

'I'm just happy Mama wasn't big on Dolly

Parton's ex partner,' Plummer explained. 'Imagine being a black guy and everyone yellin', 'Hey, Porter!''

We leaned against an ASP cruiser and did the overview thing as Waylon took notes and his partner Hugh Tandy walked the roadside looking for evidence.

'Got blood here,' a junior tech a young redheaded woman with Asian-esque features, said. She knelt and took a sample, set a marker down. The photographer whisked in and documented the find.

I said, 'That's probably from when they lifted the wounded guy into the pickup bed. Your blood trail probably ends . . . '

'Right about here,' Tandy said. 'Nice recollection for a guy getting half an armory dumped in his direction.'

'What were you doing while Kid Carson was fighting the Indians, Harry?' Waylon asked.

'I was stuck to the floor of the Vic, the brake pedal caught in my jacket's lining. I finally tore loose.'

Harry reached to the ground, picked up the jacket, one purple sleeve waving disconsolately in the breeze. It looked like a deflated elephant.

'A two-hundred-buck jacket and a seventy-five-buck replacement allowance,' Harry lamented.

'That thing's bright enough for any three jackets, Harry,' Waylon advised. 'Submit in triplicate.'

'I've tried before. The bean counters only pay in monotone.'

Waylon turned my way. 'You didn't see any features, Carson?'

I put my hands in front of my eyes as if holding binoculars. 'They were all wearing those full-face helmets used in racing. Gloves. Shades. Hell, I couldn't tell you if they were white or black. Didn't see an inch of skin.'

'Plates?'

'Taped. Duct tape. I noticed it when the bike dropped, filed it away. I did manage to note body types. I had a well-built guy as one of the drivers — the bike that stayed up — maybe six to six two. Wide shoulders, slim waist. He had a heavier, shorter passenger, leaning to fat, maybe why I hit him in the love handle. The other two bikers were pretty large, six two to six four. Shaded to the slender side. The passenger on the first bike, not the injured guy, had a ponytail out the back of the helmet. Brown and greasy, like a foot of dirty rope.'

I saw the picture in my head, but it was like I wasn't there.

'Nice memory, Carson, and the description's pure poetry,' Waylon said, writing in a neat little leather notebook. 'How about the guys in the truck?'

'The guys in the truck weren't roaring at me. Grubby clothes, medium builds. That's about all I recall of them.'

Waylon nodded, wrote a couple lines.

'Anything from the local hospitals?' I asked, figuring the wounded guy would at least be dropped in the parking lot of a clinic or hospital by his accomplices. Maybe they'd simply taken him somewhere to die. But that was at odds with the guy who'd been boosting him into the truck.

Waylon said, 'Nada. At least so far.'

I leaned against Waylon's cruiser and replayed the action with a clear head. It had been planned by someone with both intelligence and a penchant for detail. I figured the gunners had planned to blow twin barrels of double-ought through our windscreen, one guy targeting Harry, the other one me. The Harleys would roar away just as the truck zoomed up from behind, ready to handle any cleanup chores, like if Harry or I were still breathing through our headless necks.

The only fly in the planner's ointment had been the intervening freighter. Had Harry and I not been train aficionados, I never would have looked through the freight-cars, noticed the shotguns coming out. The oncoming bikers and the shooters in the following pickup would have blown us apart in ten seconds and been on their merry way.

I heard a squeal of metal over metal as the Crown Vic was pulled from the wreckage of the old train station. It would be winched on to a platform tow truck and taken to forensics for a full inspection. There were no windows remaining and the panels were pocked with holes, thankfully most of them on the trunk side with only a couple of holes in the upper quadrant of the door panels.

Harry stood beside me and watched as a worker ran up and sprayed a still-smoldering tire with a fire extinguisher. A door fell off as the winch groaned the car backward.

My hand started shaking. I jammed it in my pocket.

Dr Matthias sat down at his laptop, entering data. He'd spent the whole day inside, re-reading texts he'd already perused a half-dozen times. But one had to be sure. The texts were always interesting, dealing with the migration of early human tribes. There was a great deal of information on the measurement of nucleotides contained in DNA, the haplotypes. The diversity of the genetic variations decreased with distance from Addis Ababa, Ethiopia. This had been discovered within the incredible amount of work accomplished on the Human Genome Project, a project that Matthias had been instrumental in organizing, at least in its early days.

The HGP had generated so much information that biologists and geneticist would be analyzing it for years, drawing conclusions, building theories, making major leaps in the understanding of biology, medicine, evolution, human genetic diversity and its manipulation, accidental and otherwise . . . could the word eugenics be used any more? No, but perhaps something useful would replace it, a term that carried no baggage. Eugenics, as he had discovered, was politically incorrect.

Matthias started to close down his computer, but paused. He saw an end to this leg of his research, and there was much to do back in Mobile. Drawing threads together. Checking on Anak and Rebecca and finding them better lodgings than out in the hinterlands. Reporting his latest findings to his employer. Wouldn't that be interesting.

Matthias opened his Bookmarks list, tapped an entry. The British Airways site opened. That would do just fine. A flight to Atlanta, then the connection to Mobile. All he needed was to assemble his final report. The prices for flights were insane, he thought as he studied the schedules. But he wasn't paying, so First Class it was.

He filled in a few boxes. Reserved his seat for the return flight.

★ ★ ★

When we got back to the department, word of the ambush had spread and we had to relive the moment for the other cops, trying to keep it brief. Since there had been no eyewitnesses, the description had been minimized, morphing into what appeared to be a robbery attempt by some bad boys on motorcycles, foiled when the innocent travelers they had chosen at random turned out to be cops. There had been enough weirdness in the press of late, what with a baby found on a beach — more minimization — and an attempt to steal the baby from the hospital. We didn't want the public spooked any more than necessary, plus, unfortunately, such stories weren't all that unusual any more.

Harry decided to see if forensics had picked up anything useful from the scene, and I went along to kill time. The lab was a flurry of activity as techs analyzed shell casings, glass from a broken motorcycle headlamp, photos of tire marks on the roadway.

'Hey, there they are,' called a voice at our backs. 'I was just about to call you.'

We turned at the voice, saw Ed 'Pieboy' Blaney, the forensics guy who handled the automotive division. He took the nickname from his lunch habits, which were the same every day: a piece of pie and a cup of coffee from a bakery off Old Shell Road. Didn't matter what kind of pie it was, as long as it was fresh made. Cherry, pecan, mud, peach, coconut cream, grasshopper . . . all were fuel for Pieboy's singular passion, the study of cars.

'Hey, Pieboy,' Harry said. 'S'up?'

Pieboy ran a pink hand through thinning blond hair. He was pear-shaped, probably an effect of all the pie. Or maybe the spare tire was showing empathy for cars.

'You guys are tough on vehicles. What, you moonlight in demolition derbies?'

'You sell it for scrap yet?' Harry asked.

'About to. We're done with it.' He dug in his pocket. 'Here's why I was calling. I got something to show you.'

He picked up a metal disc, tossed it to me. It was the size of a fifty-cent piece, black anodized case, a small wire embedded in a worm of clear glue on one side. On the other was a rough patch of rubber cement.

Harry stared at the disc. 'A bug, right?'

'A GPS locator. And a fine one at that. Expensive.'

'Where was it?'

'Stuck to the rear undercarriage. I almost didn't see it. It's basically a sophisticated version

241

of tracking systems folks put on their dogs'
collars to let them know where Fido is at any
given moment. Didn't find any prints, unfortunately. This version probably cost a couple grand
with the satellite receiver. They knew your
location down to about a ten-foot circle.'

'We're two dead dogs,' Harry said.

'Arf,' I added, lolling my tongue like Mr
Mix-up.

32

When we got back to the department, Tom Mason ordered me to go home.

'Get some rest,' he said. 'You've had enough.'

'Him, too,' I said, pointing at Harry.

'I was talking to both of you.'

Harry said, 'Can I speak to you for a minute, Tom? I want to run through some details on a court case I gotta testify at in a couple days.'

'Then you're heading straight home, right?'

'Scout's honor.' Harry held his fingers in the scout salute, headed into Tom's office.

The door closed.

I went to my truck and sat there for ten minutes, rubbing my face and neck. The day was a blur, as if I'd watched a video on fast-forward, randomly freezing scenes for a few seconds before zooming ahead again. I scrabbled my fingers under my seat and came up with a bottle of ginseng tea and a few ounces of bourbon left over from my post-prison stop at the roadhouse. I swigged a bit of ginseng — the concoction tasted like boiled denim, truth be told — and replaced the tea with bourbon.

I drained off half the mix, and waited for the warmth in my belly to loosen the kinks in my back and neck. I headed out into the street, the light surreally bright and painful. Slipping on my shades, I saw a little red BMW blow by in the opposite direction, like it was heading for the

243

department. I watched it disappear in the rear-view.

Clair drove a sporty red Beamer.

It couldn't possibly be Clair, my mind said. What would Clair be doing at the MPD in the middle of the day?

I turned for home, intending to stop at the store for a tofu burger and lentil salad, but suddenly wanted food I could feel inside me, ending up with a bucket of fried chicken, gravy and biscuits. Once home, I turned on the television, set the tub on my kitchen counter and pulled out a drum, dipped it in the gravy, brought it to my mouth.

I snapped at it, missed. Tried again. The drum dodged my mouth. Gravy splattered the floor.

My hands were shaking again.

And then my knees were shaking. Followed by my shoulders. And then everything else was shaking and I found myself tight in a ball on the floor.

It passed after twenty minutes and I took a shower and lay on the bed, staring at the ceiling and trying to lose myself in the white until I heard crunching of sand and shells under tires and an engine shut off. Seconds later I heard a knock on my door. A realtor, I figured; they were always gliding through the neighborhood, trying to get their names out among residents who hoped to sell. I closed my eyes and willed them away.

The knocking persisted. I went to the door, yanked it open. 'I have no intention of — '

Harry.

'What are you doing here?' I said. 'Tom told us to — '

Behind him, I saw Clair, her eyes nervous. She rushed by and sat on the couch so fast I figured she needed to get anchored. I saw her shoot a glance at a pile of clothes in the corner of the living room, topped by my briefcase and a tipped-over bucket of half-eaten chicken. Harry sat beside her. He leaned back and stitched fingers behind his head, a poor attempt at casual.

'We want you to talk about what's bothering you. It's overdue.'

'There's nothing bothering me. Unless it's you showing up here when I'm trying to . . . trying to . . . eat chicken. You want *bothering me*? That's bothering me.'

'Things are getting worse, brother,' Harry said.

I wrinkled my brow in puzzlement. 'How can things get worse if things aren't bad?'

He nodded at the tube, a game show where people dressed as items they wanted to win. They were made up like cars, boats, and huge televisions, jumping up and down and screaming for attention.

'You used to fish, swim, kayak, run, and so forth, a dozen hours a week. Now you run home and watch television. How much do you watch?'

'I'll have to check with Nielsen.'

'You're doing things out of character,' Harry continued. 'Taking chances that are not just risky, they're illegal. If you'd gotten caught forging the warden's signature, you could have wound up in the cell beside Kirkson. I don't

245

know what the hell you did at Teasdale's place, but — '

'She asked if her kid still had that goofy lopsided face,' I snapped. 'Her own kid.'

'I have no doubt it was sad, bro. But in the past you would have blown the ugliness off, walked away.'

'I'm tired of the past.'

Harry studied on that for a moment. He looked at Clair, turned back to me. 'Today was the worst yet, Carson. Walking into those gunslingers like it was the OK Corral. I don't know why you're not dead.'

'They were lousy shots.'

Clair cleared her throat. 'Carson, you're acting erratically at times. It's getting worse.'

I walked to the door shaking my head in disappointment, put my hand on the knob. 'I think you both should go home and try self-analysis. Find out why you're projecting your problems on to me.'

I yanked open the door. Tom Mason was leaning against the railing, fanning himself with his white Stetson.

'Howdy, Carson, mind if I step inside? Hot out here.'

Without waiting for the courtesy of an answer, he walked in. I glared at Harry, mouthed *snitch*. Tom leaned against the wall beside Clair and Harry, hands in the pockets of his jeans.

'I'm pretty sure Harry wanted me to wait outside so I wouldn't hear anything to, uh, compromise my position. What this all comes down to is I'm taking you off duty and putting you on desk work unless you see the departmental shrink.'

'What? YOU CAN'T!'

Tom said, 'I scheduled your first session for tomorrow at nine in the morning.'

'No way in hell . . . ' I countered, 'am I seeing a shrink.'

Tom looked down at his hat, brushed something from the felt. 'Sure you are,' he said gently. 'Because you ain't got but one choice in the matter, Carson, and that's mine.'

I turned away and walked out to my deck, where the air was free from the stink of betrayal. I heard the front door pull shut, the cars in the drive retreat. Watching the gulls flash above the waves, I decided it had been a pissant intervention and, though my interrogators were mistaken about whatever was concerning them, I deserved better. That pathetic display was supposed to save me?

But I figured if I went to the shrink's office, sat my ass in a chair for a few fifty-minute sessions to satisfy the obsessions of my former friends, I'd pass whatever test they were imposing, and be free once again.

But what a senseless waste of time.

33

The MPD shrink wasn't the property of the Department, but rather a private-practice type who worked on retainer. The guy — a Dr Alec Kavanaugh — had his offices in Spring Hill, not far from the college, in an office attached to a private residence. The house had been built in the fifties, I figured, under the influence of Frank Lloyd Wright. An anomalous style for Mobile, the home was of dark brick, with a long single-story section at one end, a two-story section at the other. Given the landscaping and overhanging trees, the house less sat the lot than embraced it.

The office area was an add-on in the same architectural style, just on the far end of the garage. A small sign on the door said, *A. Kavanaugh, PhD, Psychology*. I took a deep breath and popped a few mints. Despite the provocations of the preceding evening, I had slept solidly and taken my vites and such. I had decided to drink a little coffee now and then, since tea — despite its many organic benefits — showed little ability to open my eyes in the morning.

I was preparing to ring Kavanaugh's bell when the door opened. I saw a woman in her fifties with . . .

No, check that. In her early forties or so, the first impression coming from white hair pulled back and bundled away. Slim, average height, a bit more nose than standard, slender lips. Her eyes were deep brown and behind large round glasses with tortoiseshell frames. She wore a dark jacket over a white silk blouse; her slacks matched the jacket.

'You must be Detective Ryder,' the lips said as the woman opened the door wide and gestured me inside. 'It's good to meet you. I'm Alec Kavanaugh. Come in, make yourself comfortable.'

Businesslike, I noted. Voice in professional mode, friend-like overtones with we've-got-fifty-minutes underpinnings. The room was large, a few planted palms breaking the space into regions: the desk region, the overstuffed analyst's chair region, the Freud-inspired couch region. The colors were corals playing against cool gray. I smelled air freshener, pine-bodied, something with a name like Winter Forest. Kavanaugh gestured between the couch — spare and futon-inspired, one end up-angled — and the big fluffy chair.

'Do you have a preference?' she asked.

'I'm a traditionalist. I'll take the couch.'

I thought it would be amusing to lay the wrong way, with my feet elevated. Doc Kavanaugh didn't seem to notice, or maybe most of her patients were dyslexic.

She took the chair, turning it to face me through five feet of winter-pine air. She crossed long legs. Her smile was clinically perfect.

'I'd like to ask a few generic questions, Detective Ryder. Or may I call you Carson?'

'No.'

She nodded. 'That's absolutely fine. What brings you here, Detective Ryder?'

'I watch a lot of TV, Doctor. Or so I am told by others.'

'How much television do others find to be too much?'

'The average American watches something like five hours of tube a day, Doctor. I average about two.'

'What do you think that means?'

'Someone owes me three hours.'

She just looked over her eyeglasses. A humorless woman. This might actually be fun, batting around words with a humorless chick shrinkadoodler.

She said, 'What did you used to do before you started watching television?'

'Masturbate.'

She said nothing for so long that I had to fill the silence.

'Fish, swim, kayak,' I said. 'Run in circles. That was my favorite. Running in tiny little circles until I could bite my tail.'

She was either writing down my answers on a pad, or pretending to. She looked up.

'When did you last do one of those activities?'

'I went fishing with Harry one week ago.'

She would have received an overview of my recent work record from Tom Mason, part of the process. Thus she'd know about us finding the kid. She'd now be wondering why I didn't mention it, then play the denial card which I'd trump by telling her I'd omitted the kid on purpose, leading to a *gotcha!* moment.

She seemed to study her notes. Looked up at me. 'Any thoughts on why you've shifted from physical activities to television?'

'Maybe I'm tired of running in those little circles.'

I heard her shift in her seat as she leaned forward.

'Do you think you have angry moments?'

I sat up quickly, slamming my feet on the floor. I shook my fist at her and screwed up my face in angry disgust.

I yelled, 'FUCK YOU!'

She smiled. 'Very amusing.'

'Thanks,' I said.

'You can leave now.'

'I uh — what?'

'You can leave now. We're done here.'

I looked at the clock on her desk; four minutes had elapsed. I was supposed to have forty-six more minutes in my session.

'It was obvious I was kidding,' I explained patiently. 'Answering a question about anger by pretending to be angry.'

She stood and walked to her desk, showing me her back. She tossed the notepad on the desktop. Stifled a yawn.

Said, 'Don't let the door hit you in the ass on your way out.'

34

On the way to the department I planned to stop at the health-food emporium and grab a toasted lentil something-or-other, but pulled into a convenience store and selected a pair of pink-frosted Krispy-Kremes. I'd been faithful to Fossie's regimen for about a week — vites and grains and juices and teas — but figured a little processed flour and sugar wouldn't be fatal. I poured two extra-large coffees for accompaniment. In the checkout line I noticed a familiar face on a tabloid newspaper beside the register: the face was Scaler's, the rag was the *World-Week News*, which had never before met a Scaler idea it didn't like.

The headline read: *Reverend Scaler's Death is S&M Scene!*

The subhead read: *Torture and Devil Worship and a Gay Black Lover.*

A starburst in the corner read: *A Tangled Web of Weird!*

Uh-oh, I thought, reaching for a copy. *What went wrong here?*

Waiting my turn at the checkout, I sucked on one of my coffees and read. The tabloid's story was basically true to the facts because they couldn't be improved upon: one of the nation's most arch-conservative, family-values-trumpeting moralists had died while being whipped by a gay black junkie prostitute. The candles at the scene were depicted as symbols of Satan. It was a leap, but then it was the *World-Week News*.

I set the paper beside my coffees. The clerk, a plump, hair-netted woman in her late forties, scowled at the paper as she rang it up.

'Can you believe that guy?' she said, not hiding the anger and betrayal. 'All those years of pretending to be holy. What a scummy fake.'

I must have been under Harry's more-generous influence and mumbled something about all the facts not yet in.

'They're in enough for me,' she said, anger bright in her face as she handed me my receipt. 'The people at my church got all his books and his sermons on CD. But not for long.'

'How so, ma'am?' I asked.

'Tonight we're gonna light up a big bonfire to lay 'em all on.'

I left the place realizing Scaler's reputation was as destroyed as if it had been ground zero at an H-bomb test.

★ ★ ★

When I hit the department Harry was mainlining coffee, chomping a danish, and trying to draw a connections line: who touched who when? None of the lines on the page went far. I waited for him to make reference to yesterday, but the event in my living room seemed to have disappeared as far as he was concerned; fine with me.

Tom Mason wandered over and held up a copy of the *World-Week News*, the Scaler edition.

'You guys seen this?'

I nodded. 'Everything's out. No more secrets for the Rev. His rep's going down in flames.'

'I talked to a buddy in Miami where the rag's written,' Tom said. 'For this to hit stands today the story and pictures had to have been ready yesterday. Who leaked and why?'

I did the money-whisk. 'The rag pays, people send the stuff in.'

Harry scanned the story, set the paper aside. 'Scaler did everything in a big way. Same for his fall from grace.'

'He's still falling,' Tom said, finger-twitching us to the window. Seeing a CNN van, we sprinted to the conference room and turned on the television.

'*First this message,*' the anchor was saying, '*then a bizarre and provocative update on the death of famed religious leader Richard Scaler.*'

'This ain't good,' Tom Mason said.

After a minute of commercial the anchor segued to a local CNN stringer in Mobile, squinting into sunlight. Her hair was strawberry blonde, her face the shape of a heart. I saw our building in the background, MPD headquarters. The stringer lifted the mic to her lips, shook back her hair, a move I'm sure they teach in Reporting 101.

'*Sources close to the deceased suggest that the Mobile Police believe the last person to see Richard Scaler alive was a black male prostitute named LaPierre O'Fong. It's been suggested that Reverend Scaler died of a heart attack suffered during . . . erotic games. In another*'

254

bizarre twist, O'Fong was one of the four addicts who died after OD'ing on uncut heroin earlier this week, adding yet another layer of infamy to the once-impeccable reputation of Richard Scaler . . . '

'They know everything,' Harry said, amazed.

'She said, 'sources close to the deceased,'' I said. 'That's not the usual line when someone on our side is yapping. Then it's a source close to the investigation.'

We heard a click as the intercom was activated. 'Lieutenant? Lieutenant Mason? Chief's on line one.'

Tom rolled his eyes. Flicked the phone to private. He said the word *Yup* five or six times, followed by an *uh-huh.* He hung the phone up.

'The Chief just got a call from the Mayor who just got a call from — '

'James Carleton the third,' I ventured, stepping into a wide-open space between words.

'That Scaler's lawyer?' Tom asked.

'The one and only.'

'Mr Carleton is nasty upset at the news reports coming out. The report goes into stuff Mr Lawyer thinks could only come from the MPD.'

'Back in a few,' I said, sprinting toward the door.

I caught the stringer standing beside the news van and applying fresh lipstick in its side mirror. Her videographer was wandering down the sidewalk singing a Green Day song along with the iPod wired to his ears. The woman's name was Nell Pomeroy; I'd met her when dating a local reporter a while back.

'Hi, Nell,' I said.

'Hey, Carson. How you doing?' Her eyes looked happy to see a potential leak. 'Are you on the Scaler case?'

'I've got too many other cases,' I finessed, suddenly becoming of no interest to Pomeroy. She turned back to her lips, making a kissy face at her image in the mirror. It reminded me of Harry in the PICU.

'Could I ask where you got the details on Reverend Scaler's death, Nell? I promise not to tell a soul.'

She dropped the lipstick in what was either a purse or a daypack. 'Sorry, Carson.'

'I'm not asking names of sources,' I said, though that's exactly what I'd hoped for. 'But they aren't inside the MPD or forensics, or the ME's office?'

She thought, measuring words. 'We're getting stuff from several places. Nothing big came from the cops or the ME's folks. I can't say anything else.'

I loped back to Tom and Harry. Shook my head.

'Not us. Sounds like it came from someone with a line into the Scaler organization.'

Harry shook his head. 'They're the last group on earth who'd want Righteous Rev.'s legend besmirched. They have the biggest stake in Scaler having an immaculate legacy. And does anyone on the inside even know all the grim details?'

'Tutweiler,' I grunted. 'I told him what

happened, remember?'

'Tutweiler would be the last person in the world to expose Scaler,' Harry said. 'Everything in Tutweiler's life is Scaler trickle-downs. The guy made his living riding on Scaler's coat-tails.'

'How d'you know that?'

'I've been back on YouTube, Carson. Scaler and Dean Tutweiler go back years.'

I nodded toward the conference room. 'Show me.'

Harry pulled down all his downloaded material. He tapped the keyboard and Scaler took the monitor by storm, bible in one hand, microphone in the other, preaching at a ball field in a park, the stage over the pitcher's mound, the crowd in the outfield.

'This is Scaler after leaving his small church up in Pickens County,' Harry said. 'I guess it didn't give him a big enough audience. He's back on the salvation circuit, pulling the bucks with that big stage presence, Wayne Newton with a chip on his shoulder. Scaler's sermons often veer close to white-supremacy rants. Watch this next scene . . . look close at the curtain behind Scaler on the stage. Every now and then a face pops through.'

I leaned close to the monitor. A woman's face parted the folds of cloth behind the stage, mouth heavy with lipstick, almost a leering face, as if amused there was a party going on in the back, while up front the faithful were falling to the floor, speaking in tongues or offering afflicted parts up to the stage for Scaler to heal.

Harry said, 'Here it comes . . . '

A face parted the curtain, eyes scanning the crowd as though counting money, the lips curling up in what? Amusement? Sneer? It was Tutweiler; no mistaking that square jaw and rack of white teeth. He turned his head backstage, behind the curtain, yelled something, grinned, let the curtain fall back in place.

'He looks like a happy man,' I said.

'He's got an early seat on the Scaler gravy train,' Harry said. 'Who wouldn't be smiling?'

I shrugged. 'What's your point? Who cares if Scaler and Tut have been buddies since way back?'

'Remember Scaler's weird tape: 'I have been led astray by false companions over years'? Tutweiler's been around for a long time. And I don't think Scaler had many real friends.'

I watched as the scene shifted to people walking across a field, past cars, folks eating chicken, drinking sodas and iced tea and lemonade. The camera panned past a small guy in a light-colored suit, the clothes making him a parrot in a field of crows. He was sitting on the tailgate of a pickup truck and spooning cake into his mouth, talking to those around him.

'Go back for a minute,' I said. 'Freeze when I say freeze.'

Harry moused back the vid to the start of the scene.

'Just a bunch of crowd shots,' he said. 'What are you — '

'Freeze,' I said, leaning forward. The guy in the suit had a half-dozen men around him, heads craned, as though between bites of cake he was giving out first-rate stock tips. I knew those guys, as a type, anyway: quintessential rednecks in white tees and Big Ben overalls, jeans and blue work shirts, mud-caked boots. They looked grown from hard soil, tight-eyed and grim. They'd been born with a grudge and life was a daily matter of nursing it.

I tapped my finger on the small guy with white cake stopped just south of his lips. 'Seen that particular piece of hate before?' I asked. 'Like maybe he was once a dozen feet from you?'

'Arnold Meltzer,' Harry whispered. 'The head of the Aryan Revolutionary Army.'

'Not back then, I expect. But it looks like he might be finding the Scaler audience ripe for recruitment.'

'Let's talk to Tutweiler again,' Harry said.

35

Tutweiler was pulling into a parking slot as we arrived. Actually, Tut's driver was doing the pulling, the Tutster in the rear seat and barely visible through the smoky windows of the black Yukon. His license tag read KING2. I bet I knew who KING1 had been.

The driver slid out, opened the rear door. Tutweiler scowled when he saw us pull in beside and get out. He looked at the driver.

'Go on along, Desmond. I'll call the garage if I need anything more.'

Tutweiler turned the chiseled face to Harry and me. Something about the Tutster looked worn, like some event had drained fifty per cent of his air out.

'Yes, Detectives?'

'A few questions, Dean,' I said. 'How long have you been with Richard Scaler?'

'We've been . . . ' he paused, as if trying to decide something. 'We've been friends for over twenty years.'

'Where did you meet?'

'A prayer breakfast in Jackson. Richard had been preaching a week-long revival. We started talking and I've been with him ever since. I started as an advance man, meeting with churches, setting up revivals, making sure we'd have enough seating when Richard came to town. It was an exciting time, doing the Lord's work out in the fertile fields.'

I stared directly into Tutweiler's eyes. 'We've come upon what seems a fertile field in the Reverend's oeuvre, a recent videotape where he speaks about something wrong with a house he built.'

Tutweiler did bewildered. 'Richard and Patricia used the finest builder available for their house over in — '

'No, Brother Tutweiler,' I said. 'House as a parable, a metaphor. Brother Scaler speaks of building under false pretenses, of false companions over years. Any idea what he's referring to? Or who?'

'Richard never knew an enemy, he only knew souls. Richard Scaler saved many souls in his lifetime. Consequently, he had many friends.'

'How much do you make a year, Dean?'

The question jolted him from his reverie. The nose lifted into the air. 'That's my business,' he sniffed. 'I run an institute of higher learning and am paid commensurate to my position.'

I figured a half-mil would be about right. With a shitload of perks worth another quarter mil, like the car and driver, paid for by the faithful. Maybe Scaler even cut Tutweiler in on royalties from souls saved.

Tutweiler broke off his pose and looked to Harry. 'This video about false friends or whatever — I suspect the recent timing means it was created during Richard's decline. When he was often distant, distracted. We've done much thinking about those days.'

'And what, pray tell, have we thought?' I asked.

'A good preacher speaks in word pictures, creating scenes in the minds of those who listen. But in the past year he sometimes lapsed into speaking of such images as if living them.'

'Like psychotic episodes?'

'Psychotic episodes. Yes, that could well be the answer. He seemed, well, almost delusional,' he said. 'That's the only word I have for it. I blame myself, of course.'

'For his delusions?' Harry said.

'I — we . . . those who loved him, should have confronted Richard about his problems. He was falling apart and we could have intervened.'

'You didn't do anything for your good friend,' I said. 'Why?'

'Richard had his delusions, we had ours. Our delusion was thinking he'd return to the Richard we knew.'

'Did you know Scaler was beating his wife?'

I expected a *What, me?* moment. But instead we got closed eyes and a slow-shaking head. 'There were times when Patricia was late to a taping; twice she was limping, once the make-up person worked half an hour to cover a bruise on her cheek. She said she'd fallen, bumped into the car door. I didn't want to believe . . . ' his voice trailed off. 'Maybe it was part of Richard's increasing anger. Or his delusions.'

We said we'd be back with more questions. Tut seemed happy we were leaving. He turned and began striding to the building.

I said, 'Excuse me, sir?'

'Yes?' Spoken over his shoulder like he had to keep moving or turn into salt.

'Have you heard anything from Arnold Meltzer lately?'

He froze. Turned. Gave us a full frown with pursed lips.

Said, 'Who?'

'Nothing. Just a name.'

Harry got behind the wheel and we pulled away from Kingdom College. Harry shot me a look.

'Indeterminate on the Meltzer ref, maybe he knew it, maybe not. And judging by the age of Scaler in that last video, Tutweiler was with the Rev. for more like thirty years. But what I really found interesting was how the once-immaculate Reverend Scaler seems to have gone from having a few problems to being angry and delusional.'

I nodded. 'The man's not even alive and he's falling apart.'

36

'Where to next?' I asked Harry. He pulled a notepad from his pocket, studied a list of connections.

'A biker wannabe tried to abduct Noelle. Bikers tried to kill us on the return from meeting Sintapirininni, checking into Noelle's start-point. Meltzer controls at least one biker gang. Do you think Ben Belker would have any more info on Meltzer?'

'You can bet he'll have whatever there is. And it'll go back years.'

★   ★   ★

While driving to Montgomery, Harry never mentioned the shrink or intervention or anything related, and I didn't volunteer info, choosing instead to watch the scenery flashing by. I didn't know if Kavanaugh was required to report to Tom Mason the details of our truncated session, but I'd done my part by showing up.

We pulled into the strip mall where the SLDP offices were located. Again, I saw the hulking bubba type smoking in a battered pickup in the parking lot, hat low over his eyes. Same plaid shirt, same hard arms blue with tattoos. Same look shot our way.

I'd called and Ben was waiting. He brought Harry and me to his office, closing the door. 'We know less about Meltzer than most of the movement leaders. He holds some of the ugliest ideas in a movement filled with ugly ideas, and he has lots of protection.'

'We're interested in his past. Where's Meltzer from?'

'He grew up in Noxubee County in Mississippi. Strict and confining childhood, from what I gather. His father was an itinerant preacher and handyman, more the latter than the former. Daddy Meltzer had odd ideas on child-rearing, and was prone to dress little Arnold in girl's clothes and make him stand one-footed on a stool when he misbehaved. His mother worked as a clerk at Wal-Mart and didn't seem to have friends. Little Arnie was very bright, but had a speech impediment that may have affected his schooling. His grades were poor.'

It amazed me how many serial killers and sociopaths had the same strange item in their backgrounds: dressed in clothes of the opposite sex.

'In high school Meltzer formed a group called the Alliance, a white, male-only club with secret passwords and handshakes and rituals. It seems adolescent, but . . . '

'But it gave him something he could control,' I finished.

'The recruits to his club were ignorant and poor. Arnold preferred strong, mean-spirited chest-thumpers. Together they made brawn powered by brains and beat the shit out of anyone who looked at them sideways.'

265

'He built a tribe,' Harry said. 'When they became a tribe, they stopped being lone outcasts and losers, and became a force to be reckoned with. All held together by whatever ideology Arnold invented.'

Ben nodded. 'Meltzer grew the Alliance like kids in 4-H grow gardens. After a few years it was a submerged but potent presence throughout a dozen surrounding rural counties; warriors for the white race. In his early twenties Meltzer branched out, writing and printing hate literature. Booklets and pamphlets and such. He's authored several books. Meltzer's managed to stay under the national radar, but if there's a hate site on the web, chances are it's traceable to him. Either he runs it directly, or has sponsorship.'

'Sponsorship?' Harry asked. 'Like advertising?'

'He lets the owners run it free from his server network, offers graphics that put more slick in the sick. He promotes products on the sites. He also sponsors recruiting rallies and even retreats, if you will, where strategy and tactics are discussed. Like what politicians might be useful to the movement — again, under the radar — and deserve help getting elected.'

Harry suppressed a shiver. 'You mention Meltzer writing books. Books I could find at the library?'

Ben reached to the bookcase on his wall, plucked out a softcover volume. He tossed it to Harry, who studied the cover.

'I saw this at Bailes's trailer.'

'It's a classic,' Ben said. 'If you're into Aryan supremacy.'

266

Harry held the book up for me to see. *Slaves By Nature* was the title, emblazoned above a color cartoon of blacks grinning, dancing, eating watermelons and, obviously from the position of the feet under a bush, having sex. The subheading was *The Truth at Last!!!*

Harry opened the book and started reading:

'*The black race is not a true race as such, but a subspecies that, when properly trained, is best suited for menial labor and low-thought operations such as simple assemblage in factories. As for constant revisionist bleatings about the injustices of 'slavery', both history and biblical reference instruct us that the Negro actually thrives in such an environment, needing constant oversight and a firm hand in matters of discipline. In this case slavery, far from being an impediment to development, actualizes the Negro . . .* '

'That was Meltzer's first effort,' Ben noted. 'He's penned a dozen others, all basically the same, all standard fare for the Aryan library.'

Harry tossed the book on Ben's desk. 'Meltzer make money at this?'

Ben shrugged. 'Not a lot, given the limited market. But he also sells T-shirts, posters, flags, key rings — '

'Key rings?'

Ben scrabbled in his desk, tossed me a stamped-metal medallion with a key loop. I stared at it, a swastika over a WP: white power.

'Yours for $18.95 plus shipping and handling,' Ben said. 'Everyone who's anyone in the movement has a Meltzer key ring.'

'Costs maybe a buck to make,' I said. 'Nice margin on Aryan nick-nacks.'

'As long as there's a difference between races, Meltzer makes money on this shit. But it's his dope muling that brings in the big bucks. Of course, he keeps himself removed from the drugs.'

'This rabbit ever pop from his hole?' I said.

Ben said, 'Funny you should ask. Meltzer's making a guest appearance tonight at a white-power rally near the border. He's been uncommonly visible the last couple of weeks, this being his third rally in as many states. It's unusual.'

'This like a Klan rally?' Harry asked. 'Sheets and secret handshakes and burning crosses?'

Ben grinned. 'Times have changed. Picture a rave, only with lots of hate and a median IQ of about twelve.'

'You have informants at the rally, Ben?' I asked.

He shook his head. 'We know time and location, but penetrating a Meltzer rally is nigh on impossible. The only people invited are the inside crowd who know one another. They're suspicious folks. Or maybe a better word is paranoid.'

★ ★ ★

We raced back to Mobile with the lights flashing. Harry had a late-afternoon meeting with the District Attorney's office about an upcoming trial. We discussed Meltzer on the high-speed run, wondering whether to pity the little boy in a dress made to stand one-legged on a stool, or hate what he'd become. Harry grudgingly opted for the former, I voted for the latter.

I dropped Harry at his car so he could run to the DA's office. He leaned back in the passenger window.

'Where you heading, Carson?' he asked.

'Home,' I said. 'Maybe take the boat out, paddle a bit.' I yawned against the back of my hand, did a tired look. 'Or maybe I'll catch a full night of Z's, be fresh and ready in the morning.'

Harry looked dubious. 'You're not thinking about Meltzer's rally tonight, are you?'

'Was it tonight?' I yawned.

'You'd get your ass caught. With no one to pull the wolves off your back.'

'Jeez, bro . . . ' I shook my head. 'You think I'm nuts or something?'

37

The rally was down a long country road, deep in the piney woods. A few guys on Harleys blew by me, did the white-power salute and I gave it back. There was another turn-off and I saw activity down the short piece of red-dirt road. I went two hundred yards past and pulled into a fire road in the trees.

Staying low, I moved through the brush until I was twenty yards from the activity. It was a checkpoint. I watched bikes and pickups and SUVs roll up, show a piece of blue paper to a half-dozen guys who looked like hell's bellhops: greasy hair, gaps where teeth used to be, chains rattling on their boots, leather holsters holding serious ordnance. I figured the blue sheets were official passes, probably signed or somehow protected against copying. Someone smart at the top, like Ben had said.

I looked in the direction of the gathering, thinking of sneaking through the woods. I discerned a couple guys in camo among the trees, holding rifles and smoking. Step on a twig and draw fire; no thanks.

It was the checkpoint or nothing.

Dark was falling. I crept back to my truck. It looked impossible to slip past the grimy crew at the checkpoint, but could I wangle an invite from someone less inclined to study me? How did the process work?

Nothing to do but find out.

I drove back to a spot a couple hundred feet from the turn-off, turned around as if aiming at the rally, pulled off the road. I got out and began rummaging through my glove box, throwing maps out on the road like they'd been tossed there in a rage. I saw a stripe of red beneath my seat: the ridiculous flag yanked from Beefer's truck: Hank Williams, Jr. on a Stars'n'Bars. How would it play to this crowd — heroic icon or Cartoonish blasphemy?

I hung it in the rear window as a big van roared up from behind, a half-dozen people in the rust-bucket vehicle, four burly men and two women. I shook my head and started jamming the stuff back in the box as the truck rumbled up beside me. My keychain dangled from my pocket, the WP medallion flashing against my jeans.

The van stopped and the driver yelled out the window.

'Problem, bud?'

I did childish rage. 'I'm turning around and gonna miss the fuckin' blow-out, that's the problem. I'm stupid. That's another problem.'

'Whaddya mean?'

'My pass. I thought I stuck it in the glove box, but musta left it in the saddlebag of my hog.' I kicked the tire, yelled, 'Fuck!'

The guy driver jumped out and moved toward me. He was six four or so, Harry's size. Wearing a pirate's beard. Hard muscles all over, with wild hair half restrained by the bandana. He sucked from a bottle of Dixie beer and stared into my face. He scratched his beard and I saw the word

KILL inked across the knuckles of his right hand.

'Where'd you get it?' he growled. 'The invitation here.'

'Sonny Rollins,' I said, figuring these guys weren't into jazz.

Suspicious eyes. 'Never heard a him.'

'Sonny's ramrodding the movement in Memphis. Sonny couldn't make it but got me a pass; thought I might make good contacts. I know Sonny through Donnie Kirkson.'

The hard eyes somehow got harder. 'How you know Donnie?'

'He got in Holman two months 'fore I got out. We helped keep the niggers off each other.'

His hands curled into fists and his eyes tightened to bunkers.

He yelled, 'BULLSHIT!'

My heart stopped. I think everything stopped. 'Uh . . . what?'

'That was a goddamn *bullshit* charge. I heard the runaway looked at least eighteen. They been after Donnie for years, finally used that goddamn bullshit charge to lock him up.' He calmed a degree or two, did concern. 'Donnie doin' all right, bro?'

'Puttin' on a little weight,' I said, patting my gut. 'Prison food. But he's hangin' tight.'

The guy flashed a look at my keychain. Studied the flag. A grin took his face. He sang, 'Are you ready to par-teeee?' echoing a Hank Williams, Jr hit song.

'I was, but now I ain't,' I said, climbing back in my truck. 'Y'all take care and party hard for me.'

The guy started back into his van, thought a moment. 'Come on in behind us, I'll vouch for ya. One of the guys on security is my cuz. We all forgit shit now'n then, right?'

'I wish you'd stop forgettin' to wear underwear,' the scraggly blonde in the passenger seat crowed out the window, provoking a chorus of hoots and catcalls inside.

'Thanks, brother,' I said. 'Eighty-eight.'

'Fuckin' yeah,' he grinned. 'Eighty-eight. Fall in behind.'

★ ★ ★

The air at the rally smelled of beer and sweat and barbecued pig. I walked to a white tent bordering the woods where a hog was roasting in a pit and three guys were pulling beers from ice-tubs and setting them on the slat-board counter. Aryan Nation flags hung from the rear of the tent. I tossed down a ten-dollar bill, took away a can of Bud and a half-cup of 'cue ladled over a grocery-store bun that was mostly air.

'Hey, buddy, you forgot your change,' a voice yelled to my back.

'Keep it, brother.'

The speed with which he jammed the bucks in his jeans told me Aryan catering units weren't used to tips. I walked away pulling strands of oversweet and undercooked pork from my teeth, thinking maybe the gratuity was premature.

Night was almost full and the fire was growing. The fire committee was three beer-swilling behemoths feeding the blaze from a stack of applewood and oak. They'd grunt in unison and launch six feet of log on to the fire, sparks cascading into the purple sky.

The growing crowd was mainly males, only about ten per cent female participation. Most of the women in attendance were biker chicks, demoiselles of denim and leather, some looking hard and some looking lost. The young girlies had punked-out spiky hair like it was the eighties, the older mamas had hair hiked high — prom night in Waco, Texas, circa 1975. The older ones all shared the same voice, a graveled purr, like buttermilk laced with broken glass. The younger ones tried to emulate the effect, failing because it was the voice of No Way Out, and they hadn't learned that yet.

A band was playing, four skinhead types in risers in front of a wall of Hi-Tone amps. It was headbanger speed metal, distorted power chords punctuated by shredding guitar leads. The musical structure was strident and anthemic, the skinhead lead singer in a white tee, torn jeans rolled to mid-calf, hightop Doc Martens. He was curling around a microphone stand, his mouth a rictus of agony, less singing than screaming.

'*Fuck the watermelon-eating niggers . . .* ' he howled.

'*FUCK 'EM!*' the crowd roared in response.

'*Fuck the tortilla-eating spics . . .* '

'*FUCK 'EM!*'

'*Fuck the goat-eating A-rabs . . .* '

'*FUCK 'EM!*'

It was sad and small and it wasn't all that long ago the singer might have called out the potato-eating Micks or the spaghetti-sucking wops. I waved my beer in the air and shrieked out the response with everyone else, using the time to scope out the crowd. I figured, given my years on the force and Mobile a half-hour distant, there was probably someone in there who I'd rousted or arrested. I pulled my ball cap lower over my eyes.

After ten minutes I needed a break from the noise and the smell of sweat and the constant Heil Hitlers and other tribal salutations. I wandered a couple hundred feet from the fray to the woods, walking into the trees until the brush softened the sound. It was almost peaceful, the moon high and bright.

I startled at the crack of branches breaking and heavy breathing and spun to see a tall, wide-shouldered guy in a black shirt pushing from the brush at my back. His arms were marbled with muscle. He was talking to himself, in the clutches of something potent, meth, acid, ecstasy, or some ugly hybrid of any or all.

He saw me, narrowed his eyes.

'They're coming.'

'Hunh?' I said. Normally I say *Pardon?* or *Excuse me?* but among this crowd, *Hunh* was the word.

'They're coming, brother. We got to stop them.'

I decided to play along. 'I know. They're right over the horizon.'

He wiped his face with his hands, shook his head. 'They're breeding them like tomatoes, using different strains.'

'You lost me.'

He looked from side to side, like there were informants in the trees. He waved me closer, leaned to speak in a whisper.

'Super niggers. They'll be able to fly. I heard it from a guy who heard it direct from Meltzer.'

'Hunh?'

'Won't really be flying, but they'll have legs so strong they'll jump like bullfrogs. They'll be bouncing all over the fucking ghetto and cops'll have to build big nets to catch 'em.'

I couldn't help chuckling at the inanity. A mistake. He grabbed me by my shirtfront and rammed me into a tree.

'Don't laugh at me,' he rasped. 'I'll goddamn kill you.'

His trip was turning ugly. I said, 'I'd never laugh at a man who knows what he's about. If you took me wrong, I apologize.'

He blinked at me so hard I could tell I was little more than a hazy shape in his addled mind. His grip fell loose and he patted my arm.

'You're OK, dude. I thought you were laughing.'

'No man, I was listening. You heard from a guy who heard it from Meltzer.'

He stumbled backwards a step, rediscovered his chain of thought. 'The guy was s'posed to keep it secret but got drunk and told me 'bout this crazy doctor who's doing a Frankenstein act with . . . I dunno, that cell shit.'

Frankenstein. Flying people. Crazy doctors. I backpedaled slowly away, making a note to be careful about laughing.

'Gotta head back to the rally, brother,' I said.

'Nice meeting you.'

'We all gotta hold together, man,' he called after me. 'Some mad scientist grew a special baby. They're gonna make clones outta it. We gotta fight for our own.'

The word *baby* had been much in my life of late. I turned back to the guy.

'You know anything more about that baby the guy was talking abo — '

'Spider, you there?' A voice from the far side of the trees cut me off. Feet were pounding through the underbrush, approaching fast.

'You out here, man? Yo, Spider?'

Spider's mouth dropped in fear. I spun and disappeared into the woods, stopping and crouching behind a clump of briar. I heard a commotion and looked back. Moonlight revealed four guys circling the druggie.

Someone said, 'You gotta learn to keep your mouth shut, Spider — ' and I heard a fist smack into flesh.

I ducked away, re-emerging two hundred feet distant in the light of the meadow. The bonfire was raging. The fire crew had stripped off their shirts. Sweat glistened on their torsos as they humped logs into flames licking twenty feet into the night sky.

I passed by a lone biker chick leaning against a tree, pushing back loops of fake-blonde hair, sucking a beer. Her eyes sparkled with amphetamine.

'Hey there, handsome,' she purred. 'How 'bout we go back in the bushes and crank off a quick fuck?'

'No thanks,' I said over my shoulder.

'Don't like to fuck girls?' came the taunt.

'Don't like to fuck quick,' I said, putting more jump in my steps.

I heard a roar at my back and turned to see a dozen bikers thundering into the parking meadow, cranking accelerators on straight-piped Harleys to announce their arrival. A roar arose from the crowd, three hundred voices howling at once. Bodies parted for the biker escort, a large white step van following the Harleys. The growling phalanx entered the field and I saw fists raised in salutes of joy.

'He's here,' said the hulking man behind me, so softly it sounded like prayer. Someone else said, 'Praise God.'

Arnold Meltzer had arrived.

I watched the step van pull in front of the stage. A ladder allowed access to its roof and two rangy guys scampered up like monkeys, unrolling a carpet across the top and setting up a microphone and PA horns the diameter of truck tires. The crowd tightened around the vehicle and I was pressed toward the front.

'*Arn-old, Arn-old . . .* ' rose in a chant from the crowd, all eyes aimed toward the van. It was a scene of tumult and exultation. A woman beside me was crying with joy.

'*Arnold, Arnold . . .* '

A cheer filled the air as a man slipped from the rear of the van followed by four others. The quartet climbed the ladder with automatic weapons slung over their shoulders, took wide-stance positions atop the van, eyes staring into the crowd. Dressed in black pants and blue shirts, they had wide black belts of shiny leather holding holstered sidearms.

I blinked, looked again at a man atop the van, close to the edge. It was the deputy from the scene at the burned house, Briscoe's man. What was his name?

Briscoe's voice yelled in my memory: '*Baker! Git to the car and you git calm.*'

I filed the name away as Meltzer ascended the ladder, the crowd deafening in its adulation. He was a small man with an imperious, military bearing, hair short and neat and black. He moved as though lighter than air, a pixie. His perfectly tailored white suit seemed an improbable choice until I noted how much it stamped him as different from the rabble below; it was, in effect, a uniform.

I was close enough to see his mouth, and its full and pursed femininity surprised me, as if someone had pasted the lips of Marilyn Monroe on Adolph Hitler. The mouth twitched and blossomed as the crowd roared, palms slamming together, fists waving, boot heels pounding the hard dirt.

Meltzer patted his hand downward in the silence motion and the crowd obeyed as readily as sheep; in seconds all I heard was breathing. He looked out over the throng and moved to the mic with catlike grace.

'*Ih-ehs-isn't it a buh-beautiful night t-tuh-to b-be white, my Aryan buh-buh-brothers and ssss-si-issssss-sisters?*'

Arnold Meltzer stuttered. Not gently, but

279

racked by the struggle to push words out, hunching his shoulders, clenching his fists, fighting for syllable by tortured syllable. Had I seen the contortions from behind, I would have thought his body gripped by epileptic seizure.

When Meltzer finished his sentence, the crowd exploded, first into joyful screams and rebel yells, then into a rising chant: *Arn-old, Arn-old, Arn-old* . . .

It occurred to me that Meltzer's acceptance of his impediment played perfectly in a crowd where all were afflicted, mentally, emotionally, economically, educationally. He may have been smarter, wealthier, and better educated, but he too was deeply wounded.

Arn-old, Arn-old . . .

He allowed a full minute of adoration, drawing energy from the vocal thunder, then waved the chanting down, the pursed lips satisfied, the mouth of a man receiving dues a long time coming. Beside Meltzer, Baker's puffed chest and wide stance might have been funny if he hadn't been holding a weapon that could cut down an oak.

The guy beside me said, 'Fuckin' incredible, hunh? Arnold is God.'

'Who's the guy beside him? The crew-cut guy to the right?'

'That's Boots Baker, brother. Boots is a monster, Meltzer's shadow. You walk up to Meltzer without being asked, Boots takes your head off.'

The guy grinned at the idea of heads coming off and turned to face front as Meltzer launched

280

into his own particular form of sermon, his voice brittle through the metal cones of the public address system.

'A *fuh-false prophet is more d-d-deadly than a wu-weapon, for a weapon can only ki-ki-ki-kill bodies, but false prophet can d-destroy souls. The f-false prophet can destroy ten thousand sssssouls with a ssssingle utterance. Wuh-we have s-seen a fu-fuh false prophet and learned of his tuh-terrible d-d-debasement . . .*'

The crowd booed as Meltzer hissed and twitched out an obvious reference to Scaler, heaping manure on the man's legacy, alternately painting him as mad, debased, delusional, traitorous. Meltzer shoveled for a few minutes, then segued to an allied theme.

'*Those who wuh-would r-r-rule us like sheep have nuh-new weapons and n-new lies . . .*' he said, feet away from Briscoe's deputy. There was a sneer on Baker's face, as if standing atop that truck next to a lump of human garbage marked the pinnacle of his existence.

'*We mu-muh-may hear terrible l-l-lies over the n-next weeks and muh-muh-months. Lies designed to-t-t-tear the wuh-white race apart. Lies designed to du-du-destroy our way of life. Sssstay strong and du-don't ever waver. It will all b-be lies. Lies. Lies! LIES! LIES!*'

The crowd picked up the rhythm and chanted the word *lies* until the ground shook. Meltzer seemed to be preparing the crowd for some upcoming news or announcement detrimental to the movement.

The speech ended with thunderous applause

281

as Meltzer performed a series of salutes including white power and the standard Nazi crowdpleaser. I wondered if successful white supremacists had to memorize salutes like NFL players memorized play-books.

I was ready to leave. My head hurt from the noise and assaults on reason and I had much to think about, including Deputy Baker being one of Meltzer's honor guard. How the rant against the dead Scaler fit into anything. And Spider's mention of a strange baby, a stream of babble reminding me of the mad screeching of Terry Lee Bailes.

The parking area was on the other side of the milling, agitated crowd, and I waded into the hoots and rebel yells and displays of the various salutes. The band had returned and was playing a heavy-metal version of Dixie, the singer howling out revised lyrics.

I wish I was in the land of cotton,
the niggers and spics dead and forgotten,
It's God's way, it's God's way, it's God's way,
Dixie land

I crossed fifty feet past the barbecue tent, looked up to see Meltzer's security detail fueling on pork. Baker was to the side, a solemn, powerfully muscled apparition in the rippling orange light of the nearby bonfire. He was scanning the crowd and looked into my eyes.

I saw reptilian curiosity, brow furrowing as neurons of recognition fired in his brain. I pulled my hat low and tight and ducked into a dozen men standing in a circle and comparing sidearms.

I heard Baker's voice. 'Hey you — stop!'

Baker was frantically waving several men to him, pointing in my direction. I sunk deeper in the crowd, staying low. I saw a group of heavies walking fast at the edge of the rally, looking in. I ducked and circled. When I looked again, I couldn't see what direction they'd headed. Should I cut to the left or right to make my break? My palms turned wet.

I ducked lower, headed for the edge of the crowd. I decided to cut left, to the east.

A nearby voice hissed, 'No. Right! Go to the right!'

I spun to the voice, saw only a wide back stumbling away under a dirty gray cowboy hat, beer bottle in hand, another drunk. But I took a chance on the strange twist of fate, dodging to the right. After a long two minutes, I emerged by the wood fence separating the rally grounds from the parking area.

I slipped between vehicles, saw an orange Toyota Four-Runner ahead and to the side. It boasted all the trimmings, roof lights, chrome luggage rack, mud guards. I wouldn't have seen the vehicle except that it was lit by twin halogen lamps. A white towel was closed in the rear gate of the vehicle, a red cross hand-painted in its center.

It was a small aid station, which made an ironic sense, given the stoners and drunks wandering through a farm field at night. It was a place to fix barb-wire gouges, burns from stumbling in the fire, noses busted in friendly fights, methedrine ODs, and so forth.

I heard a voice moan, 'Owwww. That fuckin' hurts,' and recognized the voice of Spider. I saw him in a chair beside the aid station, the medic's back to me, pulling a suture tight.

'It hurts, gawdammit,' Spider moaned. 'I hurt ever'where.'

I heard voices back in the field, the unwelcoming committee trying to figure which way I'd run. I yearned to hear more of Spider's cryptic ramblings about Frankenstein babies, but crouched and zigzagged to my truck, blowing away with lights off before my pursuers arrived with a noose.

38

I made it home at two a.m. I saw the call light flicking on my phone, pulled out my cell, shut off before the rally. Calls were stacked up on the cell as well, all from Harry. I felt a sense of dread.

'What is it, bro?' I said when he picked up.

'Noelle's gone. This time the grab was successful.'

My breath froze in my throat. 'What? How?'

'The security detail and staff were distracted by a car burning on the street below . . . '

'A what?'

'The fire trucks added to the drama, kept the faces glued to the window. The flames were twenty feet high.'

I saw the picture. 'Staged,' I said.

'Stolen car. A backseat full of rags. A soaking of gasoline and fuel oil. The staff were distracted for maybe five minutes.'

I heard voices in the background, a clattering like a cart or gurney.

'You're at the hospital?' I asked.

'The thing happened at eleven. I've been interviewing, checking security tapes — nothing.'

'What can I do, bro?'

'Go to bed. Get some sleep. There's nothing left here.'

'I'll see you in a few hours and — '

'Carson?' he interrupted, his voice ragged.

'Yes?'

'You were at the rally, right?'

When I didn't answer, he clicked off. I took his advice and fell into bed. Sleep was a series of disjointed images: a mouth talking with only the sound of thunder emerging, arachnids crawling over webs spun from faces, subhuman creatures feeding a fire so hot it burned blue.

After crawling from bed at five a.m., I climbed into my truck in the dark and drove toward Mobile, at the last moment turning east on I-10 and crossing away from Mobile, driving east into Daphne.

The sky carried only a whisper of light when I parked in Kavanaugh's drive. The house was dark inside. I approached the door of her office and sat on the stoop. There was no sound from the house, the drapes drawn and the curtains closed.

The sun began giving form to the shapes in the night and I felt vulnerable. I retreated to the causeway, the slender spit of sand linking the east and west shores of Mobile Bay, pulling off near the eastern shore, by Meaher Park.

I sat on the hood of my truck and looked across the water. Fishermen in small boats were gathering their nets. I pictured escaping fish beneath the surface, jumbled and in turmoil, much like the thoughts in my brain had become of late. Last week, the jumble and turmoil had started not just crawling into the light but ramping up into actions. I had done stupid things that seemed to explode from the shadows of my mind.

Was I going mad? Had the family curse

slithered from a hiding place in my genes?

I tucked the disquieting thoughts away for later study, then went to do my job as best as I knew.

★   ★   ★

I found Harry at the hospital, trying to make sense of the crime. He sat in an exam room with a full-size poster of a skinless human body on the wall and laid out the details of the abduction.

'The fire distracted the staff. Someone moved in, took Noelle, and made it outside — or hid until they could get outside. The doc called me at eleven thirty. By the time I got here it was a mess, everyone running into themselves.' Harry looked on the brink of exhaustion, his clothes rumpled, his breath sour.

'Nothing on the cams?'

'A few people that look like staffers. We're checking them out one by one. We're checking everyone out one by one. But no one saw anything out of the ordinary.' He looked at me. 'I really need you, Carson. I'm not sure if I'm thinking straight.'

I started to argue. 'You always get one hundred — '

He stopped me with an upraised palm. 'I'm trying to stay here as long as possible, get the investigation on fast-forward. As soon as Tom finds out I'm here, he'll pull me. Tell him I'm working the Scaler case; buy me some time.'

'Sure.'

I started away. Harry called out.

'Carson?'

I turned to face him.

He said, 'I need your head on straight, and I need it now. Don't let me down, brother.'

I nodded and looked at my feet. I said, 'I'm sorry.' It seemed a strange thing to say.

I headed downtown to the department to continue researching Scaler and Tutweiler. On the way I pulled into a convenience store to grab something to eat. I picked at the stacks for five minutes, nothing looking good, finally snatching a couple of chili dogs and a can of Dr Pepper.

A dozen customers queued ahead of me, highway-construction guys in work boots and luminous green shirts. A couple of female office workers in skirts and heels and fresh perfume. I saw a biker-gang type in ratty clothes with a bright chain slung belt to wallet. He was leaning against the wall by the door to the restrooms, talking on his cellphone. He shot me a look, went back to his conversation.

I stood in line and counted my change. I felt eyes on me, looked at the guy. His eyes shot away. Waited. Lifted. Saw me watching him.

He said, 'Gotta go, Miriam. Catch you later.' He walked back toward the restrooms.

Miriam? I thought. The guy who'd smacked me with the hospital cart had been talking to Miriam when I interrupted him in the restroom.

Gotta go, Miriam. We'll talk later.

Was the improbable name a code for, *I can't talk now, someone's listening?* I walked back to the can but saw no one inside. I pushed open the door of the women's john.

I saw no one until the guy exploded from the

stall, shouldering me into the wall as he blasted out the door. I scrambled after him. Bolting toward the front of the store I heard the roar of a Harley cranking up. As I pushed through into the lot, the guy was roaring away, shooting glances over his shoulder.

He'd been following me.

I threw a fiver at the surprised clerk and high-balled to the hospital where I told Harry about the incident. Five minutes later we were with the hospital's director of human resources, Daria Fareth, an attractive light-skinned black woman with dazzling green eyes.

'We need to talk to a male employee,' I said. 'Mid thirties. Five-eleven to six feet tall, stocky, weighs maybe two twenty. Brown hair, thinning at the top. Pushes a cart poorly.'

Wentworth flipped through personnel files with attached ID photos. 'Him?' she said, turning the book our way, slender finger tapping a head shot.

'Nope,' I said. 'Our guy's younger and uglier.'

'This fellow?' She turned another photo our way, her nose twitching like a septic odor was rising from the page.

'Bingo,' I said. 'Cart-man. What can you tell us about this guy without getting in confidentiality trouble?'

'Michael Douthitt — a less-than-model employee. Lazy, not real bright, smokes inside the hospital, and has a way of . . . ' Wentworth looked at Harry. 'A way of talking down to people who aren't white. But makes it so it doesn't sound like down, y'know?'

'Gee,' Harry said. 'I've never encountered that.'

289

39

We found Douthitt alone in a small employee lounge on the third floor, eating a bag of chips from one of the machines lining the wall. The room smelled like cigarette smoke. He was leaning back in a chair with his feet on the table, cramming chips in his mouth from his palm, licking it afterward.

'Where is she, Michael?' Harry said.

'Who?'

Harry's hand lashed out like a cobra, grabbed Douthitt's collar, pulled him to standing.

'The kid you helped kidnap.'

'I didn't do nothing. Fuck you.'

Harry reached down and grabbed Douthitt's long sleeve, pulled it high. Tats: eighty-eights and SS knives and a swastika on his forearm for good measure.

'You like them?' Douthitt sneered. 'They don't like you.'

I grabbed Douthitt by the arm and yanked him away from Harry before my partner could strangle him.

'Michael Douthitt,' I said, pulling out my cuffs, 'you're under arrest. Accomplice to kidnapping in the first degree. And one attempted kidnapping.'

I saw thoughts tumble through Douthitt's head, calculations followed by puzzlement. And sudden fear.

'I didn't do nothing but answer a phone call,'

Douthitt said. 'And not this time. Book me and I clam tight, call my lawyer. First-class, special-ordered, just for me. I'm bailed fast, out and laughing.'

What the hell did *Not this time* mean? And the bit about the phone call? I felt a prickle up my back; something was haywire.

I turned to Harry, winked twice. Our signal that I was about to go into Oscar-nominee mode.

'Give us a little time here,' I said, brusque, giving Harry an order from the Alpha Dog, showing Douthitt who was in charge. 'I wanna get some things straight with Mike. Wait in the hall, wouldya?'

Harry did dumb. 'Huh? What you gonna do with — '

'Beat it.' I shot a thumb towards the door. 'Go grab a coffee an' I'll call you when I need you.'

Harry mumbled, slouched his shoulders, and sullenly shuffled away. Wentworth had mentioned that Douthitt wasn't bright. A guy in his mid thirties making minimum wage pushing food carts? I figured the human resources director was right.

When Harry left, I went to the door and looked right and left as if making sure it was just Mike and me, two amigos, members of the same tribe. I closed the door and grinned ear to ear.

'I didn't see you at Arnold's rally last night, Mike.'

Douthitt's mouth fell open.

'Jesus fuckin' Christ. I was there. You was there, too?'

'Arnold is God,' I said. 'I never miss a chance

to see him. It was fuckin' incredible, right? Arnold roaring in behind that Harley escort, speaking from high up on that van, the fire burning below. An inspiration to white people everywhere. And wasn't that band the hottest?' I did few headbanger bows while singing *Fuck the spics.*'

Douthitt grinned. 'Goddamn . . . you really were there.'

Douthitt had been there too, pretty much nixing him for the grab. But he'd said something about 'not this time'. Had he meant the abduction? The advance work? I checked the door again, leaned close to Douthitt.

'Lotsa guys on the force are sympathizers, Mike. I'm the one in charge of going to the meetings, bringing back the news. My pipeline to Arnold used to be Donnie Kirkson, but now I'm tied direct to Boots.'

His eyes widened as much as his gaping, gold-filled mouth.

'Holy shit!' he bayed. 'Boots Baker?'

I winced. 'Shhhhh!'

'Sorry.'

I sat beside him like a counselor, put my hand on his shoulder. 'What went down last night, Mike?'

'Nothing, brother. I was as surprised as everyone else when I got to work today and heard the kid had been grabbed.'

'But the first attempt to snatch the kid . . . you were in on that, right? The inside man?'

'I got a phone call asking where the kid was. That was all.'

'You don't know who made the grab last night? You being straight with me?'

He put one hand out, palm down, the other beside his head, like he was swearing on a bible in court. 'I swear I got no idea who did the snatch. Not this time. Musta been someone else tipping them off.'

I patted his shoulder like he'd been a good dog. 'You got your directions, right, Mike? For if you got caught?'

He tapped his wallet. 'I got a lawyer's number.'

'Call him, pronto. You're gonna be fine. You gave some directions into a phone, talking casually, right? For all you knew, it was a parent or guardian, right? Getting directions to see the kid?'

Douthitt grinned, thinking I was feeding him lines. He shot some idiot damn Nazi-Aryan salute.

I said, 'You're cool, brother, a non-participatory involuntary participantosa. It's legal shit that means you were involved, but you had no malice aforethought.'

I walked to the door, opened it, peered out. Harry looked at me from a dozen feet away, making sure no one disturbed the conversation in the break room. I turned back inside.

'Tell me something, Mike. Why didn't you make the grab the first time?'

'They wanted me to, but I wasn't taking no chance of going to the pen for kidnapping. They said, 'If you can't get the kid out, kill it.' I said, 'Now I've got a murder charge. No way.' A few days went past, they called and said they'd prepared some guy to do the grab — Bailes. All I had to do — '

'Back up. 'Prepared'? Your word or theirs?'

'That's what they said: *prepared*, like food.'

Bailes being prepped with the lie that he had terminal cancer? Bailes had been prepared, all right; cooked like a goose.

Douthitt continued: 'Bailes called, said, 'Where's the kid?' I told him how to slip up the back stairs to the fourth floor, the PICU. The kid was third in a line of five.'

'No calls after Bailes failed?'

'Nothing. I swear.'

I gave Douthitt a long side-eyed glance, like I was gauging his worth for the truth.

'The caller let you in on why the kid had to go, Mike? They told you the story, right? It's scary.'

A pure fishing expedition. I wondered if Douthitt's handler had given him a reason for Noelle's abduction, or if he was an ideological soldier, an automaton.

'Oh wow, man, yeah. I heard the kid was something a doctor made in a laboratory, like a Frankenstein nigger or something. It was a threat to the movement and had to be stomped out.'

Frankenstein. The drooling wreck Spider had used that word. And similar ones, ending with the exhortation to destroy Noelle.

'You were checking the kid that day you rammed the cart into me?'

He nodded. 'When I saw two cops, I banged my cart into you for a little fun.' He held out his hand. 'No hard feelings?'

I took it, making a mental note to wash my hand in disinfectant first chance I had. 'None, brother. You gave directions and that was it. Like I said, Inparticipatory involitudinal nonparticipitude. Or, as we say in the biz, 'Scott-free'.'

I winked, put a solemn mask over my face, opened the door. Harry came in, cuffs already in hand.

He said, 'So, Mikey, you ready to take the walk?'

Douthitt smacked his lips on his palm and blew a smooch at Harry. 'I'm a nonparticipational particulator,' he grinned. 'So you can kiss my white ass, nigger.'

Three seconds later Douthitt was kissing the wall as Harry applied the cuffs. I wandered off to find some disinfecting hand soap.

40

We booked Douthitt, gave him his phone call. I convinced Harry to wait and see who showed as counsel, since Douthitt's lawyer was special-ordered. Most of these guys used bargain-basement attorneys who had grubby offices squeezed between the bail bondsmen by the courthouse.

Instead, the guy who showed up was a slender, bespectacled guy in his thirties with a tailored pinstripe suit and a creamy leather briefcase that probably cost more than thirty of the canvas satchels I used to tote around papers. Lawyer-boy was using a gold pen to scribe his name into the visitor's log.

'I know that guy from somewhere,' I said.

'So do I,' Harry said. 'Why?'

The image formed, Mr Briefcase standing silently by as a bald bulldog barked at me through a cloud of musk.

I said, 'I'm pretty sure he was with Scaler's lawyer, Carleton, the day we first interviewed Mrs Scaler.'

'Hey,' I called across the room to the guy. 'What group of shysters you practice with?'

The guy looked up, pursed his lips. Ignored me. I nodded to Harry and we walked over, stood at his side. We were both taller.

'Carleton & Associates, right?' I bayed, slapping a heavy hand over the poor guy's skinny shoulder. 'Your firm handles all the Scaler enterprises? Why's a white-shoe hotshot like your fine self even looking at a piece of shit like Michael Douthitt?'

The lawyer flinched at my touch. He looked like he wanted to ditch the fancy briefcase and pen and sprint to the street for safety. I wondered if he'd ever been inside a jail before.

'I'm trying to make partner,' the lawyer said, eyes pleading to be left alone. 'I just do what I'm told.'

★ ★ ★

We headed back to the detectives' room. Harry was agitated but trying to hold it together. We needed full investigative mode, and that meant emotionless. Emotion crippled logic, and only logic could blaze a path to the heart of this maze. Still, Harry was having a hard time keeping his heart from eclipsing his brain.

'Carson? What if she's . . . '

He couldn't finish. The unspoken was that Noelle might well be at the bottom of Mobile Bay, or in a hole at the edge of a festering swamp.

'She's fine, Harry. Hold on to that.'

'What did she ever do to anyone?'

'Keep it tight, bro.' I think he'd said the same thing to me a few days back. I hadn't kept it tight at all.

Harry took a deep breath, began: 'Assume the tithe envelope ties Noelle to some aspect of Scaler's enterprises. That he or someone in the Scaler organization knew who was in the torched house. Maybe put them there. Someone who knew there was a baby out there that was, in some strange way, special.'

'And?'

'Now we've got a group of white supremacists who've kidnapped her. Possibly targeting her for death.'

'I read you,' I said. 'But why didn't the overseers giving the orders check with Douthitt before making the second, successful attempt? How did they know Noelle was still in the third incubator? Or in the PICU, for that matter? Doc Norlin said she was ready to head to the regular neonatal-care unit.'

'Another pair of eyes in the hospital?'

'Possibility,' I mulled. 'But if Douthitt did the job right the first time, why not just use him?'

'That's nuts-and-bolts stuff,' Harry growled. 'We've got to come up with what's underneath this vat of slime. Who's keeping it cooking?'

'I think you're on the righteous road, bro,' I consoled. 'Every time we learn something, it's touching the past. Did you get that Meltzer grew up in the county adjoining the county Scaler came up in? And how about Tut? He goes back thirty years with Scaler. Meltzer, Scaler, Tut . . . all about the same age, mid fifties. Carleton, too.'

Tom Mason knocked at the door. Tom frowned, held up a call message.

'I just got word that Dean Tutweiler's dead.'

'What?' Harry and I said in unison.

Tom shook his head. 'The Dean was found in

298

his home about fifteen minutes ago. How about the two of you go take a look?'

★ ★ ★

Tutweiler owned an impressive multi-columned house in west Mobile, not far from the college. The house stood alone at the end of a street, an acre of yard surrounded by deciduous woods.

The uniforms who'd responded when the body was discovered by Tutweiler's housekeeper — did everyone have a maid but me? — had the sense to realize the potential of the situation, choosing to call the death in on a personal cellphone and not over the air and thus susceptible to police-band-monitoring media types. There were no news vans, no neighbors milling on the lawn with cellphones in hand.

Clair was on the scene as the rep from the ME's office, which showed the weight of the event. Clair only worked a scene if there was something new she might learn, or the case carried political or celebrity-style weight. Tutweiler, unfortunately, qualified as both.

Tut was sprawled in red silk boxers on a couch. His mouth was open, his tongue lolling. His eyes looked heavenward, which I found ironic. White foam had dried on his cheek. The living room boasted expensive furniture and decorations, but not a touch of personality. It was as if a door-to-door ambience salesman had sold the Dean a pre-selected grouping: the Yawn Suite.

Clair was standing by the body. She looked up from her notes. I saw a split-second struggle over

299

whether to look concerned or nonchalant, opting for the latter.

'Hi, Carson,' she said, the blue eyes as dazzling as always. 'How are you?'

'Engaged in the moment,' I said. 'I'm here. What you got?'

'An OD by the looks. That's so far. I'll know more when we get him to the morgue. Check the pillow beside him.'

I looked down, saw a syringe and an umarked bottle of solution.

'That's what makes you think OD? Maybe it's medication of some sort.'

'Look here. His feet.'

I bent as Clair carefully spread the Dean's long blue-white tootsies, the nails in need of trimming. I saw punctures between the digits. Clair said, 'Standard low-profile junkie injection sites. He's hidden them in other places as well.'

William S. Burroughs claimed being a junkie was no big deal if you had enough money to guarantee access to good dope. You were like anyone else, except you pumped a feel-good substance into your veins. Burroughs believed the deleterious effects of junk weren't the drug's doing, but caused by the typical junkie lifestyle of malnutrition and disease and living in a city's danger zones.

'So our boy's had a monkey riding him for a while?' I suggested.

'Years, maybe. His feet are riddled. Hips, too.'

'Is Tut married?' I asked, looking around. No sense of a woman's presence, hardly a sense of a man's.

Harry shook his head. 'Everything on the web said he's always been single. His standard line was that he was married to his service to God.'

Harry stood beside the couch, bounced up and down. I heard squishing. Harry bent and patted the carpet.

'There's water on the floor. The carpet's wet.'

I crouched over the carpet and sniffed. 'Just like at Scaler's scene and Chinese Red's. I'm taking bets it's sea water.'

No one bet against me.

* * *

I looked out the window, saw a dark-suited James Carleton stalking toward the house all by his lonesome, his deep-blue M-Benz in the drive. He stopped and talked to a group of uniforms for a few seconds, then pressed past, heading for the door.

No knock. He stepped inside like everywhere was his house. I turned, widened my eyes in false delight, clapped my hands.

'Look who's here, Harry — Jimmy Carleton. Lookin' good, Jimmy!' I brayed, treating the upmarket lawyer like the thirty-buck-an-hour ambulance chasers we schmoozed in the courthouse halls.

Carleton eyed us like something unpleasant into which he'd planted the soles of his five-hundred-buck Italian loafers.

'Nothing can be taken from this house without direct linkage to the scene,' he barked, cranking into payday mode, on the clock. 'Any and all items taken must be entered in a — '

'How'd you know?' I said.

He scowled. I'd interrupted his cash flow. 'Know what?'

'About Tutweiler's death. No one knows but us chickens here on the scene. It hasn't been broadcast.'

The face blanked. 'I didn't know until a minute ago,' he said. 'I had some papers for Dean Tutweiler to sign. Official papers. I saw the cars, the police. I parked and ran up, heard the terrible news. It's a horrendous shock.'

I couldn't read his face. 'Could you show me the papers?' I asked.

'Papers?'

'The ones you were going to have the Dean sign. You must have some papers in that fancy briefcase with a dotted line for the Dean to sign on, right?'

He pulled the case closer. 'Anything I have in this briefcase is subject to attorney-client privilege.'

'I'm not looking for the secret recipe for Coca-Cola,' I prodded. 'I'm just interested in seeing a dotted line ready for the Dean's pen point.'

Carleton did what lawyers and politicians do when confronted by an unruly question: changed the subject, looking at his watch and shooting me a glare.

'I suppose this will be in the news within the hour, just like the sordid details of Richard's sad death. Don't you people have any clamps on your leaks? It's a matter of humanity, for God's sake.'

'Guess not,' I shrugged. 'Do you know how the Dean died, Mr Carleton?'

'How would I know? I just got here. A heart attack, I'd imagine. The stress of the past week.'

Carleton retreated to the front porch as Harry and I inspected the scene. It seemed a typical OD, like Chinese Red's. Only this one was a world away from the apartment in the Hoople, no matter how nicely the benighted Mr O'Fong, scion of the world, had appointed his small space.

'You think Carleton knew Tutweiler was dead? Harry asked when we finally signed the body over to Clair and her people.'

'Interesting question,' I said.

I bid farewell to Clair, politely. As I climbed in the car I saw her shoot a glance at Harry. While yawning nonchalantly, he slipped his hand out the window and gave her some kind of signal.

Clair smiled at whatever it was.

41

We drove past Carleton, sitting in his massive chunk of German engineering with a phone to his ear, the darkened windows tight.

'Stop,' I said to Harry.

He pulled beside Carleton's driver's window. I made the roll-down-your-window motion. It slid down as if tracking on wet butter.

'What?' he demanded.

'How old are you, Mr Carleton?'

'Fifty-four,' he said. 'Why?'

'Just taking a survey. I'm thirty-six, Harry's forty-something.' I decided to drop a bomb, see what it took down. 'How old do you think Arnold Meltzer is?'

His eyes reacted, but not his face. A good lawyer can do that.

'We know you know him,' I said, expecting another blank-faced *Who?* or *What are you talking about?*

'So the fuck what?' he said.

I nodded toward the house.

'First Scaler, now Tutweiler. What's Meltzer's connection?'

'I don't have the slightest idea what you're talking about. Reverend Scaler, the poor sick man, died of a heart attack. It appears that Dean Tutweiler killed himself. The pretty lady in there said as much.'

'No,' I said. 'The pretty lady in there is my

girlfriend. And the pretty lady is a professional. She'd never leap to such a conclusion. I think that's what you're planning on — suicide. Where did you get your forensic training, Mr Carleton?'

'I'll thank you to remove yourself from my presence before I talk to your Chief.'

'How do you know Arnold Meltzer?'

'Anything I might say about Arnold Meltzer is under privilege. Now, if you'll excuse me.' The window started to roll up.

'Privilege?' I said. 'So Meltzer's your client.'

'Everyone is entitled to representation under the law,' he said, his voice like oil over an eel. 'You might try reading the Constitution, Detective. It actually affects parts of law enforcement.'

The window closed. I heard Harry's door open. The blue Mercedes moved ahead a yard, stopped dead.

Harry was standing in front of its grille. The window dropped.

'Get out of my way,' Carleton barked. 'This is harassment.'

Harry put his foot on the bumper. Leaned toward the window. 'Not harassment,' he said, his voice as cold as wind from hell. 'A warning. If anything happens to that little girl, I'll cut everyone involved down like a scythe.'

'I h-have absolutely no idea what you're t-talking about,' Carleton sputtered, putting the car in reverse and backing away.

We drove off feeling that somehow we were shaking things loose. We didn't know what, but experience had taught us that when high-priced mouthpieces look scared, we were doing something right.

'What next, Sherlock?' Harry said. He hadn't called me that in weeks.

'Aim for the Hoople Hotel,' I said. 'I got a hunch and that starts with H.'

⋆ ⋆ ⋆

The room clerk, Jaime Critizia, shot a frightened look when we entered the Hoople.

'Stay seated, Jaime,' Harry said. 'It's like before, just a conversation. No La Migre if you level with us.'

Critizia relaxed, nodded his understanding.

'Chinese Red, your dead boarder?' I made a syringe-plunge motion with my fingers above my forearm. 'I need to know if he ever had friends over here.'

'He had some friends that were . . . not friends. They came because Mr Red was handsome.'

'They came for sex?'

Critizia wrinkled his nose as if smelling something even worse than the lobby of his workplace. 'Ees a bad job here, but I have a sick back and cannot work the chickens or fields or gardens. I must have money for my family in Ecuador, and I can sit in this job. The pay ees no so good as the chickens factory or fields, but I can work long hours to make up.'

Critizia was telling us he only worked at the Hoople because he had no other choice. I figured he'd been a good, upstanding Catholic back in rural wherever, had seen more vice in his first day at the desk of the Hoople than he'd seen in his life. And he wasn't part of those goings-on.

'*Si*. For the sex.'

'One of the people who might have come for the sex,' I said. 'Did he look at all like this . . . ?'

I held out a photo of Tutweiler pulled from the net. Critizia took a long look before he nodded.

'He dressed to look different. A light hair thing.' Critizia wiggled his fingers over his head, meaning a wig. 'And always sunglasses, even when it rains.'

'He was here how many times?'

'One time every week, usually Wednesday in the night. Sometimes he would be here on Sunday.'

'A new meaning for Sunday services,' I said.

★ ★ ★

Heading outside, we saw Shanelle emerging from a minimart across the street, eating a sloppy po'boy from wax paper. Her green dress had required less cloth than my handkerchief. The gold clogs had turned to sparkly red pumps like she was ready to tap dance over the rainbow.

She saw us and ran over.

'Harry, you look sweet as honey today. How 'bout you and me get tickets for Rio and fly away some night and — '

Harry held up his hand.

'Gotta talk serious here, Shanelle. How well did you know Chinese Red?'

'We was friends, Harry. We'd go to the docks

307

and talk. It's so unfair he's gone.'

'Tell me about his last days.'

'Red got clean, Harry. He kicked. He was getting better.'

'But still selling himself, right?'

'When he had to, and only to a couple of high-price clients. He was putting the money away and not in his veins. He was gonna start his own detail shop next year.'

'You're sure, Shanelle?'

'I ain't ever been sure of much, Harry. But that's one of the few things I know for fact.'

Score one for Ryan's optimism, I thought as we drove away.

'Tut was a regular customer of Chinese Red,' Harry said, rolling up the window. 'If someone who knew of the unholy alliance between Dean Tutweiler and Red suddenly needed a way to destroy Scaler's reputation, putting Scaler with a gay black man with a history of prostitution . . .'

'Was the kind of inspired move I'd expect of a guy like Arnold Meltzer,' I finished. 'But Meltzer lacks the balls to slice pepperoni. He delegates. Which probably means we need to know more about Deputy Baker,' I said, pulling my phone.

I made my call to Ben Belker as Harry drove. Ben was out having lunch and I told Wanda Tenahoe we needed everything Ben had on Boots Baker. She knew who I was talking about, judging by the *Ugh* when I mentioned Baker's name. Ben would call back soon, she promised.

With nothing else to do, Harry and I picked up po'boys and headed for the causeway. He didn't want to eat, but I shoved the sandwich into his hands, let instinct take over.

We leaned against the car and ate without a word, watching the boats and herons and pelicans.

'Has it ever gotten to you, Harry?' I said. 'I mean, before today?'

My cell interrupted. It was Ben Belker. He said, 'Can rattlesnakes catch hydrophobia, Carson?'

'Why?'

'That's how I describe Delbert aka 'Boots' Baker. He got the nickname from kicking people's faces to a pulp. While others held them, of course. He's a rattlesnake with rabies.'

'You know he's a county sheriff's deputy?'

'I'll add that to his file. He must have gotten fired from his last job, guarding at a Mississippi prison. Maybe they found out about his previous prison work.'

'You lost me, Ben.'

'Baker was a guard at Abu Ghraib. One of the worst of a bad lot, a sadist. You heard about water-boarding? Baker invented watersheeting.'

'Watersheeting?'

'Not a bad idea, as first conceived. Soak a sheet or blanket in water, wrap it around someone you want to move — a mummy wrap. Ever try and wriggle from wet fabric, Carson?'

I thought of how hard it was to pull off a wet sweatshirt.

'I can imagine it.'

'Except Baker wrapped prisoners and did things like add a bit of electricity to the mix. They got pain, he got pleasure, and no proof was ever left on the bodies.'

I pictured Baker's system in my mind. 'Because the wet blankets acted as a soft restraint. The prisoners didn't flail around and contuse themselves.'

'Yep. Just laid there like screaming burritos.'

I shook my head. Saw Harry slipping on water at Scaler's death scene. The wet floor at Chinese Red's apartment. Glenn Watkins delivering the verdict of sea water and petrochemicals, like water found near boat traffic.

'You know where Baker lives, Ben?'

'Address is 432 Grayson Court. It's along the Intercoastal Waterway.'

The waterway was a canal running through the southern half of Mobile county, heavily used by commercial traffic: barges, tows, shrimp boats. The water was often shiny with oil.

'Thanks, Ben.'

I hung up. Looked at Harry. Told him we were heading south.

Delbert 'Boots' Baker lived in a ranch-style house on a short spur of the Intercoastal Waterway. It would have been a nice-looking place except for being entirely surrounded by hurricane fencing, the fence dotted with *Keep Out* and *No Trespassing* signs. I saw two security cameras pointing toward the street, knew there would be more. I looked for signs of attack dogs, but realized people with paranoiac, possibly psychotic personalities didn't tend toward keeping animals. They were so inwardly focused that animals distracted them from themselves.

'Looks like Deputy Baker's built himself a fortress on the water,' Harry said.

'A paranoid,' I said. 'Worse, a paranoiac wrecking ball.'

We got out and walked the fence line. The adjoining property was a scrap yard, beater cars hauled or driven in on their last legs to be sold for scrap, hulking piles of metal stacked close to the channel and awaiting passage to China or wherever was using our cast-offs these days.

The house seemed empty of life, no curtains parting. I figured Baker was on duty somewhere, like the day he'd had the confrontation with Al Bustamente. The thought almost amused me until it led to two others: Had Baker been the one to attack Al Bustamente last week? It made sudden and perfect sense: a sociopath of Baker's ilk would have felt the burn of Bustamente's derisive words long after the confrontation. I figured Bustamente was lucky he'd only been injured and not killed.

And had Baker been standing in the prints, not because he was ignorant, but because he was trying to destroy evidence? That he knew — or had been part of — whatever had gone down at the house in the middle of nowhere?

I filed these thoughts away, stepping over pieces of metal and car parts that had drifted over from the junkyard, half hiding in the kudzu and poison ivy.

'Look at the back of the house,' I said, pointing.

We saw a pier on the water, a sleek, thirty-foot cruiser berthed against the pilings, a boat that

311

could cross the Gulf like I stepped over a creek. I looked to a concrete pad behind the house, saw two battered five-gallon containers, the big blue plastic jobs, short lengths of rope on the handles. I had a similar container I filled with drinking water when camping in the Smoky Mountains.

'What are you thinking, Carson?'

'I'm thinking a short walk takes Baker to his pier, filling his jugs by setting them in the water.'

The rest of the scenario unfolded: Baker, with the help of one or two of his crew, soaking a blanket from the containers, wrapping Richard Scaler when he answered the knock at his door, immobilizing him for a nighttime run to the camp. Or perhaps Scaler had been lured to the camp, immobilized there. Water had pooled beneath Scaler, suggesting they'd hung him up — struggling, but making none of the marks of struggle to alert the coroner.

'Tutweiler and Chinese Red were immobilized for heroin overdoses,' Harry said. 'But what happened to Scaler? Potassium chloride? An air bubble?'

Inject either of the two into the blood and *bang*, heart-attack city. There was virtually no way to discern that the death was anything but a cardiac event.

'Fits,' I said. 'Or maybe Scaler had a heart attack from sheer terror, saving Baker a step. They whipped his back before he died, but once Scaler was in the air, he was helpless. Tie the gag in his mouth, ram the plug into his anus. Set out some candles for effect. There was nothing to be done about the water dripping off the blanket, but they probably figured it would evaporate before the body was found — a miscalculation inside a cool house.'

'Where do you think Baker is?' Harry asked, looking at his watch. 'It's late for him to still be at work.'

'He could be working a swing-shift. Or maybe he's out torturing small animals, the kind of hobby he'd have, I expect.'

'This place makes my skin crawl,' Harry said. 'Let's bag it for now. But make a note to come back real soon.'

We pulled away, both shooting glances in the rear-views at Baker's waterfront fortress.

'What's the strangest thing about this case, Carson?' Harry asked when we were back on the main highway, simultaneously veering so close to a passing gasoline truck I could have leaned out and refilled our tank.

I thought for several minutes, tumbling pictures and events through my mind.

'Why the hatchet job on Scaler's reputation?' I said. 'If someone wanted Scaler out of the way, why not just have him popped with a contract hit?'

'Then he'd just be dead,' Harry noted. 'Now he's dead and discredited. The big question is . . . '

'Why discredited?' I said, looking out into the night sky. 'It's always 'Why?' '

We got to the department's parking garage. It was quiet, the night-patrol shift out on the streets, the detectives long home.

'You going home?' Harry asked.

'I expect it's all that's left for today. You?'

Harry blew out a long breath. 'I'm going inside and sit at a computer. See if I can find anything else Scaler hid in the internet, in the Tower of Babel.'

'It's a drudge job. Why not start fresh in the morning?'

'Morning's hours away. If Noelle's alive, she may not have hours. I gotta do it now, Carson.'

He exited the car, slinging his jacket over his shoulder and trudging toward the building. In the yellow half-light of the garage, he looked like an ancient soldier, sick to death of the battles, but knowing nothing else.

He also looked desperately alone.

42

I woke up and shot a glance at my watch. It was 6.45 a.m. I unfolded from the hard office-style sofa and put my feet on the floor. Something tickled my thigh and I noted my half-hung tie flapping against my leg.

I blinked my eyes into operative mode and saw Harry across the conference room, bagged out in a chair, mouth open as he snored lightly. The computer monitor on the table displayed the screensaver, an undulating rainbow. I'd left off the chase at 3.45, Harry still running the search engine, plowing through years of Scaler sermons tucked away in various sites on the web.

I tip-toed out to the wide and deserted detectives' room and brewed a pot of coffee. When I returned, Harry was back in position at the computer.

'You find anything else?' I asked, adding, 'Good morning.'

Harry took the cup of coffee I'd brought, sucked away half. 'The usual. It seems every time Dickie-Boy preached a camera was there to capture the great man's words, sticking them on the web to bring his way and light to all. See enough sermons and you realize they're basically all the same, he's just mad about different things. You get the feeling that, at the heart of things, Scaler had little love or hope for humankind.'

'The way?' I said, making a connection. 'You

315

said Scaler was the way and light, Harry.'

'Just a joke,' he said. 'From the bible. Jesus was — '

'The way, the truth and the light, right? At least as I always heard it. Remember Scaler in the video?'

I tore open my briefcase, pulled out my notes, found the transcript of Scaler's parable about the crumbling house. I read to Harry:

"'If I don't falter,' Scaler says, 'I will tell you the truth through the Trinity, and what I now believe to be the Truth . . . '" I indicate that Scaler forms a cross with his fingers. 'He continues with ' . . . the way and the light.'"

Harry's eyes widened and he set aside the coffee mug. The keyboard ticked as he pulled up Google and ran Scaler's name, this time adding the word 'Way'.

I peered over Harry's shoulder at the results. Over a hundred thousand hits, every sermon in which Scaler had used the word 'way' or a detractor had responded with a screed like 'Scaler is the way to hell.'

'Try, 'Scaler, Way, Child',' I said.

Harry typed, said, 'Five hundred fifteen hits.'

'Make it recent, if you can. After the 'Truth' vid, before the day he died.'

I held my breath as Harry applied various filters, cutting the results to fifty-nine videos, the bulk of them anti-Scaler rants bouncing across the net daily. Harry scrolled, scrutinizing titles.

'There,' I said, 'the one titled 'The Child Shall Lead the Way'. It was put up on the afternoon before he died. Open it.'

316

We held our breath. And then we saw Richard Scaler. Not at a pulpit, but at his desk, as in the Truth video. Gone was the white suit. He was wearing a robe over what appeared to be pajamas. He was sweating, his eyes anxious. He closed his eyes and turned utterly still.

'What's wrong with him?' I whispered.

'Praying,' Harry said. 'Probably for strength.'

If he received it, I couldn't tell. Scaler leaned toward the camera.

'*I am frightened. I am weak. These past months have been the greatest trial of my misspent life. I was pitted against me. Past against future. I asked for truth, and received the answer from science, against which I have railed mightily.*'

'*But if science studies the intricate workings of the universe, it studies the workings of the Creator. Science does not destroy, it informs. How terribly long it took me to know that. I had a plank in my eyes and thought it less than a mote. But my eyes are now clear.*'

'Is that a reference to the problem with his eyes?' I said. 'He called out motes in others, disregarded the plank in his?'

'*When I tell this to the world, I will be castigated by the few, uplifted by the many. When the world understands, we will know peace. Here is the knowledge as it unfolds today . . . There came a child and its name was All of Us. The tribes of God assemble in this child. What an incredible message of love.*'

A harsh noise from somewhere intruded and Scaler's head snapped to the sound. His face

317

tightened and his voice dropped to a whisper as he leaned toward the computer's microphone.

'*A danger to my greatest project, another terrible lesson I have learned: to believe with your eyes closed means others can lead you where they wish. I close now, and again file my words deep in the Tower of Babel. Stay safe, my world-wide kinsmen all, God bless you as He has finally blessed me.*'

We heard another grating blurt of sound. Saw Scaler's fear as he reached for a computer keyboard and the picture disappeared.

'Scaler never made it to the next video,' I said, 'which should have been 'Light'. Do you think he planned it to be the video that shines light on things?'

'Makes sense. But it's never gonna happen. Did you make anything of that sound in there?'

I shook my head. 'Just a sonic blur.'

'Lemme crank it up.'

Harry pushed the volume to distortion. We listened to the burble of sound that seemed to scare Scaler, but the mic on the computer lacked sensitivity.

'How about we run over to forensics, see if the audio folks can do anything?'

We were heading out the door when Riley, the newly arrived desk sergeant, looked up. 'I didn't know you guys were here. You got a delivery a few minutes back, Carson,' he said. 'A package.'

'Where'd it come from?'

'Some redneck-looking guy brought it in. Big guy, hard-looking. He dropped it off, turned and booked.'

Riley handed me an eight-by-ten mailing envelope. No return address. I held it in front of the lamp on Riley's desk, saw nothing threatening inside. I slid a thumbnail under the loose glue, opened it and pulled out a single sheet.

I stared mutely at a photograph of Noelle. She was on a blanket. In the foreground was a *Mobile Register*. It was today's paper.

Harry saw my open mouth. I handed him the photo.

'Someone's telling us she's all right,' I said, my heart racing at the back of my throat. 'You think a ransom demand is about to arrive?'

'I don't know, and I don't care,' Harry whispered, his voice wind over dry leaves. 'She's alive.'

We continued to forensics, the photo between us on the dashboard. Something seemed off-key. I said, 'You're the one who's been pushing Noelle's case, bro. But someone sent the package to me. Why?'

'You got me.'

He stole another look at the picture, as if drawing sustenance from the image, and pushed the accelerator to the floor.

★ ★ ★

Arlis Hinton was the audio tech at the Alabama Bureau of Forensics. He was sixty years old and had run a recording studio for thirty-eight of them. Arlis was a wizard who could probably wire an iPod to an orange and make the fruit play music as you ate it. He ran the tape through

319

a DVD, listened carefully to the sonic muddle.

'I'll use voice-recognition software, the latest gen. That'll give us a statistical probability of the words, insert them. While that's going on, I'll run a copy through this baby here.' He tapped a black box fronted with dials.

'Which is . . . ?'

'The same thing, in a way, except it analyzes tonal aspects of the sound. It will recognize and filter out the sounds in the guy's office — outside ambience, the computer's motor, his breathing — then use the remaining sounds to reconstruct a vocal model.'

Arlis sat, put on a headset and began playing. After a few minutes he nodded. 'Here's the word reconstruction. It'll sound robotic. We'll fix that on round two. Coming atcha . . . '

We leaned forward toward the speakers as if that would do something.

'Rich-ard,' the flat, mechanical voice said, 'where . . . the . . . fuck . . . are . . . you?'

'Sounds like Tutweiler,' Harry said.

'Only because he seemed like such a machine,' I said.

Arlis diddled with more knobs, talking to himself in audio-engineerese. I saw a series of wave forms on the monitor. They seemed to mean a great deal to Arlis. Finally, he said, 'Got it as close as technology can make things. Ready?'

We nodded and leaned closer to the speakers on Arlis's long desk.

'Richard!' a hard, shrill voice demanded. 'Where the fuck are you?'

'It sounds kind of like Patricia Scaler,' I frowned, not matching the timid convalescent with the bark of cold command coming from the speakers. 'Sort of. Not quite. Maybe.'

'You're not sure it's her?' Harry asked.

I paced the room. 'Patricia Scaler wilts when you speak above a whisper. Computers scare her. Everything seems to scare her.'

'Acting?'

I frowned. 'No one fools me like that. I can always see through an act.'

Harry put his hands in his pockets and rocked back and forth, looking at the ceiling. Something hit and he spun to Hinton.

'What if two related people were analyzed? Like sisters?'

The audio tech tapped his chin, thinking. 'If their voices were similar in tone and timbre, they'd sound closer through the computer than in real life, where the ear distinguishes more subtlety.'

'You said Mrs Scaler has a sister? A beautiful woman?' Harry said to me. 'Does she stay at the house? Live in the area?'

'I've never seen anything but a picture from a portrait joint. A place called Blackburn Studios.'

'Portrait studio?' Harry mused. 'You've got to figure a place like that keeps address info on clients, right?'

43

The photography studio was in one of the hoity-toity neighborhoods on the west side, which seemed odd. I recalled the photo of Patricia Scaler's sister as being emotionless, as if taken by the camera and not a human behind it. Maybe cold and mechanical portraits were the new rage among the wealthy.

Harry had a call from the DA on the court case and had to sit in the car and detail his upcoming testimony. I think he preferred staying in the cruiser anyway, keeping close to the pic of Noelle.

I walked in the door, found myself in a plush anteroom with art on the walls, potted ferns, furniture upholstered in creamy leather. A woman in a nurse-type uniform sat behind a window, reading *Vogue*. It hit me that I was in an upscale dentist office, or something similar.

'Good morning,' the young woman said, showing perfect teeth as white as snow. 'May I help you?'

'Is there another Blackburn Studios?' I said. 'I'm looking for a photography studio.'

She puzzled about it, pretty little chin perched atop her pink finger. 'There's a Blackburn Motors. Sometimes people dial us instead of them.'

A man in his mid forties stepped from a back hall into the office. He was attractive to the point

322

of pretty, walking in choppy steps as if on a model runway. He wore a starched white lab coat and was holding a stack of files in a pink hand with manicured fingernails. He looked like a guy who had to be dragged out of the mirror section of department stores.

'Trisha, I need you to please put these back in . . . ' He looked up, saw me. 'Hello . . . can I help you?'

'I'm beginning to wonder.'

'I'm Dr Lawrence Blackburn. Step back here, please.'

Puzzled, I followed him into a small office with several mirrors and a large desk. There were posters of noses and chins on the wall, hundreds of noses and chins. He stepped close and studied my face like Michelangelo inspecting a chunk of marble.

'Great angles, masculine thrust. But everyone can use a little help. You're mid thirties, right?'

'True.'

'Your nose has been broken.'

'Twice,' I affirmed. 'Once in the line of duty and once in defense of a lady.'

'I can make it straight as an arrow; think of Pierce Brosnan's nose. And I can take five years off those eyes. You spend too much time in the sun. It's taken a toll. How about giving me profile?'

I did my best uprising profile, modeled after Tutweiler. 'You know Patricia Scaler's sister, don't you, Doc?' I asked as I posed. 'I don't recall her name.'

He did puzzled. 'I didn't know Patricia had a

sister. She's never mentioned one.'

'You took a picture of the woman, Doctor. Strikingly attractive. Her portrait said Blackburn Studios in the lower-right-hand corner.'

'That wasn't a portrait like a picture portrait. It's a picture of the future, a computer-generated image of what our procedures will create. Patricia's having a total reconstruction . . . a good way to start with a plain-Jane face like the poor girl's been wearing all these years.'

'Wait a minute . . . I was looking at Patricia Scaler?'

'After rhinoplasty, blepheroplasty, cheek uplifts, chin implants, collagen. Along with our facial work, she's having cosmetic dentistry by Dr Mellmen over in Daphne, implants, caps. The best in the region. Plus breast implants. She'll look twelve years younger and drop-dead gorgeous. The damage to her face is the best thing to ever happen to her, from an aesthetic standpoint, of course. We can start from scratch.' Blackburn seemed to realize he'd gone on without mentioning a critical moment in the past couple weeks, did an obligatory frown.

'Terrible thing about her husband, of course.'

'Maybe a new face will cheer her up,' I suggested.

'Better than new shoes,' the doc said, chipper again.

★ ★ ★

'We heard it right,' I said after explaining to Harry I'd been in a cosmetic surgery clinic.

'That was Patti Scaler on the video. Get this: the woman's having herself re-done, cosmetic surgery from tits to topknot. Maybe that's what she's always wanted.'

'She sounded angry in the video. And tough.'

I folded my arms and thought through three traffic lights, lost in my head. 'Tough probably isn't the word,' I muttered.

'What?'

'Try this one for a hoot, bro: Lady Scaler's in on the action. When the boyos come to hijack Scaler, spirit him off to camp, she tells one of them to work her over. Knock out those rabbit teeth and bust a few things bad. It gives her an excuse to get everything rebuilt from the beginning. Symbolizes a new start.'

'Jesus, Carson, that's freaky.' Harry thought about it. 'But it also lets her claim . . . '

'That daddy Scaler was a wife-beater, adding to his negative legacy. And sweet Patti gets to have a sexy new face installed after forty-eight years.'

Harry scowled. 'That's insane, you know. Something a psychopath would do.'

'Time to turn the camera on Patricia Scaler,' I nodded, feeling foolish. 'Like I should have done a week ago.'

44

There were two cars in the drive, the blue Toyota that belonged to Mrs Herdez, the Scalers' housekeeper, and a red pickup with a Mexican flag on the bumper.

I knocked. Seconds later Mrs Herdez's face appeared at the door. It took her a second to recognize Harry and me. She didn't look happy to see us.

'I'd like to speak with you, ma'am,' I said. 'About your employers.'

'No speak Ingles.' The door started to close.

Harry's hand caught the door and eased it open.

'You spoke it well enough to work for the Scalers. Or did the Scalers *comprende Espanol?*'

A trapped look from Mrs Herdez. We used her moment of confusion to slip into the room and close the door, as if invited into the home. Despite the second vehicle, I didn't see anyone else. The place was bright and clean and orderly, a couch and chairs covered with woven blankets, a tube-style television in the corner. One white wall was covered with photos going back years; family, I expected, far more black-and-white photos than color. Some were faded and yellowed, dark-skinned people leaning on rattle-trap cars or sitting beneath mesquite trees or gathered in a room, the walls obviously adobe.

'You're not in any trouble, ma'am,' Harry said.

326

'We just need to ask you some questions about the Scalers. Mrs Scaler, in particular.'

Mrs Herdez's face seemed overtaken with sudden joy. Her hands clapped.

'Mrs Scaler is a lovely woman. An angel. Kind and generous. She shares her things with me, gives me clothes, food. One time there was a party and she gave me twenty pounds of camarones to take home to my family.'

'How did she and her husband get along?'

'They were like children in love. Kisses, the snuggles.'

'We heard they didn't still sleep in the same room,' Harry said. 'Or talk a lot.'

'I don't know who would speak such things. They were happy like two doves.'

From the other room I heard, 'That's a load of *sandeces*, Maria Herdez. It's bullshit.'

I looked toward the door to the kitchen. A slender woman with angry eyes strode into the room. She was in her forties, probably very pretty when her face wasn't tight with anger. Her hair was in a braid and outsized loop earrings dangled from her lobes. She put her fists on her hips and glared at Mrs Herdez.

'Tell them the truth, *Tia*. Now.'

'I am telling the truth,' Mrs Herdez said, not meeting the other woman's eyes. 'The Scalers were like children in love.'

'Who might you be, ma'am?' Harry asked our surprise addition.

'I'm Luna Martinez, and this is my aunt. *Tia* Maria won't tell you the truth because she's afraid she'll get a bad mark on her work history.'

She looked to her aunt. 'Everyone you've ever worked for will give you excellent marks, *Tia*. Forget the Scalers and tell the truth.'

They lapsed into Spanish, firing sentences back and forth. It was like watching a tennis match. Harry and I turned our heads to Mrs Herdez for the serve, to Mrs Martinez for the return, back to Mrs Herdez. Boink. Boink. Boink.

Finally, a nervous Mrs Herdez picked up a square of lace from the table beside her, smoothed it with her hands, set it back down.

'It was a house like no other have I ever worked for.'

'How angry did Reverend Scaler get?' Harry asked. 'Was he a danger to you?'

Ms Martinez jumped in. 'Not the Reverend! It was that miserable wife of his! Tell them what she made you do, *Tia*.'

'Shhhh,' Harry said. 'Please let your aunt speak.'

Mrs Herdez said, 'Mrs Scaler . . . was not bad. She was just touchy.'

'Touchy? You call a hair-trigger touchy?'

'Ms Martinez, please,' Harry said.

Mrs Herdez said, 'Mrs Scaler wanted things done a certain way. Breakfast at eight forty-five in the morning, lunch at twelve thirty-eight, the dinner between twelve and sixteen minutes past six. Ees a good way to be, so I always know what she wants.'

Ms Martinez had put her energy into tapping her foot. 'And if you missed by a minute, *Tia*? Tell them what happened then.'

'I sit in a chair and look at the wall until I am needed. It was good in a way. My feet felt good to sit.'

'Were Mr and Mrs Scaler happy?' I asked.

'The Reverend spend his time in his office, working. He slept on his bed in there or one of the other bedrooms — there are five. They did not speak unless she wanted to talk. Mostly she would yell and he would do the things she asked, until it was time to walk outside the door. It was like she had the . . . *cojones* in the house.'

Ms Martinez said, 'By *cojones*, my aunt means — '

'Yes,' Harry said. 'We're acquainted with the word.'

'Tell what else she makes you do, Maria.' She looked at us. 'I didn't find out about this until last week. I work from my home, writing computer code. At noon I heard a knock and *Tia* Maria was there, not able to look in my eyes. Maria almost never drinks, but she had two cervezas y tequila and her shame wiggled out on a loose tongue. Tell them what you did for that woman,' Mrs Martinez said. 'Every morning at nine forty-five.'

'I wiped her,' Mrs Herdez mumbled.

'Pardon?' Harry said.

'After she made the . . . bathroom from behind her. I wiped her. I had to do it just right. The paper couldn't be wadded, it had to be folded and ironed.'

'Ironed?' Harry echoed.

'With the steam. To press the paper flat without losing the softness. Eight folds, then iron. When she was done I had to show her the . . . ' she couldn't say the words.

'The results?' I asked.

'It was very important to her. When I had done all that I could do, I had to clean her with mouth-wash — it could only be the Listerine with mint.'

I shot Harry a glance that said, *mouthwash?* and turned back to Mrs Herdez.

'This was daily at nine forty-five?'

'She was very much a prompt woman.'

Harry leaned forward. 'You don't work on Sundays. Uh . . . '

'No problem, *señor*,' Mrs Herdez said. 'She saved until Monday.'

★   ★   ★

'Patti Scaler is an absolute control freak,' I said as we drove away. 'My mistake was not realizing her timidity was an act. She controlled me every time I talked to her.'

'She dished out what you wanted to see. And feel.'

I nodded. 'Anger at Scaler and pity for her.'

'We're making forward motion by looking into the lady's present,' Harry said. 'You want to check out her past?'

We went to the department. Harry planted himself at the computer in the conference room, hung his purple tie over a chair, unbuttoned his yellow shirt and, using a keyboard like a shovel, began digging into Patricia Scaler's history, trying to see past the press releases and gloss, find what had been hidden in the shadows.

There was a map of Alabama on the wall, mounted over cork so thumbtacks would hold. Harry picked up a box of tacks, went to the board, began sticking tacks to indicate locations.

'Patti Scaler went to a county high school. Everyone in the county went there, no towns in the county big enough to support a school. Check this out: here's where little Patti grew up, here's where lawyer Carleton grew up, here's where — surprise! — Senator Custis grew up. Here's where Tutweiler grew up. Small-town kiddies, all within the same county, where there's little to do but drive around and mix and mingle. Everyone knows everyone.'

I studied the array of tacks. 'Where's Richard Scaler's pin?'

Harry tapped outside the map, where central Mississippi sat.

'It would be up here, a hundred miles away.'

I frowned. 'Out of the pattern, brother.'

'Unless you stick it here.' Harry jabbed the tack a bit beside the cluster of others.

'Which is?'

'The little country church he started when he was in his early twenties.'

'Proximity in space,' I said, studying the map. 'But what does it mean in time?'

'Oh, wait . . . got one more little flag.' He pressed a white tack beside the others.

'That being?'

'Arnold Meltzer. Another kid from the county.'

'OK, so you got Meltzer, Scaler, Carleton,

331

Custis and Tutweiler all in the same geographic area. It's a nice coincidence, especially since they're similar in age. But we're looking at Patti Scaler. How does this touch her? She's six years younger than the others. Not much of a difference, but it's amplified when younger.'

Harry tapped some keys, arrived at a website called Keep In Touch.

'Here's where I found a copy of her high school yearbook. Amazing what's online, right?'

'Where's the lady?'

Harry electronically turned pages. 'Here.'

The photo was black and white and unmistakably the woman who in ten years would become Patricia Scaler, though the name said Patti Selmot. Her complexion was poor. She hadn't smiled for the photographer, perhaps to hide the teeth.

'I doubt she made prom queen,' I said.

Harry handed me several sheets of paper. 'I printed the yearbook's name listings out, Carson. Now it's your turn . . . '

I didn't sit by the computer, I sat by the phone. Using a combination of charm and deceit, I spent hours calling names listed in the yearbook, sometimes being a lawyer trying to track down the recipient of a will's largesse, sometimes a guy trying to put together a class reunion, sometimes even myself. It seemed most of the former students had moved away, out of the county, out of state. I wasn't surprised, heavily rural counties lost a huge percentage of youth.

But I found a few who had stayed. A couple of

them had known Patti Scaler, *nee* Selmot. One told me all she knew; not much. The other woman sounded angry and worn and depressed. She refused to talk to me.

Those were my favorites.

* * *

Harry had to stay at the department to monitor incoming information and wait for any ransom note or other communiqué. I made the two-hour run north to the county where every major player in our case had a connection.

The woman I hoped to talk to was Nona Jett. According to the listings below the names, both Ms Jett and Patti Selmot had been in band together.

I followed my Google map down a gravel road that passed beside a rusty water tower. I bumped over a railroad crossing, pulled into the dirt drive of a doublewide modular, a decade-old Buick Skylark in the drive. Walking past it I saw half the back seat was burned away on the driver's side, generally caused by the driver flipping a cigarette out the window and the wind blowing it back inside, landing in the back seat.

There were a dozen other doubles and singles in the area, scattered willy-nilly through the fallow, sun-parched fields, a fistful of dice on a dirt-brown table.

I knocked, waited. Knocked harder. The door opened a hair. I saw an eye caked with make-up and shadow. Then I saw blonde hair, lacquered stiff as stalactites, scarlet lips, a penciled-on mole.

'Ms Jett? I'm a Mobile detective. I want to ask some questions. There's no problem, no trouble.'

'Questions about what?' the lips said. I smelled beer.

'Patricia Scaler. Patti Selmot.'

'You called earlier.' The door started to close. 'I don't know a thing. I barely remember her.'

My toes stopped the door. 'You were in the same class at a small school. You were in band together. Hard not to know at least a bit about her.'

The eye squeezed to a frown. 'Why you asking about Patti? Is it cuz her husband went crazy and took up with a fag nigra?'

'If you believe what you read in the papers.'

She sighed. 'I used to think Reverend Scaler was like Jesus' brother here on earth. He was for us white Christian people. We don't get no respect any more. We used to own everything, but now Mexicans is everywhere. I work housekeeping at the Ramada and I'm the last white lady left. It's all nigras and Mexicans.'

I didn't point out that her sentence didn't make a lot of sense. Beer does that, in quantity. It helps when you're trying to establish rapport, though.

'They started letting Mexicans in the Mobile Police,' I said, lowering my voice to secret-telling size. 'They cook their tacos on the departmental hotplate. And every day after lunch they sleep on their desks.'

She nodded. 'It's that fiesta they all gotta have.'

I sighed. 'The department makes me work

334

with a black guy, too.'

She looked past me at the empty Crown Vic. 'Why ain't he here?'

'I could tell this was a good white neighborhood. I figured you'd feel better if it was just you and me.'

She gave me gratitude. 'No one ever thinks a us any more. It's like white people are a dying breed. Come in.'

I followed her into a tired little space stacked with cast-off magazines bought for a dime at a charity store: *People, Us, Entertainment Weekly* — the lives of others to distract her from her own. I figured she cheered for people on reality shows.

'Wanna beer?' Jett said, opening the door and nodding toward the fridge. 'I'm gettin' me one.'

I was on duty, but this was pure business. I dug in my wallet, liberated a fifty, handed it to her like I grew fifties in my garden.

'Tellya what, Nona, lemme buy a couple six-packs. You can get 'em later.'

Warming to me fast, Nona Jett brought cheap canned beer in foam cup holders emblazoned with the logo of a local liquor store.

'So what can you tell me about Patti Selmot, Nona?'

She fired up a cigarette, blew a cone of smoke toward the ceiling. 'None a this ever gonna come back on me?'

'Here's my official interview notebook . . . ' I slipped a little red notebook from my pocket, opened to a page, drew a horizontal line at the top. 'That's the space for the name of the person

I'm interviewing. That's all anyone knows about where this comes from. What name do you want me to make up for you?'

She thought a long time, said, 'Britney Hilton.'

I wrote *B. Hilton* in the space. 'There,' I said. 'No one will ever know where I got my information.'

'That's good,' Ms Jett said. 'Tell this kind of thing and you could get messed up bad.'

45

I'd choked down one cheap beer, poured most of the other down the toilet when I'd used the bathroom. In the same span of time, fifteen minutes, Nona Jett knocked back four of them atop whatever she'd had before I'd arrived. I'd not gone the direct-question route, but opted for conversational, asking about high-school activities and so forth, settling in on the personalities of the kids in her class.

'I'm figuring Patti as one of the shy kids in your class, right? Quiet and solitary and — '

Ms Jett laughed, a hard, metallic sound. 'Patti shy? Patti wasn't nothing near shy. Least not with the boys.'

'She was social?'

Nona Jett circled her left thumb and forefinger, then one by one waggled her right fingers in the circle.

'Meaning?'

'Meaning Patti Selmot would fuck anything with a dick. She was plain as Hellman's with that pasty face and big buck teeth . . . but when you're dealing with teenage boys and they know sometime during the night the lid's coming off the honey-pot, you're gonna have boyfriends.'

I pictured a homely little girl trying to be popular by letting high school guys feel her up in the backseats of ragged cars.

'That's sad,' I said.

A harsh laugh. 'You're thinking Patti was like this little curl of fluff being taken advantage of? She busted balls. If a boy was gonna dip his wick, he was gonna pay.'

'Money?'

'Whores take money. Patti liked to take something outta people.'

'Could you explain, please?'

'She might make a guy steal something. Stuff that didn't mean a thing, like 'Go get me a gold-colored picture frame.' The guy'd sneak in a store and come out with a picture frame jammed down his pants. She'd look at it and laugh, then smash it in the gutter.'

'This was in high school?'

'Yep. Then she moved on to the sex stuff. She liked to do things that made people feel bad about themselves later. There was this gross fat girl in class and Patti said she'd give a handjob to any guy who asked the fat girl out then stood her up. Another time she made some boys line up and whack each other off. Said she'd make it with the first guy who came.'

I pictured a motley crew of acne-riddled slackers and dopers sniffing at Patricia Selmot's heels like dogs round a bitch in heat. It was sad and ugly and all too common.

'Were these guys the, uh, class losers?'

'Hah! A guy could be captain of the football team, but she'd get him under her thumb and twist him down. It was that hot little bod of hers.'

'You mean she's shapely?'

'She wears them old-timey sacky dresses on

the tee-vee, but she's packing heat. Got little tits, but they're perkers, nips like gumdrops. Little butt as round as a sugar-baby melon. Long pretty legs . . . '

She seemed to realize something. Stopped short. She shook her head and blew out a plume of blue smoke. 'She did that stuff for a while then moved up and on.'

'She moved out of town?'

'No. She learned what got favors from the boys in school worked even better on older guys with jobs and money and good cars. The last I saw of her, she was with one of the usual groups in a convertible, the guys in their twenties, one guy driving, the others acting like fools to get her to pay attention to them.'

'Always groups?'

'I never saw Patti with one guy, it was always three or four. She liked to walk around with them, showing off at us other girls. Them older boys always had their tongues hanging down, hoping she'd put out. She did. But only on her terms, buddy. They also had this cruel game they played.'

'Which was?'

'They'd drive into a town and Patti would hang around a Dairy Queen or a bowling alley lounge or drugstore place where guys didn't know her. She'd tease them boys with her eyes and wiggle that round butt in them tight shorts. Walk past them and rub on the front of their pants. They'd forget that pasty face and want what all boys want.'

She paused to light another cigarette,

continuing her story from a roiling nimbus of smoke.

'Patti'd get them boys to drive her out to some place in the country, rubbing against them all the way, promising they was gonna get the fuck of their lives. But when they pulled off the road somewhere, the rest of her crew would jump outta the bushes and give the guy a beating.'

I shook my head at how pathetic it all was; the rural version of rolling gays. I thought a minute, added like an afterthought, 'You ever hear of the Alliance? Or Arnold Meltzer?'

She took a suck of beer. 'It got started a few years ahead of me, but right in our very own school. Ever'body knew someone in it. The Alliance was on our side, like you and me. Mostly it was older guys makin' sure people knew America was for us and not them. Kickin' ass when they had to. Lib'rals and communists and such.'

'How'd Patti wind up with Reverend Scaler?'

A shrug. 'I dunno. Just one day I heard she was getting married to Reverend Scaler. That surprised me, cuz I'd heard she had the hots for some lawyer-boy. But then I figgured she'd doped out that the Reverend could be somebody big if she grabbed control of things. That girl loved to control. If you ask me, she controlled him all the way to being rich and famous.'

'The Reverend's church was nearby?'

'Just over in Siler, little white wood place. Scaler was in his early twenties.'

'Mrs Scaler's a big deal, being on the television and all. This story you told . . . ' I shot a look at a stack of *People* magazines on the floor. 'No one ever passed this story on?'

'There was one girl in our class, she went on to college and everything. Writes those books you see at the Winn-Dixie, romance things? She was going to do a book about Patti Selmot. She was gonna write a . . . a . . . '

'Biography?'

'Yep. But when she started going back and asking people what they remembered and all, this whole car full of lawyers showed up and told her if she wrote the book, she better have proof of everything, or they were gonna make her so poor she'd think a can of beans was a Thanksgiving meal.'

'The writer dropped the project, I take it?'

'She didn't want to be poor. But who fucking does? Patti sure didn't.'

⋆   ⋆   ⋆

Dr Matthias put the label on the tube-like container, checked the information for accuracy, slipped the tube into the shock-damping package in his briefcase. It was full. In the morning he'd FedEx the package to the lab to get the tests started, the results on his desk when he returned to Mobile.

He began packing his clothes, the long journey over, a longer one about to begin.

46

I got back to the office, downloaded my information from my head to Harry's. Mrs Scaler was looking more and more like a woman whose troubled past reached straight into today.

The desk sergeant rang my phone.

'You got a caller, Carson. Some drunk. Wants to talk to, and I quote, the skinny white guy who can't comb his hair, that cop who goes around with the big black monster.'

'Hang on a sec, Sarge,' I said, punching a button. 'Lemme put it on speakerphone so the monster can hear.'

Harry rolled his chair close. I pressed *talk*.

'Detective Ryder.'

'This is Arch Fossie,' he said, his words slurred. 'I think you better get over here, Detective. The, uh, Scaler household.'

'What is — '

The phone clicked off.

The front door of the Scaler home was open. We called inside, got no response, went in cautiously, guns drawn. Fossie was in a chair in the corner, head drooping, lips wet, a bottle of whiskey in his hand. His hair stood out in puffs where he'd been scratching at his head. There was a white residue beneath his nostrils. He was a half-step short of totaled.

'What is it, Doctor?'

He waved the bottle toward the study, whiskey

342

splashing out. Harry walked to the study door, looked inside.

'Cars? Better come here.'

I left Fossie to his whiskey and walked over. Senator Hampton Custis lay sprawled on the floor, prone, face turned to the doorway.

His face had been mangled by repeated stabbings. His lips had been sliced away. One of his ears was missing. A shotgun blast had pretty much removed one leg. The torn limb had left a wide swash across the peach carpet as Custis had tried to crawl from where he'd fallen. A series of small red triangles and dots accompanied the swash: bloody high heels. Custis's tormentor had probably shot his leg first and followed with the knife as he'd crawled, performing the insane surgery.

'There's only two things cause this kind of damage,' Harry said, his voice quiet.

I nodded. 'Hate or love.'

Custis's eyes were wide and glazed and his cheeks puffed out, a white strip of paper emerging between his lips. I put on latex gloves and tugged the paper out, a wad that someone had tried to jam down his throat. I pulled it open.

The fake, computer-generated, post-surgery Patti Scaler. The beautiful Patti, where she was smiling with the breathtaking new face.

'Where is Mrs Scaler?' I asked Fossie.

'Upstairs. Locked in her room.'

I looked at the bedroom door at the top of the stairs, heard nothing. 'What happened?'

Fossie started to put the bottle to his lips. I stopped it.

'What the hell happened?'

'Patricia called Hampton Custis. Told him to come here alone, she had news. When Hamp ran inside she showed him some picture of herself, said it was what she was becoming. Just for him. They could be together, the Washington power couple.'

'Washington pow . . . ?'

'She said they no longer had to meet in secret. Life was perfect.' Fossie choked out a sound; a laugh, I suppose.

I looked at the room where Hampton Custis's body lay torn asunder.

'The senator had other ideas?' I said.

Fossie tilted the bottle to his lips, got about half in his mouth. 'He obviously hadn't figured on whatever she had planned. But it made sense to Patti. Richard was dead and the two of them could finally be together.'

Nona Jett's words about Patti Selmot rang in my head: *I'd heard she had the hots for some lawyer-boy.* Custis had started out at a law office in Silar thirty years ago.

'Custis and Patricia Scaler were lovers?'

Fossie slurped down another drink. 'On and off. She was always trying to get on him, he was always trying to keep her off. Hampton kept his distance, mostly. She scared the shit outta him.' He laughed again, a drunken gurgle. 'I used to give him Viagra mixed with yohimbe so he could get his pecker hard enough to slip into her.'

It hadn't escaped me that Fossie seemed to know the senator on a first-name basis. Not what I'd expect from a guy who presented himself as a part-time purveyor of vitamins and herbs and low-fat diets.

'So why did Custis visit?'

'The only way he stayed in office was the votes provided by Richard's flock of robots. When the great Richard Scaler said, 'Vote for my buddy Hampton Custis,' they voted in lockstep. Patti probably told Hampton if he stopped fucking her, she'd tell Richard he was fucking her.' Fossie gurgled with mirth.

'I take it Scaler didn't know of the affair?'

'If he knew, Richard was probably happy it kept her away from him.'

I said, 'You must have been close to hear all this, Doctor.'

'I've known Patti for decades.'

Decades? I filed that fact alongside the first-name familiarity with the senator.

'No, I mean today, Mr Fossie. To hear everything that was happening between the pair.'

Fossie frowned through the substances in his head. 'Oh. I was working on her meds.'

'Medicines?'

'Uh, vitamins. She needed them to help her through what she said would be a busy day. She said she wanted her head to sparkle. I did an injection, headed downstairs. I stopped to fix a drink and get a few sparklies in my own head. A few minutes later the front door opened. I . . . ' he paused, mouth open, like his engine was sputtering. It seemed my nutritionist had other medications in his bag.

'Keep going, Mr Fossie.'

'I heard Hampton call for Patti and I hid in

345

the gym, figuring they'd go upstairs and knock out a quick fuck and I could leave. I heard talk, then angry talk, then it turned real bad: Patti yelling and breaking things. Hampton was yelling, too, like with Richard gone he was telling her how it really was. Then I heard the . . . ' he blew out a long breath.

'Boom,' I finished.

'Hampton started screaming like nothing I've ever heard. It was like he was being eaten alive. I was too terrified to move.'

Fossie made a noise like a deflating cushion. I looked at Harry, then at the closed door at the top of the stairs.

Harry said, 'You want to wait for a team?'

'Miz Scaler and I have a history,' I said. 'Watch my back.'

I climbed the stairs, stood to the side of the door. Knocked gently. 'Mrs Scaler? Patricia? It's Detective Ryder.'

'It's not a good time, sir.' Her voice sounded distracted, as if she was nearing deadline on a project and I was interrupting.

'I need to come in, ma'am. Are you decent?'

'I'm a beautiful and desirous woman.'

'Yes, ma'am. You're a lovely woman. May I come in?'

'Oh, I suppose.'

I said, 'You don't have a gun or anything, do you?'

'I put it back in the locker. I was finished with it.'

I took a deep breath and pushed open the door to see Patricia Scaler's slender back across the wide room. She was looking out the window, framed in light, her black spaghetti-strap dress cut low and hemmed high. It was an amazing body for a woman nearing fifty. She wore sling-back high heels. Scarlet smudges had followed her across the carpet.

I moved closer. Her hands were touching at her face.

'Ma'am? Are you all right?'

She made a mewing sound and I advanced another few steps, eyes adjusting to the light. Her hand was at her face, elbow jerking back and forth, like a fiddler.

Or a butcher cutting meat.

She turned and stopped my heart. The right side of her face was missing. She threw something my way. It landed on the carpet at my feet. A rag of severed flesh.

'I won't be needing that any more,' she said, her open teeth and gums glistening with blood, one eye revealed almost fully. 'I'm getting a new one.'

She started to laugh, a wet sound.

★   ★   ★

Tom Mason rolled up at the scene. He'd been working the political side, keeping the brass clued in, getting timelines down. Mrs Scaler had been transported to the hospital forty minutes ago. There were no flashing lights on the vehicles out front, kept to a minimum while things were being sorted out.

Tom held his hat low in respect as the

347

senator's body was rolled out the door on a gurney. He turned back to us.

'The senator's aides say he received a call two hours back, looked frightened, jumped in his car.'

'How's Mrs Scaler?' I asked. 'Have you heard?'

Tom shot a glance at his watch. 'Sedated. She was screaming when she arrived at the hospital, trying to tear the rest of her face off. A shrink at the hospital thinks she's gone fully round the bend.'

'She's always been at the turn in the bend, Tom,' I said, unable to shake the image of Patti Scaler turning to me with half a face. 'Today she had the current behind her.'

Tom shot a look at the techs, busy photographing and cataloging the bizarre scene. He took my elbow and pulled me to a corner.

'What's behind all this, Carson? Scaler. Tutweiler. Meltzer. A US senator, for crying out loud. What's going on?'

I could only offer my shaking head as an answer.

'I have no idea, Tom. We're sure it started in the way-back. Unfortunately, we may have run out of people who can tell us anything.'

Tom sighed, nodded, walked over to Clair. She was directing her tech staff, displaying her typical calm in the middle of chaos. Watching Clair's serene command I felt a convergence of emotions, then a sense of relaxation; strange feelings to have arise in that troubled house.

'Hello?' said a voice from behind me.

I turned to the open front door and saw a small man in his sixties, suited, his sharp face like an anxious hawk. A neighbor, I thought, drawn by the commotion.

'Yes, sir?' I said.

'I wanted to speak to Richard Scaler. I work for him.'

The man looked guileless, as if he really expected the Reverend. I said, 'You haven't been watching the news, I take it?'

'I've been out of the country. Often in isolated places. I'm not big on news anyway.'

'Who are you?' I asked.

'My name is Dr Kurt Matthias. I've been doing research for Reverend Scaler.'

I saw a name scrawled on a property transfer. *Kurt . . . Not Matthews, Masters, Mathers . . . Matthias.* Was this also the man who'd swabbed the Q-tip through Shanelle's mouth?

My heart started beating hard against my ribs. I gestured for him to step over the threshold, enter.

I said, 'What's your connection to a house below Coden, Doctor? A place near the Gulf in an abandoned shrimping village. There is a connection, right?'

A sharp frown. 'Excuse me, but how do you know about — '

'Please answer my question, sir.'

'I used the Reverend's money to purchase the property. I needed an isolated place to house a young couple and their child until finding better accommodations in the city.'

Dr Matthias's eyes strayed to the threshold of the study, saw the dark swashes of red.

'Something terrible has happened, hasn't it?' he said.

47

Harry and I took Matthias to a sunroom at the back of the house, far from the din of the investigation. It was bright and cheerful and at odds with everything the house had come to represent. We told Matthias we suspected his young couple — Anak and Rebecca — were dead, but were clinging to hope that the child had survived.

The news hit him like a falling wall. Matthias needed several moments to gather himself, seeming to drag his emotions into a box, storing them for later. He switched into a scientific mode, calm and clinical. He sat in a chair beside a potted fern, tented his fingers beneath his lips, and frowned.

I said, 'The residents of that house, Doctor . . . what was so special about them?'

'Anak and Rebecca? They were simply two young people who, by nothing more than chance, carried a wide variety of genetic material from around the world.'

'What were you using them for?' Harry said.

'Study. Trying to advance a theory.'

'Some people think you were playing God,' I said. 'Breeding people. Creating Frankensteins. What's your answer to that?'

Matthias looked at me like I had started clucking like a chicken.

'Breeding? Playing God? Making Frankensteins?

My God, man, what are you talking about?'

'Cloning a new race,' I said, stealing from Spider's addled jargon. 'Creating super-humans.'

Matthias closed his eyes and his face fell into his hands. He muttered about ignorance. He stood wearily, his shoulders slumped, and turned to Harry.

'You know people with sickle-cell anemia, Detective. Is that not so?'

'I do.'

'All are of African-American descent, right?'

Harry nodded.

'People of Jewish descent are prone to Tay-Sachs disease. Many Asians have difficulty digesting milk. Some populations have long life spans. Others are prone to schizophrenia. Some resist cardiomyopathy better than others. Every disparate population has a multiplicity of positive and negative genetic dispositions. I'm talking statistics, here. The actual differences are miniscule.'

Harry said, 'What's this have to do with . . . '

'Hear me out. What would happen if you ate little more than fatty meat, with vegetables almost unheard-of in your diet?'

'My arteries would clog and I'd tip over dead.'

'The Inuit and Laplanders eat vast amounts of meat and blubber and suffer no deleterious effects. Why?'

Harry said, 'It's not something I think about.'

'It's what I've been thinking about all my life,' Matthias said. 'I developed a theory, and I'm doing research. That's all.'

'Further research into what?'

351

'Into where the finger of God is pushing us.'

'Pardon?' Harry said. 'The finger of God?'

'Reverend Scaler preferred that phrase, which was fine. I lean toward a more historical perspective.'

'I'm listening,' I said.

Matthias walked across the room to a spreading areca palm. He touched the fronds, as if inspecting them.

'Near its beginning, the human race split into various tribes and went separate ways, geographically speaking. Over time, genetic positives and negatives arose in these separate populations. When disparate populations combine, it appears that the remediating, or, if you wish, the good genes, eventually triumph over the misfires.' He paused, showed a sad smile. 'We are, in many ways, the cure for what ails us.'

'You're saying that intermingling of these genetic pools results in . . . '

'Superior resistance to disease, which translates to better health and longer lives. Higher overall intelligence might result, and perhaps even more benefits. With the world shrinking, these tribes are coming together. Take a genetic union — marriage — between European and African genes; rare in this country until recently. But now?'

I shrugged. 'No big deal, especially to younger folks.'

'The same applies on the West Coast, but, from a statistical point of view, more Asian genes are entering the gene-pool stew. A person from Japan or China might marry a person with a black father and a white mother. Or someone from Mexico or Central America. The offspring move to Minneapolis, marry Swedish-Germans. In human genetics, this is climbing toward betterment.'

I thought of a line from the poet Theodore Roethke about a lowly worm making its way up a winding staircase. Had Roethke been analogizing Humankind crawling up the spiraling staircase of DNA?

I said, 'But there's still much more to combine, right?'

'Polynesian genes, genotypes from the Indian subcontinent, Siberia, tribes along the Amazon, genes from peoples in Andean countries . . . the list goes on and on.'

'Tell me more about the couple and their child,' Harry said.

'I discovered them in Vancouver, a wide-stanced pair, genetically speaking. She's Jewish and Oriental with significant ties to South American genetics. His lineage is Inuit and Scandinavian, Eastern Europe and sub-Saharan African just at the parent level. The child is a rainbow of genetic input.'

'You discovered this by cruising for hookers?' Harry asked.

Matthias sighed. 'I seek out all manner of people for genetic samples. I swab mouths for DNA. It's one metric to determine rapidity of genetic mingling. Port-city prostitutes mingle more widely than most.'

'Sailors from everywhere.'

'I saw Anak and Rebecca at a park, with the

child. They looked interesting so I swabbed. When testing revealed the breadth of their genetic experience, I paid them to come here. I plan to put them to work in my new genetics lab. It was Reverend Scaler's suggestion to keep the couple isolated for a few weeks.'

Just in case someone pried into the story before he told it his way, I figured.

'New lab in Mobile?'

'Part of a huge grant from Reverend Scaler — his generosity has been boundless. He called his sponsorship of my work part of his penance. I'd do the research and he'd explain it to people.'

'That project's dead now, I take it?'

'Goodness, no. The money is in place. We met quite privately at an attorney's office for the arrangements some weeks back. Not the usual attorney, I gathered, from all the secrecy.'

Carleton was cut out. Scaler was stepping fully away from his past. Carleton had felt Scaler slipping away, had high anxiety at losing a major client.

'How did you hook up with Richard Scaler?' I asked.

Matthias looked uncomfortable, cleared his throat. 'Eight years back I did prototype research. I suggested if pure African genetics were bred out of existence, it would be a good thing. I was leading to the positives of broader genetic stances and could have said the same about Caucasians, Asians, Australian Aborigines . . . ' Matthias looked disgusted and threw his hands in the air.

'You stirred up a hornet's nest,' Harry said.

'People concentrated on the math, ignored the bottom line: When races disappear into one all-consuming genetic pool, we're an improved evolutionary product. Instead, I got an immediate reputation as a racist, sentences from my paper used out of context. Drooling white-supremacist morons began quoting me.'

'Scaler called you to confirm his views on racial superiority?'

'Obviously his intent, to affirm life-long tenets. I said my research was in a final phase, that I'd send synopses in layman's language. He asked for the scientific research as well.'

'What was his initial response to your research, given that it was the opposite of what he'd expected?'

'His first instinct was falling into rhetorical evasions, rationalizations, denials.'

'Just what I'd expect,' I said.

'But in the end, Detective, Richard was smart enough to realize he was wrong. I think he found great strength in order to face the mirror and declare himself incorrect. Mr Scaler was far smarter than people gave him credit for, by the way. A more enlightened upbringing might have given us a scientist.'

I looked at Harry. He'd suspected Scaler had more depth than the man presented. I'd viewed the Reverend almost as simplistically as Scaler had viewed the world for most of his life.

Matthias said, 'My travels and sampling show a world moving rather well toward assimilation, my terms. Richard spoke of the finger of God. Of lost tribes gathering. To each his own.'

355

'How long will this assimilation take, Doctor?' Harry said.

'At current rates of genetic transfer? Thirty or forty generations. A thousand years or so.'

'Answer me this, Doc,' Harry said. 'The child. Is she different than the rest of us?'

Matthias smiled. 'The child is a single instance, and statistically insignificant, but I hope to find her discrete genetic strains have canceled certain harmful genes in favor of positive ones. She should be a rather healthy child. That's about all.'

I thought of all the doctors and nurses amazed by Noelle's resistance to infection. Then I thought of Mr Mix-up, Ms Best's poor doomed pooch.

I said, 'Noelle's as healthy as a mongrel dog.'

'Odd analogy,' Matthias said. 'But it has merit.'

We arranged to meet with Matthias in the morning when things were less chaotic. Harry and I returned to the car. He put the car in gear and pulled away, shaking his head in disbelief.

'It appears that instead of fighting, your average warring tribes should be . . .'

I held up my hands, making an O with my left thumb and forefinger, poking through with my right forefinger.

'Make Love, Not War,' I said. 'The hippies were right.'

'Imagine what Meltzer thought when he heard of Matthias's research via the ever-vigilant Patricia Scaler.'

'Race mixing is good? In an eye-blink,

everything the white supremacists ever stood for is wrong. It would cost him adoration. He didn't give a damn about anything but the symbolic kid. So he went after her. Twice.'

Harry thought about my words for a couple of miles.

'It doesn't fit, Carson. Why not use Douthitt again? He hadn't been compromised by Bailes. Why didn't Meltzer keep using Douthitt as his eyes in the hospital?'

I shook my head, perplexed. Harry drove a mile. I saw his hand tighten on the wheel. 'Jesus, Carson, what if two camps were trying to grab Noelle?'

My turn to think away a couple of miles. Two separate entities trying to grab Noelle explained a lot.

'I like it,' I said. 'It works.'

'What we do know is that white-power bikers are in the mix, and that leads to Meltzer and Baker. Let's aim a hard eye that direction.'

48

Thirty minutes later we were a half-block away from Baker's house in a 1991 Dodge Caravan with rust holes in the paint, giving it a speckled look. The left front tire was flat. The seats had springs poking through.

The van was courtesy of the metal-recycling firm next door. When we showed ID and told them we needed something looking like an abandoned vehicle for surveillance they were happy to oblige, dragging the Caravan to the watch point with a tow truck. It looked at home on the grubby, barren street.

Harry had offered money for the rental.

'You after that guy in that house next door?' Tony, the manager of the scrap yard, nodded toward Baker's property. 'The muscle-bound asshole?'

Harry nodded, pulling a couple twenties from his wallet. 'Yep.'

'We keep security dogs here at night. Or did until someone shot 'em dead. Started just after that guy moved in a few months back.' Tony pushed Harry's money away. 'Shit, man, you get rid of that bastard I'll give you cars all day long.'

We hunched down in the seats and waited. Night started to fall, a few stars pressing against the blue, the moon at the far corner of the sky. The air was still and hot and smelled of the slack-tide on the Intercoastal Waterway four hundred feet distant. A barge tow pushed up the broad canal, the throb of its diesels rattling the loose metal on the Caravan. Two windows were out on the van and we swatted mosquitoes from our faces.

After a few minutes Harry nudged me with his elbow, pointed down the street. I peeped above the dash and saw a blue truck roll by, a loaf of bread painted on the side.

'So?'

'It's the third time that bread truck's gone by. Think there's much need for bread this time of night?'

We watched the truck continue down the street, turn into a stand of trees beside a condemned house half enveloped in kudzu.

'Whoops, lights behind,' Harry said, ducking.

I followed suit, dropping toward the floor. A vehicle rumbled beside us and a flashlight lit the interior of the van.

'Anything?' a voice said.

'Hunh-uh. Dead metal.' A low laugh. 'Prob'ly ought to be hauled to the yard over there and ground up.'

'How much longer?' the first voice said.

'Ten minutes, give or take.'

'Let's book.'

The vehicle rolled away. Harry and I simultaneously let out our breath.

'You recognize the second voice?' I asked Harry.

'Sure enough,' he said. 'It's my old buddy, Sheriff Briscoe.'

We sat up enough to see the taillights of a

dark, nondescript sedan of American vintage glide past the house where the bread truck was parked. The brake lights brightened on the car for a few seconds, then it moved on.

'The car stopped for a three-count,' Harry said. 'Conversation?'

'Makes sense,' I said. 'What you think's happening?'

'Seems like we'll know in ten minutes or so.'

It was twelve minutes. We felt the presence before we saw them, ten fat Harley hogs thundering from the main road a half-mile away. We sucked in our breath and slunk low in the van. Their bouncing headlamps shivered through the Caravan and their engines rattled my sternum.

'Sounds like Meltzer's security detail,' I said. 'Wonder if he's along for the ride?'

Harry peered between the wheel and the dash. 'Meltzer like to travel in a white step van? Ladder up the back?'

'Eighty-eight on that.'

'What?'

I chuckled. 'I mean, ten-four.' Something felt good inside me; I felt light, happy. It started after we'd spoken with Matthias.

Harry said, 'Our band of gypsies rolled up to Baker's. Someone's out of the step van, walking into the headlights — Baker. He's unlocking the gate so the party from hell can drive through. I just had a thought, Cars . . . '

'Probably the same as mine. Noelle could be there. If it's Meltzer who sponsored the grab, maybe he's moving her out of his place and to Baker's.'

'There's Meltzer,' Harry said. 'He's barking orders at the bikers, heading toward the house. He's carrying something, a big-ass satchel. It's kid-sized.'

'Stay cool,' I said. 'What's happening?'

'Baker's doing a wide-foot stance like some goddamn cartoon Nazi. He's wearing a Sam Browne belt, a pair of sidearms. Meltzer's heading around back, a couple of the bikers flanking him. I think . . . uh oh.'

'What?'

'The bread truck. It's backing out, lights off. The contingent at Baker's can't see it.'

I sat up, looked down the street. The bread truck was coming at Baker's house backwards. We heard tires screech from behind us as the sedan from a few minutes back roared past, two others in its wake. Within four seconds there were three cars bouncing into Baker's front yard. And a bread truck.

We heard yelling. Orders barked. Saw lights from every direction, pouring from the cars, from the truck. Everything turned still for a half-heartbeat. Then the gunfire started.

'It's a raid,' Harry yelled. 'Someone's attacking Meltzer and the bikers.'

He started to jump from the car. I grabbed his arm, held tight. It was like restraining a buffalo. 'Stay down!' I yelled as a stray bullet whanged off the Caravan.

'Noelle's in all that,' he yelled.

'Let's go around the side,' I said, jumping out and staying low, Harry following. The melee was in the front and to the side of the house; it looked like the bikers had taken cover inside the house and on the porch. The other side was returning fire as fast as the bikers could pump it out. I heard words yelled through a bullhorn, couldn't make them out.

We scrambled along the fence line toward the waterway. I heard an explosion, like a grenade. More gunfire, volleys.

'There,' Harry yelled. I spun my head, saw Meltzer and Baker crouched low and moving through the back yard toward the boat, one of the bikers close behind, a shotgun in his hand. Baker had the satchel slung over a thick shoulder.

The fence ended at the waterline. The tide was slack and dropping, giving us a few feet of rip-rap to walk on. We stumbled over the rocks, staying in the shadows of scrub brush at the rear of the fence line, trying to move fast while not stumbling into the canal.

The pier was sixty feet long, eight wide, paralleling the waterway. We clambered on to one end as the trio was coming through the gate. I saw another biker in the distance, near the house, booking toward the boat.

'Freeze,' Harry yelled, a bull elephant on full trumpet.

The biker whipped the shotgun up, but double-taps from Harry and I hit him at the same time, punching four holes across his chest. The shotgun hit the water a half-second after his body did.

Baker turned and fired and we hit the pier. We rolled off on the side with the rip-rap, sheltered by the dock. I saw Baker jump aboard the boat, the satchel bouncing over his shoulder. I laid out three shots and leapt back on to the dock. Meltzer was frozen in front of us, eyes wide in terror. Up front, on the street, it sounded like the Fourth of July.

I saw Harry pick up the diminutive Meltzer and hurl him into the side of the boat like a rag doll. A biker in the back yard fired at us, the shots thudding into the boat behind me. Harry ducked beside the pier pilings and began returning fire.

I belly-crawled beside the boat, heard a hatch pop open, Baker suddenly above me. I launched up and into him before he could level the pistol. We fell to the dock, tangled together and rolling side to side. He was fiercely strong, pummeling while I tried to keep him clinched. Harry was thirty feet away, pinned behind a piling, firing into the yard, unable to move from his cover. I was fighting from a defensive position, lacking the strength of Baker. He slammed short jabs into my side, jackhammers against my ribs. I felt my strength fading as his hands found my throat.

My only chance was the water. I bucked, Baker atop me, thumbs trying to crush my windpipe. I wrenched again, found my head and shoulders over the water. I bucked a final time, sucking as much air as my lungs could capture.

We plunged into the murky, deep-dredged channel. Instead of trying to break free of Baker, I hugged him as tight as a lover, kicking for the bottom.

Hold on.

He pushed, pummeled, wrenched. Hands and legs flailed and grabbed. Blows rained into my sides, thankfully slowed by water. My ears filled with the sound of my heart and lungs screaming for air. *Hold on.* Baker gave up fighting me to fight for the surface. I felt his terror. *Hold on.* I heard his scream turn to bubbles. I felt his chest expand as his lungs sucked in water. Baker drew another breath of water. I felt him shudder and the weight in my hands went slack.

I slid upwards over the body and broke the surface, gasping; the oily, fuel-laden air was as sweet as honey. I looked around. Harry was a dozen feet away on the prow of the boat. He let out a long breath. There were no sounds of gunfire.

'Baker?' Harry asked.

'I'm standing on him.'

I dog-paddled to the boat, moss or seaweed on my face. I pushed it away. It kept sticking. No, not seaweed, I noted in the light from the pier lamps. Hundred-dollar bills.

Harry pulled me from the water. Meltzer lay crumpled against a piling, regaining consciousness. I saw the satchel, upside-down, beside it dozens of blocks of banded money, some of which had broken open and tumbled into the water. I also saw several kilo-sized bricks of plastic-encased white powder.

My heart fell. 'It wasn't Noelle.'

Harry shook his head. Meltzer was fully conscious now, cowering on the pier.

'D-d-don't hurt m-me,' the pink lips said. 'Puh-puh-please.'

364

Harry made a big deal of slamming a new clip in his weapon, racking the slide. He knelt beside Meltzer and pointed the muzzle at his temple.

'Where's the kid, Arnold? I'll kill you if you don't tell me.'

'I d-d-don't know. I suh-swear. Puh-please don't k-k-k-k-k — -'

'TELL ME!'

Meltzer pissed himself and began to weep. Hunched shapes moved through the shadowed back yard. A bullhorn voice broke the silence.

'Drop your weapons and lock your fingers behind your necks.'

'We're cops!' I yelled back. 'Detectives Carson Ryder and Harry Nautilus, Mobile Police. All is secure.'

The shapes moved closer. One of them was wearing a cowboy hat.

'Holy mother of God,' Sheriff Briscoe said. 'What the hell are you doing here?'

'I believe that's our question,' Harry said.

Briscoe scowled at the cowering Arnold Meltzer, then saw the stash Harry'd dumped from the satchel.

'Got the dope and money,' Briscoe yelled over his shoulder as a tall black man in a suit walked up. The suit had sand along one side, like he'd been firing from the ground.

The black man knelt, pulled a pen from his pocket, poked a hole in one of the bags of white powder. He wet a forefinger, tapped it to the hole, brought it to his lips.

He grinned like tasting the mother lode of Beluga caviar.

49

I stood in the front of Baker's yard and watched three medic vans haul off the casualties: three dead bikers and four gunshot injuries. Five bikers had surrendered. A police boat was in the channel with grappling hooks, fishing for Baker's body.

I spoke to the cops on the scene and discovered Harry and I had stumbled into a joint jurisdictional action: DEA, ICE, Staties and county force. The lesser players were driving away as the forensics types moved in to document the event.

I found the remaining cast sitting around a table on the patio. Someone had thoughtfully supplied a couple of six-packs of Sam Adams beer.

'So it was all an act for Baker's benefit?' Harry was saying to Briscoe. 'You're not a cracker asshole.'

The sheriff sighed, took a suck of brew, and pushed back his hat. 'I probably am. That's what my college-girl daughter thinks, anyway. She's at Radcliffe — scholarship, thank God; I could never afford that shit.' He looked at Harry. 'You asked about a kid?'

'I thought it was what Meltzer was carrying.'

'We been watching the little Aryan prick for months, with special emphasis on the last two weeks. We got tipped he was going to get stressed. Maybe enough to move his stash. We knew Meltzer figured big in the H and meth trade — him and his biker yahoos — but he stayed insulated. Turned out our tipster was dead-on and we got Meltzer side by side with about a million bucks of pure smack. But in all that watching we never once saw a baby, Detective Nautilus, I'm sorry to say.'

'This tip was anonymous?' I asked.

Briscoe nodded. 'But it had to be someone who really knew Meltzer's ways.'

'The tip was in future tense?' I asked. 'Meltzer was *going* to get stressed.'

'For sure. I could gauge Meltzer's activity by Baker's comings and goings, running off every time his real boss called, the miniature *Fuhrer*. Baker'd started spending half his time away lately, being Meltzer's private SS guard-boy.'

'Did you know about Baker before you hired him?'

The tall black federal agent had been leaning against the wall a dozen feet away, hands in his pockets. He stepped forward.

'Yes he did. And I asked Elvin to hire Baker. Sheriff Briscoe and I have worked together before. He was the only guy I knew with the smarts to gain Baker's trust, allowing Baker just enough leash that, when we pulled, it might drag Meltzer along.'

'And some perceived threat put Meltzer together with the dope?' I asked.

'We knew the stash wasn't near his house. Turns out dope in Meltzer's possession gets parked in the basement of a low-life ex-doctor named Fossie. His main clientele is — '

'Whoa up,' I said, startled. 'Fossie was a doctor?'

'Not in years. He lost his license for dispensing controlled substances without proper prescriptions. Plus he'd started concocting his own goofy stuff to take people up, down, in between, every which way — a real Dr Feelgood type. The past few years he's sold himself as a nutrition expert, got an online degree for fifty bucks or whatever. I think he needs to see himself as a doctor type, an authority.'

'He was Patricia Scaler's buddy,' I said. 'He made up herbal concoctions for her.'

'Nice friend to have around if you've got a taste for head travel. Fossie would have gladly zoomed the lady wherever she wanted to go. Fossie's got a grubby little office out on Hodkins Road that's big with the white-supremacist bikers and similar low-lifes. The asshole's waiting room looks like a casting call for contract killers. Think he's handing out nutritional supplements? Plus he runs a kinda Red Cross station at white-power rallies.'

I shook my head. I'd seen Fossie's back while he stitched up the hapless Spider. It hit me that Fossie's 'nutrition clinic' was two miles from the ambush, probably where the biker I'd shot had shown up. And with all the pure heroin around, it would have been no problem to load a couple of syringes with hotshots for Tut and Chinese Red, then laying a few bags of pure H into the hands of local junkies, making Red's death one of several OD's, no big deal. The conspirators dappled a pair of Red's pants with Scaler's blood and the seamy headlines were under way.

Fossie also made a perfect fit elsewhere.

'How about Fossie for a case of pancreatic cancer?' I said to Harry. 'Picture Fossie — still a real doctor to a poor, dumb SOB like Bailes — putting his hand on Bailes's shoulder: 'I hate to have to tell you this, son, but in a few weeks you're gonna die like flames are eating out your insides. Here's a few pills, Terry. Go forth and do something to make your mama proud.''

★　★　★

Harry and I traded cards with the participants, knowing we'd all soon be contributors to endless pages of interlinked reports on the converged cases. We headed off to retrieve our vehicle from the scrap yard. Harry sat in the driver's seat, but didn't fire up the engine. We sat quietly for several minutes before he turned to me.

'Uh, Carson.' Harry said. 'Fossie was mixing up stuff for you, right?'

I had been staring out into the night and thinking the same thing. My first freaky incidence was winging the table into the camera equipment at Bailes's mother's house. I'd started my day with a few of Fossie's capsules. The same for everything: the scam at the prison, my fight with the hapless Beefer, my anger at Clair, the gun-blazing march into the bikers . . . all on days I'd taken Fossie's vitamin potion. What had Ernie Hemmings said about Stenebrexin?

' . . . *mixed with a cocktail of meth and*

Prozac, the stuff interacts poorly. It can lead to odd behavior, anxiety, acting out. Doesn't take much, either.'

'Jesus,' I whispered. 'I got doped. Fossie was screwing with my head.'

'Why, you think?'

'Probably thought it would give him more control while he filled me with lies about Scaler, which I expect it did. I also expect that my herbal sleeping pills were the more traditional sort.'

Harry said, 'When was the last time you took that shit?'

'I got tired of drinking perfume tea and eating healthy things that tasted like hay two days ago. Dropped the vites, too.'

Harry grinned. 'Saved by fried chicken and gravy. That's my boy. You been feeling any different?'

I looked out the window, saw a gurney being pushed from Baker's backyard toward the ambulance out front. They'd found the body. It was draped with a sheet, the sheet soaked with sea water dripping from the corpse.

'Yeah,' I said. 'I'm suddenly feeling a lot better.'

50

Harry and I were in the swing state between adrenalin rush and total burnout. We headed homeward to try and bag some recovery time before tomorrow renewed the hunt for Noelle.

I fell asleep without Fossie's pills, but it only lasted four hours. I was up before dawn, on the deck, drinking coffee and shoveling cheese grits and bacon into my food hole. My mind felt clear and charged full, and I paced the deck for an hour, unraveling a timeline intermingled with the cast of characters. The timeline was almost four decades long.

I sat at my computer. Did a Google search. Found what I'd half-expected. I called Harry as I was driving to work, said we were running up to the SLDP's offices, I needed to ask a couple more questions.

Harry hadn't slept much either, and was still ragged from the previous night's search of the 'net. I drove to Montgomery and let him bag out in the back seat for a change. He made a whistling sound when he snored. I awakened him at a gasoline stop outside of Montgomery. He headed into the station and brushed his teeth, splashed on some after-shave. Got in the front seat and away we flew.

'So you think Ben Belker has something we could use?' Harry asked.

'Worth a shot,' was all I said.

We entered Ben's office. He gestured toward seats but I preferred to stand.

I said, 'I looked up a few things on the internet, Ben. Your father died eight months ago. I'm sorry.'

He pushed up his black glasses and rubbed his eyes. 'Thanks, Carson. I appreciate that.'

'Why didn't you mention anything?'

'I don't like to talk about it. Dad spent his life in pain. Growing up, I had to watch him try and walk, doing his best to hide his misery so we could all live something like a real life. He was legally blind from blows to his eyes. His whole life was torn away from him.'

'All in the span of a horrific beating,' I said.

Ben said, 'I hope whoever who did it pays by burning in hell.'

I leaned against a bookcase filled with hate literature. 'They're paying now, Ben. Scaler, Tutweiler, Meltzer, Custis. Maybe Fossie and Carleton. Paying it all back, right?'

A beat. Ben Belker's eyes flickered, then affected perplexed. 'I don't understand what you're talking about, Carson.'

'Your father came to the South to fight for the poor. He went to town one night, stopped at a diner. He was abducted by racists. They took him to a field and crippled him for life.'

'Yes.'

I looked at Harry, saw a frown. I turned back to Ben.

'Is that how it really was, Ben?'

'Of course. Everyone knows it. My father was a legend.'

I pulled a chair up close to Ben and sat it backwards, arms crossed on the back, looking straight into my friend's face.

'I think something else happened that night, Ben. I think a woman came on to your father. Her name was Patti Selmot. Plain in the face but with a body that'd give a corpse a hard-on. Your father went trotting after her with his tongue hanging to his knees.'

Ben leapt to his feet. 'You're *lying*.'

I pointed to his computer. 'Your father's death sent you on the trail of his attackers. Years of gathering information all came together and you discovered what really happened that night.'

Ben pointed a quivering finger at me, his face red. His eyes closed. He turned away, fists clenched, but his shoulders were slumped in defeat.

'Luring men to beatings was a hobby to that crazy bitch,' Ben hissed.

'The truth was a blow to your father's legacy,' I said, my voice low and reasonable. 'Thomas Belker beaten not over human rights, but over a hick drugstore bimbo.'

Ben collapsed into his chair, dry-washed his face.

'When Meltzer discovered my father was Jewish, he went crazy with a ball bat, getting the others to join in the fun. All the time she was laughing, urging them on.'

'What was Scaler's part in all this?'

'There was a big manhunt when Dad was

373

found, the FBI was involved. It scared hell out of the attackers. They went to their ideological twin, Richard Scaler, and told him they'd been trying to send a do-gooder Jewboy back to New York, but things got a bit out of hand.'

Harry said, 'Scaler helped them with their alibi.'

Ben nodded. 'He swore they were members of a night bible study and had all been in attendance.'

'The Feds bought Scaler's story?' I asked.

'It was almost forty years ago, Carson. Every fourth male in the county would've beaten up a Yankee organizer. The Feds had a suspect list fifteen pages long. The case went nowhere.'

I put the missing links in the chain. 'The perpetrators stayed free and helped one another through the years, bound by criminality and mutual silence. Three months ago, Scaler began re-thinking his life, having doubts, the great crippler of ideologues. Scaler hired Matthias for verification that Scaler's superior-white-folks concepts were correct. But this time, Matthias had the full story.'

Ben said, 'It shook Scaler to his core. He felt his soul was in danger. He was starting his amends through a major announcement, that the tribes of the earth were coming together.'

'How did you discover Scaler's change of heart?' I asked. 'Through your contacts?'

Harry stepped up. 'Mrs Herdez, right?'

'Close, Detective,' Ben said. 'Luna Martinez was picking up her aunt after work one day when Scaler asked for help with his computer. It had frozen while he was writing his journal. He knew Ms Martinez was a programmer. He didn't know she was a long-time sympathizer with the SLDP.' He paused. 'That's all I'll say.'

'It's enough.' I imagined when opportunity presented Ms Martinez continued to check on what Scaler'd been writing. Or planted a worm in his computer that piped his writings to her.

'Is Carleton in on this? We had him scared to death.'

'Carleton knew Reverend Scaler was changing his corporation and holdings in major ways, liquidating some, restructuring others. And that he was being left out. The bottom line is that Kingdom College was dissolving, the money quietly moving to genetic research. Carleton didn't know the why behind the move, and not knowing had him spooked. He's not part of the overall nastiness.'

'What do you know about Meltzer trying to steal the kid?'

'Meltzer is sick and twisted. He made enough money running drugs to do anything he wants. But what he needs is the adoration of his squirmy little followers. He looks at his greasy pamphlets and sees *Mein Kampf*. He looks out at two hundred people at a rally and sees fifty thousand.'

'Noelle threatened all that,' Harry said.

Ben nodded. 'She was a dagger poised at the heart of his organization.'

Harry crossed the room, head angled in thought. He sat on the desk beside Ben, studied him.

'I'm hearing individual stories,' Harry said.

'Mama Scaler losing her hold on hubby, Meltzer losing his reason for existence, Tutweiler losing a high-paying position at Kingdom College, putting his high-priced habit in jeopardy. Custis would lose the political support of Richard Scaler, dooming him in the next election. All your father's assailants are being set up to fall down.'

Ben looked up at my partner.

'And?'

Harry said, 'I'm not hearing the pivotal moment from you, buddy.'

'Pivotal moment? You lost me, Detective.'

'How did the others discover Scaler's plan? These separate stories had to reach critical mass somehow. Otherwise Scaler goes on TV, makes big news about his conversion to science and genetics. There'd be too much media light on him and the story for the others to get away with foul play.'

Ben shrugged. 'I saw conditions were right for a fire, so I, uh, threw a match.'

'Explain,' Harry said.

'Scaler left town on business and I created a bogus file that showed communiqués with Matthias, aspects of Matthias's research, the young couple and the baby. The file . . . Ms Martinez left it for Patricia Scaler to find. It suggested what Scaler was planning.'

'Which crazy Patti takes to her psycho buddy Meltzer, saying we gotta cut hubby down and tar him thick. Turn anything that might ever come to light in hidden Scaler writings or tapes into the ramblings of a twisted, lying pervert by smearing him in the media. Destroying any credibility he had or would ever have.'

Ben nodded. 'Plus I, uh, maybe wrote things a bit sensationally for added effect.'

'The couple and the baby,' Harry said. 'You sensationalized that?'

'A little.'

'How?' Harry's voice was a whisper.

'Maybe I used the words 'clone' and 'superbaby' and a few other words to suggest that . . . '

'YOU ASSHOLE!' Harry roared.

Ben Belker levitated from his chair, whirled in the air with Harry's hands at his collar, slammed high against the wall, papers flying, monitor crashing to the floor.

'YOU LIGHT DYNAMITE AND THROW IT RIGHT WHERE THE KID IS?'

'It was dumb,' Ben croaked, trying to push Harry's hands from his throat. 'I wanted to start . . . something, anything. To get the bastards . . . who broke my father.'

I jumped to Harry, put my hand on his arm. 'Let him down, bro. It's in the past.'

'You self-centered idiot!' Harry spat as Ben's feet regained the floor. 'You . . . you . . . '

Harry couldn't think of anything bad enough to call Ben. He walked to Ben's desk, slammed his hand down. It sounded like a bomb. Ben righted the fallen chair and sat rubbing his throat. He took a deep breath, collected himself. His face went blank.

'I realized my error in planning,' Ben said without emotion, his tone as mechanical as a robot. 'I discovered my mistake and made corrections. Me and me alone. No one else assisted in anything and it was all my doing.'

I stared at Ben. It was worded like a prepared statement.

'What the hell does that mean?' Harry snarled. 'You sound like a lawyer.'

'Everyone has alibis,' Ben said quietly. 'And they're damn good ones.'

'What are you talking about, Ben?' I said.

Ben closed his eyes like the recording was over. Harry grabbed my elbow, pulled me toward the door.

'Let's got outta here before I strangle the guy, Carson.'

We went out and climbed into the car, Harry still upset.

'Tossing gas on a fire.' Harry shook his head. 'No freaking idea which way it would burn, only that flames would shoot everywhere. First it burns the Rev. to the ground, then Lady MacScaler figures Custis can now ascend to Washington and they'll be the new Bill and Hill or whatever. Meanwhile, Meltzer's fuck-up bikers draw him into the suspect picture and he tries to move his stash.' He put the car in gear.

'Just a minute,' I said. The wide-shouldered redneck in the truck was still there. I jogged to the truck. The guy pulled his gray cowboy hat way down, turned away. I rapped my knuckles on the door.

'Whattya want?' the mouth grunted.

'Thanks,' I said.

'For what?'

'For telling me to go right at the rally.'

Almost imperceptibly, the hat nodded.

51

Harry and I got back to the department at eleven a.m. The sun was high and bright. White gulls keened in the air. We stood on Government Street for a few minutes to shake off our morning with Ben Belker, let the sun bake it from our clothes. After that we'd go sit our desks and wait for something to happen, hoping best, thinking worst.

I looked south. There was little pedestrian traffic, a few businessmen types, a clot of tourists with Hawaiian shirts and neck-slung cameras, typical.

A half-block away I saw a man and a woman in their early twenties walking toward the department. The man looked like an escapee from the Wild West: tall, wide-shouldered, bearded, wearing mud-encrusted denim. The woman was petite, wearing a long white dress over her slender form, the dress also smeared with dirt and mud. She had a white dressing taped to her forehead. The couple looked worn but joyful, the only people to crawl unscathed from a plane crash.

The man was carrying a bundle, held tight to his wide chest. The woman touched at the bundle like it held a magic potion.

I pulled Harry's sleeve, pointed. We ran to the pair, our hearts wild with hope.

★ ★ ★

379

It was Anak and Rebecca. And their child. The couple told a fantastic tale of being sent to the small house near the Gulf, waiting for more permanent lodging. A group of attackers had arrived from the front. Rebecca ran out the back with her baby in her arms. The man remained inside to fight, wielding a rusty harpoon from the corner. The door had exploded open and a man had jumped in firing a shotgun.

Anak's harpoon had connected.

Out back, Rebecca saw a shadowy vessel closing in on the house. She placed the baby in a boat, slipped the boat beneath the pier. When she turned and ran, a gunshot grazed her forehead and knocked her unconscious.

Tumult. Pandemonium. The smell of fire. Anak found himself with a sack over his head and a gun at his back, rushed into a watercraft, tossed beside Rebecca.

Someone yelled, *'There's no child. The others must have taken her.'*

Curses of anger. The watercraft sped away.

The couple found themselves in an earthen room, probably a hurricane shelter. Food and drink were plentiful. Their captors never spoke, save for a disguised voice that said simply, 'Have hope.'

This morning the couple had been gently bound and gagged, heads enshrouded, guided into a vehicle. They had traveled for at least an hour and been dropped off a block from where Harry and I saw them. Pulling flour sacks from their heads they saw a baby on the sidewalk, wrapped in a clean blanket.

It was a strange tale that went one step stranger. When the story started coming out, Harry asked, 'What's the little lady's name?'

Rebecca pulled her child close, smoothed her hair.

'She was born at one twenty-three a.m. last December twenty-fifth,' Rebecca said. 'We named her Noël.'

52

We followed Anak and Rebecca to the hospital. They were in good shape physically and now mentally, having been re-united with their child. The couple were worn to the bone, and we left them to sleep, many questions to come. Harry and I returned to the department to commence paperwork that, when complete, would probably need a forklift to move it from place to place.

'It's what Ben meant,' I said across our desks. 'About recognizing his error in planning. How it was him and him alone, no assistance and all his idea.'

'The people coming in on the boat weren't attackers,' Harry nodded. 'They were rescuers.'

'Told to grab the people in the house and get them safe, no matter what. Unfortunately, they arrived just as Meltzer's squad arrived.'

'What about the dead guy in the fire? One of Meltzer's melt-downs?'

I nodded. 'I don't expect anyone is missing him.'

'Like I don't expect we'll find out who came in by boat. If we have suspicions . . . '

'It's alibis all around, according to Ben. I expect hardcore SLDP operatives are a tight-lipped bunch. Especially after a nighttime gunfight. Or when a sympathizer or two spirited the kid from the hospital to keep her safe from a second attempt by Meltzer's Aryan brigades. It's legally kidnapping, but . . . ' I looked Harry in the eyes. 'Where do you want to go with this?'

He glanced at his watch and pushed himself to standing. 'Let's wait until tomorrow. See how it looks when we're writing it up. As for me, I'm going back to the hospital.'

'To see Anak and Rebecca and Noël?'

Harry pulled his orange tie from his pocket, began knotting it around the collar of his lavender shirt. 'To confirm a date with Doc Norlin. Tonight's the Jazz Club meeting. After that, Angela and I are having dinner at that new fish joint on the causeway.'

I grinned. 'Then home to . . . '

He held up a hand. 'This ain't gonna be a bad joke about genetics, is it?'

'Not any more. This your first date with the doc?'

'The third. You haven't been on your game lately. Where you headed?'

'First off, I got to make a stop and hopefully tend to some business.'

'After that?'

'I got a date with a shrink.'

Harry shot me a thumbs-up and headed to the hospital. For me, it was time for the final loose string to be tied; to see Kavanaugh. First, though, I made a stop and picked up a friend. We climbed in the car and drove to Kavanaugh's office with the windows down, the air warm on our faces and thick with the smells of azaleas and dogwood. I sipped from a bottle of water as we walked to the door of Kavanaugh's office.

'Wait here,' I said. 'This won't take long.'

I took a deep breath and walked up to knock on the door. Kavanaugh appeared. She was casual, in a loose purple dress and dark stockings, her feet in black ballet slippers, her white hair hanging loose.

'Good to see you,' the doc said. She was smiling.

I laid on the couch. Again with my feet the wrong way, but some things are sacred. Kavanaugh moved to the chair beside the couch. She crossed her legs beneath her in lotus position and leaned forward. In the purple dress with the white hair flowing loose, she looked like a lady wizard.

'The last time we met I behaved deplorably,' I said. 'I apologize.'

'No need. Your partner told me what happened. I consulted with a pharmacologist. No one had any idea that a mood-altering chemical was causing your behavior, least of all you, obviously. Stenebrexin metabolizes in hours, as I expect you've discovered. I'm happy to say that you'll be fine.'

I stared at the ceiling in silence.

'Detective?' she said.

'It goes back further than that,' I said. 'My actions.'

'Tell me.'

'I've been depressed. Not clinically. But for the past few weeks I didn't believe anything I did meant a tinker's damn. I lost my faith.'

'You know that for sure?'

'The department had been short-handed all spring, Doc, bodies stacking up like cordwood.

384

Some of the bloodiest murders I've ever seen over things like a hand of cards, a quart of beer. It seemed the world had gone insane. I had a case where the child of my first murder investigation eight years ago ended up a murder victim. It was like I'd been beating my head against the wall for nothing. Then the kid floated up.'

'The child was the final straw?'

'Harry kept dragging me over to see Noelle. I didn't want to look at the kid. All I saw was someone killing a baby by pushing it out into the ocean. It was the most inhuman act I could conceive.'

'So the child came to represent futility? The world was hopeless?'

'As simple as that,' I admitted. 'And I expect my unhappiness was enhanced by the crap Fossie was slipping me.'

'But as it turned out, things weren't as bad as they seemed.'

'Like Harry said, the story had a happy ending.'

Kavanaugh stared into my eyes so long as to make me uncomfortable. When she spoke, her voice was gentle.

'You need happy endings, don't you, Detective Ryder?'

I slung myself off the couch and walked to the window, staring into the trees. It seemed I could feel the earth turning. I spun back to Kavanaugh.

I said, 'Thanks, Doctor. I'll be back.'

'I'll be here.'

I walked outside. The sun felt glorious on my skin. A thousand years to become what we're supposed to be? Is that what Matthias said? Hell, if we've been here a hundred thousand years, we're in the last one per cent of the journey.

It's just a kiss away, as the Rolling Stones say.

'Come on, partner,' I said. 'Let's head home and go for a walk.'

I picked up the bowl I'd left on Kavanaugh's stoop and tossed out the remaining water. Mr Mix-up bounced on his front paws, yipped like a chihuahua, roofed like a basset. He tumbled to the grass, rolled over twice, and stared at me with perfect joy.

The complete mutt.

He was miles ahead of us, but we'd get there.

Acknowledgements

I thank decades of exposure to high-voltage television preachers for my basic research, making the list too lengthy to attach here. I can, however, name the superb folks at the Aaron Priest Literary Agency and the team at HarperCollins UK: Julia Wisdom and Anne O'Brien. There are many more stars behind the scenes, including the booksellers and librarians who recommend my work. I thank you all for the input and kindnesses.

We do hope that you have enjoyed reading this large print book.

Did you know that all of our titles are available for purchase?

We publish a wide range of high quality large print books including:
Romances, Mysteries, Classics
General Fiction
Non Fiction and Westerns

Special interest titles available in large print are:
The Little Oxford Dictionary
Music Book
Song Book
Hymn Book
Service Book

Also available from us courtesy of Oxford University Press:
Young Readers' Dictionary
(large print edition)
Young Readers' Thesaurus
(large print edition)

For further information or a free brochure, please contact us at:
Ulverscroft Large Print Books Ltd.,
The Green, Bradgate Road, Anstey,
Leicester, LE7 7FU, England.
Tel: (00 44) 0116 236 4325
Fax: (00 44) 0116 234 0205

Other titles published by
The House of Ulverscroft:

BLOOD BROTHER

J.A. Kerley

Detective Carson Ryder's sworn duty is to track killers down. He's never revealed the fact that his brother, Jeremy, is one of America's most notorious killers — albeit imprisoned. Now though, his brother's escaped and is at large in New York. With Jeremy the chief suspect in a series of horrifying mutilation-murders, a mysterious video demands Ryder be brought into help. What should be a straightforward manhunt couldn't be more different — or more terrifying. A dangerous cat-and-mouse game develops between Jeremy and the NYPD with Ryder in the middle, trying to keep his brother alive and the cops in the dark. But it's a game of life, death and deceit, a game with an unknown number of players and no clear way of winning . . .

COLD CASE

Faye Kellerman

The savage murder of beloved teacher Bennett Little shocked a community and baffled police. That his killer was never caught has haunted Genoa Greeves, one of his pupils . . . Eighteen years later, software billionaire Genoa reads of a similar murder involving a carjacking in Hollywood. Now, enormously influential, she pressures the LAPD to direct Lieutenant Peter Decker to re-open the case and solve the homicides. But Decker, finding only cold trails and dead leads, enlists the help of his daughter, Hollywood detective Cindy, as well as Rina, his wife. It's a decision he may come to regret as the line between cops and robbers gets dangerously blurred. Now Decker's cold case is unearthing treacherous secrets in a city where the price of fame has no limits . . .

FEVER OF THE BONE

Val McDermid

When teenager Jennifer Maidment's murdered and mutilated body is discovered, it is clear that a dangerous psychopath is on the loose. But very quickly, Tony Hill and DCI Carol Jordan realise it's the start of a brutal and ruthless campaign, targeting an apparently unconnected group of young people. Their chameleon-like killer chats with them online, pretending to share their interests and beliefs — then lures them to their deaths. But just when Tony should be at the heart of the hunt, he's pushed to the margins by Carol's cost-cutting boss and replaced by a dangerously inexperienced profiler. Struggling with the newly awakened ghosts of his own past, Tony battles to find the answers that will give him personal and professional satisfaction in his most nerve-shattering investigation yet.

BLOOD SAFARI

Deon Meyer

Lemmer is a freelance bodyguard. Lean, angry and violent, he works for Body Armor, a personal security company in South Africa. Emma le Roux wants to find her missing brother, who supposedly died twenty years ago. Convinced she saw him on the news as a suspect in the recent killing of a witch doctor and four poachers, she hires Lemmer to guard her when she goes looking for answers. As le Roux and Lemmer look for clues in the Lowveld, it's apparent that someone wants to keep them in the dark. Someone who will go to any lengths to stop them asking questions. When they are attacked and almost killed, Lemmer decides to go after whoever is hunting them — against all the odds.